Love Beyond the Ashes

First Printing: 2021

ISBN-13: 978-1-7334913-8-9

LCCN: 2022932528

For more information about this or other Grassleaf works, please visit grassleafpublishing.com or email info@grassleafpublishing.com.

For more information about the book or author, please visit www.jillannmai.com

Grassleaf Publishing was created because of the belief that good literary works, films, music, and art of all types can come from anywhere and anyone. After all, all goodness comes from He who created goodness, and He is powerful enough to display that goodness through any individual.

As writing turned from a personal hobby into a passion, I quickly realized that an author without a platform of thousands of followers has no chance to see work published. This is disappointing to writers, but should also be disheartening to readers. What kind of good works are we missing out on?

Publishers will tell us that people do not read anymore. They denigrate the old-fashioned art of reading. However, when one inspects the quality of books being printed, it is easy to see why consumers have turned away. Books are published based on the name of the author, not the quality of the content. Occasionally, a good book will make its way through, and readers will devour it over a weekend, especially young readers. It isn't the art of reading that's old-fashioned.

At Grassleaf Publishing, we believe good books can still be written. But the process of publishing must evolve. That's why Grassleaf operates differently than the traditional publishing company. Content and quality are the sole focus. The status, background, or life experience of an author doesn't matter. Grassleaf Publishing believes that if good content is made available, He will see that it serves its purpose.

As a reader, you may not recognize Grassleaf's authors, but hopefully you will recognize our logo and trust that it represents a worthwhile work.

Grassleaf Publishing was created to do one thing: contribute a verse.

Charles Brandon Wagoner
Founder, Grassleaf Publishing

Love Beyond the Ashes

Jill Ann Mai

To my husband, Donny, who has been a constant source of encouragement in this journey.

"For I know the plans I have for you," declares the Lord, "plans to prosper you and not to harm you, plans to give you hope and a future."
Jeremiah 29:11 NIV

The Cambridge of 1776.
*Adapted from original drawning by Mary Isabella James

1. Harvard Commons
   - Soldier Encampment
2. Washington's Headquarters
3. Christ Church
4. Henry Vassall House / Camp Hospital
5. Harvard Square
   - Blue Anchor Tavern
   - Tailor Shop
6. Schreier House

Chapter 1

Falmouth, Massachusetts 1775
(*Modern Day Portland, Maine*)

Abigail wiped off the dirt from her fingers and placed the last of the cabbages in the wheelbarrow. She looked at the produce, pleased. The harvest had been fruitful this year. They would have plenty for pickling over the winter months and the rest could be sold in the town square for a small profit. She took in a breath, relishing the fresh coastal breeze mixed with the cool, morning air. Despite the recent drop in temperature, it gave her a warm feeling.

"Do you think we're done yet?" Charlotte tossed a head of cabbage onto the pile. "I've got enough dirt in my fingernails and up my hemline to pass as a pig rolling in the mud."

A small laugh broke from Abigail's lips. "What? You don't like getting your hands dirty?"

Charlotte looked at her pointedly. "You know I don't. I just can't understand why you do."

Abigail shrugged. "It's not really so much that I enjoy it. I just know it needs to be done."

"That seems like something you might say—a typical Abigail answer."

"And what is that supposed to mean?"

"It's so responsible, so Abby-like." Charlotte gave a haughty exhale. "Come on. Isn't there a part of you that gets tired of this place? I mean, we do the same things day after day and year after year. Aren't you tired of toiling in these fields and caring for the animals? Don't you want to see more than our farm on the edge of this ocean?" Her arm outstretched to the east and Abigail's gaze automatically shifted with the gesture, knowing exactly what she was pointing to. "I mean that big body of water could take us anywhere if we just had the means."

It wasn't the first time Abigail thought about crossing the Atlantic or about her great-grandfather who did just that to make it to this very spot. He had endured the long voyage through severe weather, cramped quarters and risk of scurvy to make a new life with their great-grandmother, choosing to settle here in Falmouth. She glanced over to the main house, feeling both a sense of pride and devotion to its history. The humble structure had only stood for fifty-six years, an infant compared to the homes and buildings back in the motherland, but it signified something prominent: a giant leap of faith.

Her great-grandfather had started life again from scratch, choosing to plant new seedlings in a place foreign to him and away from the deep roots he knew in England. There was a part of her that wanted to see those roots, to see what they had left behind to make this good, but mundane life. Yet, how could she when she knew her family's wish was to remain here? Not to mention "mundane" might be a good thing right now. It was safe and predictable. With a war going on in the colonies chaos was inevitable. They'd have to face other unknowns and the predictable was exactly what she wanted. Still, a part of her admired her younger sister's desire for adventure when conflict was right in their backyard in Boston.

"Charlotte, you act like we don't go anywhere at all. What about Aunt Sylvia's?"

Charlotte raised an eyebrow. "You mean Portsmouth? Abby, that's been over a year ago." Had it been? Time had certainly passed. "Besides, that's not what I mean."

"Why? Did you not have a good time?"

"Of course I had a good time. In fact, I wish we would go more often. Aunt Sylvia knows how to really live. She doesn't work in the yard like we do here or even make her own clothes for that matter. And she's been to France three times already." She huffed. "I've begged Mama for me to go and stay with her over the winter but she won't let me."

Abigail had no difficulty remembering their family's visit to Portsmouth. In the span of two weeks, they had attended two parties at their aunt's estate and two more at the Lady Delwright's. It was Aunt Sylvia's way of showing her niece and nephew off, getting them into society. They were the only formal parties Abigail and her older brother had ever attended. And, unless they visited their aunt again, would probably ever attend. At the time, Charlotte had been too young to join them, though she'd enjoyed other advantages of their aunt's fortune, including hearing about her yearly trips to Paris.

Abigail eyed Charlotte with an almost half-stunned expression. So much could change in a year. Her sister's lean, adolescent features were in bloom, turning into the curves of womanhood. She imagined Charlotte in one of the dresses her aunt supplied to her for the parties and smiled to herself. Her sister would be lovely in it. Abigail knew Charlotte was entirely willing to make her debut if given the chance, and Aunt Sylvia would be just as anxious to show off her other niece. Yet, she just wasn't sure when their next visit would be to Portsmouth with a war in its beginning stages. According to their father, the Thatcher family had no plans to leave the safety of their home in Falmouth. Abigail gentled her words, trying to find some encouragement for her sister's disappointment.

"It's because you're needed here. It takes every one of us to run the farm." She gave an easy smile. "I need your help too. Mother still hasn't reached her full strength after Olivia's birth. She needs our help with taking care of her and Henry."

Charlotte frowned as she put another cabbage into the wheelbarrow. Abigail looked at the rest of the field and the work they had left to do. There was about a fourth that remained to be harvested. If she did the job alone she could probably get it done in about half an hour.

"There's not much more to do. Why don't I finish the rest while you go inside and see if Mother needs any help with Olivia? Once I'm done, we can go into town. I think Mother said she was making a pie for Mrs. Abernathy. We can take it to her on the way in."

Charlotte's eyes brightened at the suggestion before fading again. "What about Henry? Should we take him into town with us?"

Abigail shook her head. "He's with Father out surveying. I imagine they'll be back later this afternoon. That should give us enough time before we need to get back." The light in her sister's eyes returned.

Charlotte rose at an instant from her spot in the garden, shaking off the clumps of dirt that stuck to her dress. The excitement reverberated in her voice. "Oh, thank you, Abby. I'll see you inside."

Abigail reached the door of the family farmhouse with the last of the cabbages in tow. Her fingers had just grazed the top of the handle before the door flew open.

"Abby, are you done yet?" Charlotte stood at the threshold with arms crossed.

"Just finished. Did everything go well with Mother and Olivia?"

"Yes, yes. Olivia is sleeping and Mama is in her chair mending a tear in a pair of Henry's pants. I'm just waiting on you." She smiled, then frowned. Her eyes looked Abigail up and down with disapproval. "You're not going to wear that, are you?"

Abigail hesitated, now noticing the clean, blue gown usually reserved for Sunday service over Charlotte's slim frame. "I suppose not…"

"Good. Because you look positively filthy. I put some fresh water in your basin upstairs. When you're done make sure to clean up." She took a step back inside the house then stopped. "And hurry up. Mama says Abraham and Father have a meeting tonight at the tavern, so we'll have to get them an early dinner before they go. I want to have enough time in town before we have to be back." Evidently needing no reply, Charlotte stepped further inside, disappearing into the house.

Abigail went upstairs to find the basin filled as Charlotte promised. She washed her hands and face before choosing a plain, brown dress to change into then headed back downstairs.

"You're wearing that?"

"Yes." Abigail looked down at her choice of ensemble. "What's wrong with it?"

Charlotte rolled her eyes. "At least take that infernal cap off your head. I don't know why you insist on hiding that gorgeous hair of yours." She snatched for the modest headpiece, throwing it down on a side table. "There. That looks a little better."

"Don't forget Mrs. Abernathy's pie, Abigail." The frail female voice came from the corner of the house in front of the fireplace. Their mother sat in her chair still closing the gap in Henry's pair of trousers. She gave them a warm smile and pointed to the pie keeping warm by the flames. Abigail could smell the sweet aroma of the chicken pastry her mother had taken all morning to make no doubt tiring her in the process. "Mrs. Abernathy has been a saint. I don't know what we would've done without her."

Abigail returned her mother's smile, but her heart was scarcely in the gesture. It was true the midwife had done everything she could during the birth of her youngest sister, but the event had taken its toll. It had left her mother weak, partly because it was a difficult birth and partly because her mother was considered past her years in childbearing. She wasn't healing

5

as fast as they hoped, nor had her strength returned. Abigail still held to the midwife's assurance that her mother's strength would rebound in time, but doubt threatened. Olivia would be three weeks old this Sunday and there had been little improvement to her mother's condition.

"Come on, Abby!" Charlotte snatched the basket with pie inside. "Let's get going."

"Are you all right?" Abigail ignored her sister's urgency to leave, directing the question to their mother, though why she bothered asking it, she wasn't certain. Their mother would never tell them she wasn't feeling well, especially with Charlotte nearly out the door.

"I'm fine Abby, just a little tired. Olivia is still sleeping, so I might rest my eyes too for a bit before her feeding. I'll see you later."

"Are you sure? We can always go another time. Mrs. Abernathy will understand if we don't..." Both Charlotte and her mother conveyed their reproof, the latter shaking her head while the former let out an impatient whine.

"No," her mother protested with a kind smile. "I don't want my gratitude to be delayed nor do I want you here feeling sorry for me. Plus, both of you could use a change of scenery now that the harvest is done and I could use some peace and quiet while your youngest sister sleeps. I'll be fine. Now, go." Reluctantly, Abigail conceded and her mother waved them on before returning to her patchwork.

Abigail shut the door behind her, an uneasiness sinking in. Despite her mother's assurances, she could tell the morning had already been too much for her. She said a quick prayer, asking God to give her mother the rest she needed.

Charlotte was already out the door, standing near the far side of the house. Her eyes seemed almost transfixed on the view just down the hillside. Her sister's gaze resting on the ocean brought back their earlier conversation. What would it be like to sail across its wide expanse and see what was on the other side? For a moment, Abigail's heart leaped at the prospect and she drew closer to Charlotte upon the hillside taking in the best view Falmouth had to offer.

"Are there any coming in today?" Abigail continued to close the distance between them, anxious to get a view of any incoming supply ships that might be arriving this morning. When Charlotte didn't answer, she tried again. "Charlotte?" Abigail's attention veered to her sister's empty hands. The basket she'd grabbed before leaving the house was now turned sideways at her feet—the pie ruined. Worry over her mother was replaced with disproval. "I know you want to go into town, but there was no reason to smash the pie mother made for Mrs. Abernathy. It wouldn't have taken us long to…"

Abigail stopped, realizing Charlotte wasn't listening. Her sister's eyes stayed fixed on Falmouth's harbor. She followed in the direction of what held Charlotte's unbending focus and her own body froze. Confusion gripped her as her heart raced and fear sent a sharp chill up her spine.

The sea, immense in its size, sparkled under the sun's rays. Every so often a wave would break, revealing their whitecaps, while seagulls rushed towards the water, searching for the chance to grab a tasty meal. Only God could create something so beautiful. On any other day, the scene would have been welcomed as Abigail breathed in the warmth of its tranquility, but not today. Today, its beauty was tainted by five ships headed straight for their port.

"What do you think is going on, Abby?" Charlotte's voice was soft as she began to stumble from her daze.

"I don't know, but we need to find out. Abraham should still be down at the docks."

"You thinking of something?"

"I'm not sure, but right now he's our best chance. He still may have a friend he meets down there who has a good ear for what's happening with the war."

Charlotte's eyes widened. "What does Falmouth have to do with the war? We're not a threat."

"I wish I knew. Maybe this." Abigail gestured over to the side of the harbor they were talking about. "Maybe it's just nothing." She certainly hoped so. Either way, a force within her pulled at her to find out.

***

It took them under a quarter of an hour to reach the harbor. Abigail clung to the post of a gangway leading up to a frigate, her breath exasperated from the run over. A fishing boat bobbed alongside the larger ship, and she immediately wished she hadn't stopped in front of it. Both crew members gutted their fish and threw the remains back into the sea. She made the mistake of inhaling too sharply to catch her breath and almost became ill because of it. Charlotte stopped beside her, leaning against a dock post with an expression that told her she'd made the same mistake.

"We need to keep going."

"I agree." Charlotte gasped while her nose veered away from the fishermen. "But can we slow down for a minute?"

Abigail nodded, then glanced out beyond the docked boats. Her heart quickened. The ships had drawn closer in like a bad omen. Her eyes darted around for any sign of her brother. Where could he be? The sooner they found him, the sooner they'd know what was going on and whether their concern was warranted or not.

"I'm sorry, but we need to go." An urgency pushed hard and she grabbed for her sister's hand dragging Charlotte along. "I can't help thinking something's wrong. I'll feel better once we talk to Abraham."

"Hey!" Charlotte protested, pulling her hand away. "What if he doesn't know anything? What if he's not even here?"

Abigail sucked in her breath, trying to be patient when everything in her felt differently. "He's here. I'm sure of it. He's been here every morning since the rebellions began. He'll be here." She nodded for added effect, making sure she believed it herself. It did enough.

Charlotte picked up her pace again and they weaved in and out of people, scanning the docks.

It was difficult. The harbor was restless. Not that she visited often, but it seemed extra busy this morning as they maneuvered through the crowd. She wondered if news was already breaking out concerning the unexpected visitors.

They continued walking briskly along, passing ships bringing in goods. Two men were in the process of unloading a crate from a schooner with the words West Indies on it. One of them spat into the water as they lowered it off the boat. A few more yards down a man from the docks refused to let a small brig tie off. Abigail couldn't make out the ship's cargo but guessed well enough by the man's threats to its captain. The vessel must have carried British goods. That was happening more as of late. Since Parliament's decision to raise taxes through their legislation of the Stamp Act and Sugar Act, people refused to buy from the Motherland. In some cases, like this one, they prevented supply ships from even docking.

She tugged gently at Charlotte's sleeve to urge her on and away from the scene where the two men argued. It wasn't a good idea to be involved, at least that's what her father protested despite Abraham's earnest desire to join the cause.

"Abby?" A familiar male voice sounded behind her. The tension in her shoulders eased. Abraham. His eyes drifted from her to Charlotte with deciphered confusion. "What are you two doing here?" The furrow of his brow deepened, and she got the feeling he wasn't entirely pleased to see them.

Then she noticed the older man, who slouched next to Abraham as though he'd borne the weight of the world on his shoulders for some time. His unfortunate posture was due to an injury he suffered to his right leg. Was he a sailor? She wasn't so sure. Those men had to be quick on their posts. Yet, he wore a Monmouth cap that covered most of his head except for a few gray strands around his ears. Maybe his past proved otherwise.

"Abraham, we were looking for you." She paused momentarily, letting her voice soften for only her brother and Charlotte to hear. "We saw the ships." She eyed the older man, giving him a polite smile, yet indicating their conversation with her brother was meant to be a family affair.

Abraham smiled in return, showing he understood, but his failure to excuse the man let her know he disagreed.

"As a matter of fact, we were just discussing that issue right before I spotted my sisters getting a little too close to that squabble over there." She could hear the displeasure in his tone. "You know Father wouldn't like that. He wouldn't want you caught up in the fight."

"He doesn't like you in it either." Charlotte sneered.

"That's different. I'm the oldest and practically out of the house anyway."

"Abby's only a year behind you," she argued.

"Yeah, but until she finds herself a husband, she's still under Father's roof and his problem. Not to mention Mother still needs you two around to help with Henry and Olivia." He shook his head. "But there are more important issues at hand." He let his disapproval wane as he gestured to the older man. "Abby, Charlotte, this is Cleophes."

"You can call me Cleo." The man bowed at his introduction, a thick Scottish accent ringing through. So, this was Cleo. Abigail had certainly heard of the man, but until now, had never laid eyes on him. Per Abraham, he knew everything about the war, at least what news came in and out of Falmouth.

Abigail smiled, counting herself fortunate to have the pleasure of meeting the very man most likely to know what she hoped to find out. "Abraham's mentioned you before."

Cleophes gave a small chuckle. "Well, I must admit I'm glad to hear that, Miss. It's naht everyday an old man like me gets the attention o' two young ladies like yourself, though I hope it's been good things you've heard."

She let out a small laugh as the man's easy candor calmed her. "Abraham says you know everything about the war, for both sides. Is that true?"

He gave them a sheepish grin and shrugged. "Well, I don't know if I know everything about this war. Things can change rather quickly, you know, but I do tend to know more than most."

"Then do you know why there's a fleet approaching our harbor as we speak?" She pressed the question. "A Royal Naval fleet, to be exact?"

"Aye, I do, Miss, and I'm afraid you're naht going to like what you're going to hear." The Scotsman's light-hearted banter turned serious and he leaned in closer, his voice at a whisper. "A captain by the name of Henry Mowat has returned to Falmouth."

"Mowat?" The name sounded familiar on her tongue, but she couldn't put a finger on it.

"You mean that captain the militia captured a few months back?" Charlotte crossed her arms to tell Cleo this was old news and an annoyance to her previous plans.

The older man nodded but didn't seem to notice her irritation. "Aye, that'd be right, Miss Charlotte. I'm told the men used brute force in the capture and had done it while he was in the middle of arranging church services for his crew. Needless to say, Mowat didn't take too kindly to that."

Abigail's body grew rigid as Cleo went on.

"Mowat's first lieutenant threatened to fire cannon on the town if his captain was not released promptly. He even fired two blanks just for good measure as a warning he meant it. Thanks to some loyalists and town residents naht wanting to see Falmouth become a battleground, Mowat was returned safely to his ship where he made his passage back to England and the ordeal was ended." He shrugged, letting out a cool breath. "At least, so we thought."

Abigail shook her head, still hoping for an alternative explanation for what awaited them in the wharf. "But with the conflict ended and the captain returned safely to his ship, what would he be doing back here so soon?"

Cleophes pressed his lips and she read the expression well enough. It wasn't good news. "It seems the English captain left with revenge in his heart, Miss."

"Abby." Abraham chimed in, his hand clamped with a firm gentleness on her shoulder. She didn't like the grim expression he held now. "It could get really bad for us if we don't handle things right. Cleo has informed me Captain Mowat has returned and has not done so entirely peacefully."

"What do you mean?"

Abigail's heart picked up speed, thinking that very question Charlotte had the nerve to ask. Something told her she wasn't going to like it. Her brother confirmed it. His eyes seemed to center on both of them.

"Mowat plans to order firing on the town. I'm told that his orders are to punish all towns that rebel against the king, but I'm sure Falmouth is on the top of his list from the last time he was here."

Abigail's stomach plummeted. A sense of dread washed over her as she caught sight of the captain's ship now anchored just outside their harbor. The HMS *Canceaux*. Once a common merchant sloop, now full of cannon and used for military purposes under the Royal Navy and Mowat's command—the command that might cost them their town. And the war sloop wasn't alone. Four other ships were anchored just behind her, the red and white colors snapping against the wind as a warning—a warning that might have come too late.

Chapter 2

Garrett stared off the port side towards the town of Falmouth. He had no knowledge of why they'd anchored here. What he did know was Captain Mowat had ordered their fleet to follow his ship, the HMS *Canceaux*, to towns that had rebelled against the Crown and fire upon them. His stance shifted just slightly. He wasn't completely thrilled by the idea although he didn't know why, especially if it meant here. Falmouth had plenty of loyalists to the Crown. Maybe this was just a good place to stop for replenishing supplies and maritime amusement.

An agitated sigh escaped his lips. No matter. He would find out soon enough. His own ship's captain would announce their orders within the hour. He'd been a part of the Royal Navy long enough to know that. He'd served with the Royal Navy for as long as he could remember, or at least as long as it mattered.

"What do you think Mowat is up to?" Nicholas came up from behind him, to stand shoulder to shoulder with Garrett.

"I can't say for sure." Garrett continued looking at the unsuspecting town. Only a few miles of water separated them. "Probably just a place to stop and refresh. We could use some more supplies and much of the crew have complained about wanting to stretch their sea legs."

"I haven't heard any complaints from the crew." Nicholas' brow furrowed, showing a hint of worry underneath the weight of forced confidence. Garrett knew his friend's statement was out of concern for the men. Nicholas was a great lieutenant. Unlike some of the other higher ranked officers who cared little for their crew's state of health, Nicholas cared about the well-being of those who served under his command.

The mild expression of disturbance on his friend's face made him recall the last evening Nicholas had confided in him. They'd all gathered for a celebratory dinner accompanied by a bottle of claret inside the wardroom to commemorate Nicholas' promotion to first lieutenant. The small party had lasted several hours until the rest of the officers had turned in for the night, leaving just the two of them when Nicholas spoke.

"It's a lot of pressure, you know." Nicholas twirled his glass, staring into the deep burgundy of the wine remaining in it.

Garrett huffed, realizing it came out more exaggerated than he meant. It told him he'd had more than his fair share to drink. He recovered when he saw his friend's gaiety from earlier turned serious.

"Not like you do." Garrett shrugged. He'd assumed his friend was about to say his piece concerning the captain. It wasn't something he would do in front of the others, but the captain was harsh, especially to Nicholas. Every once in a while Garrett knew his friend needed to unleash. But Nicholas shook his head, letting him know he'd guessed wrong.

"I don't mean my father. It's thinking of the men on board my ship that keep me up at night. They have lives back home, some of them, wives and children they haven't seen in months."

"That may be true, but remember, they volunteered for this." Garrett eyed Nicholas squarely. "The war has been over for twelve years, now. We no longer need the numbers we did when fighting the French." He believed what he said, but he could see his friend wasn't so easily convinced. Nicholas still looked like he carried the weight of a ship on his back, stocked with provisions and a full crew.

"That doesn't matter to me. If they die at sea, they would never see their families again. That's a much greater burden than anything my father could lay on my shoulders."

Garrett looked at Nicholas from the side of the ship, remembering the despondency in his voice that night. Even under the spell of the claret, he knew his friend meant it. It was why he sometimes felt guilty when he knew things concerning the crew that Nicholas did not. He made no effort to do it intentionally, but the men just seemed more willing to confide in him rather than their commander. And it wasn't because he held a special regard for them like Nicholas did, although he did care about their well-being. Most of them did it because despite half his life being raised in a moderately affluent household, Garrett didn't come from a family of privilege. That seemed to matter to them. In their eyes, he may have been an officer of higher rank, but he was no different. They respected him in his position, without the uneasiness towards him that accompanies a feeling of inferiority that separated them from Nicholas and his father.

Explaining the situation to his friend would do no good. Nicholas came from a wealthy family and there was no changing that. Not wanting to cause his friend pain, he thought carefully about his response.

"They only tell me because they know where I come from." Garrett meant the comment as a mockery to himself, hoping it would lighten the mood. It didn't. Nicholas' expression of annoyance towards him told Garrett his friend wasn't buying it. Garrett cleared his throat. "Anyway, how's your first week going in your new position?"

Nicholas gave him a sideways glance only he could see. "Other than the fact I'm ignorant of my own crew's grievances, it's fine. There's a little more shouting involved with commanding more of the men, but I'm sure you'll find that out soon enough when you get your own promotion."

"Let's hope it's sooner rather than later."

"You're on your way."

He was. Garrett knew it, but that didn't mean it hadn't been a long road. It seemed like a century had passed since his entry into the navy, starting from the bottom as a servant for the captain of an unrated ship. He'd been young, but the captain had been so impressed with his quick wit that he requested Garrett's company the following term and promoted him to landsman. His mouth curved a degree, remembering how ignorant and excited he'd been about the advancement until he realized that only meant he'd be stuck swabbing the deck or performing some other menial tasks until he could earn his place as an able seaman. More years went by and he continued to rise in rank, discovering skills he didn't know he had: a keen eye for keeping watch against potential dangers and for steering the ship, a good sense of direction and math intelligence for navigation, a high stamina for rigging sails, and even a capacity to give an order or two rather than just taking them.

"Yeah, we're getting there. I'm just ready to command my own ship." His heart hammered thinking how close he was to reaching his dream since he'd joined the navy at fourteen. In that moment, he felt like that young kid again, full of optimism for becoming a captain to a vessel of his own. Like then, his attitude remained much the same: he didn't care whether it was a rated or unrated ship, just as long as he called the orders.

"In time you will, but for today you're under someone else's command." Nicholas' gaze moved cautiously as a figure came to meet them from the stern of the ship.

"Gentlemen, I have received our new orders." Garrett shifted his view. The strong, commanding voice rang forth from the tall, broad shoulders of the man now approaching them: Nicholas' father.

Even after two months at sea, the man's uniform was pristine: a navy-blue frock coat embroidered with gold laced buttons, a white waistcoat, and breeches. He was a man who carried himself with pride which only made him appear to tower over most of the men on board and earned his

16

crew's full attention without having to utter a word. These features elevated his esteem from those under his command while officers of equal standing and above in the Royal Navy held him in high regard. It was only a matter of time before his promotion to admiral, some said, as soon as next year.

"Captain." Both Garrett and Nicholas immediately halted their conversation to make their formal salute. Garrett could feel the muscles in his back tighten, a sign of how the man still intimidated him despite having practically been raised by him.

"We are to prepare the ship for firing, men. Captain Mowat has sent an officer to warn the inhabitants of the town of his intentions to ignite our battery on it." He turned to Nicholas in a way that did little to suspect relations of father and son. "Mister Edwards, meet me on the quarterdeck after you carry out your tasks." Without further explanation, the captain turned away from them and headed back towards the stern of the ship. Nicholas' own demeanor, too, instantly changed as he assumed his role of first lieutenant.

"Ready the gunners to prepare the cannons, Mister Ward."

"Aye, sir." Garrett's gaze met his friend's as he snapped his response. Now was the time to act. He had a part to play, and he needed to do it well if he was to obtain his own promotion. Nicholas walked away to give the rest of the men on the ship their orders while Garrett went to find the master gunner on board.

Most of the crew had lingered on deck. They talked amongst each other, enjoying the break of a stationed ship until they received their next orders. Bernard Abbot was no exception. He seemed to be engaged in a conversation with two quarter-gunners under the main mast of the ship.

"Mister Abbot, get the guns ready to fire and make sure the men know their post."

"Aye, sir. Has someone risked running the gauntlet, sir?" The man's voice was rich with an English naval accent. Normally the term referred to a more specific scenario where the guilty party was forced to walk between two lines of his crew mates while they proceeded to beat him. But for whatever reason, Bernard Abbot preferred the term for all instances of punishment, both in and out of sea life.

"Indeed, Mister Abbot. We have orders from the flagship to fire on this town at the ready of Captain Mowat." As a lieutenant, Garrett owed the men of lower rank nothing of further explanation. They were to simply follow his orders, but he understood their curiosity and he even respected it, to an extent. It had not been long ago when he'd stood in their position, wishing to know the reasons they were expected to carry out their orders with immediate action and without question. That had always bothered him, so as long as it didn't interfere with his command, he didn't mind explaining, within reason of course.

"Aye, sir. Thank you, sir." The man gave a half bow in appreciation. "We will have the guns and the men ready." Garrett noticed Abbot seemed to be debating whether to be bold enough to ask another question. To Garrett's chagrin, he was. He looked to his superior with a wary confidence as if uncertain he might be crossing a line.

"Do you know why the captain wants to set the town ablaze, sir?" Garrett's jaw clenched. The man was beginning to step out of bounds, even for him. Questioning a captain's orders was considered insubordination and punishable if caught by the right person. Garrett was not that person and apparently Bernard Abbot knew it. Nevertheless, the man's inquisitions halted progress and that wouldn't look good for Garrett. He hated doing it, but he'd have to remind the man of his rank. He couldn't risk losing his position of authority in the rest of the crew's eyes and jeopardize his own career for a single man's meddling. Not when a promotion was on the line.

"That will be all, Mister Abbot. Please assume your duties as I've ordered you to carry them out." It wasn't a request and the gunner knew it. He gave Garrett a quick salute before heading below to the gun deck with his two companions. The threat was gone.

The tension in Garrett's jaw eased, though not completely. The man's question mirrored his own. Why were they firing on the town? Mowat's orders issued from Graves were to punish towns that rebelled against the Crown. Garrett had thought the punishment just. Many of those who had left England had forgotten their homeland. They treated their mother country with disdain and contempt, rebelling like spoiled children. They acted out by refusing to purchase her goods and complaining of taxes they owed to her king. Garrett didn't understand it. Were not those things part of running a country? Were not the American colonies just an extension of the Motherland? He scoffed under his breath.

He'd heard the talk of how America was a land of opportunity, yet that's not what he saw. The people here chose to wear ordinary clothing and build simple furniture made by their own hands instead of buying the fine clothing and luxurious furnishings England offered to them. It was like they wanted no part of their past. Garrett's blood heated. England had been good to him. He'd come from a poor family and had risen to the rank of lieutenant in the most powerful navy in the world. He could only think of one reason why Falmouth would receive their fire. They had rebelled and would now have to suffer the consequences.

A memory resurfaced. In the church he'd attended with his father as a young boy, the preacher expounded on striking a child with a rod to discipline them. As a child the verse had made him feel uneasy, reminding him of the times he'd misbehaved. His father would send him outside for the biggest switch he could find for his own punishment. The recollection of it made him cringe. He had hated the verse in his youth, but today he understood it. They had a mission to discipline the motherland's children who'd gone astray in hopes to bring them back to their senses.

The tightness in his face returned with full force. Garrett hadn't expected to be reminded of his father. He hadn't known it then, but that day in the church would be the last time he'd see him alive. It was also the last time Garrett stepped foot into a church.

The sight of Nicholas hurrying towards him jerked him to the present. Nicholas had just finished speaking with one of the other lieutenants, giving the man a nod before moving towards Garrett's direction.

"Mowat has just given us orders to fire." The abrupt news came as a surprise.

"What about civilians?"

Nicholas seemed to understand his concern and nodded. "I'm told they were given a deadline to evacuate."

Garrett used his spyglass to take a survey of the town. It looked deserted enough. Not that Mowat owed the townspeople anything, but he wondered whether any mercy had been given for them to right their wrongs. "Was any effort made for reconciliation you know of?"

"As far as I know, Mowat gave them an ultimatum: swear their allegiance to the Crown and give up their arms or else."

Garrett grimaced, but not at the captain's warning. Foolish people. He was astonished at their stubbornness and defiance. Rather than committing to a simple act of obedience, they had refused their chance to save their town. Any sympathy he'd felt for these people edged away.

"I will get into position, then." He waited to see whether Nicholas had anything further to add. Perhaps he would try to continue where they left off in their earlier conversation. Garrett hoped not. No verbal response came from his friend. He simply turned away from Garrett and returned to the quarterdeck to stand beside his father.

"Shot your guns!" Garrett heard the captain yell out the order that would signal the gun crew to load the barrel of their canons. It would only be a few seconds, now. He let his gaze drift once more over to the town now within their guns' reach. All it took was one word.

"Fire!"

Chapter 3

Abigail picked up a charred piece of splintered wood from the ground where the kitchen used to stand. The black residue stained her fingertips as it crumbled into ash. She wouldn't have believed it if anyone told her. Just a day ago she'd awoken and started her chores like it was any other day. No one could have convinced her nothing, at least, almost nothing would be standing where her family's farmhouse used to be.

She swallowed, fighting back the tears. How quickly things can change. One minute she was talking to her brother and Cleo down at the harbor and then, what seemed like a blur to her now, her family had to rush to pack as much of their belongings as they could. She'd never dreamed something like this would happen, that her town would be nearly demolished, and her home gone. In the course of a single day her family now lay uprooted from the lives they knew.

"Looks like the animals made it out okay." Abraham called out to her from what remained of the barn, a hint of despaired agitation in his tone. It had fared better than the house. Parts of the frame, though badly charred, still stood and fragments of wood laid scattered around to what appeared to be part of the roof.

The move to her aunt's happened so quickly there was no time allowed for the animals. They'd made the difficult decision to leave them behind, a decision that affected her younger brother the most. At the ripe age of seven, Henry had been the one to open their stalls and untie their ropes, hoping they might sense the danger and find refuge.

The memory of it made her heart ache. He'd entered the carriage door with watery stains left on his cheeks. No doubt he'd been crying while carrying out the task, but he said nothing. She sighed with the only relief she could muster. Henry had held a special bond with the animals. He would be glad to hear none had stayed.

"There's nothing here to salvage." She called back to Abraham, the reality of the words making them hard to digest. She tried to focus on the piles of crumbled ash around her feet. The wet tears formed and she couldn't hold them back. She also knew God didn't promise an easy life, but until now, she'd been naive enough to think somehow her life was an exception. She struggled to fight against the pain of loss while a part of her wanted to stay strong in front of her older brother.

Abigail let her gaze drift out towards the water. The scene was much like she'd viewed only the morning before with Charlotte up on the hillside apart from one thing: Mowat's ships no longer approached their harbor. They were now anchored within it. The sight of them made her insides boil, and she welcomed the strength the anger gave her. The thought of crying in front of Abraham who'd shared equally in her loss was one thing, but to allow the men who destroyed her town to see her grief was something she wouldn't do.

She'd assumed they'd docked and disembarked to assess the town's damage. She closed her eyes, her lips pressed firm with the next dreadful thought. They'd take account of any dead among those that decided to stay during the attack. Whether it was customary or not for these soldiers to make their assessment, she didn't care. They had all but obliterated her town and now they had the nerve to enter it? It seemed wrong. Again, she was thankful for the anger. Although it stirred something inside her, giving way to thoughts she wasn't proud of, it served as a remedy for her loss.

She looked out again towards the sea, a fire rising within her at the sight of Mowat's fleet still within Falmouth's harbor. Her eyes shut tight to prevent the hot tears from flowing. When she opened them again, she intentionally ignored the five ships by setting her sight past the wharf. Beyond it, she could see water for miles. Even further, a vast ocean that eventually led to the other side where a land and government had approved to lay waste of the life she knew. If that's what her great-grandfather had chosen to leave, it was no wonder. What were you thinking? She scolded herself under her breath. Your family left for a reason. Why would you want to return to a place they'd chosen to distance themselves over 3,000 miles from? Now, she would never trade this life on her own accord. But she was beginning to learn more personally that life didn't always go as planned.

Her mother's words this morning at breakfast came back as a reminder: "We cannot grow if we stay where we feel comfortable. We can either change on our own or the Lord will do it for us."

Abigail wished she could be as trusting and hopeful as those words came out, spoken with conviction. It seemed the Lord had made the decision for her, but her heels were still dragging, reluctant to make the change. She had not been ready for this.

"Abraham, what are we going to do? Our home is completely gone." Her brother had left the ruins of the barn to meet her in the remnants of their kitchen. His expression was solemn yet thoughtful. She didn't know how he could be so calm when she felt like her whole world was falling apart. She wanted to scream, cry, or both, but repressed it.

He looked at her, his brown eyes dark. "The only thing we can do now. You'll stay with Aunt Sylvia until we can rebuild."

She looked at him doubtfully. "Don't you mean, 'We'll stay'?"

He bent down, taking some of the dust from their home and rubbed it between his fingers. "I'm going to Boston."

She gulped. She wasn't entirely surprised. After all, Abraham had been involved in the town's meetings concerning the rebellion. She even presumed he'd join the war effort at some point, but something about his announcement made it hard to swallow.

"You're going to fight?"

He nodded. "I'm going to join Washington. Our town is the last thing I can take."

"But what about Mother and Father? You're going to leave after all this?" Her body pointed to the debris left of the farm. It was her attempt to keep the rest of what she loved safe. The truth was, her parents might not have taken allegiance to a side of this war, but they knew their son had. They wouldn't be surprised by his declaration, especially after this.

His jaw went taut as grief mixed with anger shone in his eyes. "Abby, I can't just stand by anymore."

"There has to be another way." She tried to think quickly. "Petitions, boycotts…" Abraham shook his head, gesturing back towards the ruins of their home.

"We're way past that, Abby. First, Boston. Now, Falmouth. Look what they've done. Did you know two boys were killed during the massacre in Boston? They were only 17. One of them wasn't even involved."

The intensity grew stronger in his eyes. There was no talking him out of it but she had to try.

"What if you have to go into battle?"

"I'm counting on the chance I will."

Her mouth gaped open as her mind searched for excuses. "But Abraham, you've barely handled a gun. You'd be facing an army of trained soldiers."

"Hey." He looked offended. "I can handle a gun well enough. Not one of those coyotes managed to get close to the hen house since we started having trouble with them."

"Coyotes are not the same as a company of His Majesty's men. You could die." She shuddered to think how likely that could be.

"We all die sometime, Abby. At least I'll be doing something I feel strongly about. I'm not the only one that feels that way, either. I hear there's plenty of untrained men willing to join in the fight."

"When are you leaving?"

"Tomorrow."

She half-choked. "So soon? Why not wait a little longer? Even if it's just a few more days. Stay with us at Aunt Sylvia's until then."

"I'm not waiting, Abigail." His words came out harsh. It was evident he was done with her weak attempts to coax him otherwise. She tried to remember he wasn't aiming his anger at her. "I can't stay here another minute pretending things are fine when they're not. I have to do something. I have to go." He sucked in a breath and his voice softened. "Let's just keep moving towards town. I've seen enough here."

They said little on their way as what seemed like an ominous cloud hovered over them. After the sight of their home's destruction, whatever damage the town suffered, wouldn't surprise her. She couldn't be more wrong. She gasped, hardly recognizing what was left.

The cannons had done their work. Faint patches of black smoke leftover from the fire still wafted towards the bright, blue sky. The scene seemed paradoxical. Here they were, walking past the dark ruins of their lives while the radiance of the sun glistened overhead.

Beneath their feet shards of glass from broken windows crunched, making them mindful of where they stepped. With every few yards, large chunks of mortared brick from one of the town's buildings blocked their path.

They passed by several homes, all of which had been reduced to rubbish. The meeting house, though technically standing, was missing its entire front side from where a bomb had exploded and torn it to pieces. A few buildings still stood but even those were left hollowed by shattered windows and walls. Abigail's heart sank as they approached the foregrounds of the church. She was sorry to see it had suffered the same fate as the others.

She couldn't help but tremble. Abraham's own silence communicated how deeply the scene disturbed him too. People had taken what they could quickly gather, leaving the rest of their valuables behind. What was once a fine-tailored waistcoat, prized by its owner, now lay tattered and blackened on the side of the street. Card tables that once displayed details of their skilled craftsmanship and expense lay mangled beyond repair.

Some broken pieces of china reminded her of her own mother's set, a gift from her great-grandmother. Her mother had displayed them neatly above the cupboard, but no remnant of the collection her mother cherished so much had survived. Had this set, too, been handed down from a loved one and could not be replaced?

"There's someone over there."

Abraham scrunched his brow and gave a slight cock of his head towards what remained of a Georgian style home. "What is he doing?"

Abigail scanned the area her brother indicated. The man's back was turned towards them, but he was picking up garments leftover from the aftermath. He tossed them aside haphazardly one by one and out of his way. He stopped at an embellished woman's dressing gown, appearing to examine it as if he planned to barter it off for a good price. Either that, or he was debating about trying it on. She couldn't jump to conclusions, but admitted the act looked suspicious. She considered other explanations while she took into account the house the man rummaged through belonged to Mr. Gentry. Unlike the esteemed businessman, burly and polished every time she saw him, this current man's smaller stature and disheveled state, proclaimed he was neither Mr. Gentry nor his twelve-year-old son.

"Perhaps he's related or a friend?"

Abraham gave a low scoff. "I don't think so, Abby. He doesn't exactly scream Gentry material if you ask me."

Abraham had a point. The man was indeed a ghastly sight. His trousers were aged and tattered, beyond mending and tarnished with black residue. His shirt, in no better condition, the material newly ripped and charred. Of all the pieces of clothing, if you could still call them that, his boots had fared the best. They were largely scuffed and the soles wearing thin, but both buckles remained intact. He looked more like he'd been in the line of fire, if it was possible. Thought rushed, Mowat had given the town time to evacuate. So why would someone stay behind?

When the man reached down as he continued to explore the materials left in the debris, she recognized the Monmouth cap and the tufts of now singed hair poking out below his ears. Returning to his stance, though with some difficulty on his right side, he seemed to ponder over the dress again.

"Cleophes?" She murmured the name under her breath.

"What did you say?" Abraham raised a brow at her.

"I think that's Cleophes."

He shook his head. "Can't be. Cleo was the one who warned us about the attack. He would've had plenty of time to get out of here before they started the cannon blasts. That man looks like he was right in the middle of it."

"I know, but I really do think that's him. I remember his hat. And look at the way he stands. He has a limp on his right leg."

Abraham squinted his eyes, zoning in on the subject at hand. He rubbed his chin. "I'll admit, that's all there, but I still can't imagine that's Cleo. He'd be a fool to stay behind."

Abigail shrugged, having nothing more to offer.

"All right, then." The air came out sharp from his lungs. "Let's settle

27

this."

Abigail followed her older brother close behind until they arrived in the middle of the Gentry home to meet the man. His back was still turned. He didn't seem to notice them as he continued to examine the dress.

"A fine choice. The Lady Gentry would approve in your taste of women's fashion." Abraham's remark did the trick.

The man turned round and revealed a mischievous grin. "Why, Abraham. You half spooked me. What are you doing sneaking up on old men minding their own business?" His eyes brightened. "And Miss Abigail. What a wonderful sight. I'm glad to see you're safe and well. The rest of your family make it out too, I trust?"

One side of Abraham's mouth raised. "We're all right, thanks to your warning, Cleo, but I can't say the same for you. You look like you were in the heat of it all. What happened?"

Cleo looked down assessing the conditions of his current wardrobe. "Oh, this? I reckon I'm lucky to be alive. One of Mowat's cannons almost sent me to the grave if you can believe it."

Abraham offered a smug expression. "I can believe it. You look like you were fired out of one. Why didn't you leave after you warned us? You should've been gone way before we left town. You don't have a farm or family to pack up."

Cleo flinched. Something about her brother's last comment hurt even if it hadn't been his intent. Had Abraham caught it too?

Cleo certainly didn't appear affected now. "Aye, I know. I suppose that's part of my problem and why things happened the way they did." He looked to her. "You see, Miss Abby, I don't own a lot of belongings. What I own is what I can carry." He held his arms outstretched and open as if the gesture better modeled his point before he continued. "Since my packing was done, I decided a farewell drink was in order. After all, I've lived in this town for ten years now, the longest I've ever lived in one location, and I've had a merry time in it. I thought it would be a shame to leave without a proper goodbye."

Abraham frowned. "So, you went to the tavern alone?"

Cleo nodded. "Aye, that I did. Lucky for me, Fanny was still there, the keeper, tho' she was clearly on her way out—had already stocked up most of the good stuff but left me a few pints as a farewell present; in case I didn't make it, she said." Cleo let out a snort of laughter. "Turns out the lass was nearly right. I almost didn't. The next thing I remember was being roused by the sound of violent blasts—sounded like they were coming from the tavern, like they were right there in the very room with me. My eardrums still ring from it." He grabbed his ear for an instant as if checking to make sure it was still attached. "I wasted no time. I bolted out of the door as fast as my legs could carry me in my state and without a second to spare too. After hurling myself out, a cannon ball tore through the tavern, landing right where I sat." He pointed to a large mound of debris where the tavern used to stand. "I'm lucky this was all it did to me."

"But Cleophes," Abigail butted in. "That still doesn't explain why you didn't leave like the others." The Scotsman's cheeks took on a dark hue of pink on his fair, weathered skin.

"Oh, Miss, Abigail. It's naht a part of my life I like to speak of, but we've come across hard times since this awful conflict between the colonies and the king in England. It's more than a challenge to make a profit from the English goods I buy off the ships when they make port. No one wants to support the Crown or purchase materials from the Motherland these days. The truth is I thought it would be to my advantage to stay behind." He held up the dress he'd been examining when they came over. "I might be able to make enough from this and a few other items I found to get me through this winter. From what I hear, it's going to be a hard one."

"What's the meaning of this?" Two men approached them, dressed neatly, each in a white waistcoat complimented by white breeches and stockings. A blue frock draped across their shoulders lined with golden buttons that ran down each side of their white lapel collars. There was no doubt who these men were: soldiers, or rather officers of the Royal Navy.

The man who spoke was tall and thin, wearing a tricorn hat that covered most of his sandy, blond hair. He spoke with authority, though his eyes appeared kind in nature. The second officer held a slightly broader build than his companion. The sideburns that adorned his face made him appear more rugged than the polished look of the first. Instead of a hat, he'd chosen to leave his hair exposed, revealing ebony curls trailing to the nape of his neck. He gave them a hard stare that only ignited Abigail's own contempt, wanting to blame these men for so much loss.

How could he look at them like that, like they didn't belong here, like...Abigail caught her breath. Did he think she was rummaging through what pieces remained of her townspeople's lives? Heat fumed inside her at the thought. It was she who should be angry towards these men. They were the ones responsible for her town's downfall. The anger gave her courage and her eyes locked with the second officer's, mirroring his judgmental stare in challenge.

"I say, again, what's the meaning of this?" Abigail caught the flinch of irritation in the first officer's calm, but firmly repeated question. He made a stern gesture towards Cleo. "I don't imagine that dress will be very becoming on a man such as yourself. I would let the lady have it." A touch of light humor rimmed his voice.

"There's naghin amiss here, sir. We were just going through to see what remained of our belongings."

The two officers exchanged glances. Abigail wasn't so certain they believed Cleo. Even when the man wasn't covered in dust and blackened debris, he didn't exactly give the impression of a person who owned the high-end, sage frock that'd been tossed to the side earlier because of its singed sleeves.

The second officer peered over to Abigail. She could feel his gaze roam from her head all the way down to her toes before his expression turned smug. Her face went hot, but not with anger this time.

He spoke to her. "And I suppose the dress is yours?"

Abigail caught the cynical brow. She didn't know what to say at first. Clearly, the dress didn't belong to her. She didn't fit the profile and these men knew it, though they didn't know how much. She stood silent in her plain work dress, her apron tied at her waist and her white cap that covered most of her hair. She was dressed for work as she was most days, typical of her life on her family farm. But it wasn't just the necessary clothing she'd grown accustomed to for getting the job done. It was the fact her family couldn't afford anything remotely close to the fine, silk dress belonging to Mrs. Gentry that Cleo still held onto. These men didn't even know her and yet she felt exposed. She hated it.

"I don't think that matters in the light of things." Abraham put his arm protectively in front of her and stepped forward to meet the second officer in challenge. His eyes narrowed. He snarled like a dog ready for a fight. The officer's attention drew away from her. She would've been relieved if she wasn't concerned for what Abraham might do.

"In light of things? Do tell." The officer met her brother's challenge with an unbothered smirk.

"For starters, your Parliament thinks it owns us, when it doesn't. We've made a new life here in the colonies since our families arrived over 100 years ago. We have our own legislations here. We have our own government. We don't need your Parliament to tell us what to do, especially when it won't let the colonies be represented to serve in it."

Her brother's boldness made Abigail's stomach turn over. What would these men do to someone so daring as to speak with such defiance? Simply revealing his own side could get him arrested, she sucked in a breath, or *hanged*. All the officers had to do was ask the question she feared her brother might be brazen enough to answer.

The second man shifted his gaze to her and then back onto her brother, his expression agitated but his tone even. "You've forgotten where your families came from in the first place. Parliament allowed them to settle here. You wouldn't be here if it weren't for your mother country's provision. You've lost sight of that."

"This is my country." Abraham stomped the heel of his boot into the dark, ashen soil. He looked ready to spring. "And I'll fight for it." The officer met her brother's defiance with a scowl, his patience at its limit. Now, he appeared just as eager to test whether Abraham stood by his words.

"Gentlemen, let's remain civil." The first officer tried to intervene.

"Civil? Is that what you call what happened in Boston? Five dead and two of them just seventeen?"

Abigail's heart raced. Her brother's rage was only building and she longed to bring it down. What would these officers do if things escalated any further?

"Sir, do calm yourself." The first officer frowned. "Boston was a tragic mistake, but we have run off course to the initial reason for my comrade's and my interference." He turned towards Cleo, putting the man back on trial. "The dress is clearly not yours, nor the rest of the items in the pile you've constructed. Why do you have them?"

Cleo gave an uninterested shrug. "They may naht have been mine to begin with, but no one else has come to claim 'em. It would be a shame to just let all these wonderful items go to waste."

"They've hardly had time to claim them. It's been little over 24 hours. Give them three days. If the items remain, consider them yours."

"Three days?" Cleo shook his head. "But sir, anything can happen in three days. What if the weather doesn't hold? I can't get a penny for 'em if that be the case. Or worse yet, what if someone else comes along to snatch 'em up? No, sir. That's naht fair. I was here first. I should be the one to have 'em."

"They're not yours." The first officer's kind disposition turned to one of irritation. "As far as I'm concerned, we can confiscate them or trash them. I'm offering you a courtesy for even the chance to have them. I could arrest you for disrespecting an officer if you prefer."

Cleo shut down. He didn't even try to argue further. Instead, he gave the dress to the second officer who held his hand out expectantly. The first officer kept his sight on Cleo while the second focused on Abraham, his glare warning him to stand down. For the moment her brother obeyed but she could still feel the intensity within the ruined foundations of the Gentry home. Cleo also looked less confident now with beads of sweat starting to form on his forehead. She wondered if she gave any telling signs how she felt. She tried not to, but the butterflies in her stomach wouldn't take a rest.

"What did you say your name was?" The first officer addressed Cleo again with a pointed look.

"My name?" Cleo hesitated. "Well, I didn't say, sir." Expectant eyes appeared on each officer, no doubt waiting for him to oblige them with his full answer. He didn't appear desirous to give it. Cleo's voice shook. He was uneasy about something. Did it have to do with these men? Officers of the Royal Navy?

Abigail compared the two men, dressed neatly and unflawed in their uniforms against the backdrop of her destroyed and disassembled town. Cleo had warned them about what would happen beforehand. He gave them enough time to gather what they needed before they had to leave. For that, she felt she owed him somehow.

The second officer's gaze shifted to her and for a brief moment their eyes locked. The butterflies fled as her blood boiled. This man, *these* men, were responsible for what happened here. Her courage stirred. She just hoped she wouldn't regret what she was about to do.

"Gentlemen."

The word caught in her throat, but she quickly recovered and squared her shoulders. She ignored the men's surprise, even Abraham's. "This is my Uncle Samuel. He was just helping my brother and me go through some things we hoped to salvage from the destruction you and your men caused."

Abigail let the words come out cold. She was determined to appear convincing, although mindful her boldness towards these men would not be taken lightly. To insult them was to insult the Crown. Her anger exposed her feelings, not thinking about what consequences might result. But it was too late. She'd said it and now she wouldn't show them fear, even if that's exactly how she felt.

"Miss, we have no quarrel with you, but be that as it may I'll have to ask to see your deed of the estate." She caught the officer's mouth tighten.

The reply came easy enough in her rage, her body shaking.

"And where do you think that might be, sir?" The sarcasm in her tone rang as she peered over the grounds of the ruined Gentry home. "There is nothing I can show you that will prove I once lived here. You've made certain of that."

"We simply carried out our orders, miss." This time it was the second officer who replied. His voice was strong, but his eyes had softened from earlier. "May we be of service and offer you transportation home?"

She did her best to hold back a scoff. Because of their actions, her home was gone. No, they couldn't offer her transportation home because she no longer had one.

"Your services are not wanted." She worked hard to force the words past the lump in her throat as she said it.

"Abby?" It was Abraham. He stood down from the two officers. Perhaps his confusion over her intercession had led him to do so. At least she'd been able to calm him. Cleo's mouth went slack. He too, looked less bothered and more perplexed by what had taken place, but stayed silent. She was ready to move past this, to get away from these men. Just seeing them ignited the pain inside her.

"Please move on, gentlemen. I'm sure you have more orders to follow." The words came out bitter. For a moment, both men flinched as if her comment had somehow wounded them. She doubted that was the case.

"Very well, miss." The first officer bowed before he assumed his dignified posture once again. He looked to his comrade, who stared at her. She didn't read challenge in his expression, but she dared not flinch. "Let's go, Mr. Ward. There's still more to cover before we need to report back."

The man he called "Ward" nodded, displaying a mutual understanding and then turned towards her once more. His features were now just as dignified as the first officer's.

"Take care, miss." He too gave a regal-like bow, but not before she thought she caught a smirk wipe across his face that both surprised and infuriated her.

Chapter 4

Garrett found himself playing the fantastic scene over again in his mind. The defiance of the young woman had taken him by surprise. He couldn't decide whether she'd been reckless or courageous in the way she expressed her unfortunate opinion of him and his fellow comrades. He remembered the fine-arched eyebrows extended just above those sharp green eyes. Their ferocity had burned an impression upon him he could never forget, and that was before she had uttered a word of her displeasure.

Until they'd happen upon the two men and woman, the morning proved uneventful. Sailors within the fleet were ordered to disembark into Falmouth to properly inspect the damage and report. They were given permission to loot if they desired, but violence towards any townsperson they came across was strongly discouraged. Wanting a change of scenery, most of the officers followed suit, happy to set their feet on dry land while also maintaining a presence of authority for keeping their men in line. Garrett and Nicholas usually ventured together unless ordered otherwise on such excursions. That morning had been no exception.

They'd started on the lower part of town and worked their way through until they reached the upper end. It was evident their mission had been a success if that's what you would call destroying a town. The place was all but obliterated. Buildings and homes on the lower and middle areas were leveled, or at the very least, deemed unrecognizable. Most of the homes in the back street and upper end had shared in the same fate.

Inside the town some residents had returned, no doubt working to digest the reality of their loss and salvage what remained. The navy had reduced nearly three quarters of the area and he suspected these townspeople were going to have a hard winter unless they managed to find a place of lodging elsewhere. But as much as they lost, Garrett hadn't changed his mind about them. They'd brought their own ruin by their lack of action. They had neither accepted Mowat's terms, nor took arms to defend their homes. This was the consequence to their passivity.

It was the old man that captured their attention initially, or more so his grossly disheveled appearance. He looked like he'd had the unfortunate experience of being loaded and shot from one of their own canons. And that wasn't all that seemed strange. He'd been holding up a woman's dressing gown as if he was about to try the piece on. Both Nicholas and Garrett had assumed the same thing. They'd seen it all before.

The man was looting from the wreckage. It was one thing to take items as a soldier. That was expected as part of the terms that came with the rules of war. This man, however, was not a soldier, nor had he ever been one, he'd wager.

When the other man and woman crossed over to accompany him, Garrett and Nicholas decided to act. They little tolerated lone persons who partook in the spoils of war but had no part in the fighting. A group was even less welcomed. It wouldn't last long. It never did. Seeing the royal colors had a way of making people comply. Or at least it used to. But this group was different, and he didn't like it.

And the man near his own age? Garrett's jaw clenched. His insolence for the uniform reeked of rebellion. He wanted to arrest the fool and take him in for treason. If only the man would've swung at him or even just threatened him. Garrett could sense he wanted to and was almost there before Nicholas stepped in to save the man's neck.

And the woman. What part did she play? She looked disturbed by the whole ordeal like she wished it was over. He almost felt sorry for her and even decided not to ask whether the fool she was with was a Whig or Tory. That would have sealed the man's fate, but when he looked at her, something told him to hold back.

He couldn't explain why, except maybe he didn't envy her for whatever relation she had with such insolence. However, that was before he'd learned she had more gumption than the two men combined.

Garrett blinked as the water lapped against the starboard side of the ship. The anger in her eyes pierced into his, catching him off guard. It seemed like minutes had passed before he felt he was able to tear himself free from that unforgiving stare. A chill sprang up his spine at the memory of it.

"Your mind on the stars tonight, Garrett, or something else you'd like to talk about?" Nicholas approached him by the side of the ship. No doubt he'd come from the wardroom where the other officers remained socializing from their evening meal. Garrett could smell traces of alcohol on Nicholas' breath, a routine part of their dining he himself partook in on occasion, but not tonight. Tonight, he wanted his head clear.

Nicholas knew the answer to the question before Garrett said anything. The two of them had grown up together. Not only that, but his friend also had a keen sense for reading people. It was another great quality for commanding a ship. Even if he didn't know exactly what part of it, he knew already Garrett's mind remained on the confrontation they had within the town. Regardless, Garrett really didn't want to discuss it.

He chose the safer topic instead.

"The stars."

Nicholas gave a short laugh; acutely aware he'd been blown off. He didn't look offended.

"All right, have it your way. We'll talk about the cosmos instead of what's eating at you."

Garrett smiled. He took a deep breath of fresh sea air, letting it go slowly and angled his eyes towards the wide expanse above them. Not a cloud in the sky prevented the stars and moon from illuminating the water. It was a sight he could never grow tired of even after all his years at sea. He didn't know why, but something about them seemed to demand his attention and he willingly complied.

As a boy, his father had told him God had created them in a single day. Looking at the vast amount of them now, scattered across the blackness overhead, he had trouble with such a belief. But if it had been true, he shuddered to think what else a god like that could be capable of.

"I never get tired of looking up at them," he finally said.

"There is something about the stars, isn't there? It makes me wonder at times if there's more out there beyond them, beyond us."

Garrett gave an uneasy shift. It wasn't like Nicholas to bring up the topic of God. Sure, they'd attended weekly chaplain services, but that was mostly for appearances and rules. In the time he'd known Nicholas and his father, he'd never seen them utter a prayer outside of public display or mention things above. Strange how he'd just been thinking about the very subject moments ago. Nicholas knew him well, but he didn't know him that well.

Why would a topic he'd pushed away all these years now suddenly creep its way back into his life? Was he feeling guilty for Falmouth? He hadn't before the attack. Not only that, he stood firmly behind Mowat's decision. Garrett's jaw firmed, not thrilled where this rabbit hole was about to lead.

"If there is something else." The cynicism rang in his voice as if challenging the supernatural being to come forth. It didn't.

Nicholas laughed. "You don't think there's more out there after going through what we've gone through? Seeing things that we've seen? I know you don't think that's true. Your father had a knack for talking about God. He should've been a priest rather than a carpenter."

Garrett shrugged to keep appearances, but the dagger pierced through his chest at the mention of his father. No matter how many years passed, he still couldn't shake the images from that day. His father's brutally beaten body on the floor of his shop with the money gone. He never knew when it happened, only that a bad feeling crept up when his father was an hour late from his usual return home. Garrett couldn't make himself wait any longer and decided to make the walk just to make sure everything was all right. But it wasn't.

Garrett fists clenched. He didn't understand it now and he certainly didn't understand it then. His father had been devout in his faith, never missing a Sunday sermon, yet God had let him suffer and die without just cause. Irritation wet his lips. "I'm not sure what I believe anymore." He might have asked Nicholas why the change in interest towards God with so many years not caring, but the reminders of his father put him in a bad mood. He was more than ready to do an about-face with this subject.

Again, Nicholas didn't press him. Over the years doing so only reinforced Garrett's walls. The two of them stood there silent for a moment, gazing out into the openness of the sea.

On a night like this the ocean looked black and sinister except for the constellations and moon above them reflecting within it. It could easily crush their ship with its mighty waters and take their crew as prisoners to a murky grave if it wanted to. With the time he'd spent at sea, there were always a few lost by a violent storm or when battling in the open waters. He'd come to respect it and hoped it would not claim his own life one day to leave him tossed back and forth and alone in its deep.

"Do you recall that older fellow we met today on land?"

They'd only come across one group of persons. Much of the town was still desolate from the life that lived there before the navy laid it to waste. But even still, Garrett knew instantly who Nicholas meant. The man was unforgettable, in his butchered clothing and soiled state. He looked just as bad as the town they set fire to. "He looked vastly familiar once I got a good look at him."

Garrett nodded. He'd thought the same thing. And why did the young woman choose to defend that man? Perhaps she'd known him, but he highly doubted he was truly her uncle. He couldn't put a finger on it, only that the whole ordeal seemed off. One moment she was wide-eyed and tense, as if ready to bolt. That was when the young man decided to oppose them. Before Garrett knew it, her whole demeanor changed, growing just as obstinate as she defended her so-called uncle. Surely, she recognized he and Nicholas were not so foolish. The man was clearly guilty of something. It was evident he'd been anxious while they were present. They could sense that much. They merely lacked the proof otherwise to arrest him and taking him on the grounds for hearsay would have been a waste of time. The young woman had saved him for now, but once they found out who the man really was and what crimes he committed, Garrett highly doubted the king's army would be so lenient again. He certainly wouldn't.

"I'm afraid I don't know either. He didn't look familiar to me, but he looked guilty of something. You certainly startled him."

"Yes." Nicholas' brow furrowed. "I noticed that too. I'll check my logs and inquire of my father about the man. Perhaps he knows more on the matter." Nicholas gave a wry smile. "The young lady didn't care for you, did she?"

Garrett only offered an uninterested shrug, pretending not to care. "I don't think she liked either of us. In her eyes, we are the ones responsible for what happened to her town."

"I venture you're right. But I do think she and the other townspeople will come to see we had to follow orders. It wasn't meant to be personal."

Garrett disagreed. He knew what losing something meant. It was hard not to take offense when it seemed like something was snatched away from you.

For him it was his father, back when he was young and the possibility of the Navy wasn't an option.

Garrett shook his head, still gazing at the dark openness surrounding them on all sides of the ship. "Everything in this war is personal."

Nicholas offered no reply as the waves broke easily against the stationed vessel. They both knew it was the truth. No matter which side a person was on, war was always personal.

Garrett eyed Nicholas. He seemed focused out across the emptiness. Unlike his friend's uncanny ability to know him so well, he couldn't discern what was on Nicholas' mind in that moment. Maybe the idea of God had returned, though he couldn't imagine why. Nicholas had done well enough without the Almighty this far. He was top of his class in the academy and top ranked in the field. He was honorable and respected like his father, though less harsh in executing his orders. Most people liked him. Women were attracted to him. He had it all. So why did he think there was more? And did he think God could somehow give it to him?

Garrett's fists tightened again at the reminder of what God had done for his father. The man had been naive. He'd trusted God with his life and God let him suffer at the hands of robbers. He wasn't about to let his best friend go down that deadly path.

"I wouldn't look too hard for something that's not there, Nick."

Nicholas smirked. "And here I was thinking I was the one who knew you so well."

Garrett shrugged with some disappointment. He didn't think he'd be right on his guess. He'd hoped he wasn't. "I suppose we've spent plenty of time together to know one another well enough."

"A brotherhood of it." Nicholas let out an exasperated breath, his face grown serious. "Which is how I know where you're coming from."

Garrett flinched at the pain he worked so hard to force away every instance the issue was brought up. As time had gone on, it was talked about less and less. Even so, the hurt still lingered deep.

After his father's death, Garrett tried asking God why he would let something like that happen. He never got an answer. Instead, he only felt angrier, so he stopped asking. While alive, his father talked about God like He was his best friend, always looking out for him.

"He is all-powerful. He knows everything and everyone and He is everywhere. You can hide from me, Garrett, but you cannot hide from God."

It was something his father would say to him when he'd been caught in a lie or had done something else to get in trouble. Garrett often struggled with why a god so powerful would care to take the lives of both of his parents when he still needed them. Some best friend.

His perspective of God was more like that greedy thief who murdered his father. He'd taken away the little Garrett had left in the world, leaving him with nothing to salvage—a boy without a family. What kind of god would do that to a child? He didn't care how much his father believed. He had bought into a lie, and Garrett wouldn't fall for it. He didn't want Nicholas to, either. He didn't want his best friend to feel the bitterness that filled his own soul at times. He didn't deserve that.

"I'm just saying to be careful, Nick. I wouldn't want you to end up disappointed or waste your efforts. You know what happened to my father."

"I know." Nicholas didn't offer his condolences. They'd already been down that road more than enough times when it first happened. Garrett cringed just remembering all the looks of pity he'd received in the past.

"Not that I'm condoning your father's death, it's just part of me wonders if there was more to it."

Garrett angled his head, his brow in a defensive raise. "What do you mean?"

"I don't know. You were only a friend of mine at the time—one I didn't particularly like but tolerated because our fathers were such good friends. Now, you're my brother. It was challenging at first, suddenly having one, but I wouldn't trade it for anything. Not to mention, you're on your way to becoming captain of your own ship. Maybe God just changed the direction of your life."

Nicholas meant no ill intent, but bitterness coated Garrett's throat. "If that's true, He has a twisted way of changing one's life direction." It made Garrett feel like his worth to the Almighty was as shiftless as the wind, changing courses constantly. If that's how much God cared, he didn't want any part of him. Garrett wanted to tell his friend he was wrong. God had left him an orphan. He didn't care enough to have any part of Garrett's life, except to take it away.

Garrett wholeheartedly disagreed. "Your father is the one who changed my life, Nick, not God. I'm thankful they'd remained friends for so long even with my father's lower social standing."

Nicholas breathed in heavy then out again. "Yes, well now you know firsthand, now how strict the man can be."

"Maybe, but I'll take that rather than having to fend for myself in an orphanage. Besides, I still felt like a second son. Because of him, I'm a lieutenant in the Royal Navy working my way up." It was more than what Garrett could say for the so-called "Being" who peered down on him from heaven. No, God wasn't looking after him. It was Nicholas' father and the Navy that gave him a second chance at life.

Still, he often thought about what life would be like if his parents were alive. Being a son of a carpenter, he would've learned his own father's trade, living under humble means. Perhaps he would've taken a wife by now. He wasn't so sure he would mind such a life if it meant he could talk to his father once more. But that was not at all the life he now knew with growing up in a captain's household and, apart from his parents being gone, he didn't mind that either.

He'd been given a chance to work his way up in society through the Navy. With his status came privileges he wouldn't have otherwise known. He'd attended multiple parties with some of the elite of society and had earned their attention in conversation just by being an officer of rank. And even if his rank wasn't apparent, there seemed to be something about a man in uniform that always grabbed the ladies' attention.

Even so, Garrett hardly pursued the invitations anymore. He'd come to find such ladies of nobility were much the same, busying themselves with trifling matters, and he'd grown bored of their company. If he had been a simple craftsman, they wouldn't have given him a second glance and for some reason, that bothered him.

When Garrett offered nothing else to Nicholas' topic over God, the first lieutenant broke into an easy smile.

"All right, enough of that. I can see you're as tense as if our ship was being overtaken by pirates. I won't say anything more about it." Nicholas looked back towards the officer's cabin. A bolster of laughs bursted forth from its closed door. "Why don't you join the rest of us back in the cabin for some merriment this evening? They were wondering why you left so early after dinner—had me come out here to check on things. I said I would try to convince you to return, but no promises."

The change in topic caused Garrett's shoulders to relax. The bitterness in his mouth waned as the corner of his lips raised.

"Thanks, but I prefer to be out here for now." He'd been enjoying the solitude of the upper deck when Nicholas came over. Until then, he had only heard the whispering voices of a few crew members. Apparently, they'd also chosen the quiet of the nearly abandoned main deck to that of the mess where the rest of the crew members dined. It had given him the chance to think. "Maybe I'll join in a minute," he said, feeling somewhat truthful about the statement.

"Sure." Nicholas shrugged with a nonchalance. "Don't let that brunette take up too much of your time out here."

Garrett startled as his friend gave him a chiding smile before turning towards the stern and back to the wardroom. A moment later, he heard the door open. Loud and obnoxious singing from what he recognized as "God Save the King" breached through. The men had butchered the song with their slurred speech. No doubt the product of far too much wine, rum, or both.

For most of the crew it was a time of celebration after an assignment had been successfully carried out. On any other day Garrett would be right there with them, drunk and giddy with the taste of victory, but tonight all he thought about were those green eyes staring back at him. Or at least they had been until Nicholas brought up the subject of God. Now, there was more on his mind than he cared to think of. He chose the image of the brunette over the latter, preferring the copper undertones of her chestnut hair as it danced in the harbor wind instead of the deity that let him down so many years ago.

He thought again of the woman's brow, her lips pursed in anger. Now that he'd obtained a moment to reflect, he realized just how impressed he was with her, even if he hadn't agreed with her opinion. She had a boldness that intrigued him. She had spoken her mind, surely knowing he and Nicholas could have reported her for treason.

Had one of those homes belonged to her? Garrett already knew. He'd recognized the burden of loss she carried. Which one had it been? Perhaps she had grown up on the lower side near the harbor or maybe more towards the middle part of town. Had it truly been in the pile of rubble where he and Nicholas had found them?

Garrett could hardly swallow. It was nearing the beginning of November. Winter was quickly on its way, and he didn't know if she had taken up shelter elsewhere. Not that she wanted their help. She had made that clear enough. He wasn't certain why he cared so much. He thought of her icy tone towards them and felt a sense of justification at the memory of her refusal. Maybe if she hadn't dismissed their help so prematurely, they would've done more to offer their aid. Still, he knew when he wasn't wanted.

With his concern for the lady beginning to diminish, his spirits for celebration began to return and the echoes of the men in the mess singing had stirred his desire to join in the gaiety of the night. He gave the stars one last glance before retreating to the captain's cabin where he welcomed the distraction of his drunken fellow officers.

Chapter 5

Cambridge, Massachusetts 1775

"Abigail, hand me that needle over there."

Abigail did what she was told and grabbed the small instrument from Doctor Adam's medical satchel. She didn't know why she'd been placed at the doctor's side, but her experience in witnessing two of her mother's births somehow qualified her to be a camp nurse. She handed the needle to Dr. Adams along with a small amount of thread that would be enough to get the job done.

"Really, Thomas, you should be more careful instead of getting yourself into trouble you don't need. I doubt your mother would approve of your brawl against your soon to be comrades on the field." Dr. Adams threaded the needle, giving his young patient a disapproving glance.

"It was just for fun, sir."

"That's what you call fun? Getting your own handed to you? What happened to the days of playing a game of cricket? At least you could try hitting something other than each other."

The boy, Thomas, responded with a sheepish glance.

"Never mind, I don't pretend to know the mind of today's youth, nor do I intend to. I'd rather just focus on getting you taken care of." Dr. Adams drew his attention to the minor injury, a cut just above the boy's eye. "It looks like Jacob didn't rough you up too badly. I can't do anything about the bruises. Those will heal on their own in time, though you'll see some discoloration as they do. The cut is minor, but just deep enough to require some stitching." He looked towards the needle and back at Thomas again. "This will sting a bit though I doubt much compared to what you've already been through"

Thomas gave a shaky nod before his eyes shot wide at the needle that began its approach to his forehead.

Abigail took hold of Thomas' hand. It amazed her this young man could so easily find himself caught up in a fight that left him bruised and beaten while the small point of a needle made him squeamish. She gave his hand a gentle squeeze and offered him a reassuring smile. "Tell me about your family, Thomas. Are you from here?" She hoped the question might divert his attention.

"No Miss." He winced as Dr. Adams started his procedure, the needle penetrating the skin. "I've come from Salem. We have a farm there. It's a lot of work, but I have a pretty big family to help out."

"Is that so? How many of you are there?"

"There's seven of us kids including me. I'm the oldest." A pained smile crossed his mouth as Dr. Adams continued to pull the needle through, the thread working to close the open wound.

Abigail imagined it would've been more of a proud one if he hadn't been going through what he currently was. She reflected on his answer and considered just how young he looked himself. The youngest age to enlist in the army was 15, but Thomas barely looked even that. His face was clean, showing no sign of whiskers and he was quite smaller than his peers. His blonde, curly hair also made him appear youthful still and reminded her of her youngest brother, Henry. If Henry was a few years older, they would've been mistaken as brothers. That very thought made herself want to wince, but not at the needle. She couldn't imagine Henry here in Cambridge learning how to stand face-to-face against British soldiers. She became aware the encouragement in her expression had weakened and tried to strengthen it again. "I'm sure your parents are proud of your bravery for being here. Did you come with your father?"

"No, Miss. It's just me." He averted his gaze both from the needle in-between his eyes and her.

"Alright, Thomas. That should do it, lad." Dr. Adams tied off the thread before he wiped away a small amount of blood. "You'll probably have a scar when it heals, but it might serve you well. Maybe the other boys won't give you as much trouble." He gave the boy a hearty wink with a hint of a smile. "Now, off you go."

Abigail's gaze lingered, watching the slightly older image of her youngest brother walk awkwardly out of the medical tent.

"Don't pity that boy." Dr. Adams took hold of a partially soiled cloth and used it to clean his needle. "It's the last thing he needs."

The piece of advice directed to her came out of the doctor's mouth more like an order. Abigail scrunched her brow. "I don't understand."

"Thomas' reason for being here has everything to do with his father not." Dr. Adams must have sensed her confusion for he went on. "The boy's family has a small farm in Salem, but his father was a fisherman by trade. We crossed paths in Salem when I treated him from a minor injury he'd acquired at sea. He was a good man but was killed unexpectedly while on the job. As far as I know it had something to do with a scuffle between British officials. I highly suspect that's why the boy is here in the first place. That, and the small funds he'll collect as a soldier. His mother could certainly use the money to be sure, but I'm quite certain it's revenge that's behind Thomas' motivation." He placed the needle back in his satchel. "Frankly, I wish the lad would go home. His mother could use the help as most of the children are still too young to be of any good to her aid. The boy's father was no giant, but he was plenty tall and his mother average. I'm certain he'll catch up to his peers in time, but for now Jacob and his gang use the delay for sport. Thomas could do without that especially when his father's death was only three months back."

Abigail didn't say anything, only feeling a sadness for the youth.

Dr. Adams must've sensed it easily enough. He gave her a stern look. "Like I said, Miss Thatcher, the boy doesn't need your pity. He'd probably deny anything I just said to make certain of it. If anything, he could use a friend."

"Dr. Adams." The flap opened to the medical tent to reveal the very subject of their discussion. Thomas. The doctor and Abigail shared a weary glance. How long had he'd been outside the tent?

"Everything okay, Thomas?" Dr. Adams looked over at the recently treated wound, appearing to examine it again. "The cut still looks fine. Is there something I missed?"

Thomas shook his head. "No, sir. I've actually come for Miss Thatcher on Officer Haywood's orders." The boy looked to her with a gained confidence he hadn't possessed before leaving their work tent. "He requires to see you, miss."

Abigail nodded, not entirely surprised by the order. She'd been in the continental camp for hardly a week and quickly understood her role as a camp follower was a versatile one. On her first day she'd helped cook and serve all the camp meals and on the second she'd worked to wash and pin half of the men's clothes to the dry line. It was on her third day here when she was placed with Dr. Adams after Abraham casually disclosed her attendance of their youngest siblings' births to another officer. It was becoming clear she was needed wherever she could be of use and now it seemed Officer Haywood had found another area.

Abigail exited the medical tent with Thomas at her side as they walked along the Commons of Harvard Square. She thought about what Dr.

Adams said concerning the boy's father and still wondered if he'd overheard anything, but she didn't ask. Instead, she remembered what the camp physician said about him needing a friend.

"Officer Haywood didn't give you too much trouble about the cut I hope?" The hint of a smile touched Thomas' cheek with her jesting tone. He looked like he could use a touch of light-heartedness right about now.

"He didn't like it one bit. He said I was lucky Washington was forgiving enough to allow me to stay. If Mr. Haywood was in command, he said he'd throw me out before I could explain myself."

Abigail gave a small laugh. She wouldn't have expected much different from the shrewd officer. "I don't suppose he did."

"No. To be honest, I was more nervous about what Haywood might do than my mother. She'd be a little cross I got myself into a fight, but not for too long since she's looking for any excuse to bring me home. I'm just thankful he doesn't have the authority to dismiss me."

Abigail gave him a glance full of warning. "He doesn't now, but he might not need to if you get yourself in another fight. He does make a good point about the commander. Washington might be more forgiving, but he comes from the same Virginian upbringing that Haywood does. I doubt he'll tolerate such behavior for long."

Thomas let out a sigh. He put his hands in his pockets and scuffed his foot against the ground. "You're probably right, Miss Thatcher."

"Abigail," she gently corrected, "But my friends call me Abby." She smiled before she gave him a telling glance. "And I hope never to find out if I am."

He beamed and again she was reminded of Henry, the two sharing that youthful innocence that lit their expression. "I'll do my best." His face fell. "But Jake and those boys make me so mad at times. When I first got to camp, I found out they were my age. All I wanted to do was befriend 'em. You know, be a part of their group." He kicked a small rock lying in their pathway off to the side. "I don't know what I did to 'em but

52

for some reason they don't like me and do everything but shout it off the rooftops to make sure I know it. I try to ignore their jeers, brushing it off as best I can. Honest, I do, but I don't know…" His eyes rose to hers, a struggle between anger and remorse within them. "This time I just blew up." He shook his head. "I hardly remember doing it."

Abigail tilted her head towards Thomas as they continued to walk. "Do you remember what it was about?"

"Not really. Something about Jake knowing girls with more whiskers than I've got. Just another jab with how young I look. I don't know why I got so mad then. I didn't really care about what he said. It's not like I haven't heard it before. I suppose I just got tired of it all." Thomas brushed his fingers across his forehead where'd he'd received his stitches. "A lot of good that did me. Jake barely got a scratch on him."

They were getting closer to Haywood's tent. Abigail could easily spot it if it without the slightest effort. That wouldn't be the case in the British army where the tents were more uniform and exact. Here, however, the cacophony of makeshift dwellings that served as living quarters for the men made the orderly structure stand out like a well-polished, sore thumb.

Abigail would've laughed under her breath at the absurdity if she still hadn't felt a crushing astonishment walking along the camp. She was sure the British army would if they ever caught sight of the spectacle. And why wouldn't they? It wasn't uncommon to pass by a shelter that looked like it was thrown up quickly with whatever could be found; stone, turf, brush and sometimes brick. She frowned as they passed by an older gentleman who wore only his breeches and stockings and stood outside his own housing comprised of sailcloth with some boards used as its main support. The reminder easily gave way to her first day in Cambridge, the sheer sight of the encampment stealing her breath, and not in a good way.

She hadn't expected the group of men Washington would be leading to be as formally trained as King George's army. That thought was highly impractical, especially since most of the soldiers of the continental army held no military background whatsoever, but according to Abraham, Washington had a reputation. He was a man of discipline and tradition, yet Abigail couldn't help thinking if that were true, the men he led in battle were anything but the reflection of their commander. Many were rough, unclean, and unshaven, mirroring more of the disarray of creations in which they took shelter rather than the well-fitted Virginian plantation owner.

They were merchants, tradesmen, and farmers. Many were born in the colonies, but some had come from elsewhere. All fought for freedom from the English King, but some also fought for personal freedoms that had been hijacked from them since birth. They were anything but uniform and Abigail wasn't so sure if that was to their advantage against an army that was the very definition of the word itself.

"Your brother's Abraham, isn't he?" Thomas asked the question with enthusiasm like her brother held the status of the patriot general himself.

"He is." She smiled with mild intrigue. "Do you know him?"

"Never met him, but I know he's only been here a week and there's talk Washington has already had him in one of the officer meetings."

Abigail didn't say anything at first. The truth was she'd been so busy herself at camp since their arrival she hadn't spoken with Abraham to know the information firsthand. She had to admit, the news startled her to a degree. Abraham was just a farmer and with no training as a soldier. What would Washington want with him? She made a mental note to look for her brother later and ask just that.

"Are you all right, Miss Abby?" Thomas' expression was dappled with concern. It was then she realized she hadn't given a response. In truth, she wasn't completely sure if she was all right. Something about Abraham's quick rise in popularity made her muscles twitch, but she didn't know why.

"I didn't know that...about Abraham I mean. I'm sorry to say I haven't spoken with my brother since our second day here in Cambridge. That was five days ago."

"I wouldn't worry too much about it, Miss Abby." Thomas' eyes lit with confidence. "I doubt it has anything to do with him being in trouble if that's what you're thinking. Washington wouldn't waste an officer meeting on something like that."

Abigail appreciated his effort of reassurance even if her concern for her brother had nothing to do with punishment. All she could think of was what Abraham aimed to do now that their town had been destroyed by the Royal Navy. She knew what the impact had done to her. Before she'd lost her home, she had no desire to join the rebellion. Her wish to avoid the war altogether was even pressed upon Abraham as she tried to talk him out of it upon the debris of the place they grew up. But that all changed at their encounter with the Royal Navy officers. A fire of anger burned within her that was enough to bring her here and do something. It was her way of fighting back for what had been taken from her. Abraham was ready to fight for the cause before the attack on their town. Who knows what he was willing to do now?

"I certainly hope you're right, Thomas. Otherwise, I'm going to have to make better acquaintances here in camp. I'm not sure it would do me well to associate with men constantly getting into trouble." She gave him a light-hearted smirk letting him know she was fine.

Appearing to believe her, Thomas went ahead a little, disappearing into Haywood's tent. He came back out half a minute later to let her know she could enter. When he was dismissed, he gave her an expression as if to say 'good luck' before leaving.

Abigail sighed. She'd been in the presence of Officer Haywood enough times to know the drill. She'd be ordered to take a seat in the single chair across from him. At a little over six feet tall he would tower over while he looked down at her from where he stood.

The first time she'd encountered the ritual, Abigail felt herself blush from embarrassment, sensing the state of her belittlement. But the several occasions thereafter for each new order she received, whether it be serving the breakfasts and dinners, laundering, and mending the men's clothes, fetching firewood, and her most recent assignment with aiding Dr. Adams—the state of the officer's scorn towards her grew tiresome. Still, even if she'd been standing, the man had a way of making one feel small.

She cast out another breath, steadier this time as she readied herself for what else Haywood could throw at her before she entered the regimental officer's tent. At no surprise, Haywood stood expectantly in his navy-blue uniform. The ensemble was nearly identical to the general's and stood out among most the camp who had no means of such official dress. His regimental coat was well-pressed and pristine even against the wardrobe of the King's soldiers.

Haywood's eyes told her to take a seat and she did, but not before she noticed a Negro woman who also took part in their meeting. The woman's hands were folded at her waist and her eyes soft and hopeful. She gave Abigail a quick glance but averted her attention back on the man in charge.

Abigail did the same, drawn to how the officer's facial features seemed to come to a point apart from his round eyes that almost looked complacent.

"Miss Thatcher." Haywood gave her a cordial nod that lacked any degree of warmth. "A small matter has come up that has left me to pull you from your duties to assist Dr. Adams today. However, I'm certain the skilled doctor can handle things without you."

The comment was apathetic and bit, but she couldn't disagree with it. Dr. Adams was entirely capable of handling things by himself. Her recent position by his side was more of a student then of any aid at present. Yet, she did hope with time and learning she could be of some assistance to the doctor after all.

Haywood began to pace the area behind a small table that served as his desk. His clean-shaven chin was held high, a gesture that pulled at Abigail to straighten her posture and force her shoulders back.

"This is the housemaid of a Mrs. Schreier, a woman who lives here in town and with child, I'm told." Haywood eyed the dark-skinned woman who nodded willingly before he returned his gaze back to Abigail. "It seems the lady's doctor, a loyalist, has fled the town for Nova Scotia. I'm told Dr. Adams has agreed to treat her but won't be able to see her until later this week." The officer cleared his throat, Abigail sensing agitation in the act. "To concede to her wish to be seen and grant the lady a gesture of good faith. That is, that we don't mean her any harm despite her preference to have a citizen of King George treat her, the doctor has agreed to send you."

A jolt rushed up Abigail's back, her already quickened heartbeat accelerating. "But Mr. Haywood, I'm not a doctor, sir."

The officer gave her a sharp glance. "I know that, but Mrs. Schreier's condition is not pressing at the moment, according to this woman here." His eyes shot at the lady's housemaid for confirmation and again the woman granted it. "However, it seems her lady's opinion feels differently."

Abigail stood, unaware she had done so, but she had to object. "Mr. Haywood, if I may…"

"Miss Thatcher, no you may not." His eyes went dark as he stopped her cold. "If you recall on the day of your arrival to our camp, I made it clear that each follower must work to stay within its confines. They must pull their own weight. We don't have enough rations and I don't have enough patience to keep those that don't. You can either follow your orders or leave."

Her first meeting with Haywood had been brief, but Abigail was able to learn three things about the shrewd officer. He didn't like camp followers, only tolerating them as part of a necessity to take care of the men in the army; Washington had placed him in charge of the those he protested to dislike; and he was a man who expected his orders to be followed. If they weren't, the man held no problem enforcing his command over the guilty party.

Abigail was informed later that six camp followers had been dismissed by Haywood two weeks after they'd arrived for not meeting up to his standards. What would she have to lose if she tried to fight her own case now that her reservations clashed against his expectations? To be discharged from the camp meant she would have to go to her Aunt Sylvia's until they could rebuild their home back in Falmouth. It wasn't something she wanted to do, living comfortably in her aunt's large estate, as if pretending the war wasn't upon them—as if their town had not been demolished by British forces. A conflict within her quickly rose at the image of playing cards with her aunt and her sister in the parlor and attending parties in the evening as if her world hadn't changed when it clearly had. She understood what Abraham must've felt like when she first tried to talk him out of joining the cause.

She swallowed, forcing down her resistance and took her seat again. "I understand, sir."

"Good." Haywood's tone softened to the slightest degree as he waved the lady's housemaid over.

"Here's the address, miss." The woman's tone was warm as she handed Abigail a piece of paper. "The lady wrote it out for me jus' in case. She's hard-pressed to see someone. When do you think you can come?"

Abigail tucked the paper into her apron pocket. Her eyes were fixed on Haywood despite her answer being meant for the woman. "I'll make it my next priority. I just need to do something first."

A relieved smile brightened the woman's face. "Thank you, Miss. I'll hurry on and let her know you're comin'."

After leaving Haywood's tent, Abigail crossed over the separation that eventually led to the other side of camp where the followers stayed. When she arrived at her own tent, one she shared with four of the soldiers' wives and one child the age of three, she reached for her satchel, but fell short to obtain it. What should she put in it? What would she need for a situation like this? They were questions she didn't know, and why would she? The only experience she had was watching her mother carrying Henry and Olivia.

Olivia. Abigail's breath caught at the memory of her father's hard-pressed eyes over the strain her mother was almost unfit to bear. He shouldn't have even been in the same room, the custom for each birth prior, but the midwife insisted the exception. Abigail could still picture her father's anguish that day along with his fear she had slowly and painfully come to understand. Why else would the midwife call him when three other women, including Abigail were there to help with the delivery? She shuddered at the first and only time she'd witnessed her father's helplessness, watching his wife's exhaustion and pain almost take her from him. If her father, the rock of their family had felt so, how much more did she as the fear of losing her mother gripped her tight?

"Everything alright, dear?"

Abigail's body went taut at the interruption but grew less tense when she saw Mrs. Bates at the opening of the tent with a stack of firewood in tow. "Yes, just a little overwhelmed I think."

The woman's lips pressed with disproval. "Don't tell me Haywood has something else he's put you to. Doesn't he know even the Lord himself took a day to rest?"

Abigail offered a weak smile. "I'm not sure. He wants me to see about a lady who's expecting." She took a moment to recall the name. "A Mrs. Schreier. Dr. Adams has agreed to treat her, but my impression from the meeting is she wants someone sooner. I just don't feel right about it. I'm not a doctor after all."

Mrs. Bates laid the kindling on the ground just outside the tent. "Is that why Rebekah was here today?"

"Rebekah?"

The woman half-rolled her eyes and put her hands to her hips looking like she was about to shame someone. "For a Virginian gentleman, the man sure does lack manners. Rebekah pretty much runs the Schreier home." The side of her mouth turned upwards, and her tone lifted. "I was wondering why she'd set foot in a continental camp knowing full well her ladyship is a Tory."

"She supports the Crown?"

Mrs. Bates nodded. "Mmmhmm. Her husband is off as we speak doing who knows what to aid King George. I'm sure Washington would be interested to know what that might entail with the man's background in military service."

Abigail shook her head, but little convinced by her own gesture as she began to see the point her companion was making. "Officer Haywood said our involvement was to show her the army meant her no ill will."

Mrs. Bates shrugged; her eyebrows raised. "Oh, that's not to say he's not telling the truth, but there could be a double agenda. This war has a lot counting on it including the cost of both freedom and finances alike. I wouldn't put it past Haywood or the general to gather any information they could."

Could it be true? Now she was an informant and without her own knowledge? Abigail had come to Cambridge to do something, to act by seeking justice for what happened to her town, but to deceive a woman who had to turn to an army camp because her doctor had fled, stirred an ill-feeling inside her.

"Oh, dear. I can see I've upset you when that wasn't my intent." Mrs. Bates shook her head, her voice growing soft and tender. "You shouldn't give mind to what an old woman like me says. Haywood is many things, but he isn't a man who would put you in such a compromising position unless you allowed it. And you're not the sort." Her eyes glistened with sincerity. "Don't you get yourself hung up on your visit today, dear. I know of the lady you're to see. She has some time yet before the child comes, and the doc will take care of things after he meets with her."

Abigail rallied herself with no alternative but to accept the older woman's assurance while knowing she was due at the lady's home in the near future. Dr. Adams would be there to see Mrs. Schreier this Thursday. That was only two days from now, which meant Abigail's encounter with the woman might be limited to just today. A fresh sigh eased the tension in her shoulders she hadn't realized she had. Why was she getting herself all worked up over what was nearly a guaranteed one-time visit? All she had to do was make sure the woman was all right, that she wasn't winded of breath or in pain, and she didn't need to be a doctor to do that.

"You're right, Mrs. Bates." Abigail returned her satchel to the space on the floor she'd been sleeping. "It looks like I won't be needing that after all."

It took forty minutes to reach the Schreier estate that, a little over a mile and a half from the Harvard Commons. Abigail surmised in the unlikely scenario where she'd have to make it again the walk would take her less time, given she wouldn't slow her pace again to admire the beauty of the Georgian-style homes that lined Watertown Road. She pulled the piece of paper from her apron, making sure she had the address right. It was just a quick visit, and she'd be back with enough time to check in with Dr. Adams before dinner needed to be prepared for the men. Striking herself forward on the brick-laden sidewalk, she tapped at the door and was met by none other than Rebekah.

"Miss Thatcher, so glad you came." The light in the woman's smile was more radiant than the one she gave Abigail this morning, perhaps feeling more at ease outside a meeting under the scrutiny of a continental officer. "Please, come in and take a seat in the parlor. I'll go fetch the lady and be down soon."

Abigail removed her gloves and cloak to put them onto a hall tree before she chose a wing-backed chair adjacent to the fireplace. A grandfather clock stood at the far wall reading a quarter past three. Behind it, a plain tapestry of egg-shell white outlined the room, complementing the array of shapes and patterns that were otherwise ornate. Along the edges of the ceiling, small projections protruded, embellishments of crown moulding to give character while an elegant, gold chandelier hung in the center. A picture depicting an enchanting river landscape decorated one wall while a portrait of who Abigail surmised to be Mr. Schreier himself mounted on another. She looked out the window, the floral drapes and crimson tassels framing it along with the trees she could see outside. The leaves were all but gone now.

A little later, Rebekah entered, accompanied by a lady who Abigail assumed to be Mrs. Schreier. The lady was fashioned in a robe a la francaise that was suited to her social standing, but not overly stated like the ones Abigail had seen on some of the women in Portsmouth while visiting her aunt's estate. She was fair in complexion with strawberry-blonde curls teased tall and pinned about her head. Abigail took note her figure shared features similar to her own mother's physique, though Mrs. Schreier's being at least ten years the younger if not more.

The lady strode into the room, her gown having been let out to accommodate her transforming figure. She chose the open chaise across from Abigail and close to the fire. Abigail held back her relief to see the woman was not in any danger of delivering a child soon.

"I was told they'd be sending a woman." Mrs. Schreier's tone was dry, the unwelcomed response causing Abigail's cheeks to burn. "Not that I should be surprised. Tell me, does your camp doctor refuse to see me because of my allegiance?"

Abigail nudged down her embarrassment. "No, ma'am. Dr. Adams has agreed to treat you but will be by later this week."

The lady gave a slow nod. "I see." Her brow bent with scrutiny. "And why did they send you? Are you a midwife?"

"Hardly, ma'am," Abigail answered truthfully. "I've been present and of some use for two of my mother's births, but that's the extent of my knowledge and experience on the subject."

Mrs. Schreier gave a tiresome laugh as she accepted a China teacup from Rebekah, the housemaid adding two sugars to it. "Forgive me." The harshness in her tone faded, though the tenseness of her jaw did not. "It's just that since Mr. Schreier's temporary leave along with practically all of Cambridge's loyalist population's flight to Nova Scotia, it's been a rather lonely time for what most tell me should be a joyful one."

"Hey now, miss." Rebekah looked back at her mistress, not missing a beat as she handed a cup to Abigail, filling the vessel to the brim. "You've gone and hurt my feelings talkin' like that, making Miss Thatcher here believe you all alone in this house and that nobody cares for you or that babe you carryin'. You lucky I don't just leave. Then, I'd like to see how you do."

Abigail couldn't hide the quizzical expression she knew both women before her could easily read. Could Rebekah truly leave? As far as she knew and despite her own objections to it, slavery was still very much present in the colonies. Abigail shuddered under her breath just thinking of what the lady of the house might do to Rebekah for speaking to her mistress in such a direct way. A few seconds of silence went by, but neither lady addressed the question that was all but voiced by her.

Instead, Rebekah laughed, the gesture all but pushing Abigail against the back of her seat. "Don't give it another thought, Miss Thatcher. Maybe my lady doesn't appreciate everythin' I do, but I would never leave that child."

Mrs. Schreier put a hand as if instinctively on her abdomen and smiled in a way that let Abigail know she knew it too. "We do our best not to speak of it openly, afraid we'll get more problems than we already do, but the troubled look on your face begs for an explanation. I don't know what your impression was of us when you arrived here, Miss Thatcher, but Rebekah isn't my slave. She's free to come and go whenever and wherever she wants." She shifted with some difficulty, putting her finished teacup on a side table. "It's really something, you know, you rebels fighting for freedom when you don't see the lives you're still oppressing yourselves." Another silence hit, the weight of the truth growing heavier by the minute until Mrs. Schreier averted her gaze to Rebekah, her eyes softened with what Abigail read as gratitude. "I do hope you'll stay for a while, though."

A smile came effortlessly on the housemaid's face. "Of course. I wouldn't miss seein' that child grow up for anything. Not to mention you gonna need a little help with giving that babe the affection it deserves."

Mrs. Schreier returned Rebekah's comment with a bemused smile before turning to Abigail. "Rebekah doesn't believe I'm the motherly type, though I can't exactly disagree with her. I never saw myself as a mother until fate proved me wrong." She glanced down at her protruding stomach. "Even as the child grows, I still have trouble believing it." A small chuckle gave way before the lady's brow raised with curiosity, Abigail feeling the weight of the interview resurface. "So, you're not a doctor or a midwife and it's obvious you're not of social standing." She gave an up and down glance at Abigail's ensemble.

Despite the judgement in the woman's tone, Abigail remained composed. She wasn't ashamed of who she was. She blinked, holding back all the feelings of loss that still burdened her, or who she had been. Abigail's gaze dropped only momentarily to the uniform she wore every day, the plain blue work dress and white apron. It was perfectly suited for life on a farm and now it was perfect for life in an army camp. The only reason for her discomfort to her clothes was the fact they weren't as clean as she'd have liked it to be for this particular meeting.

Mrs. Schreier clasped her hands together while her eyes narrowed. "Tell me, who are you and why did they send you?"

Honesty seemed best. "To answer the first part, ma'am, my name is Abigail Thatcher. My family has…" she forced the knot in her chest down, her feelings along with it as she tried to get through this meeting. "had a farm in Falmouth. Most of them are in Portsmouth now."

"And you decided to join the rebel army." The fine-arched brow of Mrs. Schreier dropped.

"Yes, ma'am, I did. And as for the second part of your question, I can only guess it's because my experience of such kind, as limited as it may be, is more than anyone else at camp at present."

Abigail still couldn't believe that could be true. Of all the wives who followed their husbands here, had they only been present for their own childbirths? Then again, it probably had more to do with her new apprenticeship, if one could call it that, with Dr. Adams. Who knew her stomach for blood and her mother's instruction of the needle would mean she'd be expected to provide medical care for injured men of battle one day?

Abigail decided not to tell the latter part of her theory but did want to offer more for the woman's concerns than what she just had. "But take courage, ma'am. Dr. Adams will make his visit later this very week."

Abigail eyed the grandfather clock: half past four. This was taking longer than she thought. Dinner would already need preparation and if Mrs. Bates didn't have help, the men would start grumbling. The light outside was beginning to fade and she still had to walk back. With this being her first and hopefully last time at the Schreier estate, she'd be completely lost in the dark if she didn't leave soon. Time was running short and she needed to complete this visit.

"I'm sorry Dr. Adams isn't able to make a call today, but I'll inform him of our meeting and tell him you're getting along...well?"

Mrs. Schreier took in a long, tired breath, adjusting her body weight again in the chaise. "I'm uncomfortable and my nerves along with my belly are stretched and my feet ache and..."

"Now, miss, I think Miss Abigail here is jus' tryin' to make sure you be all right until the doctor can come." Rebekah eyed Abigail urging her to answer her unspoken question.

A smile touched Abigail's lips and she nodded. "Yes, that's right. He'll want to know how you're doing even if he can't be here today." She was about to announce her departure when Mrs. Schreier cut in.

"I was skeptical, but I have to say you are certainly kinder than the rest of those so-called patriots who've taken this town as their headquarters. I'm beginning to like the idea of having someone else to talk to other than Rebekah and I'm sure she feels the same." The lady gave a telling grin and her housemaid mirrored the gesture with a nod of approval along with it. "It'll be nice to see you more often."

Abigail's heart sped up over the misconception she was about to correct. She didn't want to disappoint, especially as their conversation grew more amiable, but she saw no alternative. "I'm sorry, Mrs. Schreier, but I'm quite certain my time here in your home is a limited one. In fact, I wouldn't be surprised if this is my only visit. You see, there's much work to be done within the camp and unfortunately," she caught the irritation in her breath, wondering if they had too, "not all of the camp followers or soldiers for that matter, seem willing to take part. In fact, I should return before…" The chime of the grandfather clock bellowed their attention. Five o'clock. Now, in the early November sky of Massachusetts, the sun was at its last stage of descent.

When the chimes had ended their song, Abigail could see the lady of the house was not pleased with the recent news.

"Well, that's quite a shame," Mrs. Schreier said, her tone even. "It would've been nice to host some decent company again." Her eyes drifted to the window before she gave Abigail a cold smile. "I can see it's become late and too dark for you to walk back alone. Nikolai will take you back in the carriage."

At this Abigail didn't object. She rode sheltered inside the carriage walls, aware her cloak was no match for the drop in temperature the dark brought with it along with her inability to navigate her way, yet she gulped with discomfort. It was never her intention to give a false impression of what her role was during her encounter with Mrs. Schreier. She'd made every effort to be honest, even when having to admit her shortcomings. In truth, she never thought the lady would want her as a companion again. The thought of the contrary only echoed how isolated the woman must've felt to want to befriend someone like her. They were from opposite worlds, of different social classes and more obvious, different sides of the war. The fact she'd even considered Abigail now spoke volumes and a part of Abigail's heart crushed.

Abigail closed her eyes, her lips pushed firm. She couldn't think of that. Dr. Adams would be there soon enough, and Mrs. Schreier would be in good hands. Her priority now was to let him know the details of her visit and give Mrs. Bates reprieve from the hounding that was sure to be going on by the time she got back. Abigail hoped Haywood wouldn't take their disgruntlement out on the older woman, using it as an excuse to rid the commons of another camp follower. The very thought was like a knife to her chest, so when Nikolai dropped her off in front of Harvard Square, she ran.

Chapter 6

Garrett awoke to a "tap, tap, tap-tapping" outside of his cabin window. A white-breasted nuthatch had somehow wedged a nut into two of the planks and was trying to crack it open for its next meal. Stretching, Garrett dismounted from his hammock, perplexed a bird who favored forests and trees was out on the water with an oak frigate as its only source of wood. That's when he remembered. He was in Boston.

He stowed away his hammock, securing the canvas to a beam above. It was a habit he'd done since his start at sea, the action a necessity to make room for battle, but he also liked how it gave him more space in his cabin now. He gave an easy sigh at the change of scenery. It felt good to spend the added days on dry land. Not that he minded the months at a time at sea. He'd been on the water for most of his life and the ocean felt more like home the more he ventured on it. Still the change of pace was welcomed, wanting to experience something more than the open water and see some new faces other than his crew's. There was only so much a man could take, even him, cramped on a vessel like that of His Majesty's ships.

Garrett waited for his new orders that would no doubt be coming from Samuel Graves himself since they were now in the city where the admiral was headquartered. To make use of his time, Garrett thought he might try to explore the area, at least the parts of it where they had fortified it from rebel forces. He also wanted to see for himself just how bad the lack of support for the Crown was by the people who lived here.

For soldiers of the Crown, Boston was becoming like a bad taste in their mouth they couldn't get rid of. Most of its residents were not in favor of Parliament issuing laws on their behalf and apparently made their dissatisfaction known in creative ways like the so-called "tea party," where some of the colonists disguised themselves as Mohawk Indians and dumped entire chests of tea into Boston's harbor. What a waste. He knew these colonists liked tea just as much as his countrymen did. Most of these people were English after all. Soon the cry of the rebels would wane. When that happened, they would want their tea again. Garrett couldn't wait for that day. Maybe then they'd finally see how foolish they'd been and cease this futile rebellion. He let out an irritated sigh. As if only dumping tea was all they were up to. They'd been calling their mother country's attempt to bring order "intolerable acts." Garrett had to scoff at the idea. Intolerable acts? Only intolerable people would come up with such a name.

He grabbed his coat and secured his tricorn hat. He would need them both. The weather had recently taken its toll, signaling that winter had set in. In the last few days at sea, they'd run into trouble manning the ship. The sails had turned stiff in the freezing temperatures and the crew had trouble exposing their hands long enough in the biting winds to perform their duties aloft. It had only begun, but he could tell it was going to be a brutal season. For a brief instant, the young brunette woman came to the forefront of Garrett's mind, and he wished she hadn't. Had she found lodging yet? He shook the thought away and left the officers' cabin, about to disembark the ship when Nicholas stopped him.

69

"Where do you think you're off to?" Nicholas' boots were wet with the rain leftover from last night. He'd already been out. His friend's outfit did much to match Garrett's own, almost like looking in a mirror. Almost. The only difference between the blue and white combination of their undress uniform and Garrett's yet to be soiled hessian boots, was a silver pin Garrett wore on his chest in the form of two intertwined hearts. Though he had no knowledge of the design's significance, if there was one, the pin had been given to Garrett by his mother as a child. It was the only thing he had left of her and the only thing he remembered about her.

"Seeing I haven't received my orders yet, I thought I would explore the neighborhood."

"On your own?" Nicholas' brow raised. "Do you think it wise after all the protests we've had? You might want to take another officer with you just to be sure you don't run into any trouble."

"Yeah, all right. Fine." Garrett reluctantly consented. He wasn't in the mood to quarrel. Not to mention he wanted to explore before he was called in to Graves' headquarters. And he didn't know when that would be. "You want to come along?"

Nicholas shook his head. "Not right now. I'm trying to catch my father before he meets with the admiral. I want to ask him about that man we came across back in Falmouth."

"Which one? The rebel fool or the disheveled thief holding a lady's dressing gown?"

Nicholas smirked. "I don't think I need to clarify, but the old man just so we're clear."

"Looks like I'm on my own then." Garrett shrugged, about to step out again.

"You could take Billy," Nicholas gestured over to William III, sound asleep on his bunk. He was the only other company on the ship while the rest of the crew was probably at the Green Dragon tavern having a pint or two. Other than the ship it was the only place they didn't feel the cold stares of rebel sympathizers.

Garrett glanced at the freckled-faced boy who was only 14 and already a midshipman since his start two years ago thanks to his uncle on the naval board. It was old news he'd be attending the Royal Academy back in England, a school that only made room for sons of noblemen and gentlemen. It paid to have connections. Garrett grunted. "I'm not in the mood to babysit. Besides, I'd hate to wake him from his naptime."

Nicholas frowned with caution. "Careful, Garrett. One word to his uncle and you'll find yourself demoted to serve under his command one day. I don't see that going well, especially for you."

Garrett thought about that. He'd worked hard his whole life to get to where he was now. To think all those years could just as easily mean nothing if some high-born kid played tattle-tale rubbed him the wrong way. He turned to leave, heeding his friend's advice. He didn't want to say anything further to make sure Nicholas' warning stayed just that. "In any case, I'll take my chances alone."

For Garrett, walking through Boston as a king's soldier was a bit like walking on thin ice. One had to be careful where one stepped, especially in the company of those who weren't wearing the traditional uniform. Even if they'd fortified most of the city, you could still cut the tension with a knife. It was loyalist against rebel, patriot against Tory, soldier of the Crown against soldier of the colony. The poor citizens who wished to remain undivided were caught in the middle of it all.

He'd heard that riots and protests were common and if caught on the "wrong side" one might find themselves "tarred and feathered", a detestable practice of public humiliation. The wretched soul under punishment was stripped and covered with feathers, but not before hot tar was poured on their person, allowing for a proper adhesive.

That was the way of war. It was ugly, turning neighbor against neighbor like it so often did. But today, Garrett saw no evidence of division's brutality, just the residents' eyes glaring at him as he walked through the streets of the city. He knew his presence was unwanted, but he ignored the scowls he received and made his way north to the site that intrigued him the most. Breed's Hill.

Garrett took a moment to examine the landscape when he got there. It wasn't what he imagined it would be. The hill in sight was fairly steep to the east and west sides, but the neighboring hill north of it would have made a more formidable foe for the rebels' advantage. Still, he knew he now stood on sacred ground. Many lives from each side had been lost here, and he wanted to respect that. It was hard to imagine just months before the grass had been covered with the blood of the slain. Rain had wiped away any signs that may have once held evidence of it. Even now, he could hear the raw crunch beneath his feet from where winter was making her mark.

Garrett closed his eyes, trying to visualize the battle on that sultry summer day just four months ago. He imagined the men in their red coats, their bayonets fixed on the tops of their muskets, advancing upon the enemy in orderly lines. He cringed at the next thought. Rebels stood waiting for his fellow soldiers to approach until they were no more than ten rods away before they fired their guns and caused several men, including officers, to fall. Again, the men are reassembled in formation to march on to assault and again they are torn down by the militia. The battle continues in this fashion until his fellow soldiers begin to retreat in disarray, agitating their officers who feel inclined to threaten them with the sword and to continue in the attack.

Garrett opened his eyes, fully acquainted with the truth. It was only after the rebels ran out of gunpowder and ammunition that his countrymen were able to win the battle. But the price had come at a great cost. Over 1000 British casualties, 200 of those lives lost. The thought of it discouraged him. No doubt, the rebels saw this as their own victory of some sorts, boosting confidence in their agenda. It would make it harder for them to relent.

He started to make his way back towards the ship through the cobblestone streets of Boston. Thinking of Breed's Hill had ruined his spirits. Maybe joining most of his comrades at the Green Dragon would set his mood straight again. He lifted his eyes from the pavement to see Nicholas had caught up to him.

"You need to return to the docks. Graves is ready to give you your orders." Nicholas' face was resolute, taking on a form of officiality that hadn't been there earlier back in the cabin.

"All right. Did you find anything out about the old man?"

"Not yet. My father was already gone to meet with Graves. I suspect you might see him on your way there."

"Okay, I'll ask and see what he knows if he's still there."

Nicholas pushed his chin forward as if urging Garrett on. "You better get going. I was given the information by one of the admiral's runners."

Garrett pulled back and angled his head. "Why didn't you just send him to me instead of passing the information on yourself? You're of higher rank."

Nicholas shrugged, his mouth curving into a slight smile. "I didn't mind. I was planning to head this way sometime while we were docked. Might as well do it now." He gestured behind Garrett towards Breeds Hill. Garrett should've known Nicholas also wanted to pay his respects.

Garrett nodded. "All right. I'll see you later."

***

It didn't take him long to find himself inside the admiral's cabin on the HMS *Preston*. Garrett curbed the urge to let his eyes boggle, taken by surprise at both the warmth and invitation of his superior's quarters. He imagined Graves had made the room reminiscent of what might be found in his own home office back in England.

In the center, grand and masculine, was a mahogany desk, embellished with claw-like footing that sat on top of an ornamental rug. The floor piece, once beautiful, was faded by either years of use or harsh conditions

73

from sea life and salty air. Maybe both.

Cognizant his gaze had held the floorboards for far too long, Garrett lifted his eyes to a handsome spyglass that stood mounted next to a group of windows where the light gradually faded from the day's approaching end. He imagined the perfect view the admiral had of the rising sun from his quarters. Not a bad way to start off the morning. He made note of it for later in the chance one day he'd acquire such a title of his own.

Graves was already seated at the desk that did well to match its owner's rank. The admiral appeared to be in the middle of writing something, perhaps a letter of correspondence when Garrett entered. Having yet to have laid eyes on the man before today, Garrett wasn't sure what to expect, only that the man had a reputation for being good-tempered and held prior experience in the Americas during the Seven Years War. It was also said he'd even sympathized with the colonists during that time, earning their respect. Because of it, Parliament knew he'd be the perfect individual for his position. In fact, they made sure of it by stationing him here in Boston.

Without really meaning to, Garrett began to compare the man in front of him to Nicholas' father. In appearance, they had little that resembled each other. Even behind the desk he could see Graves was hearty in build and inferior to the Captain's size. But that wasn't saying much since most men were. Graves was dressed in his informal uniform, a double-breasted blue coat with white lining he chose to wear open. Unlike his attire for more formal occasions that was trimmed in gold lace, his current ensemble was a bit more relaxed, if you didn't count the nine golden buttons running down his coat. Still, in all the years he'd known Nicholas' father, not once had he seen the man out of his formal wardrobe for a meeting of any kind.

"You've come from Captain Mowat's fleet; from Falmouth." Graves motioned for Garrett to take a seat in a chair across from the desk. He did but stayed silent. The man's words held no question. "I've heard you're close to becoming captain of your own ship."

Garrett's ears perked at the acknowledgment. Could this be turning into an opportunity for his advancement? He only hoped. He had to bite his tongue to keep himself from sounding too excited before he was able to give an answer. "Yes, sir. I just need a chance to prove myself."

Graves nodded as if showing he understood Garrett's dilemma. A man in his position had surely done his research to know the men who served under his command, or the very least, one he'd have in his office. He must've known about Garrett's background, making the promotion nearly unattainable through means of influence. Even if he'd been partially raised by Nicholas' father, Garrett knew the man could only do so much without being of blood relation and with no assets of his own. Thankfully, in the Navy, there were other means by which he could prove himself worthy of the position. And if the admiral backed him...Garrett's chest quickened at the possibilities. He just needed the opportunity.

"Well, you may get a chance to have it."

"Sir?" Garrett's heart took on a gallop just thinking of the prospect, all the while trying to maintain composed as he sat in the admiral's presence. It wasn't easy, but he didn't want the man to have any reason to take back what he just said.

Graves continued. "But first I want to see how you do commanding your own ship in your current rank. Right now, we need all the help we can get in the harbor. We are in desperate need of supplies, especially with winter right on our heels." Graves' tone shifted from a man in angst to one thoroughly annoyed. "It seems Washington has financed a small fleet of his own who are capturing our much-needed supply ships. I need you to go and make sure those supplies get here."

"Yes, sir." The acceptance came out more eagerly than Garrett intended. He straightened. "When am I to leave port?"

"Yesterday, Lieutenant. This task is of the utmost urgency." Graves took to his seat again, straightening the gold-laced buttons of his coat. His gaze reverted back to his desk and the admiral resumed whatever he'd been working on. There was no question about the gesture. Their conversation, no matter how brief, was over.

Chapter 7

"You better get a move on, dear." Mrs. Bates approached Abigail with a second basket of baked bread, the first for the morning nearly consumed.

"I know, I will soon. Let me just finish the rest of these in line." Abigail scooped up a piece of the French loaf Mr. Porter, the baker, had donated to the cause and smeared it with butter before she placed it on a man's plate. The line this morning was longer than usual, but she knew why. Washington was having his lead men teaching formations and handling firearms. How long would that take with an inexperienced group like this one to learn? All day? All winter? That certainly explained why there were so many men eager to get the first meal of the day.

"Don't worry about me, Abby. I can handle the rest of these men." Mrs. Bates began slicing a new loaf, pausing to hold her knife up like she was using it as a lecture tool. "The work certainly does go faster with the two of us, but they'll just have to wait their turn and learn a fine lesson in patience. The Lord knows they could use it." She eyed the next man in line as she handed him the bread. "Isn't that right, Mr. Shaw?"

The thin man with the weather-stained straw hat nodded, his lips drawn tight before he carried his breakfast to a group of men around an unlit fire heap.

Abigail leaned in, her voice falling to a whisper. "Is that him?"

Mrs. Bates gave a low huff, her stare still drawn on the man that just left them. "It is." She put a rigid hand to her hip. "Yelling and throwing a fit like a child. If he treats his wife like that there's no wonder she isn't here." Mrs. Bates shook her head her disapproving countenance withdrawing. "Sorry, Abby, I shouldn't have said that. The man just got under my skin that night."

"I'm sorry I couldn't get back in time."

The older woman looked at her without an ounce of contempt. "It's all right. I know you tried. I'm just thankful nothing more came of it. Though I've been meaning to ask, how did your visit go with Mrs. Schreier?"

Abigail took another tablespoon of butter, dividing it between four more loaves. "For the most part, it was fine. She doesn't seem to be ready to have the baby just yet and Dr. Adams has been over twice now."

"Good." Mrs. Bates let the hand on her hip fall and smiled. "It sounds like that's one less thing you'll have to worry about now, or at least until Haywood puts another order on your plate."

Abigail thought about how she left the lady's estate, both perplexed by the woman's admission of wanting such company and sorry she couldn't provide it. Mrs. Bates was right. It was only a matter of time before Haywood would call her into his tent again and give her another assignment.

"Mornin' Miss Abby, Mrs. Bates." Thomas wore a beaming smile across his face.

"Why, good morning, Thomas. You seem like you're in a good mood today."

"I am, Mrs. Bates. We start some real trainin' today." His grin grew wider with pride. "I'm gonna be a soldier."

Abigail hesitated but she gave a smile just the same. She didn't like the idea of Thomas being on the battlefield despite how much it mattered to him. "Then you'll need your strength." She gave him a double portion of bread and butter. He returned the gesture with a look that was a mix of delight and wariness. A group of boys stood a few men down the line about his same age, one with tousled brown hair and a slightly taller frame leading them. They sneered when she gave Thomas the extra portion. Jake and his gang.

Thomas looked back to see their disapproving glances before he turned back to her. "Miss Abby, that might just get me in another fight I wasn't looking to start this time."

"Oh don't you worry yourself, Thomas. You just go have a seat over there by my husband. He's alone at the table and won't mind the company. He'd do well to be around a young man like yourself."

"*That* man is your husband?" Thomas gave a weary nod over to the table Mrs. Bates referred to. The man at it had a large scar just below his eye that traveled down to his jawbone.

Abigail smiled to herself. The first time Mrs. Bates revealed her husband Abigail had held almost an identical reaction. Pure disbelief. The man was large and broad, over a foot and a half taller than his wife who stood nearly as tall as Abigail. Age had taken away most of his muscle, but the slight definition that still stood within his physique gave the impression he could do well enough in a quarrel if need be. Having arrived too late to help Mrs. Bates on the night she went over to Mrs. Schreier's house, Abigail had seen him part the crowd and take his stance between his wife and the disgruntled party. He didn't even have to say a word and neither did the officers who seemed fixed where they were, perhaps wondering if they should intervene or avoid the certain chance they'd be injured themselves. Thankfully, the stance didn't go beyond that. Mr. Shaw walked away defeated and even more disgruntled, Abigail guessed, with no supper.

"Yes!" Mrs. Bates reacted the same way she did when anyone else begged the question. Shocked. "I don't know why that surprises everyone. The man's a teddy bear if you just get to know him."

"A giant teddy bear." Thomas' eyes still held caution.

Mrs. Bates met them with a reprimanding glance, her hand returning to her hip. "Oh shoosh! Now, go over there and sit yourself down."

Reluctantly, he did so. When Mr. Bates turned around to look back at his wife, she gave him a curt nod as if urging him to make the relationship work. He nodded back like the two were thinking the same thing before finding his interest back on his food and his new company. The two women shared a giggle, both knowing he was just the thing the young man needed.

"He'll be fine."

Abigail nodded, in full agreeance. "I doubt Jake and his friends will give him too much trouble."

"Let's hope not." Mrs. Bates' gaze shifted from her husband and Thomas to Abigail, the older woman's grin turning hard-nosed. "Now go, child go!"

From the edge of the Commons, Abigail cut through Christ Church, heading in the direction of the Vassall house and where Dr. Adams began taking his patients. When she took her time, she could make the trek in less than 15 minutes, but now she picked up her pace down Brattle Street.

Breathing in deep the crisp autumn air, Abigail let it fill every part of her lungs. It was always a nice change from the camp where a good stock of men somehow forgot their back home morals and cleanliness was not always necessarily a virtue. She sucked in another breath, relishing its freshness again and thanked God for it.

When she arrived at the Vassall estate, Abigail went straight to work starting with the chamber pots. Dr. Adams was in the middle of examining one of the soldiers from camp as she emptied one and placed it back near an occupied cot.

"Anything else you feel?" Dr. Adams put his palm to the man's forehead, checking for a fever.

"Other than burnin' up? Yes, sir. My body feels achy, especially my head. My stomach doesn't feel too good either." The man sank down into one of the cots on the floor.

Dr. Adams gestured to Abigail, and she sat a new chamber pot at the cot's side. A moment later the man lurched himself forward into it. When the doctor motioned for her to carry on, she began to re-dress an injury another one of the men received earlier that week.

"How's the hand look, Miss Abigail?" George Neville, a blacksmith by trade now turned soldier lounged in his cot.

Abigail took her time to look it over. New skin had started to form on the wound from when the man's gun performed a hang-fire. After pulling the musket's trigger without the firing of a shot, Neville made the mistake of examining the gun with the muzzle aimed towards his right hand. He was lucky two of the five fingers were still attached. "I think better, Mr. Neville, but you'll have to ask the doctor." She crossed her arms playfully. "You know I'm not the expert."

He laughed. "I know. I'm just glad you're doing the bandaging these days. You're gentler." Neville nudged his head towards Dr. Adams who was still with the same patient when she came in. "That man may be the physician but boy was I in a sort of pain when he was fixing me up."

Abigail tied the bandage off like Dr. Adam's had shown her the first time and the times she'd taken the task over since. She took the pillow behind her patient, fluffing it a few times before she placed it behind his head again. "Well, just remember I'm only able to change your bandages because Dr. Adams has done the hardest part," she gave him a pointed smile, "given it a chance to heal."

Neville leaned back into the cushion and gave another chuckle. "I suppose I should be thankful I didn't blow off the whole hand. The doc at least left me my trigger finger. I'll still be able to shoot at those redcoats."

Abigail stiffened. "You mean, you're not going home after this?"

"Go home?" The man shook his head adamantly. "Hardly, Miss. I'm not about to be sent home before I even get into the brink of it. Those lobsterbacks may have Boston for now, controlling our ports, but that's going to change. I want to be here when that happens—when they no longer control us. Isn't that why we're all here? Fighting for our freedom?"

Her eyes went intently to his. The man's never wavered. She understood his question was meant to be rhetorical, but it made her reflect on her own decision to be here. Why was she here? She had no quarrel against the king of England, at least not about things that had to do with liberty and protests on taxes. Like most of her family, she chose to stay out of the conflict.

Except that was before King George's naval fleet left her town devastated. Abigail sucked in a desperate breath. The image of the two Royal Naval officers came to mind and a heat rose inside. She'd received her answer. Anger. That was why she was here. She wanted revenge for the destruction of her home much like Thomas wanted revenge for the death of his father. Without putting herself on the battlefield, this was her way of doing that. She could at least help the soldiers that would be.

"Abigail, a word, please." Dr. Adams had finished with the new patient, directing her out of the room and into a nearby corner.

"Is everything all right?" She could read little in his expression, but his voice was low and soft.

"I'm afraid not. It seems I have some bad news to tell the general."

She couldn't see the man Dr. Adams had been examining from where they stood. None of the patients were in view. Nevertheless, the instinct to try and peer over kicked in and she did. "Does it have to do with the man you were just seeing?"

He nodded. "All the symptoms I've noticed and from what he's declared point to smallpox."

"Smallpox?" Abigail put a hand to her mouth, trying to control her voice from climbing. She'd become well enough acquainted with the disease to recall the lingering pain throughout her body and fatigue mixed with the high fever. She'd developed the rashes on her face and arms, but the scars those had left behind were faint. Others hadn't been so lucky.

"Have you been exposed to the disease?

"Exposed?" She furrowed a brow, unfamiliar with the term.

"What I mean is, have you ever had it?" Doctor Adams studied her like she was a new patient. "You have some light scarring around your nose and near your ears."

Her hand went to the side of her nose at the place that always served as a reminder to the sickness, before she pulled it back to her side. "I had a mild form of it when I was a child."

He let out a determined breath. "Good. I've had it too, but I'm not certain about the other patients. In any case, we'll have to isolate him, especially if I'm right. He hasn't developed a rash, but I don't want to take the chance to find out if I'm wrong. In any case, I'll need you to deliver the message to Haywood right away while I stay and monitor him." He put up a hand, his glance full of warning. "Let's keep discretion, though. Washington needs to know, but not the rest of the camp, at least not just yet. We'll tell them, but for now we need to see how His Excellency wants to handle things in the chance we're looking at a possible epidemic. In the meantime, keep a diligent watch out for symptoms."

Abigail's face faltered again. "Symptoms, sir?"

"Sorry." He gave an encouraging smile. "You're doing so well with picking things up here I forget you haven't had formal training. Signs of the illness. If you spot any, bring them immediately to me to be examined."

***

A mixture of dread and panic pounded in Abigail's chest as she walked with urgent swiftness in her step. She thought about running, but decided against it, the act only raising suspicions that something was wrong. And that was precisely what Dr. Adams told her not to do.

When she reached the tent, her heart's pace climbed. Abraham. She hadn't seen her brother since her first week in Cambridge. She'd been so busy trying to keep up with her own chores she hadn't had an opportunity to confront him. Then again, he hadn't come to see her either. Was he just as busy? And if so, with what? Excited relief to see her older brother became tainted by perplexed dismay.

Abraham was in the middle of shaking hands with Officer Haywood. The action wasn't exactly a display of comradery like between friends, but more of something that portrayed a mutual understanding. Nevertheless, the fact Haywood, a trained officer who followed the rigid structure of decorum to perfection, took hands with her brother, sent the alarm bells ringing.

"Abraham." Her throat caught as she ran up to him. "I'm so glad to see you." She scanned him over. As far as she could tell, he seemed the same. "Are you all right?"

He took her hands between his, preventing her from the hug she was about to give. "I'm fine, but I have to go. There's somewhere I need to be." The sudden halt to her embrace made her heart stop cold along with her brother's dismissive gesture. Was what Thomas had said true? Was Abraham really going to officer meetings? And more importantly, why? She stepped back from him and gave him a critical eye.

"Does that somewhere involve an officer meeting by chance?"

Abraham raised an inquisitive brow. "Actually, yes. How did you know?"

"A friend told me as much. I hoped it was only a rumor."

He shrugged before he stepped to the side of her like she was a trivial nuisance in his way.

She pulled him back by his arm, her eyes pleading with his to tell her more. "Abraham, you can't just leave me with nothing. I haven't seen you in two weeks. Is that really all you're going to say?"

He gave an exasperated sigh. "All right, Your friend's right."

Her breath caught midway in. "But, Abraham, you're not an officer, or at least you weren't when we arrived here. Has something changed since then?"

His mouth went flat. "No, I'm not an officer."

"Then why are you in those meetings with Washington? It's not like you're friends with the man."

"No, I'm not." His calloused expression softened and though weak, he laughed. The sound lifted her heart. "At least, I don't think I can call myself a friend to the general just yet."

"So why are you in there at all?"

He gave an uneasy glance around them and bit his lip. Maybe he didn't want to give up the information, but she wasn't going to let it go either. She was his sister, his family. She had a right to find out, didn't she?

"I happen to be privy to some things that Washington might find helpful, but that's all you need to know. In fact, that's the end of talking about it at all." His muscles relaxed if only minutely and he exhaled, the tone in his voice gentler than it had been. "I'm sorry, Abby, but I can't say more. Trust me, it's for the best. The less you know, the better."

She put a rigid hand on her hip. "And what about Officer Haywood? I didn't realize you two were such good friends." His brow furrowed. When she recognized he was clearly not following what she was getting at, she let her hand drop again. "I saw you shaking hands when I walked up. I don't see many of the other common soldiers doing that and I doubt they'd be so equally received if they tried."

The side of his mouth gave a smug tip. "Haywood and I have a common goal, that's all. Which is more that I can say for you and I right now. Really, Abby, I have to go. And I assume since you were on your way to Haywood's tent, you have somewhere to be too."

Her eyes shot wide, reminded of her own mission. She could feel her body tense and judging by the gleam in her brother's eye, he could sense it too.

"Looks like I'm not the only one with secrets." A brow lifted as he crossed his arms over his chest.

She didn't say anything at first. She couldn't. She'd promised Dr. Adams and as much as she wanted to know what Abraham was up to, the point had been made. It was better if neither one of them knew the other's secret. "At least tell me this and I'll let you go."

He frowned but allowed her to go on.

"Are you putting your life on the line?"

His lips bent further downward. "We're all putting our lives on the line, Abby." Eyes stricken with resolve for whatever he was involved in, Abigail watched with absence of any comfort as her brother walked in the direction of the general's headquarters.

***

With her mind divided between Abraham's involvement so close to Washington and a possible epidemic within the camp, Abigail completely forgot her superior's rules of etiquette to sit as the officer expected her to. She handed him the message Dr. Adams provided, noting his own signature at the bottom as Haywood unfolded the paper holding the unfortunate news. She knew he was done when his eyes locked on hers.

"Does anyone else know?"

"No, sir. Just Dr. Adams, myself and now you."

A crinkle surfaced on his brow, the only sign of his uneasiness. "Are there any more cases?"

"Not that we are aware of."

He nodded. "Good. I'll deliver this personally to His Excellency. Stay here, Miss Thatcher. There's more we need to discuss when I get back."

When Haywood returned, Abigail saw the message from Dr. Adams was no longer in the officer's hand. Haywood's mouth pressed with irritation. It was only a second later when she understood why. She was still upright. But her nerves were doing anything but letting her feel at ease enough to take a seat. Other than the man's agitation with her lack of protocol, he seemed back to his formal self. Even now, the fold on his forehead from earlier disappeared. If there'd been an ounce of worry over what might be a disease that could leave over half of the 14,000 soldiers unfit for battle, he left nothing visible behind of it.

"Something new has come about for you."

She drew back, her head angled to the side. Haywood didn't miss a beat when it came to camp work. "New, sir?"

"The Lady Schreier seems to have taken an interest in you, which is good fortune for us. As you already know, her husband is on an assignment elsewhere for King George, but we have yet to know more than that. You can find that out."

Abigail frowned. "But Mr. Haywood, I've already explained to Mrs. Schreier my inability to visit further, especially now that Dr. Adams…"

Haywood held up his hand, stopping her short, his tone uncompromising. "I get the impression the lady is used to having things her way. She has requested another visit from you and because it just so happens to have the potential to benefit us in turn, I'm allowing it until we get the information we need."

Abigail swallowed, forcing a knot down her throat that landed in the pit of her stomach. Mrs. Bates had mentioned this the day she'd visited Mrs. Schreier. She'd brushed the possibility aside, never thinking she'd see the woman again. But now…

"You mean I'm to spy on the lady," she asked, trying to come to terms with what this meant.

Haywood nodded. "Yes, just until we have what we need."

Her mind went back to her visit. The woman's admittance of her loneliness still gripping her heart. A part of her wanted to go back, but not like this, not when there was another agenda at hand. Her decision was easy. Mrs. Schreier might be the enemy as far as politics was concerned, but even so, the woman was vulnerable. Abigail wasn't about to take advantage of her plea for help. She shook her head with an adamance behind the gesture. "I'm sorry, Mr. Haywood, but I can't do that."

It was the first time she'd seen the man flinch. "You mean you won't?"

"Actually, both. I can't and I won't." She raised her chin despite the butterflies darting around inside her stomach. "The last time I went to the Schreier estate, Mrs. Bates was left alone to feed the camp and Mr. Bates was nearly drawn in a fight with another man because of it. I can't chance that again especially with what I know now from Dr. Adams this morning. I need to be here. I need to keep a look out for…"

Haywood's eyes breached the distance between them, narrowing on her. It took all her will not to avert her own from them especially as his tone grew more agitated. "You need to mind your place, Miss Thatcher, and remember how easily it can be removed from here. This mission comes from the general himself. You would do your best to take it unless you're willing to risk the shame of being publicly kicked out for laziness."

A heat coursed inside her. Laziness? Abigail felt anything but lazy trying to keep up with the man's demands, even considering being sent out of camp might not be such a bad thing. She wasn't willing to deceive Mrs. Schreier and to leave now before the Smallpox spread, did have something appealing about it.

Abigail's heart went heavy, recalling Charlotte's last letter. According to her sister's account, their mother's strength had not improved. Despite their hope of the change in scenery Portsmouth and everything that came with their Aunt Sylvia's luxurious estate: ample food provision, fresh air, and comfortable bedding, their mother's condition actually seemed weakened since their journey over. Charlotte encouraged Abigail to stay put, insisting the help from their aunt's housemaid, Betsy, their aunt, and Charlotte herself would be more than enough. Yet now, a part of her craved to be at her mother's side. Abigail breathed in deep, her anger turning into concern.

And what about Mrs. Bates and the workload that was impossible to carry alone? What about Dr. Adams? She couldn't leave right when he would need her help the most. Her chest tightened, trying to know what to do. Was it better to help one person like Mrs. Schreier or potentially the whole camp? Lord, help me. How do You see it?

She breathed out, letting whatever came next flow freely. "Fine. I'll go over to Mrs. Schreier's, but not as a spy." She eyed Haywood, making it clear she wouldn't be swayed. "I won't deliberately ask her questions or try to get the information you need. If it comes up that's one thing, but I won't be the one to do it especially under false pretense." She knew she was past the point of overstepping her bounds, but the next component was a must. "And Mrs. Bates will need someone else to help her with my time divided between the lady's estate and helping the doctor with our new situation. I know most of the women are stretched, but maybe there's someone you can ask to help when I can't be there."

Though still composed as a Virginian gentleman's reputation was expected to be, Haywood's eyes went ablaze. "Miss Thatcher, you are in no position to negotiate terms and as far as Mrs. Bates is concerned, she'll have to manage on her own. If she doesn't, like you, she knows the consequences."

The muscles in her jaw quivered, trying to curb the edge in her tone. "Yes, but unlike me she has followed her husband here. She has no other family and until the men are paid, no money to speak of."

"Then she'll have to find a way to keep up."

Abigail pressed her lips firmly together. There was so much more she wanted to say to the officer's cold words. Mrs. Bates' was in her early seventies. Her drive was certainly there, but her body wasn't always inclined. Just at washings alone she had to take breaks to rest her fingers, only mildly complaining of their pain and stiffness while trying to handle the garments and her overall pace in the activity was slow. The job at home wouldn't have been a problem, but for the 14,000 men the camp followers had to keep up with, speed was of the essence.

And what if Mr. Bates couldn't be there the next time Abigail was late to help? At the very least the complaints would reach either Haywood or Washington's ears and she had no trouble believing neither man would be as intimidated by Mr. Bates as Mr. Shaw was, big and broad or not. With no desire to risk her friend from having to find her way to keep up, Abigail found another solution.

She squared her shoulders and forced out the words she knew would be ill-received. "Then I refuse to go to the Schreier estate, Mr. Haywood. You'll have to find someone else."

Haywood's mouth drew thin. His eyes pierced into her own, but she wouldn't relent. She wasn't willing to take a chance at the alternative. "Then you're almost certain to be sent out of the camp."

"I understand, but I'll take my chances." Without waiting for the officer's permission, Abigail excused herself in the most uncustomary fashion, storming out of his tent and with her eyes fixed forward.

A tear grazed the side of her cheek. She swiped at it quickly. Of all the people to stand up to, Haywood was the worst choice. Washington had the final decision, but he probably had no qualms if the man wanted her out. Now, Mrs. Bates and Dr. Adams would be left short-handed. She had only made things worse.

Chapter 8

Garrett let out a forceful breath, feeling like the wind was knocked out of his sails. Nearly two months had gone by with his brig patrolling along the Massachusetts coastline and he had nothing to show for it except for a ship full of disgruntled men who were all but too eager for some excitement.

He twisted his spyglass between his hands before finally bringing it to rest at his side. At least getting a crew rounded up had been easy. After spending a few days in Boston, some of the sailors expressed their eagerness to get back in the water. It turned out they were ready to be in an environment where they were less harassed by their captain than having to face the coldness of the rebel cause on shore. Some that knew Garrett from serving alongside him during the Seven Years' War had also joined in. He took that as a good sign. And still yet were also a small handful that came from the *Halifax*, the ship he had been on under the command of Nicholas' father.

Garrett found out the captain was serving as Admiral Graves' right-hand man since their arrival in Boston. From what he gathered the admiral valued the captain's opinion. As he well should, for not only did the Captain have a long-term experience of war, but also success in the capture of enemy vessels. He'd no doubt be staying put for a while. Even so, Garrett confirmed with Nicholas' father just for good measure before agreeing to take his men on board. He didn't want any trouble. Proving his capability as a lieutenant by commanding his own ship had been just the opportunity he needed. He wasn't going to let anything get overlooked, not when he was so close to being promoted to captain and finally about to obtain his own ship.

Garrett shut his eyes. The salty air swept past him and soothed him even as he felt the yearnings of an impatient child inside who hadn't gotten his way. The admiral had given him a brig to take command of the HMS *Piper*, a smaller ship compared to the traditional three-masted sloop of the day. She carried only a pair of masts, but she was fast and easier to maneuver than the bigger vessels and equipped with eighteen guns, prepped and ready at his disposal—perfect qualities for an anti-invasion assignment like his own. What he did lack, however, were any details concerning Washington's fleet. The admiral seemed to have little, if any knowledge of it, only the confirmation of its existence. Not much to go on. He'd have to go with what he knew. And one thing he did know was the supply ships would be flying British flags.

Garrett's goal was to locate those ships along the Boston harbor and lead them into port, to ensure they'd make it to their designated destinations. The mission seemed pretty straightforward: intercept any attempts Washington's fleet was trying to make on their supply ships. Sounded easy enough. Compared to the superiority and experience of the Royal Navy, how bad could a ragtag group of enemy vessels be?

Garrett glanced back in the direction of the harbor. He didn't have a good view of it, but he didn't need to. They'd anchored themselves out to get a better glimpse of who was coming in, making sure to keep a watchful eye. It wasn't easy. The harbor had been busy with maritime activity along the ports. Boston had become the Royal Navy's American headquarters with Admiral Graves in command of nearly fifty British vessels. It was hard to believe with so many ships and capable men, they had trouble obtaining supplies for the soldiers.

Outside the wharf was a different story. Plenty of fishing boats and other small ships passed through the waters, but nothing capable enough to intercept a well-manned vessel by the Navy.

Garrett began another pacing around the forecastle, impatient with the lack of activity. He'd spent years at sea, staring at the ocean's infinite waters for often months at a time before making port again. It had never bothered him then. Why now?

He knew why. He was anxious to prove himself, but that required a reason to react. So far, there'd been nothing that called for his action and frustration propelled through him. He looked once more through his spyglass with an irritation to his grip. It was the same view he had a minute before when he carried out the same motion. Nothing. A low growl clung in his throat. Just what he needed. Another day with nothing to show for it and on top of it, his crew's favorite provisions were getting low.

Garrett had supplied the ship with enough rum and grog for two months' voyage, but he hadn't planned on the unfortunate circumstances that led his men to drink their boredom away. They were used to life at sea where the water was unpredictable and exciting, not where the nearness of the coast provided them with safety and predictability. His crew didn't ask for much, but if they ran out of their "spirits" he might have a whole other problem to deal with. If they didn't see any action today, he'd have to make the decision to head back to port and gather more supplies. And if he did that, it was likely he'd lose half his men as well. No doubt life back on land seemed more appealing than the one he'd given them these two months at sea.

"Mister Cutter, anything yet?"

"No, Captain." His lookout called back down to him from the crow's nest. The sound of the title even from the man's hoarse vocal cords was like a satisfying melody to Garrett's ears. He knew the title was only temporary, depending on the length of his assignment, but the time they'd been out, he'd been captain and he reveled in the recognition. "Nothing out of the ordinary, sir." Cutter called down again from the main mast. "Looks like it might be another quiet day."

Garrett groaned, lamenting his ill fortune.

He couldn't understand it. Was he doing something wrong? Had he missed something? No, surely not. He went over the information in his head again as he paced back and forth, now along the quarterdeck. He received verification that the HMS *Briley* was on its way from England and would be carrying 127 quarter casks of wine and ammunitions for the soldiers in Boston. Finally, something worth pursuing. The letter stated the supply ship's estimated arrival, but according to its message, that had been nearly three days ago. So far, no supply ships had been seen. With little exception, most of the boats they'd observed were smaller vessels used by the local fishermen. Had something happened to the *Briley* under his watch? His chest knotted at the thought of it. No, it couldn't have, he silently protested. He was just getting himself worked up. He'd been diligent in keeping his post, to the point of obsessive, eager to carry out his duty and prove his worth. If something indeed happened to the *Briley*, it had to have been before they reached his coastal waters.

"Captain! There she is!" Cutter yelled down from his station. Nothing was apparent to the naked eye, but the man had been using his spyglass. Garrett quickly applied his own, viewing the direction his lookout pointed. Indeed, there she was. He couldn't help but grin as his heart galloped at the site of the HMS *Briley* entering his territory. Now, it was his turn.

"Excellent, Mr. Cutter." Garrett quickly removed the glass from his eye, now addressing the rest of his crew with both officiality and pleasure.

"Men, let's get that ship to port. Our brothers in arms are counting on us."

The men looked to their captain, though appeared less than half enthused by the news. Apparently, escorting a supply ship to the safety of the Boston harbor was not quite exciting enough to completely resolve their boredom. Garrett understood but ignored their lack of response. He turned his head over to the lieutenant who stood adjacent to him on the quarterdeck, about to give an order.

"Captain!" Mr. Cutter broke in. "We've got us another ship, sir. Looks like it's headed for the *Briley.*"

Garrett's lips pursed. What? Another ship? Where did it come from? Merely a moment ago the only ship in sight was the *Briley.* No matter. He had a job to do and he was going to see it through. He took up the spyglass again, half believing it could be true but his lookout was right. Sure enough, there it was, a three-masted schooner in the distance almost halfway between him and the supply ship. And from what he could tell, things didn't look good.

The ship was not one of their own to be sure. Its colors displayed a white flag with a green emblem he could not distinguish. Even with his aided vision it had been difficult to tell. What he could see, however, was the schooner heading straight for the HMS *Briley* as if intersecting the distance between his ship and the supply ship, looking to get there first. Garrett clenched his glass. Whoever they are, they're not getting to that ship, not without a fight. He looked to his lieutenant with strained determination.

"Mr. Ashby, full speed ahead."

With the lieutenant's call of his captain's orders, the crew's state of boredom instantly vanished. They leapt to their feet, each manning their positions with renewed diligence and strength. Together as a unit, they worked to make their ship press on ahead and reached closer to its goal. Garrett was thankful for the brig that'd been chosen for him. In this dire

95

situation, the speed of the *Piper* was exactly what they needed. Still holding onto his spyglass, his grip further tightened as if letting go of the thing would somehow jeopardize the fate of this mission.

"Come on, get there." The words came out strong under his breath as he tried to keep his resolve for the benefit of his men. He knew as all of them worked at their stations, they'd also be looking towards him, seeing how their captain responded under pressure.

Garrett pulled the glass back up to get a better gauge of the distance. The *Piper* was closing fast, but he wasn't sure if it was going to be fast enough. The schooner had started to position to prepare to fire on the *Briley*. Garrett could now see the emblem of the flag it flew, flapping amidst the backdrop of the wind. Against the white background was a green pine tree and an inscription above it that read, "An Appeal to Heaven."

What seemed like every muscle in Garrett's body constricted. "Washington." He sneered the name under his breath. This was the reason the admiral had assigned him his post.

"Mr. Ashby, ready the guns." Garrett fixed his eyes on the schooner in front of them as the lieutenant carried out his second strand of command. With it, ordered chaos seemed to have filled the ship as men below deck prepared the guns while those above manned sail. "Get us broadside to that ship as soon as we're close enough to fire."

"Aye, Captain."

"I want those guns ready as soon as we're in position, Lieutenant." On edge, Garrett recalled the only time he'd prepared a cannon for a single shot. Even with an experienced crew the process took over a minute and under these circumstances, every second counted.

Garrett felt the *Piper* turn under his feet, maneuvering itself so it would be parallel to the schooner. No need for a spyglass now. Both the schooner and the HMS *Briley* were close enough to feel the effects of a cannon blast. Garrett's jaw clenched then relaxed again. Despite their vast progress to catch up to the vessels, the schooner now sat perpendicular to the *Briley* and had already started to fire on the supply ship. Thankfully, the schooner had misjudged the distance and most of their shots proved futile as the cannon balls plunged into the depths of the sea. For those that'd achieved impact, the damage had only been severe enough to take out the top yard and sail of the foremast.

Garrett allowed a breath in before he thrusted it out again. It was time for his next order. "Fire at the hull, Lieutenant." Damage to the hull was the most effective way to sink a ship. He could've chosen to have the men aim higher, damaging the rigging and the ship's ability to move, but there was also a risk of killing unsuspecting crew members. There were certainly casualties in war, but if circumstances allowed, Garrett did his best to prevent it. In sinking the ship, the crew would at least have a choice: to die at sea or come aboard as prisoners.

The *Piper* was almost in place. Once they were set, the schooner would have little chance for a favorable outcome against both the *Briley* and his brig. True, the angle at which the schooner approached the supply ship had been well calculated, doing well to avoid the broadside of it where the battery cannon would've managed in their defense. However, now, the maneuver had left the schooner's unarmed side open, a perfect target for the *Piper*. No doubt noticing their error, Garrett saw the schooner begin to change course. Perhaps it was their attempt to escape or change position, but it wouldn't do them any good. The action had come too late. His brig was on them and ready.

"Let fly!" Garrett yelled and his heart went reeling. At the command a charge of cannon fire proceeded forth in different intervals, blasting towards the direction of the continental ship. He heard the crackle of the schooner's wood as one shot hit the railing and skidded across the main deck, heavily wounding two men. Another blast hit just above the hull, near the port side, but was too high for the waterline. More blasts ensued, smashing into the enemy's ship and Garrett heard the screams of more men. "The hull, men! I said to hit the hull!" Garrett's frustration only lasted seconds, knowing the difficulty of firing a three-ton gun in the middle of the sea where the waves rocked the ships back and forth. Still, he was hoping for less casualties.

The HMS *Briley* began repositioning herself parallel to the schooner, her broadside left exposed. The two British ships had the rebel vessel sandwiched, leaving it with very few possibilities, none of which if it were Garrett, he would've found agreeable. It wasn't over yet, but he couldn't help but smile a little at the turn in their favor. Smoke produced from the gunfire drifted across the sea in-between the line of ships like a fog hovering over the water.

"Captain, they're looking to cut and run." Lieutenant Ashby came up beside him after he'd carried out his previous instructions.

The news wasn't surprising. Something told Garrett these men would be too hard-pressed to surrender their ship, but they'd surrendered their cause. The schooner, having an extra sail than his brig, was beginning to outrun the *Piper*.

"There's still a chance." Garrett's excitement mounted. "Keep firing." He wasn't going to let them get away. Not when he was so close. Another series of cannon fire ensued, this time one hitting below the waterline. "That's it." He couldn't help but relinquish a smile. "We've got her now."

The smoke had made it difficult to see the size of the hole, but the damage had been done. Where the shot had hit, water poured in while its crew scrambled about, jettisoning its guns and sails along with the rest of its shots. "Mr. Ashby, prepare to board that ship."

At the sound of Garrett's order, an explosion of yells rang out from his crew, they too feeling their triumph. Elation set forth. The victory of the day had come easily enough, but Garrett would take it.

An hour later, Ashby came quickly by his side on the quarterdeck, an expression of consternation in the lieutenant's brow. "Captain, you better take a look at this, sir."

The recent exhilaration Garrett took hold of from their success dropped from his grasp. "Is everything all right?"

"Hard to tell, sir. A ship is approaching straight for us and flying our colors. Should we prepare for them to come aboard?"

"Not just yet, Mr. Ashby. Let me see for myself."

"Captain, it appears one of His Majesty's ships is coming our way." Mr. Cutter had seconded Ashby's news from his post above in the crow's nest.

Garrett didn't need his spyglass to know what the men described. He too could see the white, red, and blue of the Royal Navy colors floating in the breeze. He didn't recognize the ship as the *Hinchinbrook* or *Nautilus*, two others the admiral had assigned to find the *Nancy*. He'd been a part of the ship's crew on the *Canceaux* and even from this distance he could tell the ship didn't belong to Captain Mowat. Admiral Graves had also ordered three more ships along for the mission. Perhaps it was one of those, but the question remained: Why were they were approaching his ship rather than looking for the ordinance brig?

"They must have run into a storm and had some trouble," Garrett said, without truly knowing. "We'll have them come aboard and give them what we can. In the meantime, we'll keep a lookout for our supply ship." He focused his attention solely on his first lieutenant again. "Mr. Ashby, signal for her to come alongside. I assume you can manage without me?" Garrett gave the man an unwavering eye and left him with no other alternative. It was an easy matter of comrade relations that the man was more than capable to handle while Garrett's own body's charge from earlier now lay depleted.

"Aye, sir. Certainly."

"Good. I'll be in my quarters. Don't bother me unless absolutely necessary."

When he'd reached the captain's cabin, Garrett freed himself from his blue, woolen coat and hung in on a nail next to the door. Despite the cold air, the garment was half-soiled with sweat. A smile came easily, one he'd kept hidden until the battle and its aftermath customs were finished. Fifty-one men captured, bound and ready to take back to Boston. They, along with the casks of wine and ammunition would not only please the soldiers, but Garrett couldn't wait to be in the presence of the admiral again now. This was what he needed. This had been the opportunity he'd hoped for.

Garrett took in the quaint desk that'd been left for him while he took command of the *Piper* and thought back to the one in Graves' headquarters. Now, if he could just secure the *Nancy*, an ordinance brig carrying more supplies to Boston. Graves hadn't disclosed what those supplies were, but Garrett could instantly recall the admiral's tense expression back in the man's office.

"She carries material of great importance for our men," were his words.

The admiral must've stood by them too because other than the HMS *Piper*, he had ordered at least five other ships to look out for her, including the HMS *Canceaux*, the ship under the command of Mowat. She would certainly be a prize, particularly for Garrett if his ship was the one to escort her in.

While the two ships anchored, Garrett resolved to get some sleep. Nearly 48 hours had passed since he last rested and the adrenaline in his body from earlier began to wane, leaving but a pleasant satisfaction of victory in its place. He glanced at the cot that sat in his cramped quarters and looked ever the more pleasing in his tired state before he settled into it. He placed his hat over his eyes as the waves gently moved the ship, rocking him back and forth until his lids became heavy. Darkness took over the light and without an ounce of effort he began to drift further and deeper into it.

***

"Captain! They've taken over the ship!"

Garrett nearly jumped out of his skin; the exaltation jolting him from his slumber. The sound of alarm had come from Mr. Cutter, of all persons, letting Garrett know his first lieutenant was otherwise indisposed. Of whether Ashby was fighting, captured, or dead, the details remained unclear. Garrett pressed a hand to his forehead. How long had he been asleep? His last memory had been the sight of a schooner's approach flying His Majesty's colors and his own orders to Ashby granting the ship permission to board before he'd allowed himself to nod off. Now, instead of the voice of his first lieutenant, the disturbing outcry from his primary watchman who'd barged through his cabin howled with every breath of his lungs.

Garrett shook himself out of his stupor, getting to his feet. "What do you mean, they've taken over the ship? Explain yourself, Mr. Cutter and make haste in doing it."

The lookout did, almost tripping over his words in the process. "Sir, the other ship, it fooled us. She's a privateer, sir—hoisted her true colors just before coming alongside. None of us thought to look, seeing we assumed she was one of our own and were getting ready for her men to board." Cutter looked at Garrett apologetically as he shrugged his shoulders. "I suppose the night also did a number on us from the skirmish. We weren't alert as we should be—many of the men quite tired from it. Though I dare say since our current takeover, they look pretty awake now."

How the man had managed to get out of his crow's nest without capture, Garrett liked to find out. But that would be a story for another day. At least he hoped. At present, there were more dire circumstances that required his attention, mainly being trapped in his own ship's cabin. Garrett had still been absorbing the blow when he heard the voice from the other side of the cabin door.

"Captain, by the order of the Continental Army under the command of George Washington, I have seized your ship and I order you to surrender your quarters."

The voice was deep with authority. For a moment, Garrett stood there as if in a trance, his body stiff like the shock of it all prevented him any immediate movement. Was this a nightmare? He was still trying to process how the whole thing happened in what could only have been minutes of him asleep.

"Captain," the same voice bellowed again through the door, this time louder and impatient. "I've been instructed by His Excellency to treat you with civility, but this will be my final request for you to exit your quarters without the means of force."

Garrett nearly flinched at the continental general's reference to His Excellency, as if the man was a king. He would have been glad to give his own opinion about what he thought pertaining to Washington and his army if he wasn't in such a difficult position.

"What should we do, Captain?" His watchman's eyes glowed with earnestness as if Garrett might somehow get the two of them out of this predicament. He was sorry to disappoint the man. There was only one way out of his cabin and that was straight through the door and right into the hands of his captors.

"Aside from jumping ship, Mr. Cutter, I'm afraid the only thing we can." Garrett gestured for the man to follow suit, both knowing trying to escape might as well be a death sentence either by the unpredictable waters or the men they faced now.

"Ah, yes. There we are!" The deep tenor of the man's voice from behind the cabin door seemed to perfectly match his person. He was a burly fellow with his face partially hidden by a coarse mustache connecting to dense sideburns and equally thick eyebrows. The areas that remained exposed: his cheeks and nose, were weather-beaten like the rest of his crew, no doubt from the frigid temperatures and icy winds, but his seemed particularly rosy. "Captain Ward, your lieutenant here has informed me of your position. I'm glad to see we can handle this with civility even within the bounds of war."

Garrett said nothing, acutely attentive Ashby stood by the man who spoke, with two other men at his sides. He was glad to see his first lieutenant was still alive and other than the strain upon his face, doing well enough. In fact, if Garrett was correct, all his crew appeared to be accounted for.

Garrett did his best to fight the scowl coming he knew wouldn't serve him well. His men sat gathered on the main deck, their hands bound while Washington's group of ragtag men guarded them with their pistols and muskets. It was humiliating, really. Here he was, a well-trained officer of the king's Royal Navy furnished with an equally skilled crew who'd been taken captive by this ordinary group of misfits. Most of them were probably fishermen and whalers with some stray landsmen who rushed for the opportunity of adventure at sea.

He looked about his own crew again. Most of them averted their gazes as if their capture had somehow been their fault, but Garrett knew the truth. He was the captain and as such, the blame was solely on him, though he was surprised there hadn't been the slightest hint of a scuffle. No shots fired or signs of powder residue from the preparation of loaded ammunition. Other than their bounds, his crew appeared unharmed, nay except for Jacobs, his cook, who wore a shiner on his left eye. But the man was known for confrontation. Who was to say he didn't obtain it in the mess hall by a fellow crew member before the takeover? No, as much as it pained Garrett to admit it, they'd taken his ship completely without the use of a single means of combat.

Vexation made his skin crawl as Garrett's gaze fell to the other ship adjacent to his own, looking for answers. He found exactly what he was looking for. There on the mainmast, now replacing the Royal Naval colors, flew that infernal white flag. The pine tree illustration and its patriotic inscription in the wind like it was dancing to her victory over his British vessel.

It was a cheap trick, a ruse de guerre, but acceptable by those at sea, nonetheless. To elude or deceive an enemy ship, it was deemed fair to fly false colors as long as the nationality's true colors were raised before engaging in warfare. The rules in the timing were even more obscure. A ship might only be seconds from firing and the ruse would still be legitimate. Even if he would've been awake, Garrett had to admit in his state of weariness at the time, he too may have missed the transition before it was too late. But it was too late. His enemy had caught him off guard, whether by skill or fortune, it didn't matter. He was now a prisoner of war.

Chapter 9

The wheels of the wagon crackled and crushed over dead tree branches and leaves that lay scattered throughout the Harvard Commons. A shiver ran up Abigail's spine. Whether it was the winter chill now among them or the sight of Mary Russel and her two-year-old son being wheeled out from the camp she couldn't determine. Mrs. Bates stood alongside her as Abigail's stomach churned awkwardly for being a spectator of an event that only reminded her of an awful ceremony of sorts. She hugged the hood of her cloak tight around her head, feeling both the bitter wind and procession take hold before looking up, though painfully, at the woman and child.

Mary sat quiet, her eyes locked down at the distant path as if to avoid the gaze and some sneers of her onlookers. Her son, David, clung to her, his red shaggy hair wild and eyes wide in wonder at what was happening to him and his mother.

A lump caught in Abigail's throat as the wagon drew past, continuing to part the well-trodden path of men and women as if God parted the water of the Red Sea.

"An unfortunate thing, that is." Mrs. Bates whispered gently as the wagon proceeded forward. "The poor dear doesn't have anyone outside of here. I'm not sure what is to become of them."

Abigail managed to find her voice, though it came out unsteady. "What about her husband?" Is he not here in camp?"

"I'm afraid not, dear."

Abigail didn't know Mary Russel, except for the handful of exchanges they had held in passing, but those had been superficial and limited on time. She always assumed Mary had followed her husband here like many of the other wives did. Not that there wasn't some other explanation. She, herself had come on different terms after all.

"Then why is she here? I just thought with David…"

Mrs. Bates shook her head apparently knowing enough of what Abigail was about to say. "I don't know the details, only that she's not married and sought to join the army for safety."

Abigail pulled back and frowned. "Safety? I would think being part of an army would be anything but safe, especially once the men go to battle."

"Oh, you'd be surprised, dear." The woman's eyes fell further than they had been, a sigh trailing along with them. "Unfortunately, that's not how things seem to work in this fallen world. I've heard rumors some of the British soldiers have ransacked homes and defiled the women. My cousin in Newport has confirmed as much in a letter I received from her last week." She flinched, her whisper growing softer still. "But I've also heard our side isn't innocent of such cruelty either. Her daughter in Greenwich mentioned a house belonging to a family of loyalists a few miles down had bricks thrown into its windows and was set on fire. Part of me wonders if this war is bringing out the worst in some of us."

Right then the sharp pain of conviction nudged at Abigail's heart and her own reason for being here. Anger. She lifted her eyes back to the wagon, now almost out of the Commons. Her view caught site of Officer

Haywood who stood resolute with nothing to interpret upon his face, only that his own gaze seemed to be on the wagon.

"That man." Mrs. Bates looked like she was preparing to charge for the officer, the derision in her tone unmistakable. "Shame on him and his superior, throwing a woman and toddler out defenseless. Even if she didn't take part in the work, it's hard for me to swallow I'm here aiding men capable of such cruelty."

Abigail looked to Mrs. Bates, the awkward churning in her stomach turning into vexed bewilderment. "That's why she's being sent out-because she didn't complete her chores?"

The woman gave a single, stiff nod. "She's being acquitted for laziness."

Laziness? Abigail gripped the fasten of her cloak, the raging beat of her heart thumping against it. Her confrontation with Haywood a few days prior came surging forward.

"You would do your best to take it unless you're willing to risk the shame of being publicly kicked out for laziness."

It was clear to her now what he meant, and he meant it well enough. The horrific display she viewed in this moment was proof of that. Even as the wagon lurched ahead, she could still see the image of a woman in it, but this time with no child for company. This woman was alone in her shame. *She* was this woman.

Abigail sucked in the cold air for relief, but it only left her raw. Sensing eyes, she looked over where she thought they came from and for the briefest instance, she couldn't breathe. Haywood's glare was indisputable. She was next.

An hour later, Abigail was at the Vassall estate, trying to find anything to occupy her mind other than the unspoken threat she saw in Haywood's countenance that morning. It didn't take much of an effort. Though few, more cases of smallpox came in and they had their orders for how to handle the sickness.

She set to work, gathering the linens she'd washed the day before and the ointment Dr. Adams had laid out for her to use before she left the estate to go next door. There, she arranged the straw bedding along with the newly cleaned sheets. It wasn't luxury that was for sure, but it would be comfortable enough, or at least as comfortable as one could get with smallpox. She cringed, feeling a momentary ache in her head and back just thinking of the disease's manifestation before she placed the ointment in the top drawer of a secretary that occupied one of the main rooms.

From what Abigail understood and Dr. Adams explained, there were two main ways to combat the disease. Either they could purposely expose it to the camp in a controlled environment where symptoms were likely to be less severe and they'd risk the month of recovery, or they could isolate individuals who have it, hoping to keep the spread down. Washington chose the latter and so that's what they were starting to do. Since their first case, three more persons came in to see Dr. Adams, describing complaints of a similar nature in less than a week's time. Those individuals were already in quarantine in the upstairs of the Vassall house, but if the rate continued, it wouldn't be long until the space would prove insufficient.

That's when they'd turned, literally, to the house next door that was left abandoned by a loyalist family who'd fled for Nova Scotia. And that's where she was now. Dr. Adams hoped the isolation might prove early enough to stop the spread, but in the chance it didn't, at least they'd have a little wiggle room before they'd have to find somewhere else. Despite the simplicity of the set-up, she scanned the rooms over just to make sure she didn't forget anything.

"Oh." Abigail gasped, checking the pockets of her apron but came up short. "I forgot the laudanum." She doubted the patients having to undergo through their symptoms of aches and pains would appreciate her failing to remember. She walked back to the Vassall estate to grab the vial, coming across an unexpected visitor in the process.

"I'm sorry young man, but you can't just walk in there." Mr. Douglas, the man on guard, put his arm protectively across the door of the Vassall home, giving his intruder a wary eye.

"You don't understand, sir. I have to see someone in there. I've got orders to…"

"And I've got my own orders which say no one is to enter this house other than the doc and Miss Thatcher and that comes from the Commander himself."

Thomas looked like he didn't care if God made the commandment, and he might barge in past the man at the next opportune time, or at least try.

"Thomas!" Abigail quickened her step, waving to him as she strode up to the door where the two men quarreled. She offered him a look of caution though laced with a smile. "I see you have met Mr. Douglas. He's here to help Dr. Adams and I try to make sure the disease doesn't spread, at least from our end." She turned to the robust man who looked like he wanted to shoo the boy away. "Mr. Douglas, this is Thomas Moore, a friend of mine."

The guard only lifted an eyebrow, while the rest of his features remained flat. "Charmed."

Thomas glowered at Douglas before he turned to her, his features softening and his eyes imploring her own. "So, it's true, then? Smallpox has hit the camp?"

How quickly word could spread. Abigail just hoped the smallpox wouldn't do the same. "It's true," she admitted willingly before refracting her tone to a more optimistic one. "But Dr. Adams knows what he's doing and that's why we're making preparations." She grinned towards the door. "Like Mr. Douglas, here."

The guard gave a dull nod. "Charmed again."

When her explanation proved little to change the downcast shadow of her young friend's expression, she had to ask. Her voice grew soft. "Have you ever had smallpox, Thomas?"

"No, none of us ever got it." He shook his head, before his eyes grew larger, peering into hers. "Have you?"

"I had it when I was young, but I don't remember. I suppose I should be thankful for that." When she saw her account wasn't helping to improve his uneasiness, she grabbed his shoulders gently. "But don't worry, Thomas. You'll be okay. Dr. Adams is hopeful we can keep the number infected low. We're keeping a watchful eye in the camp for signs of it every day and are being cautious with what we find, even if it's just a cough until we know for sure." She smiled, her hands giving his shoulders a firm squeeze. "And if you do get it, I'll be right here to make sure you get everything you need."

Thomas looked up at her, a glimpse of light, though dim shone in his eyes. "Okay, well, I'm gonna hold you to that."

Abigail's smile deepened. "If it happens, you can count on it." She put her hands to her hips candidly as her gaze went to the door of the Vassall estate. "So, who were you needing to see in there?"

"Actually, you, Miss Abby."

"Oh?"

Thomas gave a sure nod. "Yes, Miss. Mr. Haywood sent me. He said he wanted to see you."

With those words, any escape Abigail had relished for keeping her mind distracted on the epidemic came to an abrupt halt. "Oh."

"I'll be happy to walk you back."

She almost declined Thomas' offer until she considered this might be the last time she'd see him. Her smile came out more forced this time. "I'd like that. Thank you, Thomas."

Despite his invitation to escort her, Thomas was quieter than his usual, talkative self. She had a feeling the conversation they had about the illness earlier might be to blame. When they crossed back into the Commons and he still hadn't said a word, Abigail decided it was her turn.

"How are things going with Jake and his friends? Have you had any more trouble from them?"

"Not since I sat with Mr. Bates that morning at breakfast." Thomas' gaze seemed more focused on the ground than their destination.

"That's good, right? Are you and Mr. Bates getting along well?"

He raised his shoulders with a disinterest in the question. "We get along fine. He's nice enough." When Thomas' gaze finally lifted to her own, she gathered he must have caught her off guard by his response. He began to go on as the pace of his words grew hurried. "Don't get me wrong. I like him and it's true, I haven't had any run-ins with Jake, but the guy's pretty quiet. I guess that's why he and Mrs. Bates get along so well. She can talk all she wants around him and he doesn't feel the need to say a word." He raised the side of his mouth before letting it fall again. "I know it's crazy, Miss Abby, but I guess part of me just wishes the other guys would take to me. Having them not mess with me was kind of nice for a while, but I dunno, I wish we just got along better, you know."

Thomas' desire tugged at Abigail's heart. Of course, he wanted the comradery of the other boys. What 15-year-old wouldn't want to be accepted by and even friends with those his own age? The impact of such a basic need even at a time when war occupied most of their thoughts hit lightly at her core until it began to lapse into an iron fist that punched frantically at her gut. Haywood's tent. They'd arrived.

This time Abigail sat, though rallied every ounce of courage she could muster to keep her head level with the officer's sharp gaze. Like usual, Haywood stood and unsurprisingly wore a hardened expression across his brow. At first, nothing was said, the quiet between them feeling like an eternity for Abigail, but she wouldn't dare be the first to speak. Part of her wasn't entirely sure she'd need to, everything but the man's own voiced confirmation telling her she'd be packing up her things soon. Her heart pounded so violently she wondered if Haywood could hear it across the small space of dirt flooring between them.

"Miss Thatcher." The greeting was anything but warm, not that she expected differently, but the combination of the close quarters and her foreseeable future made her feel like a mouse cornered by a lion. "I believe you and I have more to discuss from the other day when you so unceremoniously left before being properly dismissed."

Abigail's throat went dry. Not that she knew what to say at her defense, only that she'd been upset, but she doubted that was a good excuse.

Haywood went on, his glare penetrating. "Please understand that is ill-advised and I won't tolerate such behavior further."

Her ears perked as her breath cut short. "Further?" She hadn't meant to say it out loud, but the implication that there was more for her here than just today left her puzzled.

Haywood's tone and features carried a flick of annoyance. "Yes, in the future, but for now you need to hear something from me." He stepped back as if unintentionally giving her more room to breathe while his hardened expression weakened. "Though I didn't approve of your choice concerning Mrs. Schreier, I should've done a better job of respecting it. Instead, I let my anger get the best of me and that's not something I'm proud of or a gentleman should allow, especially in the presence of a woman." He leaned over his desk and extended his palms to it as if pressing it to the floor. "We need every advantage we can get to win this war and I recognize in my desperation of that I said things that weren't true of your character. According to Dr. Adams you are anything but lazy, but I don't necessarily need his account to see that on my own." A long sigh drew forth. "I admit, my frustrations with the general assigning me in charge of the camp followers when my rank as a lieutenant colonel should allow me more has been most infuriating. You see, Miss Thatcher,

In the French and Indian war I was in command of 300 men under the Virginian Regiment who followed my every order. Now I seem to be in charge of the women and other misfits who both keep the men's spirits high on one end while they inhibit their attention for becoming soldiers ready for a battle that's all but upon us on the other." He gave an irritated sigh, his focus still on the desk. "Yet, without the followers who knows how many of our men will leave after their contracts are up when we need every last one of them. I suppose they are a necessary pain."

Haywood's eyes raised to Abigail's again and he cleared his throat, the action making her wonder if he forgot she was still in his tent.

"Excuse me, Miss Thatcher. I've veered off course." He released his hands from the desk and straightened back into his regimental stance. "What I mean to say is I was in the wrong with you and I hope to make it right."

Abigail blinked, still in the process of digesting what she was almost certain would be her dismissal turned into an apology, of sorts anyway. She peered into Haywood's eyes and saw nothing but sincerity. What bothered her, however, was how this man who admitted such a fault to her and seemed genuine in doing so, could also send a single mother and her young son out to defend on their own at a time when they were so vulnerable.

"Of course, sir. Thank you for saying as much." Abigail swallowed hard, not wanting to ruin what was starting to feel like an olive branch. It wouldn't be a bad idea to accept, yet the image of Mary and David this morning was something she just couldn't get rid of. "But may I ask of Miss Russel and her son? What is to become of them?"

Haywood frowned and she almost scolded herself for asking the question.

"As you saw this morning they've been discharged. My words the other day may not have been true for you, Miss Thatcher, but nonetheless they were true." The clear-cut tone of the officer she knew returned promptly. "Refusal to work will not be permitted in this camp, not while we're limited on rations as it is." His eyes locked squarely on hers. "I stand by my error concerning our previous meeting, but do not think for one minute you have somehow bypassed the rules of the camp pertaining to this." So much for that olive branch.

"What will happen to them?"

"That's something you don't need to worry about." Haywood's calloused expression told her the subject was over. "At any rate there's one other thing I need to ask of you before you're properly dismissed."

"Yes, sir?"

"It has to do with Mrs. Schreier." Abigail's neck went stiff. The mention of the woman's name brought back their dispute at an instant and her face went hot. Even with Haywood's apology, she wasn't about to give up her stand against spying on the woman.

The officer raised his hand, encouraging her to keep her seat this time. "Before you object, hear me out and consider a second refusal will not look good to His Excellency no matter what connections you have."

Abigail scrunched her brow. What did he mean by connections? As if she knew anybody...unless...The image of Haywood shaking hands with her brother instantly appeared. Abraham?

Before she could inquire, Haywood went on to business. "We've captured a man outside of Boston from the opposing side. He'll be staying at the Schreier estate for the meantime. Mrs. Schreier has allowed the arrangement, but he'll need his basic provisions including meals as the lady's housemaid is not a part of the agreement. Since Mrs. Schreier is already akin to you it seems best for you to carry on the task."

Abigail tilted her head, eyes narrowed. "And I wouldn't have to forsake her trust?"

Haywood's lips went firm. "If you mean obtaining the intel about her husband we discussed at our last meeting, no. That's not a requirement this time."

Abigail sat back a little more easily in the chair as she took a moment to consider. There was still a part of her that wanted to see the lady and now that she didn't have to do it with an alternative agenda she was against, she just might agree. Except, there was one thing. "But what about my chores with Mrs. Bates? I'm not just going to leave her stranded to take it all on herself."

Haywood didn't flinch. "Mrs. Bates' fate pertaining to this camp will still be up to her. I won't make any special accommodations for anyone, but if you can find an alternative solution I consider acceptable, I'll allow it."

Again, Abigail weighed the proposal and the pressures behind it. Whatever connections Haywood meant, she'd have to find out later, but that didn't seem to matter now. If what he said was true, she'd better accept it otherwise her fate might be closer to Mary Russel's than she thought. At least this time she didn't have any qualms against it. She lifted her chin, the matter decided. "All right. I'll do it."

Haywood gave the slightest of smiles. "A good decision."

"Is the prisoner over at the Schreier estate now?"

"No, I'm informed he'll arrive tomorrow morning."

That still didn't give her much time. She'd have to act fast to make sure her part with Mrs. Bates was covered. Abigail squirmed in the chair, remembering Haywood's warning against a self-dismissal. She wasn't about to do that again.

The corner of his mouth raised a degree higher and for an instant it seemed like the hard-pressed rock dividing them began to crack. "Thank you, Miss Thatcher, you may go."

Chapter 10

"No, no, gentlemen. Put him down over there on the bed." Abigail reprimanded the two men carrying what she hoped was a living body to the upstairs chamber of Mrs. Schreier's estate. Though feeling bad about the freshly cleaned bed linens, she didn't have the heart to leave the man on the floor as the two privates from camp seemed set out to do. Officer Haywood had assigned this man to her responsibility and enemy or not, her mother's fierce instruction wouldn't allow her to treat him any differently than if it were her own grandmother she'd be attending to. As far as the bed clothes, she'd just have to add those to her items for washing tomorrow morning or at least until he woke up.

She looked at the new occupant of the Schreier household and winced. The dark, unkempt hair that shaded his eyes was equally met by a neglected overgrown shadow on the lower part of his face. Even half covered, she could easily distinguish a large purple bruise on his right eye. He'd made somebody mad, that was certain. And from the looks of it they'd knocked him out cold. Just to make sure, she leaned in and almost wished she hadn't. An awful stench of rotten fish mixed with stale water flooded her nostrils. Where had he been? She pinched her nose tight. No use trying to hear him breathe. She wouldn't be able to get close enough without gagging. A different approach would have to do.

Abigail put the palm of her hand slightly above the man's mouth and watched his chest. It wasn't long when the warmth of air hit her hand and she saw the even rise and fall of his breast. Satisfied she wouldn't have to tell Haywood his prisoner was no longer alive, she set up the washbasin to the right of the bed, leaving a spare razor of Mr. Schreier's and a full pitcher of clean water she hoped would be taken advantage of. After kindling a fire, she laid out the white shirt and waistcoat along with a pair of breeches the man of the estate was also lending unbeknownst to him while he was away.

Abigail carefully eyed the clothes, comparing them with the figure passed out in the bed. It wouldn't be an exact fit, but the man was fortunate to get anything at all. At any rate, it would have to do until she could get his own attire washed. She frowned at the small heap under her arm. It might take more than one try and she could already see some patch work needed to be done around the lapel and cuffs of his blue coat. No, more like Navy, she thought again, much like the color she'd seen Officer Haywood wear so many times. Strange that it wasn't red like the majority of the king's soldiers she'd seen patrolling on some of the roads that led into Boston. At least, that's what she would've guessed to find when Haywood mentioned he was picked up just outside of the city. Then again, Haywood wasn't the type to miss such a detail. If he said this man was a prisoner, then so be it. She didn't plan to find out the rest of the story and frankly, didn't want to know. Her job with the stranger would be done soon enough when the time came.

Abigail placed the boiled beans and pork stew close to the fire on a small mahogany table. She took one last look at her new assignment, sprawled out in the canopied bed. The warm fire now beginning to envelope the room made her keenly aware of how extraordinary the scene seemed as the backdrop of the cold barracks of the Commons came to her thoughts. She shook her head, the absurdity giving way to a small laugh.

"You must be someone special, sir." The soldier offered no reply in his unconscious state. "Either that or I'd like to see how Washington treats his friends if he treats his enemies like this." Abigail stepped out of the room's threshold and shut the door behind her, leaving the man to his slumber.

When she got downstairs, she found Mrs. Schreier in the parlor occupying the chaise in the same manner she had for their first meeting.

"How's our new arrival doing?" Smiling, the lady motioned for her to take a seat.

Abigail chose the high-backed chair next to the fire. The cozy setting was a luxury apart from the damp, cold of her own quarters back in camp and she intended to take every advantage of it while she was here.

"I'd say comfortably. He has better sleeping arrangements than most of Washington's army." Abigail retrieved a vial from her apron pocket. "Here, Dr. Adams said you might need this. It's a spearmint infusion."

Mrs. Schreier scooped up the vial to look at it, her eyes brightening. "For my sickness."

"He mentioned you get ill sometimes throughout the day. That's normal."

"The mornings have been the worst, but it doesn't seem as severe as the day goes on. Thank you."

Abigail's own smile came naturally. "You're welcome. I hope it helps." She angled her head, the even line in her brow crumpling. "So how did a prisoner end up here?"

The woman gave a tiffed roll of her eyes. "Well, none of the other rebels wanted him under their roof, so I guess Washington chose mine."

"I'm surprised he's even in a house at all. Why not in the barracks or somewhere at the camp?"

"He's an officer, so I'm told." Mrs. Schreier offered a pointed look. "Your general doesn't take the customs of prisoner exchange lightly. I'll give him that. He's treating the man according to the rules governed by the European states, by the man's rank and title. It's all standard, I assure you."

"An officer?" Abigail pulled back, her tone weighted with bewilderment she could see Mrs. Schreier sensed as the lady's mouth lit with a grin.

"He doesn't look like it, does he?"

"I wasn't going to say anything, but…"

"I couldn't believe it myself when Officer Haywood told me."

Abigail blinked. Her interest in the prisoner upstairs was thwarted by the mention of her superior. "Officer Haywood came by?"

"He did. He was the one that came to see if I'd agree to house the man if he could make the right accommodations for me with my condition." The corner of her mouth raised. "I suppose that's where you come in."

Abigail returned the smile without effort. "I guess so. Dr. Adams also wanted me to check on you." She thought of the smallpox spread. "He's been tied up at camp and may be for some time."

"Well then it's to my fortune things have worked out for you to come to the estate. That is, just as long as he's here when I really need him to be."

"Yes, ma'am. He will be."

The lady pressed her lips, a slight frown formed upon them. Since you'll be around here more often, why don't we skip the formalities. Call me Margaret." She smiled, then looked at Abigail with expectation in her expression. "And what pray tell may I call you?"

"Abigail is fine, but I prefer Abby from my friends." She'd let the woman decide that stance on her own.

"I see." Mrs. Schreier's eyes sparkled with amusement. "And does that mean you're willing to be friends with someone on the other side of the battlefield, so to speak?"

Abigail couldn't help but laugh. "I wouldn't exactly call our arrangement a battlefield scenario."

"True, but you're already informed of where my loyalties lie, and you know my husband is out as we speak on a mission for the king. That doesn't make you leery?"

Abigail shrugged. "I could ask the same of you. You know I'm from the continental army camp, and there's no question your status in social standing is superior to mine." She stopped, recalling the woman's disappointment at their first encounter when she thought her visits were limited to a one-time arrangement. "Yet, I can't forget how pleased you seemed with the false impression that my visiting at the time would be a regular occurrence." Her cheeks grew warm. She hadn't considered the woman's desire might have altered since then. "Unless that's changed."

"No, Abigail, I'm still as lonely as ever." Mrs. Schreier gave a droll look. "Or should I say Rebekah and I are glad to have some new faces rather than staring at each other for the remainder of how long this war goes on." She put a tender hand to her abdomen. "As you might expect from my current physical state and the state of my loyalties, I don't get out much and Rebekah only goes out for things needed.

Abigail let the air escape through her lips, determination in mind. "We might not see eye to eye on things, but that doesn't mean we can't respect one another. In any case, I'd be willing to be friends with anyone, or at the very least, try."

"Good. Me too." Margaret leaned towards the fire or as best as her body would allow in her temporary state.

Abigail took hold of a nearby throw and placed the wool blanket around the lady's shoulders.

Gratitude filled Margaret's eyes before she angled them towards the ceiling. "Do you think our new guest is still asleep?"

"I wouldn't expect him to wake up anytime soon. Part of me thought he was dead until I checked for his breathing." With invitation, Abigail took a seat beside Margaret on the chaise.

"Just as well. Something tells me he might not be in a good mood after being kept in the hold of a ship for two days. Having to sleep in such a small space is cramped enough, but at least the air came through. His quarters would have been less pleasant, I'm afraid."

Abigail grimaced. She imagined the man had been picked up somewhere along the route to Cambridge where horse, a carriage, or even just by foot did the traveling, not a ship. "I thought he was captured outside of Boston?"

"He was, outside the Boston Harbor."

That certainly explained the horrific smell. But if he wasn't a soldier on land, then that meant… Abigail inhaled sharply, remembering the blue coat.

"Did I not mention he's from the Royal Navy?"

The final detail pricked at Abigail's skin and left an impression that was hard to forget. The very mention of the infamous naval fleet brought back images she'd tried to move past from: the ash left from her home that slipped between her fingers and the skeleton of singed wood that remained of the barn. And that was only her family's farm. What about the rest of the lives they uprooted that day?

"Abby, are you all right?" Margaret stared at her with blue eyes full of gentle inquisition.

Abigail gathered herself, smoothing away the wrinkles in her apron like they were the thoughts she worked to keep at bay. She had to remember even if the man upstairs was part of the Royal Navy, there was little chance he'd been there that day when her town was hit. After all, Britain's prestigious Navy had at least one hundred ships. What were the chances the man was on one of the five she saw? At any rate, he was here now, a prisoner of an army that had no navy at all. Feeling somewhat encouraged by that point, she nodded.

"Yes, I'm all right. But there is something that piqued my interest you mentioned earlier. You were talking about the man's sleeping conditions like you knew firsthand. Have you been on a ship before?"

Margaret gave a bemused smile and looked over her shoulder to the flames of the fire. "More times than I'd like. I was born in Brandenburg, but my husband and I came from Germany after the Seven Years' War to see the colonies. It took me six weeks to learn English and its customs while we awaited our departure in Bristol. Thankfully, while there, we were well-received in English court, but I can't say the same for the public spaces." Her mouth went tight after she sucked in a quick breath. "I was informed much too late my German fashions were being mistaken for French ones. With the rivalry between the two countries, you may imagine that didn't bode too well for me. I had to sell some antiques in England to pay for more suitable dressings but there was enough money left over to help pay for our final trip to the colonies. Our ship docked in Philadelphia where we spent some months with friends who'd also settled from our home country."

"And where you ran into me." Rebekah entered the parlor, plopping into one of the high-back chairs across from them.

Margaret's smile resurfaced. "Yes, before settling here in Cambridge."

"I'm surprised you didn't end up in Boston or even Philadelphia where you first arrived. With your husband's travels, it would be nice to have a port close by."

Margaret gave a slight bow of her head, indicating she understood Abigail's point. "We spent time in both cities. Much of Brandenburg is untouched by society with beautiful landscapes and nature. Though we enjoyed our time in Boston, we prefer the peace and quiet of Cambridge, even when the students are in session here. Besides, it's less than an hour ride to the city on horseback if need be." She gave Abigail a pointed look. "And what about you? You mentioned on our first meeting most of your family is in Portsmouth. How did you end up in Cambridge? Did you follow your husband here like most of the women in camp?"

The heat rose in Abigail's face. "Actually, no. I followed my brother in part."

Margaret's fine-arched brow lifted. "And the other part?"

A wave of emotion hit Abigail as the image of her destroyed town came into view. She choked it down with more effort than she liked in front of a woman she was just now beginning to know. Yet, Margaret had shared some of her story, how could she expect to build a friendship with this woman if she wasn't willing to do the same?

Abigail let out a flustered sigh while she closed her eyes. "Was on my own accord." Just thinking about the next words made her cringe, but she didn't know how else to say it. "To get revenge in a way."

Two pairs of eyes stared back at her, but it was Rebekah who spoke, her voice soft and absent of judgement.

"Revenge, miss? What for?"

Abigail clasped her hands as she worked to stop them from trembling. "My town was fired upon by the British and my home along with it. As I mentioned earlier, my family made it out all right and are in Portsmouth staying at my aunt's estate. I'm thankful for that. It's just that everything we knew is gone. I thought coming here to Cambridge to help the army was a way I could find peace somehow."

"You mean fight back." Despite the bump in her midsection, Margaret leaned in, her remark filled with accusation and truth.

"Maybe," Abigail confessed. It was still unclear even to her. "I want restitution for my town, but even more, I just want to know why it happened. Falmouth is a peaceful community. We didn't make an attack on the British, so why was such an order made?" The warmth in her cheeks began to increase, but this time not out of embarrassment.

"Miss Abby, I'm not sure you're gonna find that answer. And somethin' tells me even if you did you probably won't like it."

"You might be right, Rebekah." A defeated smile formed across Abigail's face, suspecting there was wisdom behind the woman's warning. "I suppose that's why I'm still here and not with my family in Portsmouth." Mrs. Bates and the smallpox epidemic also came to mind, but Abigail decided those details weren't on course with their current conversation. "I need to feel like I'm doing something about it, even in my own small way."

"I understand that, miss." Rebekah's mouth curved with tender sincerity. "Sometimes we need to be able to do somethin' even when everything's really out of our control. You know what that's like too, don't you, Margaret?"

Margaret rubbed her hands methodically over her stomach and lifted her chin slowly. "Yes, I know what you mean. I imagine we all have to face what we can't control sometimes." Her eyes caught on a pair of men walking past the window, a rifle slung over each back as they laughed to whatever topic they conversed over. Margaret stared at them, her gaze and body tense. "Including being surrounded by a group of rebels."

"Oh, Margaret pay them no mind." Rebekah shook her head, giving the lady of the house a stern look. "Besides, you know that's not what I mean. What about all that trouble you and Alex went through to get here?"

Abigail wanted to ask more that pertained to what the lady of the house revealed earlier. She'd brushed over it like the detail was minute when in truth Abigail found it intriguing. How skilled the woman must've been to learn another language and custom so quickly. Her German accent was hardly detectable. Abigail's lips broke, but the compliment she was about to give never made it out. Instead, the sound of a rhythmic thumping above them stopped her short and her heart took on rapid speed.

They all turned a curious eye up towards the ceiling. Footsteps.

"Looks like we'll be adding one more to our party this afternoon." Rebekah jumped up and glanced at the grandfather clock. "It's close enough to teatime. I'll get a pot goin'." She left the room and proceeded down the hall in the direction of the kitchen.

Margaret smiled, a touch of humor in her tone. Any signs of scorn from moments ago now vanquished. "Well, this should be fun."

Abigail couldn't say the same. In fact, she was at that moment trying to think of an agreeable way to excuse herself from the estate and more importantly, the awkward meeting of the Royal Navy officer. She may have agreed to supply the man his meals, but Haywood didn't say anything about having to speak to him. "You'll have to tell me all about it. I need to…"

"You're not leaving, are you?" Margaret frowned; her question covered with disproval. "Really, Abigail, I must insist you stay. You won't want to miss Rebekah's apple strudel. It's almost as good as my mother's, and I only say that because my mother would be cross if I didn't. Don't you want to see…?"

The lady of the house beamed at the entryway of the parlor as her words vanished.

Abigail followed Margaret's gaze, curious if the woman's delight was over Rebekah's return with her beloved dessert or something else. In a moment too soon, her question was answered.

Abigail's pulse rocketed. Even with the black eye she instantly recognized him and before she could turn away fast enough, she saw a keen recollection staring back at her.

***

Garrett awoke, his face and shirt half-drenched with sweat. It had to have been a dream, a nightmare: his boat fighting against the storm, his men bound and tied, his capture. Strange, the smell of mint had somehow permeated into his dream, making it if nothing, a little more pleasant.

He sat himself up, shaking his head as if to send the remnants of the nightmare away when he the feel of the soft bedding beneath him made him take pause. He wasn't on his cot. He wasn't in his cabin at all, let alone his ship. He got up from the bedding. It was softer than what he was used to, and it didn't give in to the movement of the waves to which he'd grown accustomed. It was plain enough; he wasn't at sea anymore. But if he wasn't on the *Piper*, where was he?

He looked back at the canopy bed, an upgrade from the cot he was used to lying on, but the thought made him weary. How had he come to it? A washbasin stood next to the bed's headboard while a chest stood at the foot of it. Garrett made a mental note in case he might need it for storage. But what pleased him most by the unexpected accommodations was the fireplace on the adjoining wall. It had been kindled. A wonderful, and even he dared say welcoming, addition compared to the drafty cabin he'd been housing of late.

Garrett winced, trying to remember how he ended up here. The last thing he remembered was black. Everything had gone black. Beyond that his head jarred from the pain. His insides coiled as the events of his last night of the *Piper* came back with a vengeance. It hadn't been a dream. His ship had been taken.

After the enemy's captain had made his preliminaries, he ordered Garrett's crew below deck. Garrett was granted permission to stay above, but only under the condition he wore a covering over his head. It was a condition he out rightly refused. He knew the need for such action was unnecessary, merely a ploy for the enemy to make sport of him and Garrett would have none of it. He would have gladly joined his crew below without quarrel if it weren't for what he presumed to be the captain's lieutenant trying to force the head covering against his will.

That was when his composure broke, releasing the anger that had been mounting over the course of the takeover as he sent the lieutenant back a few steps, leaving the man with a knocked jaw. The action was completely dishonorable, especially for his standing, but Garrett didn't care. After all he'd been through: the denials for his promotion, the difficulty in procuring the *Nancy*, and now his ship taken by a group of misfits, the rush had felt good. That was, until everything suddenly went black.

After devouring the boiled beans and pork, Garrett went over towards the mirror that hung just above the washbasin and grazed his fingers over his right eye. It felt tender. Not only that, but it was also swollen and partially bruised from the impact. Even without a black eye, he looked awful, barely recognizing the face in the looking glass. He couldn't do much to improve his eye, but a shaving and a good cleaning would help. Thankfully, someone had left a razor and a filled pitcher by the basin he was glad to make use of.

When he finished, Garrett took a quick examination of the clothes laid out by the fire. They weren't his, yet the way they were neatly placed by the warmth of the flames was like an invitation he decided to partake in. They were a size too large, but they were clean and dry, which was more than he could probably say for his own. Speaking of…He looked about the room and frowned. His boots and hat occupied the same space as the clothes, but where was his coat? He checked the chest at the foot of the bed. Everything of his belongings were there except for his uniform and his mother's pin. Maybe he shouldn't be surprised at them being stolen by the rebels, but why did it have to be the two things he cared most about?

Garrett took the liberty to exit the room, seeing no one was around to prevent him otherwise. That was strange. He wasn't expecting the place to be unguarded. And he certainly wasn't expecting to wake up in a place so comfortable and inviting, especially after the quarrel he had back on his ship. Maybe he'd been hit harder than he thought. In any case, he intended to find out just what was going on. He touched his eye again, the pain still throbbing. And where was his crew? Hoping to gain some answers, Garrett ventured his way down a set of stairs at the end of the hall.

A pair of female voices captured his ear and eased his tensions. He followed their sound into what he surmised to be the parlor and beheld somewhat of an odd scene. The woman who spoke and whom he guessed to be in charge of the estate by the fashion of her jade dress was directing an amiable conversation to a young woman he would've guessed to be a servant of the household or maid. That is, if it weren't for the way she sat beside the lady of the house in a velvet chaise across from two empty chairs.

"Captain!" The lady looked up at him from the couch, her eyes bright and like the room he'd just come from, inviting. The woman beside her also turned round, then back again, but not before he caught sight of her, and his breath caught. It couldn't be. Yet, he recognized those green eyes from anywhere as the image of them still haunted his heart. "Well, I must say that is an improvement from when you first arrived. You clean up nicely."

He gave the lady a cordial smile, remembering how he first looked in the mirror. "Thank you, Mrs..?"

"Mrs. Margarethe Schreier. My husband and I own this estate. I imagine you woke up with some questions in mind, am I right?" Her head tilted as she revealed a smile tainted with fancied amusement.

"Actually, yes. You've answered the first, of which I'm grateful to you for allowing me to stay thus far. I'd like to extend my gratitude to your husband in kind."

"That won't be necessary, but I'll be sure to mention it in one of my letters to him. He's away on a particular mission for the king of England."

Garrett felt the tension in his back ease. That answered another question. She wasn't a rebel. "The last thing I remember is my ship being taken." He purposely didn't mention how he got the black eye.

The lady's smile faded. "Yes, that part is true. You're a prisoner of the continental army, under George Washington, I'm afraid."

"And my crew? What's happened to them?"

"That, I don't know. I'm sorry. They don't exactly tell loyalists everything that's going on as you might imagine."

He nodded. "Well, thank you for the dry clothes and the stew. That and the bed and fire was certainly unexpected, but much appreciated."

"I'll take credit for the bed, but the rest I'll have to assign to Miss Thatcher here." The lady gestured to the woman next to her, who from the way she struggled to turn in his direction, told him she didn't care for the sight of him.

"Thank you, Miss Thatcher."

She smiled, but Garrett could tell it was feigned. "You're welcome, but I only did it because it's part of the camp arrangement for Mrs. Schreier's benefit." She said it as if to say, "and not yours."

"All right, tea's ready." A Negro woman entered, carrying a Chinese tea kettle with a strudel of some kind. The smell of baked apple, cinnamon, and did he detect...a hint of rum?

"Please, Mr....?"

Garrett hesitated at Mrs. Schreier's address, forgetting he hadn't made his own introductions. "Ward. Garrett Ward at your service, Madame."

"Lovely. Please take a seat, Mr. Ward." Mrs. Schreier motioned over to one of the empty chairs across from the elegant couch.

With purpose, Garrett took the high-back chair directly in front of Miss Thatcher.

The Negro woman poured him a cup of tea, a scent he recognized from the Motherland, before she placed it on a nearby table. "Would you like a piece of cake, sir? It's real sweet and tasty."

He nodded. She wouldn't have to convince him any more than that. His prolonged hunger hadn't been filled from his time on the rebel ship even after the stew he'd just had, and the delectable aroma made his taste buds water. After cutting him a piece, she went over to the lady of the house and then to Miss Thatcher. The latter looked as stiff as a plank, and he didn't miss her continued avoidances as he tried to make eye contact with her.

"Miss Abigail, are you all right?" The Negro woman scrunched her brow as she plated a slice of apple strudel for the her. "You look like you've seen a ghost, miss."

A slight pinkish hue flooded Abigail's cheeks as all eyes went directly on her, including his own.

"Abigail, I know I'm the patient, but really are you all right?" It was only then, Garrett understood Mrs. Schreier was with child. If it weren't for the blanket laid across her abdomen, he might have deduced it sooner. Then again, his attention between the lady of the house as she spoke to him and the woman he remembered from Falmouth sitting alongside her, left it more than a little divided. The unease in Miss Thatcher prompted him to do something, though, he wasn't sure if she was going to like it.

Garrett cleared his throat. "I believe Miss Thatcher and I know each other, in passing that is." He quickly corrected, not wanting to leave room for any ill presumptions about their relationship. "We crossed paths in Falmouth. Is that correct?" This time he gave her no choice but to acknowledge him.

Her eyes locked onto his with mouth tight. "Yes, that's true. I'll admit, Mr. Ward, I didn't think I'd see you again."

She pasted on a smile that read, "And I didn't want to." Not that he could blame her. But what was she doing here in Mrs. Schreier's estate? He recalled what she said about her being a part of Mrs. Schreier's arrangement with the camp, but what did that mean? She was a part of

Washington's camp? If that were true, what did she have to do with a loyalist household in which she seemed content? What was the commonality he was missing?

"Well, isn't that something, then? It looks like you two will be able to get better acquainted." Evidently unaware of the tension between them, Mrs. Schreier passed a container of sugar over to Abigail, who declined the offer. "Abigail is going to be…"

"Going, I'm afraid." Abigail stood up, interrupting whatever the lady of the house was about to reveal. "I'm sorry, but I've already stayed far too long. Dr. Adams will probably be looking for me, and I have some other things in camp I need to take care of." She turned to Garrett. "Mr. Ward, Officer Haywood will be over sometime today to brief you. He did mention if you happened to wake before his arrival, which indeed you have, you are forbidden to leave this house until the general orders otherwise. You may go outside, but if you leave the premises, I'm afraid it would count against you as trying to escape."

Garrett wasn't surprised by the order, only that she was the one that relayed it. So far, it seemed to be the only proof he was indeed a prisoner.

"I imagine he'll also be a good person to ask regarding the rest of your crew and other questions you may have."

"Thank you, Miss Thatcher." He was eager to learn about his crew's fate, and he wanted to ask her more about Officer Haywood, but before he could, she turned from him and bid the other two women farewell. With added curiosity, Garrett watched as she marched out of the room and towards the door, but not without catching sight of a navy coat tucked tightly under her arm.

Chapter 11

"Miss Thatcher, it is not a frequent occurrence that we get to decide how we will serve during war. We simply help where we are needed. As you know, I am not highly pleased with my own assignment, but that's where the general needs me, and the Schreier estate is where I need you."

"But Mr. Haywood," for the second time Abigail tried to plead in desperation, "you don't understand, I can't continue to visit Mrs. Schreier. Not while Mr. Ward is..."

"Is a nuisance. I know, but we must honor the laws of war, especially if we're going to be taken seriously by their Parliament. Remember, we all have a job to do, and as I said before, there's only so much to be allowed before even someone like you is driven from camp."

Abigail sealed her eyes shut in frustration. Someone like her? She still didn't know what that meant, but at the foreseeable moment, it wasn't her priority. What she needed was to find a way out of ever having to see that Royal Naval officer again.

She remembered how her breath caught, her body paralyzed when she saw him in the entryway, though thankful she'd already been sitting in the chaise lounge with Mrs. Schreier when it happened. At least then, when

her body went limp, something had been there to catch her fall. That wasn't the man she'd seen earlier in the upstairs guest bedroom. It couldn't be. And yet, somehow an unfortunate truth inside her spoke plainly that it was. Just when she thought her heart was healing. Now she had to see him every day?

Trepidation stirring, Abigail almost pressed again, until she saw the unrelenting scowl on her superior's face. The image of Mary Russel and little David in the wagon wheeled through her mind. Haywood wasn't going to budge, and if she tried he would stand by his word. Defeated, she left the officer's tent with head hanging.

"Why, don't tell me my Highlander eyes are deceiving me! That would be a sore trick if I ever saw one!"

The familiar Scottish accent sounded like music to her disheartened ears.

"Miss Thatcher, it *is* you." Cleophes stepped towards her, a smile from ear to ear. "So, you decided to join the cause after all." He frowned. "But you don't look too happy about it. Anything an old man like me can help you sort out?"

She glanced back at Haywood's tent. "I don't think so. Not unless you can speak to the general on my behalf."

Cleo gave a long, drawn-out whistle that made her cheeks flush with the attention it drew. If they didn't have any spectators before, they certainly did now. "Sorry, Miss Abigail, that's a bit higher than my rank allows."

Unsurprised, she nodded. "Then it looks like I'll have to figure it out on my own." She pursed her lips, fully cognizant the British sat in Boston and Washington was here in Cambridge, less than five miles down the road. "Abraham said you wanted to stay out of the war, so what are you doing at the very heart of it?"

He laughed while he twisted a worn-out, Monmouth cap, but one much less singed to the one he had in Falmouth, between his fingers. "I suppose you could say I'm a man who doesn't take well to a quiet life like some. I gave it a good effort, Miss Abigail, I did. Went to North Carolina where some of my kinsman settled and tried my hand at extracting sap from the pine trees for naval stores. I couldn't tell you how many barrels I filled. I hope they appreciate all that resin and turpentine there in Wilmington for their ships. I stayed awhile just to give it a good chance, but me past is so filled with…" Cleo's eyes dropped from hers.

She put a tender hand on his shoulder, sensing whatever was on his mind wasn't easy to say. "Filled with what Cleo?"

"Complications, Miss." He sighed before a weak smile pushed through. "Let's just say I couldn't put roots down. Naht to mention, that works mighty boring. While I was working on those barrels, I had time to think about what happened in Falmouth and my own account. Enough of it to know there might be more for me to do." He straightened, tilting the gray patches of his chin upward. "Abe was always hellbent on signing onto the cause, so I thought I'd do the same."

Abigail grimaced, recalling the last time she'd seen her brother outside the very tent she now spoke with Cleo. What was Abraham up to? "I'm sorry, but I haven't seen much of my brother since we arrived in Cambridge. I'm not sure where he is."

Cleo shrugged. "It's all right, miss. I'm confident I'll have a chance to catch up with him in due time."

She hoped so. If Cleo spoke with her brother, she could at least rest knowing he was all right.

"Miss Abby."

The sight of Rebekah in the Commons again made Abigail's heart quicken. "Rebekah?" She searched the woman's eyes for a sign of distress. "Is Margaret all right?"

Rebekah strode up beside her and Cleophes to make their duet a trio. She smiled easily. "Yes, miss, the lady's fine. As a matter of fact, I haven't seen her this elated since before all her friends left town for Nova Scotia." Rebekah pulled out a sealed piece of parchment from her apron pocket. "Since I don't know where you sleep, I was going to deliver this to Officer Haywood in hopes he'd pass it on, but seein' we ran into one another I'll just give it to you now." Rebekah looked at Cleo with expectation in her gaze.

Abigail hesitated, now keen to both her curiosity about the letter and her lack of manners in failing to make an introduction. "I'm sorry, Rebekah. This is Cleophes Lockhart. He's a friend of mine from Falmouth."

"Pleasure." Cleo tipped his cap while giving an effortless grin.

Abigail liked the warmth of the man, never seeming to come across a stranger.

"Nice to meet you, Mr. Lockhart." Rebekah pulled out another envelope and Abigail could see it was addressed to Officer Haywood. "I better get this inside and back to the house. I'll be needing to get things ready."

"Ready?" Abigail broke open the red engraved seal to see what was inside. Below her name read:

Please accept this invitation on behalf of Mrs. Schreier to accompany the lady as her guest for a dinner party this very evening.

Abigail's eyes veered from the letter to Rebekah. "A dinner party?"

The woman beamed. "Yes, miss, tonight."

"Tonight?" The impossibility of the situation poured over like a cup of water spilling past its brim. Even with the extra help Abigail had acquired for Mrs. Bates by asking some of the other women to take up shifts, she still had plenty to do. A few more smallpox cases came in and it was no surprise that word spread within the camp of the malady, which she was sure Washington was not happy. Some of the recruits left for home for fear they'd chance catching it.

And then there was the thought of sitting at the same table with Mr. Ward that made her skin crawl. What could the two of them possibly have to say to each other? Abigail could just imagine it. Something along the lines of:

"Oh, do you remember that day you fired your cannons on our town, completely destroying it and leaving most of its residents destitute right before the onset of winter? Thanks for that."

The sarcasm in her thoughts penetrated deeply. She would do well to keep her mouth shut if she didn't want to offend her hostess or make a scene. But even better she would do well not to go in the first place. In all reality, Margaret was the type who would require a more formal style of dress for such an occasion, something Abigail learned at her Aunt Sylvia's estate last year and something she did not possess, especially here at camp.

"A party, Miss Abigail? Well, it seems like you've made some good friends here in Cambridge."

Abigail forced a smile towards Cleo before her gaze engaged on Rebekah again. "I appreciate the invitation, but I don't think Mrs. Schreier is going to want me in…"

"That?" Rebekah raised an eyebrow to Abigail's current ensemble, her daily work dress and apron. "You're absolutely right which is why the lady has requested you come by earlier this evenin'. We'll get you properly ready then. I had my share of work on those women in Pennsylvania and the Madame herself. I'll make sure you're well-prepared. Don't you worry about that, miss. And don't worry about that Mr. Haywood either. I'll be lettin' him know the details in that matter as well." She smiled, a twinkle in her eye. "I'm sure the officer wouldn't mind agreein' to tonight's occasion, especially with the Madame housing one of your prisoners. I'll have Nikolai come by later to bring you to the house."

As Rebekah disappeared into Haywood's tent, Abigail sighed. If only her fashions were the thing that bothered her.

"Well, it looks like you'll be having a busy evening, which might be starting soon if your friend, Rebekah is right, Miss Abigail." Cleo tugged at his cap as if to straighten it. "That's fine. I better be getting along myself. I've got my own business to take care of anyhow, but I'm sure I'll be seeing you around. That is, unless you're going to be tied up with all those fancy dinner parties from now on?" He gave her a mischievous grin, but this time she couldn't pull herself to match his countenance. She was pretty certain after tonight and the awkwardness she suspected that would follow, there wouldn't be another invitation to a dinner party at the Schreier estate, but that was fine by her.

Parting ways with Cleo, Abigail went to her own quarters and retrieved the naval uniform she'd kept hidden away. She'd sewn the repairs overnight, not sure how her bunkmates would respond if they saw her mending an enemy's coat when there was plenty of their own men's clothes that needed attention.

She dug through her satchel and pulled out the brooch she'd found in the inside pocket of Mr. Ward's coat, though how it managed to stay there was a wonder in intself. The pocket was only half attached and the brooch itself was missing both the pin and clasp. She turned the cross-shaped piece of jewelry over, admiring the gold base inlet with four small ruby stones near each point and a dark blue that rested in the middle. It was beautiful, a piece for sure to be treasured. Yet, it was not something she'd ever seen a British officer wear as part of their uniform dress. For an instant, she thought of Mr. Ward and what reminded her of an heirloom piece of jewelry, may have meant to the man. She'd seen similar pieces, though not as handsome, displayed proudly on collars of ladies in Portsmouth and those with a higher means to fashion in Falmouth. She even recalled Margaret having one on the first day they met.

"Well, there you are, dear!"

Abigail wrapped the brooch in a spare piece of cloth and stuffed it inside her satchel.

Mrs. Bates had both knuckles to her hips, giving a suspicious eye to the blue coat that still lay on Abigail's pallet. "I was beginning to think you decided to join your family in Portsmouth after all. I didn't see you come in last night and no one was on your pallet this morning when I awoke. Don't tell me you're sleeping elsewhere? I'll tell Anne she needs to mind that noise. That Eli is much too young to be snoring like a grown man."

The sides of Abigail's mouth raised easily, thinking of Mrs. Brumley's three-year-old son. "No, I just had a late night that's all. I'm still around. Trust me, you'll be the first to know if I leave town. How are things working out with Mrs. White and Miss Townsend?

The older woman's fixed stare broke from the clothes and shifted to Abigail, her countenance relaxing. "Very well at present. Mrs. White and I have much in common, seeing we're both from Concord and Miss Townsend has a fine work ethic. I know Haywood has you stretched between Mrs. Schreier's estate and Dr. Adams and even back here sometimes with me. I'm thankful you found them. Otherwise, I'm not sure how well I'd get along, even with Mr. Bates at my side."

Abigail gave a heartfelt smile. "I'm just glad it's helping."

"It is. Say, what's that?" Mrs. Bates' gaze lingered on Mr. Ward's uniform again, tucked deliberately under Abigail's arm.

Abigail's arm stiffened with the clothes at her side. "Nothing, just something I'll be glad to be rid of when the time comes." And the sooner the better.

"It looks nice. The blue is a little different, but it reminds me of the coat the general wears and Officer Haywood too." She gave a critical eye. "Now, don't tell me Mr. Haywood has you as his personal seamstress?"

Abigail shook her head although she would've preferred that alternative. "No, nothing like that. It belongs to the prisoner staying at the

Schreier's estate."

"Oh?" Mrs. Bates' pulled back slightly, her eyes bright with curiosity. "I was aware you'd be bringing the man his meals, but I didn't suspect you'd be handling his laundering too."

"I don't believe it's part of my assignment usually, but the lady has lent her husband's clothes. I don't know when Mr. Schreier returns home, but I bet when he does arrive, he wouldn't want to see a stranger in them."

"I could see that as a possibility." Mrs. Bates shifted her attention downward, her sight focused on something that no doubt intrigued her.

Abigail gasped when she followed the woman's gaze. Her invitation from Mrs. Schreier had somehow slipped out of her apron and was tilted against the side of her pallet.

"And what is that? Did you get another letter from Portsmouth? I hope there's good news about your mother in it."

Unfortunately, there wasn't. The letter she'd received from Charlotte yesterday had confirmed that much.

Abigail picked up the invitation, this time putting it securely in her satchel. "Actually, I guess you could say it's part of my assignment, but one I'm still hoping to get out of." She took a moment to recall her meeting earlier with Officer Haywood. Maybe she couldn't get out of her orders that concerned Mr. Ward, but there was still a chance she could get out of tonight. She didn't exactly see Haywood delighted over an evening with two persons loyal to the king of a government he fought against, and she counted the man's strictest sense of duty to his own country would be in her favor. If it was, Abigail just couldn't see him having her go to a party when there was still so much to do here at camp.

She peeked out the slip of cloth that served as their shelter's doorway. The sun was on its descent. Nikolai would be here soon. She let the fabric fall back in place, rushing to grab the uniform beside her bedding and gave her friend a swift glance. "I better get going. If I don't, I might just lose that opportunity."

***

Wide-eyed, Abigail let out a sharp, quick breath that was anything but expected.

"Sorry, Miss Abby. Did I get it too tight?" Rebekah loosened the stays a tad and Abigail's lungs thanked her. "I'm used to Margaret. She likes her waist like those Pennsylvania women: nice and small." Rebekah picked up a pair of panniers and began to tie them around Abigail's hips. "They even add these silly contraptions just to add more attention to it."

"It's good to accentuate the waist." Margaret eased herself slowly onto the bed before she swung her legs up into it, settling in a lying, propped position. "A man likes an hour-glass figure."

Rebekah rolled her eyes. "And they say men are fools."

"I suppose they'd have to be if they think this is what I really look like." Abigail scanned her body from the chest down and the added enhancements that were of fashion attached to it.

"Trust me, Mr. Ward is a man who's used to such particulars. I'm sure he's had a woman or two on his arms for parties and not just because of his station. The man is downright handsome. That black hair, those dark eyes...even with his bruise he looks dangerous in a way I'd like to get to know. That is, if I didn't love my own Alex so much." She peered over to Abigail, her brow lifted. "Wouldn't you say so, Abby?"

Abigail shifted her position, but not because she could blame the stays this time. Even in her anger she could see at worst the man was attractive and at best—an unexpected warmth flowed through her body starting from her chest reaching down to her toes. She straightened her shoulders, not ready to pay the officer such a compliment just yet, even if it wasn't directly to his face. "I do think the blue and purple of the bruise does bring some color to his eyes."

Margaret gave her a cat-like smile and a hint of laughter along with it. "Is that all you have to say? Really, you looked so uncomfortable this morning upon seeing him. I was certain it meant there was more between the two of you than you let on."

She wasn't wrong, but Abigail sensed she meant something different than his involvement with her home's destruction. She averted her gaze from Margaret, clutching her fingers to the stays. It was still hard to believe Haywood had accepted his invitation for tonight and his insistence she do the same with her own. "That's all I can say that's good of the gentleman so far. The rest remains to be seen."

"And we shall see." Margaret propped up from the bed and went to the wardrobe, pulling out a silk, green gown.

Abigail stilled. "Margaret, I can't wear that. It's beautiful."

"Which is why you must wear it. Trust me, I don't mind. My stomach's too big to let the lacings out of it any more without ruining it." She held the dress up to Abigail, seeming to take a quick study. "And the color goes exquisitely with your eyes."

Having finished pinning her stomacher in place, Rebekah took the gown from Margaret. "Come on, Miss Abby, let's get her on."

A moment later Abigail stole a glance from the looking glass, hardly recognizing herself. It was a conflicting sensation, the feeling of gratitude for the long overdue bath she had earlier and the borrowed clothes she might never wear again all the while thinking of Mrs. Bates and the other women who worked in the damp cold. She imagined some, if not all would leap for such an opportunity, one she would do anything to trade for because of Mr. Ward. So why was it her?

"I'm gonna help Margaret finish gettin' dressed. You just come down when you're ready, Miss Abby." Rebekah smiled from the doorway, Margaret already gone to her own chambers.

Abigail inhaled sharply. When she was ready. If Rebekah only knew the weight of those words and what they carried. She wasn't certain if she could ever be ready to be in the same room with Mr. Ward again.

Chapter 12

With the lady of the house's permission and what she assured him extended to the lord of the estate, Garrett found himself in Mr. Schreier's study. Reading wasn't a pastime he particularly enjoyed but he respected the practice all the same. Being on a ship for months on end, it was one of the handful of ways one might spend leisure time and one he picked over the gambling most of the crew thought they were doing in secret.

Astronomy was a notable subject Garrett found an interest in. It was useful at sea and to his delight, Mr. Schreier had a copy of Whiston's *A New Theory of the Earth* sitting on top of one of the bookshelves. Whiston, not only a mathematician, but an active theologian, used science and astronomical events to explain his take on scripture such as Noah's flood and the detrimental effects of Adam and Eve. Regarding the earliest Genesis story, the scientist concluded the couple's sin was what set Earth in rotation and the great flood of Noah had been caused by a comet. Though Garrett rarely agreed with the author, or the reality of such stories, he quite enjoyed his thoughts, finding them deeply entertaining. The idea that the act of just two people could change the world so drastically was certainly amusing.

Garrett smiled at both his discovery and the familiarity to see the work in a place that felt well, so unfamiliar. He snatched the book up from the shelf and began to thumb through its pages, remembering the material almost by heart. Somehow the work made him feel more at ease, even improving his nerves about tonight.

He wasn't sure how things would go in a room with two loyalists and two rebels. It was more like an even opponent matchup than a dinner party. He did have to admit Mrs. Schreier was right when she told him her idea of it this morning after Miss Thatcher took her leave. It would be entertaining. That was for certain. But would any of them be brave enough to mention the white elephant in the room—the politics they clearly disagreed on, and, if so, how heated it might get? Mrs. Schreier and Miss Thatcher seemed companionable enough, but what about this Haywood their hostess decided to include just to make an even number? If the man was an officer of the rebel camp, then Garrett didn't exactly see them becoming best of friends, not like Mrs. Schreier and Miss Thatcher seemed to be. Maybe that was something female he didn't understand.

According to Miss Thatcher, Haywood was supposed to stop by for a briefing yesterday regarding his imprisonment, but the man never showed. From the impression Garrett received from their hostess, tonight was meant to be of a more amiable nature, a time to put their conflict and formalities aside, yet the question remained whether the rebel officer might break that unspoken rule of decorum and speak of it anyhow.

Garrett's stomach grumbled, continuing to aid in his distraction. He'd been used to portioned meals at sea, but it still hadn't recovered from the time he'd spent in the hold. He'd been to enough of these parties to know dinner didn't always mean a hearty one especially as the number of guests grew. He just hoped with their small count this evening, the Schreier household might provide something more substantial.

Flipping to the *Lametta*, the first book from Whiston's work, Garrett noticed the underside of his right cuff was stitched in a slightly lighter shade of blue than his left. He hadn't seen her return it, only that he recognized it easily draped over the wingback chair he'd occupied yesterday morning in the parlor. How Miss Thatcher managed to wash and mend it in that amount of time made him marvel, but it felt good to have it on again. He checked the inside behind his lapel. The pocket was fixed too, which made the side of his mouth curve up until he remembered his mother's brooch was no longer in it. Still, he would have to thank her. He was grateful to have had something to wear in the meantime, but nothing was as good as a man's own skin, or in this case, a tailored coat he'd worked his whole life for.

"Mr. Ward, I presume."

Garrett raised his eyes to the male voice directed at him. The thin lines of the man's face and slim figure resembled nothing like the boisterous jaw and physique of the portrait he'd seen of Mr. Schreier in the parlor. "That's right. Mr. Haywood, I take it?"

The man gave a stiff, cordial nod, his eyes centered on Garrett with infuriating annoyance like he'd stepped in something foul. Garrett knew the look. It was how he imagined his own appeared when he saw his enemy and he could bet Haywood saw it now staring right back at him.

"As you've been informed, you are a prisoner of the Continental Congress."

Garrett straightened, biting the inside of his cheek. It looked like Haywood was a man of taboo after all.

"While your comrades currently refuse to acknowledge our soldiers as prisoners of war and have instead, crammed them into ships with intolerable conditions, our great general has been adamant about respecting proper protocol." The officer's face went sour. "Therefore, by my commander's orders you will be treated with the civility according to

144

your rank as an officer."

Garrett was familiar with the customs of captivity in war. European states granted prisoners certain liberties based on their rank. Officers were generally permitted freedoms that included the absence of supervision and comfortable lodging, provided they gave their word they wouldn't try to escape or engage in combat. The fate of common soldiers, however, depended on the availability of space and food. Usually, they were housed in camps or prison ships, expected to receive humane treatment, although that wasn't always the case. Garrett understood the conundrum his fellow countrymen were in concerning these revolutionaries. Following the traditional customs would be acknowledging their independence and presence as a legitimate nation, something to which the king was currently opposed. However, executing punishment to those accused of treason would not likely bring about the reconciliation his nation had hoped for.

"And my crew? Where are they?"

Haywood gave him an irritated scowl. "They've been distributed to other towns, some to Maryland and some south, where they will be subject to labor there." Again, the man's tone turned bitter. "Be satisfied to know they're not being housed in a prison ship or camp." The rebel officer paused to take in a breath before releasing it as if to expel his anger into the air. "You, yourself, Mr. Ward, will be of service to Mrs. Schreier, seeing her husband is otherwise occupied fighting against us and in no condition to carry out his tasks in his stead."

Garrett agreed, at least the part concerning his hostess. Whether Haywood had given him the official order or not, Garrett had already planned on making himself useful. "And what of my officers? Have they been scattered too?"

Haywood nodded. "Yes, but like you, they will also be treated according to the protocol our general seems fit to instill upon them."

Garrett was getting the impression Haywood didn't always agree with his general's orders at least when it came to English prisoners. He was glad this man wasn't leading the rebel army, especially while Garrett was a captive in it. Garrett didn't know much about Washington, not from his own experience, anyway. He'd never met the man, but he knew of the Virginian's reputation. Even among his enemies, he had been called a gentleman, and if the rumors were true, upheld the laws of war. If that were so, Garrett could be assured his crew would be kept alive, particularly out of the confines of a disease-infested ship or prison camp. With Washington at point, they had a chance.

Instinct to shake his head was ruled out by his urge to stay unbending to Haywood. Garrett didn't want to let this man see him flinch while he pondered over his crew's probable fate. Even with the best measures taken, the conditions were never good for prisoners. War was complicated and those captive were often subject to the majority of those around them. Even trained soldiers didn't always follow proper protocol when it came to their enemies, and Garrett was willing to bet these rebels would be even less abiding. Rather, it was more likely his crew would face theft, contempt, and possible starvation.

"As Miss Thatcher may have already pointed out to you, you are forbidden to leave the estate until His Excellency says otherwise." Haywood barked, barging into Garrett's thought process concerning his crew. "Any perceived attempt to escape will be considered dishonorable conduct and will result with immediate punishment. Do I make myself clear, Mr. Ward?"

Garrett relinquished a reluctant nod. "And how long am I to be detained?"

"That is up to your general, sir."

Garrett frowned. "I don't understand."

The side of Haywood's mouth tipped, his demeanor looking annoyingly amused. "Your capture has come at a most opportune time. General Howe now houses nearly ten of our men from the Breed's Hill attack and might be persuaded to give them up with a trade once he learns we have one of his officers." The other side of the man's mouth raised to join the former, the gesture irritating Garrett more than unnerving him. "That's where you come in."

"Mr. Haywood, Mr. Ward." Rebekah knocked at the entry of the study even though the door was open. If she'd heard any course of their conversation, she didn't show it. "The women will be comin' down soon and dinner's almost ready. Why don't you come on out of Mr. Schreier's study and bring that lively conversation with you." She gave them both a grin though her eyes flickered with warning. "The lady was hoping you two would put aside your differences tonight. She'll be glad that you have." She offered them a cordial of sherry. They both partook, but as far as their conversation, that was over, or so Garrett thought.

"Oh, yes, Mr. Ward," Haywood turned round as they made their way towards the parlor with Garrett lingering behind. He didn't want to be any closer to the man than he had to.

Haywood gave a curled smile. "Be advised the general has set me in charge of you. If I hear the slightest complaint from Mrs. Schreier concerning your character, you can be sure I am at the ready to execute the swiftest of punishments."

***

"It looks like we're seated together, Miss Thatcher." Garrett couldn't have received a better distraction from his conversation with Haywood. He nearly choked on his drink as she descended the stairway, seeing her in a new light. And was that a new dress? She'd always been attractive to him, in a way she didn't flaunt, but the way she looked now was like a rose in its full bloom.

"Isn't that something, Mr. Ward?"

Garrett could read the complete lack of enthusiasm in her remark as she stood beside him, waiting for their hostess to make her formal welcome.

"You look radiant this evening, miss." He tried to keep his eyes from falling below her neckline and managed it with some great effort. The dress, though modest, fit her in all the right places and the emerald shade of it as the backdrop of those green eyes took his breath away, even if he could still read contempt in them.

"Thank you." With tone barren of any pleasure from the compliment, a forced smile if ever he saw one took hold.

"And thank you for my coat. It looks almost as good as the day I received it."

"You're welcome, Mr. Ward. I have to say it certainly suits you better than Mr. Schreier's clothes. At least now we can see you for who you truly are."

Garrett was pretty certain she didn't mean it as flattery, but he didn't bruise easily. "How is your family since we last saw each other?"

"They're fine, Captain. Thank you for asking."

The emphasis of the title stung coming from her lips as the unspoken truth rang between them like a gong. Not that he could blame her. Even if he hadn't called the order that day, he'd still played a part, one he wasn't proud of. "I'm glad to hear it, truly."

A chime was heard at the end of the table as Mrs. Schreier approached it, tapping her glass with a spoon. "Thank you all for coming. It's been too long since we've hosted a party here at the estate. Nevertheless, let us do our best to put aside our differences for tonight if we can and enjoy one another's company." She took her seat next to Officer Haywood.

Garrett offered the chair next to him for Miss Thatcher before taking to his own. He glanced at the silver flatware laid elegantly across the table that was meant for fine dining and thought he'd extend the olive branch a little further. "Let me know if you need any pointers." He gestured good-humoredly to the table and its arrangement. "Sometimes these sorts of functions can be overwhelming, especially the first time."

Miss Thatcher's eyes went wide, then narrowed. So much for that olive branch. "Thank you again, Mr. Ward, for your concern, but I can assure you I am perfectly capable of attending a dinner party, even an intimate one such as this."

Mrs. Schreier spoke between them. "Well, you certainly look the part, my dear. That dress on you is becoming. Wouldn't you say so, Mr. Ward?"

Yes, he certainly would say so, agreeing with Mrs. Schreier, yet Garrett got the impression that wasn't necessarily a compliment in Miss Thatcher's eyes.

"Yes, Madame, but I have a feeling Miss Thatcher knows much more than looking the part."

Their hostess' eyes grew with interested satisfaction. "Is Mr. Ward correct, Abigail? I thought you said your family had a farm? From the farmhouses I've seen here in Massachusetts, I have trouble envisioning a gathering like this one or much bigger in such a small space."

Miss Thatcher gave a polite smile. "We did, Ma'am. We hosted many parties, however, you're correct. The space inside is limited and most were done outdoors when the weather was agreeable to it. But none of them were formal in nature. Even still, I attended a handful of parties of this particular kind last year visiting my aunt's estate."

"Your aunt in Portsmouth?"

"The very one."

"Whom your family is staying with since the attack?" Garrett felt his chest go tight at the lady's questioning that revealed a glimpse of the pain he'd seen before back at Falmouth.

Miss Thatcher's smile weakened. "Yes, Ma'am."

Mrs. Schreier exhaled deeply, shaking her head. "It's truly a terrible thing. Mr. Ward, I don't know if you've received word, but Miss Thatcher's town was attacked in October by some of your fellow comrades. According to her, many were left destitute this winter."

Garrett took an uneasy sip from his water glass, working to clear the knot that was beginning to form there. "I'm aware of what happened in Falmouth, and I'm sorry that's been the case, though I'm glad Miss Thatcher's family is provided for."

"Yes, that certainly is a blessin'." As if on cue, and to Garrett's relief, Rebekah entered the dining room, carrying plates crammed with food.

Garrett thanked her as she put a dish in front of him on the table. The thick slice of juicy venison filled his nostrils with craving, and his mouth watered.

Mrs. Schreier finished a bite of potatoes on her own plate before she directed her attention onto him again. "Captain Ward, do tell us about life at sea, would you?"

Garrett bit the inside of his cheek, knowing full well he was unworthy of the title the lady addressed him by. "Actually, madame, I should let you know I'm not deserving of that title, though I hope to be one day." The correction had startled everyone at the table, a mix of wide eyes and furrowed brows upon him, but the critical smirk Haywood now gave made Garrett's insides boil.

"But Mr. Ward, it was my understanding that you were the one commanding the ship when it was captured."

Garrett winced as the nerve of his humiliating imprisonment struck again. "Yes, madam, that is correct. I was given command of the *Piper* as a sort of loan you see, but I have yet to make post nor granted my own ship. That is the goal, however." He strained a smile that was anything but easy.

"Mrs. Schreier, let me take this opportunity to mention again that if things are not to your complete satisfaction with Mr. Ward here, do let me know, especially in light of this new information." Haywood gave a smug smile, patting the corner of his mouth with his napkin. "Do remember that he is a prisoner of the continental army and not someone you have to feel the need to entertain. He has been properly briefed of his rights and informed of the repercussions of them if broken. However, if you so choose, ma'am, I could make arrangements for him at camp that in my opinion would be more suitable for such a man."

The sides of Mrs. Schreier's mouth lifted cordially, though with an agitation that was all but spoken. "I don't think that's necessary just yet, Mr. Haywood. Mr. Ward has only been an occupant in my home for just a little over a day and seems civil enough. Though he did not correct his station at a proper time during our introductions yesterday, he has done so now. He may not be a captain, but a lieutenant is still an honorable achievement. Not to mention, admitting his shortcomings is a quality to be admired. I think we'll give him a little more time to reveal his character." She sighed. "And let's not forget, Mr. Haywood, your commander may not have called me an official prisoner, but I know better. As long as your men parade around my town like I'm the outsider when that is not the truth, I may as well be a prisoner too. As far as I'm concerned, Mr. Ward is as decent company as any compared to your ragtag group of men you call an army."

Garrett smiled to himself, cutting into the venison for another bite as Haywood began to back step. "Now, Mrs. Schreier, I only meant to ease your discomfort by taking the man off your hands…"

Their hostess raised her hand in the most genteel way possible that still gave a clear message. "If your true intention was to ease my discomfort, Mr. Haywood, you would tell your general he is not welcomed by me and can do well to leave this town so things can go back as they were before." Her lips tightened. "Or at the very least, sir, you could've informed me of the disease that is currently festering in your camp."

The man's face fell. "I wasn't aware you knew of it."

"Indeed, sir, I have. It seems your camp doctor is a man who respects his patients and keeps them informed about anything that might affect their treatment, or in this case, well-being. I was thankful to inform Dr. Adams I'm immune to smallpox."

Garrett was in the middle of taking another sip from his water glass when Mrs. Schreier announced the epidemic that could take the pressure off Boston if word got out. It took all his strength to keep the liquid from spewing out of his mouth. Smallpox. He swallowed hard as the pressure went down.

"That's good news, Mrs. Schreier. I'm glad it hasn't created complications while you're with child." Haywood folded his napkin, before he took an abrupt stand at the table.

Garrett caught the slightest twitch in the continental officer's eye, a sure sign the man had been bested. He almost felt sorry for him. Almost.

"Excuse me, Madame." Haywood bent his head to their hostess with a stiffness Garrett recognized from their encounter in the study. "I'm afraid a matter has come to my attention I need to inform His Excellency about. Thank you, Mrs. Schreier for your hospitality."

Now accompanied by an empty seat, Mrs. Schreier drew in a frustrated breath. "I was hoping to stay away from politics this evening, but I see now that was asking for too much." She gently handed her finished plate to Rebekah before her attention went to Garrett. "You mentioned yesterday you and Miss Thatcher crossed paths in Falmouth. I didn't realize the Royal Navy made port in Falmouth regularly."

Garrett's stomach did a somersault. Just when he thought the topic was dead. He shook his head. "We don't, not unless the king tells us otherwise. I've only set foot in it the one time I was there." The hair on the back of his neck began to stand on end. He wasn't feeling good about where this conversation might lead, though he was a bit surprised Miss Thatcher hadn't mentioned the details yet. It would be the ticket she and Haywood needed to make sure his stay as a prisoner was a lot less to his liking.

Mrs. Schreier raised a probing brow. "Doing what, if I may ask?"

Garrett sighed; now confident it was all but told. He was going to have to admit the awful truth. Might as well give it to them straight and own to it. "We were going through town to…"

"When we ran into each other."

Garrett turned to Miss Thatcher, who looked just as shocked as he felt but who also seemed to recover more quickly.

She managed a smile. "Mr. Ward and his fellow officer offered my brother and I a ride home, which we declined of course."

"Of course, you did." Mrs. Schreier laughed. "I suppose I couldn't blame you with your allegiance in conflict." Her gaze seemed to draw to both of them. "But how amazing that is you've run into each other again. It makes me wonder if God Almighty had his hand in it."

Garrett liked to think there was something or someone watching over him, to care for such a small detail of his life like running into Miss Thatcher again. He sometimes saw glimpses of that when the sea was smooth and the wind carried them easily for miles on it, but at other times it felt more like he was at odds with God like the waves climbing and ultimately tumbling over his ship while he tried his best to hold on. It had been like that when his mother died and his father too. Now it only seemed more so considering he'd worked so hard just to end up a prisoner of a group of men he could barely respect as an army.

He noticed by the way Miss Thatcher had yet to respond also and the slight shift in her seat, she too didn't know what to make of Mrs. Schreier's notion. At least they could agree on that.

Garrett cleared his throat. "I don't know what to make of it, Mrs. Schreier, only that I'm glad I'm fortunate to stay in your household while I'm a prisoner here. As Mr. Haywood has already informed you, and the rest of the table so it seems, things could be worse for me." Though in his private thoughts, he felt things were still pretty bad. He was just glad Haywood wasn't in charge or he'd really be in trouble.

"Never mind that, lieutenant. It's good to have some decent company again. As long as you're an honorable man, which at the moment you seem to be, you're welcome here, sir."

The corner of his mouth raised at their hostess' comment. "I'd like to think I am, but I'll let you be the judge of that."

Chapter 13

Garrett wasn't certain how to feel about the dinner last night. On one hand, Mrs. Schreier didn't seem to hate him, something he counted to his good fortune, but on the other, Miss Thatcher and Officer Haywood clearly did. It was hard to make out the reason behind Miss Thatcher's intervention on what felt like his behalf. Why had she come to his rescue when he'd come so close to being exposed, especially if that meant he was no longer her problem? And, he was pretty sure, he was her problem. Even so, Garrett was glad for it. As much as he hated what had befallen on the rest of his crew, he wasn't in a hurry to join them.

In his effort to make time pass more quickly, he decided to take advantage of his current restrictions, utilizing them to their fullest extent by venturing out to the estate grounds. Even if he couldn't go far, he could use the fresh air. He still felt heated by his conversation last night with Haywood, and he needed to get his head straight before he happened on the officer again. If he didn't, then he might never have his boundaries extended, which meant he might never get out of the estate grounds and get anywhere close to Boston.

That was Garrett's plan, anyway. It was rough, but it was a start. Once Mrs. Schreier announced smallpox was in the camp, a malady known to spread, he knew he'd stumbled onto something to his advantage. By the way Haywood made his quick departure, Garrett was also willing to bet the officer knew it too. His restrictions would remain for a while if that were the case, but Garrett could be patient when he needed to be. When the time was right and he'd proven himself, he'd be able to find a way out. That's when he would make sure to tell his comrades in Boston Washington's men were weak and his numbers to fight were low. It was time to move in.

On his way out, Garrett couldn't help but notice the heap of firewood, though by the looks of it, running particularly low. He imagined the lady's husband had procured the pile before his leave, making sure she'd be comfortable enough for the winter. But with the temperatures already dipping, the winter had started earlier this year, and Garrett hadn't recalled the mention of the man's expected return. And even if Mr. Schreier had accounted for the child soon to come, it was unlikely he anticipated lodging another addition in his household, such as a prisoner like Garrett. The precious fuel's use for cooking and heating alone would not be enough. Garrett took a quick look around but came up short. The pile stood on its own. He sucked in a breath, letting the cold pressure fill his lungs before he removed his coat and placed it on a nearby hook. He grabbed the wedge.

It didn't take long for the activity to warm him, sweat beading at his forehead. He chopped at the wood, over and over, letting the exercise absorbed his strength. It felt good. With each strike of the axe, Garrett's blood churned. His mind drifted in the activity, wondering all the way back to his childhood when he lost his father.

He'd been grateful Nicholas had taken him in, but somewhat resentful their climbs thus far up the ladder had been different. Nicholas worked hard, Garrett couldn't deny that, but his friend had affluence on his side, whereas Garrett had to work his way out from the shadows, always struggling to prove his worth. He thought about all those years of hard work, proving himself repeatedly just to be refused a promotion and instead, taken prisoner by an army that barely qualified as one.

The heat inside him grew hotter. He'd been so close. All he had to do was bring in the *Briley*. Not only did he fail, but all those provisions that were meant for his own men in Boston ended up in the hands of rebels who didn't even have a navy of their own. Garrett clenched the handle of the wedge tighter, as if his grip was the only thing keeping him grounded, and continued to hack at the pine.

As his strength began to dissipate, so did his anger. His breath now heavy, he wiped away the sweat from his brow. He wasn't sure how much time went by, but in it, he'd managed to go through two cords of wood. It wasn't enough, but it was a start. As his breath grew more even, he noticed the sun's position had changed. It was midmorning. That's when Mrs. Schreier said she'd be expecting Miss Thatcher, and he imagined his breakfast along with her. He hoped to see her and thank her for not outing him last night.

Garrett returned the wedge to its place at last, his strength nearly depleted and his anger, too. It was when he looked up he had to stifle a smile that started to nudge its way out from the corner of his mouth. As if fate had known his thoughts and was smiling too, there she was, Abigail Thatcher, looking at him now.

"Mr. Ward." She was dressed in her work clothes, her apron tied neatly about her waist and hair hidden modestly beneath her cap like last night had all been a dream. If it weren't for the remnants of venison still digesting in his stomach, he might have convinced himself of it. A single strand of chestnut hair touched her cheek and he felt a different kind of heat rise through him than when he'd been using the ax, reminded of those same color locks falling about her neck the night before.

157

"Good morning, Miss Thatcher." The displeasure he still read in her features smothered the fire. "Is that for me?" He gestured to a basket hanging over her arm.

She nodded. "It is actually. Some rice porridge and a couple of slices of bread."

"Sounds delicious."

The tiniest smile turned her lips. "Don't get too excited. We're out of maple syrup at camp." She eyed the cords of freshly cut wood while seeming to take him in too. He had to admit, he didn't mind her scrutiny, even if he did feel a little foolish while under it. She put a hand to the basket. "I'll just put this inside next to the fire until you're ready to eat it."

"Excuse me, Miss Thatcher." Garrett stopped her just as she stepped towards the back door before she could enter its threshold. "I wanted to talk with you about something."

***

Abigail stepped back down from the doorway, wishing she would have walked on and pretended she hadn't heard him. Unfortunately, that thought came to her a second too late. She should've just entered through the front of the house instead of investigating the loud crack that seemed to be coming from behind it. She breathed in deeply, catching the scent of male sweat mixed with fresh pine before setting the basket down beside her feet. Her gaze drew to him expectantly, though what she could talk with this man about she hadn't the faintest. Not without being reminded of what he had done.

"Yes, Mr. Ward, I'm all ears."

"I just want to thank you for last night, for not stating the full details of how we know each other." He ran his fingers through his jet-black hair, looking a little uneasy like the next part he was about to say might not be to her liking. "Though if I might ask, why didn't you say something or even let me finish doing the work myself? We both know I deserve whatever happened next at the very least."

Abigail pressed her lips and considered his question; the same one she'd asked herself since last night. Why had she spoken up when a defining truth was about to be revealed? The only explanation she could come up with was doing so meant preventing what she suspected would become the ruin of their already less than amiable dinner conversation and no doubt of Margaret's expectations for an enjoyable evening.

She swallowed, letting her pride answer for her. "It's easy, Mr. Ward. I simply wasn't willing to find out whatever happened next, knowing it might very well be the downfall of what Mrs. Schreier hoped to be a pleasant evening. As far as what you deserve, I take no responsibility. I'll let God be the judge of that."

He frowned. "I think I'd rather you be the judge. God doesn't seem to want anything to do with me." He grabbed his coat from a nail stuck into the side of the house. "In any case, thank you. I know it would've been easier to just let me walk into the hole I had already dug that day in Falmouth."

He stepped closer to her, his dark eyes full of both strength and compassion. Despite herself, she felt her pulse quicken as he narrowed the distance between them. Meeting her on the step, and about an inch away from being too close for acquaintances, or even friends for that matter, he snatched the basket from her feet. Her cheeks went warm and right then she wanted to bolt.

"Now, why don't we get you inside. Working an ax is one thing, but it's too cold to be out here otherwise. Here, allow me." He opened the door, providing her enough space this time to proceed comfortably, yet she noticed he followed behind. Not wanting to risk the chance he'd trail her to his room, she decided to take the safe route where they'd be exposed in the parlor, and placed his porridge next to its fire.

"Lieutenant." She was going to excuse herself, remembering Mrs. Schreier was another reason she was here, but the tip of his mouth curved

159

into a smile and stopped her short of it.

"I think in light of what we know between us and the fact the misconception of my rank has also been revealed, we can move onto a less formal way of talking with each other. Please, call me Garrett." His brow raised with a gentle imploration. "That is, if you don't mind."

She smiled despite herself. "You mean the fact you fooled us into thinking you were a captain this whole time?"

His smile broadened. "Precisely."

"Well, it sounds like you're close, at least from what you conveyed last night."

"So, you were listening?" His eyes lit with pleasure "I was pretty certain you had blocked everything I said out, not that I could blame you. I'm not sure how I would feel if someone came and destroyed my town, but I can wager it wouldn't be understanding." His smile faded as another reminder to the current state of her home pulled her under again. "But yes, I'm close, or at least I think I was. My last mission was supposed to bring in a supply ship. I was under the impression I'd make post after that. The admiral gave me a trial run with the *Piper*, the ship I commanded and that didn't end up going as well as I thought it would have."

He only shrugged, but Abigail could sense there was more weighing on his shoulders than he let her to believe. She didn't know anything about what it took to become a captain, only concluding it wasn't something just anybody could achieve. Surely such a position took hard work and experience, and more often than not, that also meant time.

A small strand of hair she'd missed that morning while she'd rushed to get ready tickled the side of her cheek. She brushed it behind her ear and with interest favoring over prudence, she let the former win this round. "How long have you been in the Royal Navy, Mr.—uh, Garrett?"

He smiled in a way she couldn't tell if he was more delighted by the question or her acceptance of his suggestion to refer to each other more informally. "Most of my life. I entered into it when I was thirteen, starting as a servant for a captain."

"Did you follow your father's footsteps in it? I've heard that's how some men get started."

"Actually, no." Garrett sunk into a seat in one of the wingbacks and against her better judgement, she descended onto the chaise. Even now she could still see the remnants of sweat as it glistened in his black hair. "I was sort of forced into it when my father died, but it has become a family of sorts."

A breath caught in Abigail's chest. She was letting the man reveal too much. If she continued, her anger towards him might wane and she couldn't afford to let that happen. Not yet, not when she needed answers, not when she still needed someone to blame. Putting her guard back in place, she could hear the coolness in her tone return.

"Then I can see why it must be important to you."

"It is." He inhaled sharply. "The Navy has done everything for me. Without it there's no way I'd be who I am now. You might disagree, but I like to think I've become a decent man because of it."

She strained a smile. "I suppose we'll see. Lucky for you, it's Mrs. Schreier's opinion that matters."

He frowned but nodded. "For the foreseeable near future, yes, you're right. The lady's opinion is the one that counts. It would be nice to venture out of the estate grounds. Something tells me after meeting Officer Haywood last night, she'll be my only way to do that. I'll do my best not to do anything foolish, or else I'll never see the outside of this fine, but still restricted homestead."

Abigail was about to wish him luck, even if feigned, at his endeavor before she needed to excuse herself and see the very lady they spoke of. When he caught her eye again, his jaw was fixed, and he wore a thoughtful expression about him that pulled her attention back again.

"Abigail." Hearing her name from his lips made the length of her spine shiver. "There is something else I wanted to ask you about, again, if you don't mind."

Her own brow furrowed. What else could there possibly be? They'd only known each other for an instant. "Yes, Garrett? What is it?" She could hear the spitefulness in her voice and immediately felt ashamed of it.

"That older man you were with in Falmouth, your uncle Samuel, is he with your family in Portsmouth too?"

The mention of Cleo took her back a few steps, if only in thought. She just hoped it didn't show. "No, he's not."

"Do you happen to know where he went after…" Garrett let the words die between them and the resentment she'd tried to repress ticked up another notch.

"I believe he went to the Carolina's after the attack."

"I see." He gave a slow nod.

"Is there a reason why you ask?"

"He just looked familiar, that's all."

Abigail got the feeling that wasn't all, but she didn't pry anymore for Cleo's sake. She didn't know what this man had on his agenda regarding her friend, but better to play it safe. She didn't want to give him the chance to figure out she knew Cleo's whereabouts. What she did want to do, however, was get away from Garrett Ward as soon as possible.

Chapter 14

Garrett shut the copy of Whiston's work, tired of having read it twice over since he woke up in the Schreier household. Despite the more than acceptable conditions and ample space, he longed for the comfort of his small cabin. At least there he could be free. He veered his eyes to a small, decorative clock on the bookshelf and grumbled. What he convinced himself was an hour had only been half that. Time seemed to stretch with every page turned.

He'd been a prisoner of the continental army for a little over a week now, give or take a few days for the time he'd been unconscious. He'd worked to keep his toes in line as far as Mrs. Schreier was concerned and hadn't broken any rules pertaining to his current restrictions of captivity. So why was he still bound? Why hadn't Haywood been back? Garrett huffed. Maybe he wasn't as patient as he thought.

He couldn't wait for his freedom and what he was going to do with it. If anything, at least the time had given him an opportunity to finalize his plan. First, he needed to find a route or two to Boston. Easy enough in itself but throw in the complication he was an enemy captive with the near certainty the main routes would be guarded, made things a bit more problematic. Toss in the fact he knew of the smallpox and that made it downright impossible, assured Washington wasn't about to let word of it get far.

Garrett pulled out the map of Cambridge he'd acquired from Mrs. Schreier. Boston was only a little over three miles. He eased back into the desk chair. It was a good thing he was up for a challenge. Maybe then he could put this embarrassment behind him. With his information, maybe it could even mean his promotion was within reach again. When he thought about it that way, he'd merely taken a few steps backwards, but no true harm had been done.

Except for one thing that gnawed at him like a dog chewing clean its favorite part of a bone. Why hadn't he been traded yet? He'd left the captain and Nicholas in Boston fully aware of his mission and no doubt now fully aware of his capture. Yet, Garrett hadn't received an ounce of news to bring him home. He was never certain about Nicholas' father, only that things were to be done the captain's way, but Nicholas—he was his brother. If the tables were turned, there was no question what Garrett would do.

He shook his head to rip the doubt away. It had to be something or someone here in Cambridge to blame. That was where the fault laid. Maybe the Seven Year's War hadn't seasoned Washington as Garrett thought. Agitated by his speculations and his confinement, he knew it was time for some air. There was a part of the estate he hadn't seen yet, so he decided that was just the place he'd go.

Several yards out, Garrett arrived. The barn was small, nothing like he'd seen in the countryside of London, but there was life in it. A chestnut mare stood calm in her stall; her eyes fixed on the stranger he knew he was to her. Garrett extended his arm, offering the back of his hand and the mare consented, letting him pet the soft fur of her neck.

"I see you've met Athala." A dark Negro man appeared, his eyes wide and inviting. "She's a gentle soul." He gestured his head to the stall over at a brown horse, it's coat darker than the first with a black mane. "And there's Greta. She's a little less gentle, but friendly enough."

Garrett scratched his head, a little embarrassed to think he hadn't been alone with the animals. "Sorry, I didn't know anyone was here, other than the horses, I mean."

"I'm here most the time, seeing Mrs. Schreier puts me in charge of 'em." The man extended his arm. "The name's Nikolai."

Garrett took hold of Nikolai's hand and gave it a firm shake. "Garrett."

The man smiled big. "You're the reason Miss Abigail has come to call."

A sudden laugh drew from Garrett's breath. "I wouldn't exactly put it that way. Miss Thatcher isn't too keen on me for reasons I fully accept."

"Oh, is that right?" Nikolai's thick brow furrowed, then released again. "I thought I heard there's somethin' between you two."

Garrett shook his head. There certainly was something, a wall as high as the stars and as thick as the ocean was wide. Still, he wondered. "I'm interested to know what gave you that impression."

Nikolai shrugged before picking up a piece of squash from a small crate on the floor. "There's not much here. The lady and Miss Rebekah like to keep me informed whether I care to know or not." He handed Garrett the squash and gestured towards Athala. "Why don't you try and give her this. She's bound to take to you if you do. One of the only women I've come across that's easy to please."

Garrett accepted and held the vegetable out to the mare. She didn't hesitate.

Nikolai smiled as if unsurprised by the outcome. "You want to take her for a ride?"

Garrett frowned. "I thought they were carriage horses?"

"They are, but even carriage horses like to run. Whether bound or free, it's in their nature."

"Believe it or not, I've actually never been on a horse."

The whites of Nikolai's eyes expanded. "Really, sir?"

Garrett shook his head. "Never needed to. Most of my time is on the water—don't need a horse there. And when I'm on land, I can usually go where I need to on foot."

Nikolai walked closer to the animal and stroked the horse easy on her back. "Well, if you ever decide you want to try, you're up for a real treat. I don't know what it's like on a ship, sir, but Athala here is as smooth as they come."

Garrett gave the horse another pat as she continued to tear into the squash. She leaned into his hand and already he sensed a connection between them. "Thank you, Nikolai. I might just take you up on that sometime." He took a quick scan at the remainder of the barn, noticing a flat sheet of hay that laid low to the ground like it'd been arranged as a makeshift bed. "You mentioned you're here most of the time. I haven't seen you in the house." He motioned over to the haystack. "Is this where you sleep?"

"I do from time to time when the weather's fair, but not right now. I stay over there." Nikolai pointed to a small cabin. "It's less drafty than the barn."

Garrett had heard about the slave ships that left port for Africa, destined for the colonies. They'd crammed and cuffed as many lives as they could in conditions that were unthinkable for any human life to endure. Yet, somehow, some of them did, only to find their lives shackled in other ways. It always bothered him to think the end result of such a horrendous passage was a life still bound. Garrett hadn't seen a lot of the colonies but what he had in some of the ports had been enough to get an idea. More times than he cared to witness were owners treating another human with an inferiority Garrett little respected. It wasn't a life for him.

He'd also come to understand these men and women usually stayed in separate quarters from the main house like Nikolai pointed out. Yet, Garrett couldn't help but notice the interactions he'd witnessed between Rebekah and Mrs. Schreier were a little bit different. He'd seen examples of that each morning as the lady of the house and Rebekah shared breakfast in the parlor, relating to each other more like friends than owner and slave.

Garrett went over to Greta to offer her a piece of the squash leftover Athala hadn't completely devoured, but the horse didn't take to it. "Mrs. Schreier is one of the more lenient ones I've come across. I've never seen a master let someone like Rebekah speak so freely."

Nikolai's easy expression contorted. "Master, sir?"

Instantly, Garrett tried to recover, but tripped the whole way. "I just thought…"

"You thought I was a slave. Is that it?" Nikolai crossed his arms, his mouth pinched as he made the charge against him.

Garrett was pretty sure every part of his expression read he'd made that very mistake, but he choked out the only answer he could come up with: the truth. "I'm sorry, I did."

"Well, you'd be wrong. I've got my papers to prove it."

Garrett's words continued to flounder at his misjudgment. "Again, I'm sorry. I shouldn't have assumed."

Nikolai's dark eyes seemed to study him for a moment before finally the man's expression relaxed. "It's all right. I don't like to be in the habit of holding any hard feelings. I just wish the current war dealt with everyone's freedom and not just a select few. Who knows, maybe if it did, I'd join those fools in the Commons."

"Now, don't say that."

A burst of laughter from Nikolai brought ease to the tension in Garrett's shoulders. "That's right. You're one of the one's they're fighting against."

Garrett gave a bitter smile. "Not currently. Right now I'm not a threat at all."

"I wouldn't be so sure about that, sir. He sure seems to think so."

Garrett followed Nikolai's gaze to a young blonde boy who'd apparently decided to drop in unannounced. The scowl on the youth's face aimed directly at him told Garrett enough; the boy completely disdained him. Was he from the camp? An uneasy chill ran throughout Garrett's body at the possibility, noting he was only on the brink of developing whiskers. Had he looked as young when he'd joined the navy? Had the pit of someone's stomach twisted for him like his was doing now as Garrett imagined facing this youth on the battlefield?

"What can we do for you, young man?" Nikolai went over to the boy, intercepting the hard stare he'd been burning into Garrett.

"I'm looking for Miss Abigail. I was told she'd be here. I tried the front, but no one answered. I heard some voices this way and thought maybe she was back here with somebody."

Nikolai scratched the back of his head. "Well, I haven't seen Miss Abby yet today, but if she's here, she'd be at the main house. She usually goes upstairs to see about the lady. Rebekah might be with them and if that's the truth, it would explain why no one came to receive you. Sounds get a little muffled up there sometimes." Nikolai glanced at the stalls, then back at the boy again. "I'll tell you what, let me finish feedin' these horses and then I'll take you to find her myself. We'll get this all sorted."

The boy frowned, his tone imploring. "But sir, there's a problem in camp she needs to know about and I'm sure would want to know of since it involves somewhat of a close friend."

Despite his shirt and knee breeches Garrett could see urgency wore on him like a full-out uniform.

"Why don't I take him into the house," Garrett offered, a little surprised that he did. There was little doubting he wasn't' the boy's first choice, or even second when taking the horses into account, but Garrett could see easily enough he wasn't wanting to delay whatever message he had to deliver. He tried to match the youth's wary expression with a smile. "Don't worry. We don't have to say a word to each other if you want. I'll just get you inside and show you where you need to go."

The adolescent paused as if to weigh his options but finally nodded.

As promised, the two walked into the house without a hint of conversation, yet even so Garrett could sense the boy's piercing eyes behind him. Thankfully, it was a short walk. They entered through the back and walked down the hallway towards the front of the estate where the stairs connected. As Nikolai suggested, Abigail had started her descent.

Garrett hadn't seen her since the morning after the dinner party, yet somehow his meals continued to pop up in his room. She was clearly avoiding him, but how she managed it and exactly why he couldn't pinpoint. He assumed she was still cross about her town, but he wondered if there was more to it than that, thinking back to their last conversation. He was almost certain she was starting to relent, until he mentioned her uncle Samuel and the wall that divided them was made stronger than ever.

Abigail caught sight of them, both recognition and bewilderment in her features. She seemed to avoid Garrett, directing her attention instantly to the boy. "Thomas, is everything all right?"

"I'm not sure, Miss Abby, but that's why I've come to see you. I was supposed to have breakfast with Mr. Bates this morning, but he didn't show. When I went to his shelter, I could tell he wasn't himself. He didn't look so good, like he wasn't feeling well. Mrs. Bates told me to run and fetch you in light of the…" Thomas stopped short, a full-on look of distrust in his eyes aimed straight on Garrett.

"It's okay, Thomas." Abigail gave a gentle smile. "Mr. Ward is aware of what's happening in camp. He knows about the smallpox."

Thomas stepped back; his young eyes wide. "He does?"

"Yes, but I wouldn't let yourself worry on it. For now, at least, Mr. Ward is detained here to Mrs. Schreier's estate and even if that were to change, Officer Haywood is also knowledgeable of the fact."

The boy responded in a way that showed his full confidence in the rebel officer's capabilities to handle the situation. There was an annoyance about it that crept in, but Garrett wasn't about to let it show.

"Why don't you head back to camp, and I'll be there shortly." Abigail placed a hand on the boy's shoulders.

Thomas looked between them, and Abigail smiled again as if to reassure him. He nodded. "All right, Miss Abby. Mrs. Bates also said to tell you she'd take him to the hospital if she could, but I don't know how much luck she'll have getting him in if that Mr. Douglas is standing guard, especially if Dr. Adams isn't there."

"Don't worry, I'll be there soon. I promise."

Watching Thomas go, Garrett could no longer suppress his curiosity, hoping his initial instincts of the young man would prove wrong. "Does he live in town?"

Abigail sighed, already confirming his suspicions. "I'm afraid not. He's part of the continental camp, and he's as eager to fight as any of them."

The image of Thomas holding a rifle came again along with the ache in Garrett's gut. He didn't care if the boy was on the opposing side, he didn't like it.

Abigail seemed to read his expression and he could tell for once they were thinking the same thing. "I've tried to urge him to go home, but he seems bent on being here for reasons that aren't mine to disclose."

"Maybe there's nothing you can do. Sometimes people make up their minds and you can't change them. I know I was stubborn when I was his age."

She shook her head. "I just don't think I'm the right person for the task, even if I wish I was."

Garrett frowned. "It seems like you have enough tasks already on your plate. I don't know what all you do in the camp, but just coming here for Mrs. Schreier and myself is certainly a job."

A small laugh escaped from her mouth and Garrett's heart pulsed at the sweet sound, encouraged by it.

"I keep busy, but everybody has a part to play." She sighed. "And right now mine is to get to Mr. Bates."

***

An hour later, Garrett was in his room, finishing the beans and pork Abigail undoubtedly left by the fire while he'd been out in the barn with Nikolai. He scooped in the last bite, his stomach more than satisfied. As for everything else, well, that remained to be seen.

"Mr. Garrett, sir." Rebekah stood at the doorway. "Mr. Haywood is here to see you. He's down in the parlor."

It took him nearly everything to resist the urge from jumping out of his seat at the prospect of good news the officer might bring. What kept him restrained, however, was also thinking of the alternative.

"Lieutenant." Haywood was on his feet, his hands grasping a tricorn hat behind his back as he shifted his eyes off the portrait of Mr. Schreier and onto him.

Garrett could hardly decipher what news the man's stone-like expression brought with him.

"I've come to inform you your boundaries have been extended. Seeing Mrs. Schreier has not issued any complaints and the general wishes to stand by the rules that concerns prisoners of war, your rank as an officer grants you access into Cambridge." Haywood gave Garrett a hard-pressed stare. "Beyond its borders, however, you are not to cross or try for that matter. If you do, you'll be subject to execution. Do I make myself clear, Mr. Ward?"

Garrett listened to the officer's warning, almost with an indifference.

171

He wasn't surprised by the consequence. Death for desertion, even under an enemy's captivity was standard enough if caught, but he wasn't planning to get caught if it came to that.

"Undoubtedly on that issue. But what about a trade? You mentioned Howe has ten of your men from Breed's Hill. What of that?"

Haywood's expression went smug. "So we thought. As far as that matter is concerned, I have no obligation to give you any information, only that I wouldn't count on a trade if I were you, Mr. Ward" The rebel officer secured his hat, a clear sign that was all he was willing to give, leaving Garrett with more questions than answers.

As Haywood turned left down Tory Row and back towards the Commons, a wave of doubt flowed back and forth in Garrett's mind. What did Haywood mean about the trade? Had something happened with the negotiation? Surely something was being done to get him back, if not by the admiral, then by the captain or Nicholas. Garrett squeezed his fists tight with something beyond frustration, putting the fault again on, in his opinion, the lesser army. He might never get back if he waited on those insurgents to do things right.

His knowledge over the camp's illness came to his attention. It was a detail worth noting for the delay. Perhaps Washington was keeping him for that very reason. Still, ten of his men for one man? Garrett put his hand to his chin as if doing so would help him think better. It didn't. He shook his head. There was no use dwelling on it. He'd have to find his own way out. At least he could do that now that he'd been given a little slack. Even with a rope still tied, in his case, that might just be long enough.

Chapter 15

"Oh, thank goodness! There you are, dear." Mrs. Bates sprang from a Rococo style settee and from her husband's side. "I can see Thomas gave you my message. I'm so sorry to have interrupted your morning at Mrs. Schreier's household, but I felt much better if you were here."

Abigail looked beyond her friend, noting how fixed Mr. Bates seemed to be in the French piece of furniture that occupied the room Dr. Adams now used for his study. "I'm glad to see you made it inside."

Mrs. Bates scoffed, her head turning towards the door of the Vassall estate. "I wasn't so sure if we would with that gentleman out there who patrols the door. He was quite adamant about our non-entry. It was to our good fortune Dr. Adams was on his way out the premises to grant us entry to see about Mr. Bates." The woman's face fell. "But that has been an hour ago, I fear."

Abigail scrunched her brow. "Is Dr. Adams upstairs? Most of those who've come in for smallpox stay next door, while those coming in for other reasons stay down here. However, we do have a few patients up there that came in first complaining of the disease."

Mrs. Bates shook her head. "Oh, no, dear. Dr. Adams isn't here at all. He was on his way when we arrived. Mrs. Johnson's water broke while she was laying out the laundry on the grass. Mr. Johnson will have to have his shoes cared for, having been beside her when it happened, but I suspect he won't mind too much when his babe is in his arms. Should be any minute now."

Abigail nodded. She was familiar with Mrs. Johnson's condition, but Dr. Adams didn't have her involved with the woman's care. Part of her was thankful, not sure if she'd have the time to assist with the new cases of smallpox they were getting each week. Not to mention her other camp chores that kept her occupied, including her responsibilities for Garrett Ward, but she sensed the doctor knew that.

Though still demanding at times, it was this kind of work at camp she didn't mind, enjoyed in fact. It made her heart swell to help people in a way she never imagined she could. To see them heal, to make the pain go away and comfort them in the process of whatever malady they'd acquired, was a fulfillment to her soul she hadn't realized she wanted. Had Jesus felt the same way when He'd healed so many? Maybe she couldn't make a blind man see or bring a dead man back to life--talk about healing, but there was a deeper connection she was starting to feel for her Savior than she discerned she had missed until now.

"Would you mind taking a look at him, Abby?" Mrs. Bates' eyes implored hers. "I know Dr. Adams is in charge and we'll do everything he says, but I can't just sit here not knowing, especially with Mr. Bates like this." She gestured at the settee. A sprawled-out version of Mr. Bates laid on it, looking anything but the tall, able-bodied man Abigail had come to know. "You've seen several cases by now to give us an idea of his state."

Abigail considered the request thinking better of it without Dr. Adams present, but the deep shade of earnestness in her friend's gaze made her yield. She regarded Mr. Bates again, his eyes closed tight, grimacing on

174

and off again like pain coming and going.

Abigail went over to him and placed the back of her hand gently to his forehead. The sensation was warm, too warm. "He has a slight fever. How long has he been like this?"

"Just today. He was fine last night, but Thomas and I couldn't seem to get him out of bed this morning."

"Anything else he's complained of that you know of?"

"He just says he aches all over and he's gotten sick twice today."

Abigail bit the inside of her lip. "I can't be sure without doctor Adam's saying so, but in light of the disease spreading in camp, his symptoms do resemble the beginning stages of smallpox."

"Symptoms, dear?"

Abigail offered an apologetic smile, keenly empathetic with how the woman felt. "Sorry, that's just another way of saying signs of the disease. I learned that last month."

"And it's sticking on top of many other things I see."

Abigail froze, the blood rushing to her cheeks to hear the male voice of her mentor. "Dr. Adams. I'm sorry, sir, I was just…"

"You were just taking an evaluation of Mr. Bates even though you're not a doctor."

She swallowed hard, now sure her face resembled a bright crimson. It was never her intention to step outside her limits, but that's what she'd done. She couldn't deny Dr. Adams was right. She wasn't a doctor, nor had she had the training to be. At best, she was simply an aide to the camp's physician. Once more, Abigail fought to find the words to provide an explanation, but nothing good seemed to come. "Again, sir, I am so sorry. I didn't mean any harm."

"Those trying to help someone never do, Miss Thatcher. Please keep that in mind for your future in the field."

"My future, sir?"

He gave her a fleeting grin, before he was back to business. "We'll discuss that topic later. For now, finish your examination of Mr. Bates. Have you come to a conclusion yet?"

She gave a quick nod. "I think so. Based on what I see and Mrs. Bates' own account of her husband, I think he might be in the beginning stages of smallpox. He's quite warm, sir, and I can attest this man here is not the Mr. Bates we know." She gestured to the settee; a shell of that man now hunched over in it.

Dr. Adams followed her motion until his eyes did a swift assessment on the unfortunate man. "Yes, I agree, especially in light of the growing cases this week. Either way we'll be cautious just to be sure. We better get him a cot. He'll have to stay here or next door for a time until he comes out of it."

"We have some space next door." Abigail turned towards Mrs. Bates, who looked more than a little flustered by the declaration pertaining to her husband's diagnosis. Abigail softened her tone, not wanting to shatter the woman's spirit completely. "It would be best if you stayed as well, Mrs. Bates. Smallpox tends to spread."

The woman shook her head. "Oh, Abby, don't worry about me. I've had the speckled monster years ago before Mr. Bates and I were married, although I was punctured in my arm instead of having it go its own course." Her gaze shifted to her husband; her lips pressed firm though trembling. "But I'd like to stay put, that is, after I have to run an errand in town for the camp. If you don't mind, I want to come back here if Mr. Haywood might allow it. I don't know the first thing about healing, but I'd be happy to help in any way I could with the other sick here."

Dr. Adams smiled. "I'll speak with Officer Haywood and let him know you'll be helping out. He knows things have become cumbersome with the numbers growing. Perhaps if it comes from me he'll be more apt to consent to it." He glanced back over to the settee. "Abigail, why don't you get Mr. and Mrs. Bates set up. The parlor and library are already occupied, but there should be room on the second level. As far as the man's current state, well, you know what to do. I'll make my rounds here to see how the others are doing."

Minutes later, Abigail helped to accompany a feeble Mr. Bates and his understandably troubled wife to an upstairs bedroom next door. Only a single bed stood in the middle of the room and a washbasin beside it. "We've cleaned out most of the furniture to make space for those who come in but thought the bed may prove useful. I'm sorry Mr. Bates has turned ill, but I'm glad to see that it the bed is here. You'll have the room to yourselves for now."

Struggling, the two women managed to get Mr. Bates to the bed, still richly fashioned by the estate's owners who left with the rest of the loyalist for Nova Scotia. Abigail pulled out a vial from her apron pocket she'd grabbed from the secretary downstairs in the study. "Here, this should help with the pain." She gave him a dose of the laudanum.

"Thank you, Abby." Mrs. Bates took a seat by her husband's bedside. "I don't know what we would have done without you."

Abigail put her hand on top of her friend's wrinkled fingers, her eyes unflinching. "You would have done just fine. Dr. Adams would have seen you on his return and given Mr. Bates the same thing I'm giving him now." She was certain of it, thinking of how many times she'd watched the doctor do just that, she only mimicking his actions to the exact measurements since then.

"Still, it's good to know he has someone else he can turn to when he's otherwise engaged. It's just an added benefit that person happens to be you." Mrs. Bates smiled, giving Abigail a tender pat.

The gesture, though small, reminded Abigail of something her mother might have done as a means of comforting her. Strange to think of when it was the woman's husband that was ailing. With effort, Abigail tried to keep her grip loose as she became mindful of her mother's state. She was glad she could do some good here and fortunate to have learned what she had from Dr. Adams thus far, yet the yearning to see her mother beckoned.

With heart divided, Abigail forced a smile. "I don't know about that. I do what I can, and he's certainly a good teacher, patient too, but he's still the camp physician. There's plenty I don't know, though I'm glad I can help."

Mrs. Bates raised a skeptical brow. "Maybe so, but don't sell yourself short, Abigail. It sounded to me there might be more for you on this path, and I got the impression he wasn't just talking about here at camp."

Based on Dr. Adam's reply back at the Vassall house, Abigail wondered that too. She just didn't want to read too far into it and have what caused her heart to take bound, suddenly plummet. After all, future was a very broad term. What exactly did he mean by it? She wished she knew, a spark inside her wanting to find out. She glanced over at Mr. Bates, noticing by the deepened contortion of his face, his condition had declined since his assessment. She put her palm to his head again. Warmer. His fever had climbed.

"I'll get some water boiling in the kitchen. He'll need a balm infusion to help the fever go down. I can make a tea for him." Abigail reached inside her apron and pulled out another bottle but stopped short to see the contents in it were empty. How had she not seen it when she'd pulled them out of the secretary earlier? "I'll have to see if Dr. Adams has more lemon balm on hand. I'll be back as soon as I can."

Mrs. Bates looked again to her husband with a wariness Abigail could decipher. Her friend felt torn. She remembered the comment Mrs. Bates made earlier about having to complete an errand in town for the camp. No doubt, one of Haywood's orders. Abigail set to put the woman's mind at rest as best as she could in the present moment. She placed a soft hand on her shoulder. "Don't worry, we'll take care of him. Do what you need to do, and I'll see you back here later."

Mrs. Bates nodded; her eyes full of gratitude.

Abigail watched her friend go then put the empty vial back in her pocket and retraced her steps next door. She waited with forced patience while Dr. Adams finished with a patient upstairs, still working on his rounds before she caught his attention. The young man was one of the first cases they'd seen of smallpox enter the camp. His rash had recently developed into raised bumps but hadn't scabbed over yet.

Dr. Adams finished treating the rashes with a salve before he walked over. "How is our new patient getting along?"

"He and Mrs. Bates are in one of the rooms upstairs. I gave him some laudanum for the pain, but his temperature seems to be rising. I was going to make him some lemon balm tea." She pulled out the empty container. "But the vial of herbs is empty."

Dr. Adams frowned. "I'm afraid that's the only bottle I had. I wasn't exactly planning for a smallpox outbreak." He used a spare rag to wipe his fingers clean of the leftover salve. "Most of the plants are now dormant this time of year and not effective, but we might be able to get something in town to bring down Mr. Bates' fever. There's a place I stopped by on my way into Cambridge for supplies. They might have what we need." He jotted down an inscription hastily on a sheet of paper before handing it to her. "Here's the address."

Abigail read it over then tucked it away into her apron pocket along with the empty vial.

"While you're there, we'll need some more of this too." He passed her the container holding the salve. "The rashes are starting to come in on the others. We'll need plenty more of that to calm the itching."

She added it to her apron before she turned her gaze next door, her mind on Mr. and Mrs. Bates. Would they be alright? When she turned back to Dr. Adams again, he gave her a tender smirk.

"Now, I know I mentioned you're a quick study, but don't worry, Abigail. I think I'm still capable enough. Your friends are in good hands.

I'll just finish up here then I'll go check on Mr. Bates to see how he's doing."

Abigail's chest swelled at the man's good nature, the crinkles at the corners of his eyes showing nothing but genuineness. The feeling faded, a sense of fear mixed with desire probing her to find out more. "Dr. Adams, what did you mean earlier by my future?" She pressed her lips firm, not entirely sure how to ask what was on her heart. "What I mean is, were you simply referring to my work here as an aide to you in camp or did you mean something else?"

He took his time before an answer came, the delay causing every hope inside her to crash. Silently, she scolded herself. Who was she to think there might be more behind the physician's meaning than tomorrow's duties? Abigail inhaled a breath, determined to hear the truth with dignity.

At last, the doctor gave a long sigh filled with apprehension. "I certainly think there's work for you to do in camp, including here at the hospital, but beyond that, Miss Thatcher, the truth is I don't know."

The hope that poured in and filled her all but evaporated as Dr. Adam's words knocked her over like a forceful wind.

As if reading her mind, he put his hand up as if to stop her thoughts from beating her down further, offering an encouraging smile. "I don't say that to discourage you from that path. You're a fast learner and I can tell your heart is in the right place. Plus, you don't let a little blood scare you off like the other ones Officer Haywood has sent my way. With the proper training and education, I think you'd be a fine physician." His smile faltered a degree. "What I don't know is how you can get there. War has a way of bringing out change, and we may see that in time. However, for the present, the overall attitude of a woman who practices medicine outside her own home is not entirely approved of. You're just going to have to find your own way if that's the road you want to take. It's a lot of trouble to think about." The sides of his mouth rose again, the compassion in his stare giving her a sense of renewal. "But let's just focus on Mr. Bates and today instead of tomorrow. Today has enough trouble of its own already."

***

Abigail strode down Brattle Street towards Harvard Square. Her heels clipped away at the ground beneath her feet, each step growing heavier with each plant of her foot. How encouragement and discouragement could occupy one's thoughts at the same time, she didn't know. Her heart lifted a degree with Dr. Adam's evaluation of her capabilities, and somehow seemed to sink again at the obstacles he presented before her.

Yet, she knew in her gut he was right. Other than her makeshift apprenticeship with the doctor, acquiring the knowledge she still needed would be more than a challenge. Harvard, like all universities of her day, didn't allow women to enroll and she doubted those in Britain were an exception.

In Britain? Abigail wrinkled her nose with self-contempt. She pushed the thought away as soon as it came, hoping even God hadn't noticed, though knowing better. How could she even let her mind wander there? How could she even consider going to England when she was still part of an army that was fighting it?

What about her great-grandfather and his choice to leave for a better life? Maybe the exact reason for her grandparents leaving the motherland remained unknown to her, but life on the farm was good—so good to the point she hadn't considered an alternative to depart it until the war. But what would happen after the war was over when she went home? Could she return to that life again, knowing she could help others, that she could do more? A hunger inside growled for what seemed like an impossible decision. She wasn't so sure she could.

"It's always a pleasant surprise running into you, Miss Abigail."

Abigail flinched, the unexpected intrusion to her dilemma causing her to come to an abrupt halt.

181

Cleo came up beside her, though from where, she hadn't been paying attention to see. He gave an apologetic snort of laughter. "But I can see I was the one that did the surprisin'. Sorry to give you a startle."

"No, it's all right. I was just thinking…" She stopped short as the urgency to warn Cleo about Garrett's interest in him rallied itself with a vengeance. "It's good we ran into each other. I tried looking for you all last week." She didn't know the reason behind Garrett's curiosity towards her friend, only recalling Cleo's own discomfort at the introduction of the two Royal Navy officers back in Falmouth following the attack. Yet, her gratitude towards the older man for giving them enough warning to flee made the choice easy. Whatever Garrett had planned, even if harmless, she wanted to keep Cleo in the light of it.

"For me, Miss Abby?" His eyes brightened and gave a wide grin that revealed a missing tooth. "I'm obliged. What can I do for you, lass?"

"Actually, I'm hoping I can do something for you. Do you remember the two officers in Falmouth on the day after the attack?"

He removed his Monmouth cap and scratched his head. "Aye, I suppose I do."

"Well, you might not believe this—trust me, it came as a surprise to me too, but one of those officers is here in Cambridge. His name is Garrett Ward, and he seems to be interested in you for some reason. I thought you should know."

Cleo replaced his cap back to the tufts of gray hair on his head, nodding slowly as if still taking in the information. He gave a dimmed smile even as it lit with appreciation. "Thank you, Miss Abigail. I'm grateful for the news, but might I'd ask, how did you come across it?"

"Mr. Ward is a prisoner of the army and staying at the Schreier estate here in town. Part of my duties at camp include taking him his meals."

Cleo let out a long, drawn-out whistle which only made Abigail look around for any passersby that couldn't ignore the sound if they tried. Her cheeks flushed.

"You mean you're having to feed one o' the men who blasted your town?"

She sighed, then nodded. "I'm still coming to terms with it myself, but it might turn helpful. I've had some minimal conversations with Mr. Ward. Apart from the attack, he seems sensible enough. Perhaps I could talk to him on your behalf in some way."

Cleo shook his head in a way she almost felt bad for her interference. "Oh, no, Miss Abby. Don't trouble yourself with that. I know why the man is askin' even if he may naht know it himself just yet. At least I gathered that much back in Falmouth when those officers didn't arrest me on the spot."

Abigail pulled back. "Arrest you?"

He nodded, a sense of melancholy in his features. "I've run from my past a long time, Miss Abby, but I'm afraid it's finally starting to catch up with me."

Cleo had suffered too on that day in Falmouth, but the pain in his dappled gray eyes told Abigail there was more to his story. Even as she longed to know the truth behind them, she couldn't bring herself to pry further, not when the ache of the past cut so deeply in his features.

The two walked in companionable silence towards the town square until Cleo took off his hat again and rimmed it between his fingers. "I gather someone ought to know my story in the chance I do get caught. If that person be you, Miss Abby, well, I could certainly be content with that." He paused before he went on. "It's just that, I've been goin' so long at this game, I don't know where to start."

She looked at him, her heart already squeezing inside for what the man had yet revealed. "Well, why not start at the beginning? Sometimes that's as good a place as any. How did you come by the colonies, Cleo?"

The Scotsman let out a slow, methodical breath. "The how has a lot to do with my story, but I'll get to that. It was more of a why my family and I left the Highlands in the first place."

Abigail blinked. "You have a family?"

The despondency in his expression made her wish she hadn't asked the question.

"Aye, that I did, Miss Abby. We left Scotland after the Jacobite conquest, hoping to leave our hardships back in Argyll." The edges of his mouth raised for an instant, then dropped again. "Only we found we traded them for worse ones. The year I crossed the Atlantic I'd been in the company of my bonny wife and three-year-old daughter. Like many in our position, we too felt forced to leave our home in Scotland. Life had already been hard for the Mrs. and I, barely making enough to scrape by, but after losing the uprisin', things got awfully worse. What we did have was no longer enough and like many Highlander Scots, we feared for our lives. As much as we loved our own country, our best chance for survival was to come to the colonies." He closed his eyes tight. "I learned all too well that conditions at sea are naht for the faint-hearted. And I would naht recommend it for any child. Neither my wife nor daughter made the passage over."

"Cleo, you don't have to…"

He gave an adamant shake of his head, though tears began to glisten in his eyes when he'd opened them again. "No, Miss. It's just been a while since I've spoken of them, and they deserve better. My darling daughter, Catriona, came down with measles along with many of the other children on board. She was naht the only one to die from the sickness." His lips tightened again. "And my Eulah, my wife, she was so overcome with the loss of her only child, she could naht find the will to live and died naht long after of what I suspect was ultimately a broken heart. I had to bury both my child and my wife in the depths of the sea, though I too longed to join them." On top of the despair a cloud of defeat loomed over him. "But the God of the heavens must've had different plans for me, for despite my efforts to die I had indeed survived to see the coastline of where I thought would be my family's sanctuary. Now, it is only but my constant reminder of what I've lost. Still eager to unite with my family in that watery grave, I looked for opportunities to work at sea, hoping the mighty waters would somehow take me too into her depths where I might find my peace, even now I do the same." He sighed and the disappointment that drew from his breath wrenched at Abigail's heart. "But as you can see, I'm still here as if the sea scoffs at me and refuses to take my sacrifice."

Abigail wiped away the water from her own eyes. There were no words of comfort she could offer that would hold up to the weight of life this man carried and had been carrying for some time.

"Now, I was afraid I'd do that." Cleo rummaged through his trouser pocket and pulled out a half-soiled handkerchief. He offered it to her.

Not wanting to refuse the kind gesture especially as she considered his vulnerability, Abigail accepted, barely dapping at a tear before handing it back to him. "Does Abraham know?"

He returned the handkerchief back to his pocket. "No, naht that part of my tale. Such things don't come up between us."

She nodded, though she still wondered about the other part of his story, the one where Garrett Ward was somehow involved. Yet, how could she press him further in light of what he had shared?

"Now, don't have me regret telling you." Cleo gave a sad smile, any sign of the pain that had been in his expression now nearly gone. "I don't want you to feel sorry for an old man like me. I see how people look towards folk who've been through a lot with their eyes full of pity." He stared into her eyes, his own hard-pressed. "I won't have none of that, especially from you, Miss Abigail. Not when I have to face your brother this evenin'."

Abigail stilled, her sadness turning into alarm. "You're seeing Abraham today?"

"Aye, that I am. Tonight."

"Tonight?" Again, the unease to hear of her older brother rammed its way through. She'd seen Abraham less and less in the past three weeks. Part of the blame went to the smallpox spread and her involvement, but even within the camp grounds she hadn't so much as seen a flicker of him pass by. And Cleo was seeing him tonight? Abigail's thoughts went back to the last location she'd known concerning a meeting her brother was to attend. "At the Longfellow house, Washington's headquarters?"

"Aye, miss, the very same."

The confirmation only stirred up worry for reasons that continued to remain unexplained. She couldn't come up with a good excuse for why Abraham, and apparently now Cleo, were attending officer meetings where neither of them held such rank. "What's the meeting about, if I may ask."

Cleo frowned. "I'm sorry, Miss Abby, I'm happy to disclose my own life but what happens in those meetings is to remain tight-lipped I'm afraid. It's better if you don't know anyway. Less to worry about."

Abigail couldn't say she felt the same, frustration gripped hard to discover what Abraham and now Cleo were involved in. It didn't feel like a good sign when things weren't out in the open. She wanted to press, the concern of a sister and friend taking lead role to make the war's efforts step aside.

Cleo came to a firm stop in the road just outside the town square. "It's lookin' like it's time for us to part ways, both for your benefit and mine."

Abigail was about to protest, until she followed his gaze, and it all became clear even if her own mind had trouble believing it. Garrett Ward was in town. She blinked once to make sure and another time for good measure, but unfortunately wasn't deceived. He'd just stepped foot into the mercantile but nothing about his demeanor on his way in indicated he saw them. A pressure in her chest that quickly built at the recognition of the Navy soldier released and she turned to Cleo to share in their good fortune, but he was gone.

Chapter 16

"Come on in, sir. I'll be with you in just a minute."

A middle-aged man outfitted fashionably in a kimono motioned his invitation to Garrett with the tilt of his head. The rest of him was busy with a customer, taking a measurement across his client's shoulders.

Garrett stepped further into the store, rectifying his face quickly to cover his disappointment. "Do you have material here for purchase?" He asked the question, though fairly certain of the reply. The tailor shops in London he'd visited often displayed their fabric on shelves easily seen by those that came into the establishment, but here he saw no evidence of that. Though, he had to admit, those visits were always accompanied by Nicholas and his father, the latter expecting nothing but the finest in all things, especially the person who'd be fitting his clothes.

The tailor cut a notch in his measuring tape and gave a slight shake of his head. "I'm not a merchant tailor. They carry clothes in the store. I focus more on the craft. You'll have to purchase the fabric you want a few doors down at the drapers."

Garrett nodded and thanked the man for the information as he was about to retrace his steps back out the door.

"What are you in the market for?"

Garrett stopped. The tailor never flinched from his task, yet by the lack of other customers, Garrett deduced the question was aimed at him. "A coat and a pair of breeches."

"What about a waistcoat?"

"The pants and coat for now." In truth his funds were limited, but the fact he had some at all was a godsend. It had been a pleasant surprise to discover the coin in his satchel hadn't been robbed at his capture and was still hidden behind a piece of sail cloth he'd attached to the inside lid of a storage chest he'd kept in his quarters. He'd got the idea from another seaman early in his career in the chance their ship was captured by an enemy vessel or taken over by pirates.

The rest of the chest had been rummaged through, leaving him with a needle and what remained of the thread he'd packed. What did appear to be missing were his extra clothes, a navigation manual, and his pistol. No surprise on that last one. He was just glad his captors supplied him with the chest, even if nothing else, or so they must have thought.

The tailor made another notch in his tape before he gave his final pleasantries to the client he'd been helping and sent the man on his way. He looked to Garrett now with full attention. "Were you wanting a wool coat? It'd be much warmer than that one you have on."

The cotton of Mr. Schreier's coat was ill-suited for the colder months. Wherever the man was, he no doubted took his winter clothes with him. Garrett's gaze caught a young man sitting cross-legged on a platform in front of the store window, his sleeves raked up nearly to his elbow. He appeared to be finishing the stitching to a pocket of an olive-green coat. The fabric looked warm, but not overly bulky, good for a long walk if need be. Garrett pointed over to it as the young man continued to work. "Actually, I'd be interested in something like that."

The tailor nodded. "Broadcloth. A good choice. It'll take me three

189

days, maybe a week to complete them, but that's only once you've purchased your material." The merchant put a pair of glasses to his nose, appearing to assess Garrett's current ensemble.

Garrett swallowed hard under the man's scrutiny.

"Who did you say did these measurements? They're quite off, I must say."

Garrett cleared his throat. "I'm not sure." He'd borrowed Mr. Schreier's clothes again, mindful his Royal Navy uniform might not be taken well in a town hosting the enemy army. No use starting trouble when it could be prevented. "In truth, the coat is a loan until I can get something more suitable."

"Yes, something more fitted will do you better." The tailor went behind his work desk, grabbing a fresh tape. "Since you're here, why don't we get your measurements. I can let you know how much material you'll need, and you can go to the draper's after." Without waiting for a reply, the man removed Mr. Schreier's coat from his shoulders and hung it on a hook before he began his assessment.

Garrett stood still and upright as a statue while the tape stretched from his nape to the middle of his back. The short silence between them made his mind all too apt to wander freely, stopping short on Haywood's last visit. He wanted to blame the rebel army for the delay of his trade, but a stone sank deep to the pit of his stomach, telling him there might be more.

The tailor made a cut into the tape to keep record of the measurement, moving on to his shoulders. "Are you a part of the army?" Another cut was made. "I don't recall seeing you around town, but a lot of new faces have popped up since the continentals made their camp here."

Garrett tried to relax his shoulders, but the tension of his predicament proved it difficult. He was certainly with an army, but confident the man didn't mean the king's army. "Actually, I'm on my way through to Boston."

The tailor paused, and even as the man stood behind him out of view, Garrett could feel the strain of apprehension between them. Garrett instantly recalled what Boston's fortification by his comrades probably meant in the eyes of a citizen hosting the opposing side. He quickly recovered, thinking of Nicholas, and hoped he wasn't too late before the man's alarm ruined the first part of his plan. "I have family I need to get to there."

The measurements took on a more relaxed rhythm again and Garrett's heartbeat followed suit.

"I have family in Boston too. My brother and his wife opened a shop a lot like this one, only they carry fabric in their store like some of the bigger cities are doing. I suspected when you came in here, that's more of what you had on your mind?"

A shot of embarrassment ran through Garrett. Thankfully, the tailor showed no ill expression that told him he'd caused too much offense. "I was trying to be discreet. How did you catch that? You were still with a customer."

"In my line of work, one has to have an eye for detail." He stretched the tape around Garrett's chest, cutting another notch.

"Do you see your family often?"

"Not as often as I'd like. It's hard to get into the city these days with the British occupying it. A casual family visit can turn into more than an unpleasant interrogation." He stopped to recoil the rest of his measuring device as he shook the pair of scissors towards Garrett. "You should know that before you go."

"Thanks. How long is the journey?"

"It's about three miles, but you'll have to cross the river."

Garrett frowned. "So, I'll need a boat."

The tailor shrugged before he grabbed for another tape, moving on to Garrett's breeches. "You could if you wanted to, but it's not necessary. The Great Bridge connects the two, then you'll have to go through

Brookshire and Roxbury to get to the city."

"Good to know."

"That should do it." The merchant made a final mark. "What name should I put these down for?"

"Ward will be fine."

"All right, Mr. Ward, it looks like you'll need four yards of the broadcloth from the draper. I'll put your measurements aside until then. Just tell whoever's working Hart sent you."

"Thank you, sir. I'll do that." Garrett gave an appreciative nod, determined to follow the tailor's instruction and head right over.

"Oh, Mr. Ward."

Garrett turned back, the friendliness in the man's features somewhat faded, even as a slight smile still wore fashionably across his face.

"You might want to consider a different pair of boots. Those are much too nice for a traveler on his way to Boston. They might be mistaken for ones the king's men use if you're not too careful." The unspoken truth in the man's eyes told he knew more than what he chose to express outright. "There's more than a few smugglers along the route. You wouldn't want to catch their eye with those."

Slowly, Garrett released his jaw, taking in a silent, yet cautious breath. "Thank you, Mr. Hart. I'll heed that advice."

With nerves twisted and a shaky breath, Garrett stepped out of the merchant's store. He inhaled again. The cold sting of air filled his lungs and sharpened his senses, even if a little too late. He hadn't considered his boots, another gift along with his coat he'd received from the Royal Navy and no doubt a telling sign of his allegiance. He was lucky the merchant inside didn't fully call him out even when he could see plainly in the man's eyes his own cover was already blown.

He checked the coin in his pocket. A little more than a pound. It might just be enough to supply him with something that drew less attraction.

Determined to give caution to Hart's warning, he scanned for the cobbler. Better to take care of that now than risk running into someone else to call him out and who was less discreet about it.

"Mr. Fike, the men are supposed to receive a pound of bread a day. This is only enough flour for half that."

The desperation in the older woman's tone towards the merchant drew Garrett's ear.

"Then you better get word to Congress to pay up. I have my own family to think of ma'am."

"But sir," she pleaded, "think of the young men fighting for our independence."

"I respect what those men are doing, Mrs. Bates, but unless you have the money, I can't hand it over."

The woman pursed her lips, looking ever the more resolved to implore him further. "Mr. Fike, please think of the women and children. Is it not your Christian duty to help provide for them?

Mr. Fike hesitated, scratching his brow, then shook his head with an unrelenting firmness. "With all due respect, ma'am, I am trying to do just that. If I had enough to give, I would, but I must think of my own family. They count on me, especially in these hard times. As it says in Timothy, "take care of your own household first.""

A flustered Mrs. Bates let out a short, defeated breath.

Garrett couldn't help but be drawn to the scene. Maybe it was the woman's distress or the man's devotion to his own family that pulled him in. Whichever was the cause, didn't matter. He was already on his way to approach them. "Maybe I can help."

"I wouldn't waste your time, sir." The woman crossed her arms, her mouth pressed. "Mr. Fike here seems fixed on his opinion."

"It's not just opinion, Mrs. Bates," the merchant argued, "the fact is, we're not getting goods in like we used to with the British in Boston."

Conviction poked sharply at Garrett's sides, a sense of responsibility for the struggle these people were now dealing with. Thomas too, came to mind along with the other children the woman mentioned. Garrett didn't exactly like the idea of helping his enemy out in any way, but he liked worse feeling responsible for the plight of the innocent. Divided, he let the children win out. "Here, this should do it." He gave what he had left to the merchant.

"That's right, sir, not a pence more nor less."

Garrett nodded while the man put the coin away and gathered the flour. He handed the sacks over to him who in turn gave them to Mrs. Bates.

"Oh, sir, you're an angel." She put the sacks into a basket she carried at her side.

Garrett smiled, never thinking of himself in such a light but strangely the term appealed to him. "I'm happy to help."

They turned from Mr. Fike, taking a few steps away from earshot. Mrs. Bates' voice went to a whisper. "It's hard to find good help around here these days. I'm grateful when God sends me it. Thank you, again, Mr...?"

Garrett tipped his hat, giving a slight bow he was glad to see she took delight in. "Garrett Ward at your service, ma'am. And you're Mrs. Bates?" He recognized the name from Thomas earlier that morning back at the estate while the boy searched for Abigail. He would've inquired about her husband's state, but thought better of it, not certain how much of him Abigail disclosed.

"It's nice to see there's still some decent men here in town."

The side of his mouth raised. "I'm sure there's plenty of decent men. War just puts everyone uneasy, not just those on the battlefield."

"It certainly does, Mr. Ward. At least Officer Haywood won't be this evening now that his men will have the remaining portion of their breakfast tomorrow."

Garrett tilted his head, his interest inclined. "Officer Haywood?"

"You know the man?"

He suppressed a scowl as best he could, thinking back at the only two encounters he'd had with the man and how unpleasant both of those meetings had been. "We've met less than a handful of times."

Her eyes smiled in a way to tell him the secret was out. "I can tell from your expression you have. He's a sort of obscure fellow, rigid on all fronts, hard to get to know. You don't want to get him out of sorts. Some of the officers are a bit more lenient, but not that man."

"That Mrs. Bates, I have no doubt." Garrett gave her an easy grin, feeling the warmth of their conversation flow effortlessly.

"Mr. Ward, are you a part of the camp? I can't say I've seen you around."

Garrett struggled to keep his smile from falling too quickly. So much for effortless. "No, ma'am, I'm hoping to be just passing through." He thought of Mr. Hart and the aforementioned time it might take for his new ensemble. The man said it could be a week upon the receipt of fabric, a task which Garrett had yet to complete. "Though I'll be here for at least a couple more weeks I imagine."

"I'm glad to hear it. You seem like a fine young man. I'd like to introduce you to someone I know, Miss Abigail Thatcher. She's a lovely young woman who works at the camp, but I'm afraid our dear friend, Haywood has her stretched to her limits for now."

Garrett smiled to himself at the older woman's attempt to make a match and his own agreement to Abigail's lovely character. If Mrs. Bates only knew how much that young woman loathed him. "You never know, Mrs. Bates, Cambridge is a small enough community. We might cross paths at some point while I'm here. I'll be sure to mention running into you if we chance to." It was a promise he was set on keeping, knowing the chances were guaranteed.

The older woman beamed before a flake of fluster appeared in her expression. "Please do. Now, I best be off. I need to get this back to camp and see to Mr. Bates." She hugged the basket still hanging from her arm. "Do take care, Mr. Ward. I hope to run into you again."

"An occasion I look forward to, ma'am." Garrett waved good-bye and let the distance between them grow before he turned round to face the draper's store. He still needed to buy the broadcloth and the sooner he did that, the better. Aiming both his sight and his step towards the door, he made a direct path for it until the petite figure of Abigail Thatcher entering an apothecary shop knocked his focus off course.

"Garrett?" She was already at the counter, her eyes lit with consternation. Though clearly surprised to see him, she recovered quickly. "I see you made it out of the house."

He smiled, grateful she hadn't referred to his imprisonment so openly, especially with the apothecary just on the other side of the counter. "I did. Haywood paid me a visit not too long ago with the good news. I guess you'll be seeing more of me now."

She frowned, and, though he hated to admit, the reaction bothered him more than he cared for it to.

"Well, congratulations." The corners of her lips turned upward into a forced smile he recognized easily from Mrs. Schreier's dinner party. "Does that mean you'll be leaving Cambridge soon?"

Again, he appreciated the subtlety, thinking of the trade she knew about. "Not yet. Things are still being worked out."

She nodded, appearing to understand enough.

"Here's the salve, but I'm sorry, miss, we're all out of the lemon balm." The apothecary handed her a small container.

Abigail took it, but Garrett could read the alarm clearer than his spyglass could search for land. "But ma'am, I need the lemon balm too."

"I understand that miss, but the fact is we don't have it."

"Do you know when you'll get it?"

The woman across the counter shook her head. "Things are hard to come by between the winter season and the block on the harbor. We just don't get things in as fast as we used to and sometimes not at all."

A sigh pressed through Abigail's lips before they closed again. The small gesture was enough to let Garrett know that was not the answer she counted on hearing.

His knowledge concerning anything to do with medicinal properties was more than limited, but he did know a little about the herb from his experience at sea, particularly of its use for fever. That and the fact smallpox was currently in the camp made him almost sure that's what it was being used for. "If the use is intended to bring a temperature down you could try sumac as a substitute."

Abigail's gaze shifted from the apothecary now focused on him. The woman behind the counter was also inclined to hear more, her eyes full of what he read as surprise mixed with inquisition.

He cleared his throat. "I've seen plenty of it around here. The roots can be boiled to help combat a fever."

"I thought sumac was poisonous?" Abigail's green eyes pierced into his with skepticism.

"Some are. You just have to make sure you're getting the right plant. Look for red berries that sit upright instead of white or light-green ones that sag downward."

Abigail looked from him to the apothecary as if waiting for confirmation.

"I believe this gentleman here is right, miss. If a fever is what you're aiming to take care of, that is."

"Do you have it?"

Again, Garrett could hear the strain in Abigail's tone as she spoke to the apothecary.

"Not currently. I haven't had time to gather the stuff. It may be another day before I get to. But he's right on the plant's location. You can find it around here. Look for the berries. They stay crimson through most of the season."

Abigail's eyes faced the floor and another defeated breath pushed forward. "Thank you, but even with that information I hardly know what I'm looking for and I don't have the luxury of time. I need to get back with it as soon as I can."

Garrett stepped forward. "I'll go with you since I know the plant and I think I remember seeing a shovel in Mrs. Schreier's barn. It shouldn't take too long."

She hesitated, seeming to look for any sign of deception in his eyes.

"Don't worry, it's not like we're going out of town. I can't, remember?" The faint traces of a smile tipped upwards.

"All right." She gave a slight nod as if she'd relinquished something she hadn't wanted to. "Let's go."

Garrett waited while she paid for the previous container. He thought to offer his arm on the way out but decided against it. Her hesitation spoke volumes enough and he didn't want to force her into doing something she might feel she must do simply out of social obligation. He'd rather the gesture come easily anyway. Instead, he opened the door and let her pass through it. He followed her on the way out and to his own amazement, felt heartened despite the discouraging news he'd received about his trade.

Chapter 17

Abigail's heart raced, though whether it was brought on by her urgency to bring down Mr. Bates' fever or the man walking beside her now she couldn't completely decipher. Why she had agreed to let Garrett Ward help her she didn't know either, only letting herself attribute it to his knowledge of the plant and his ability to get the job done faster than she could do on her own. She'd have to lie to herself if she didn't think he was strong enough, recalling the way he swung that axe hard against the firewood when she found him behind Mrs. Schreier's house that day.

The image of him bringing down the blade was like it held a personal agenda against him he wasn't about to allow take place. His muscles strained to show a sailor who not only commanded the ropes but worked them as well. Abigail was quite aware a man's worth came from more than just what he looked like, but she couldn't help from staring, the overall action seeming...well, just so manly. Now she found herself back at Margaret's carriage house only a few yards away from the scene she'd had trouble veering her eyes from.

"I take it you know where we're going?"

Garrett grabbed a shovel next to one of the horses' stalls in the barn. Nikolai didn't seem to be around, but the two mares stood in the stalls, their eyes full of curiosity. Abigail gave them both a gentle pat, each nudging back towards her like they received it with pleasure.

"Not really, but I have an idea where to look."

Her eyes narrowed, already regretting the decision she'd made to let him help her. "I thought you said at the apothecary you've seen the sumac around here?"

He didn't even flinch. "I have, here in the colonies."

"You mean you haven't seen any in Cambridge?"

He gave her a dry smile. "I haven't exactly had the freedom to stroll around to find out but the apothecary seemed assured we would. I'm placing my wager on that."

She shook her head, her teeth set on edge for what was starting to feel like a wild goose chase. "Garrett, I have to get back to the hospital. I don't have time to go on a treasure hunt."

A slow grin stretched its way upward on his face. "Considering I'm using a map, that's a great way to put it. But like I said back in town, it won't take long. I know you need to get back, but I think Mr. Bates would appreciate it if you didn't do so empty handed."

Abigail exhaled slowly as she worked to let her frustration diminish and try again. There was truth in his logic. She couldn't deny that. "All right. I see your point. You have a map of Cambridge?"

"I do. When you're constantly in parts of the world you don't know, you sort of make it a habit to get one if you can."

"You make it sound like you've been all over."

"Not everywhere but I have been to a few places I doubt I'd ever visit unless I was in the Navy. I suppose that's the tradeoff of being at sea for months on end compared to living a life on land." With the shovel in hand, Garrett started to walk out of the carriage house.

Abigail followed behind, the two of them wandering again off the Schreier property and she still not completely convinced he knew where he was going, map or not. She gained in step beside him. "Is that where you learned about the sumac?"

He nodded. "We were on a mission concerning the East India Company, making port in Bengal. Some of the crew came down sick with dysentery from the voyage, including my friend and brother, Nicholas. A group of natives brought us a sort of tea for those ill. With Nicholas and I being so close, I made sure to know what they were giving him. I didn't want my best friend to end sewn up in his hammock just in case they had another agenda. As you know personally not everyone is a fan of the Royal Navy."

"Nicholas is lucky to have you as a friend."

"If we'd been switched, he would've done the same for me." He sounded so sure like the bond the two men held between each other was stronger than just friendship or at the very least, friendship at its finest. She knew that feeling, the feeling of certainty to be able to count on someone knowing that person had her best interest in mind. For her, that was Charlotte. Despite her sister's youth and desire to go out into the world, Abigail rested assured she'd also made her mother's condition a priority.

"He sounds like a good man."

"He is. One of the best I've come across." Garrett stilled like he truly considered the thought. "In all my travels really. I'm just thankful he's been in so much of my life. I'm not sure how I would've turned out otherwise."

Abigail wavered, not sure if she should knock at that unopened door between them but the question seemed to beg at her as she tried to fit the puzzle pieces together. "Is that what happened after your father died? Is that how you joined the Navy?"

A slow, weak smile drew across his face, trying to cover the spark of pain in his eyes. "Yes, Nicholas' father, our captain, took me in after and helped me get started. My mother had already passed away, so if it wasn't for him, I would've ended up in an orphanage. Who knows where I'd be then."

Without a sign of irritation on his part, she nudged the door a little further in. "May I ask what happened to them, your parents?"

He drew in a long, slow breath and she decided to change her mind. Why did she care to know any more about this man than she had to? Yet part of her did.

She shook her head, her speech coming out hurried. "Never mind, Garrett. I shouldn't have asked. It's not my place to…"

He raised his dark, brown eyes to hers and for the first time she could see a kindness in them. "I think it is your place—what I mean is, I'm okay with telling you." The soft smile from before returned. "I hardly remember my mother. She died from consumption when I was four years old." His face fell. "My dad, unfortunately I remember his all too well. He was murdered when I was twelve. He had a carpenter shop in east London and would work late sometimes, but when it got too late that night, I got worried. I was the one that found him, the coin bag taken and my father on the floor. That's when the captain took me in. He gave me a different life, and I embraced it, never looking back except to glance occasionally at the man I still miss."

"I'm sure he would be proud of you."

A corner of his mouth raised. "With reaching just short of becoming captain?" He let out a forceful breath. "Maybe, but sometimes I'm not so sure. He wasn't a man who cared for such titles and reputation. Part of me still admires him for that."

"And the other part?"

"Just misses him." He reached into his pocket, pulling out a square fold and undoing it to reveal the same form but four times the larger.

She eyed him. "Your map."

"My map." His eyes gleaned from the paper to her, a rueful smile along with them. He pulled his gaze back to the drawing. "Let's go this way. There should be a field close by."

With no alternative, but to follow, she did. They passed a house, cutting shortly inward after it, Abigail's pulse rising at the event of being discovered so near to the property until their steps continued to drift in. She hiked up her skirt a little past her ankles, the tall grass of the field sifting against her dress and making it otherwise harder to walk.

Garrett returned the map to the pocket of his trousers, a satisfied expression on his face. "Keep your eye out for the berries. This should be a good spot for them to grow, but if not, I have another idea."

She gave him a keen eye. "Which is?"

"To just keep walking for now and let me know if you see anything. Aside from that, Miss Thatcher, I think in light of now knowing my life story and ambition, it only fair to share some of yours." He gave her a warm smile. "But only if you want to."

"I suppose you do make a good argument, Mr. Ward," she said, deciding to play along. Still a range of emotions filled her to capacity, not certain which one would prevail. With her eyes set forward, more to cover the doubt that lingered in her heart than to look for the sumac, she began. "There's not much to my life story that you don't already know. As for my ambitions I hadn't given them much thought until lately." She felt her cheeks flush warm. "To be honest, I'm not sure I would have if it weren't for my travels to Cambridge. I always just pictured my life on my family's farm and whatever farm came after that if I got married."

"I guess I helped put a damper in that plan."

She gave him a look. She wasn't willing to go down that dark path today especially when he was helping her now.

"Sorry, I shouldn't have said that." He offered a conciliatory smile. "Tell me more of what's changed since you came here because it sounds like something has."

Abigail's lips began to part, but then faltered. Why was she about to reveal such a desire, something that now felt more like a forbidden secret to this man? Saying it out loud only deepened the longing, making it ever the more difficult to suppress, yet she wanted to. Not just to put it in the open and admit there might be more for her life than she'd ever expected, but to do so in front of this man.

She looked again into his eyes, a warmth about them pulling her in. "In a way, it did. Not who I am, that part still feels the same, but what life will be like once I go back home. I wonder about that a lot. Before I came to Cambridge, I was content, happy even with the life I had, but I don't know if I can go back to that life after being here. Something about it just feels wrong." She let out a forceful sigh, the dissonance between the two outcomes pushing against each other like two bucks clanging their antlers. "Yet, wrong not to do so at the same time."

Garrett tilted his head, the wrinkle in his brow telling her he was interested. Either that, or completely confused.

Abigail went on, hoping it was the former of the two. "You mentioned you were sort of forced into the Navy."

"That's right."

"I want to say being in Cambridge has done the same—forcing me into roles I wouldn't have otherwise done back home or even thought I was capable of." She swallowed, letting the truth fly free. "And want to explore further after my work here in the camp is done."

His wry smile appeared again. "I have a hunch it's not babysitting army prisoners, so I can only assume you mean your work with the doctor."

She nodded. "I wish I could do more after this."

"Why can't you?"

She thought of the obstacles in her way, reaching higher than what seemed like the heavens themselves. "For one thing, I don't see how it's possible. The doors of the universities are closed to women."

"True, but surely there are other ways around that. Don't let one obstacle get in the way of something you obviously care about."

She shook her head. "That's not the only obstacle, Garrett."

"Go on."

Abigail's thoughts flew, the weight of the second problem heavy on her heart as she thought about her great-grandfather's sacrifice. Falmouth would be resistant to the idea of a woman treating its townspeople, especially with the rise in men to become doctors. She'd have to try elsewhere. But if she pursued her dreams, what would that mean for her great-grandfather's making a better life where he'd planted them? A languid sigh came forth again. "It's just not the role I was designed to have. My place is on the farm."

Garrett raised a critical brow. "From what you've told me so far I'm not so sure it is."

She challenged his theory with a look, but he didn't falter and in a strange way, she appreciated that.

"I was supposed to be a carpenter, but my father's death put me on a different path. Maybe Cambridge has done the same for you." He tipped his chin, a sparkle in his eyes. "But it seems like you already know that."

"Maybe. I suppose I just have to pray about it and see."

His face fell, but he didn't say anything as a small wave of silence rolled over them. "Well, I think we've found what we're looking for."

Abigail followed the direction of Garrett's focus, leading to what looked like a border into a forest at the end of the field. Clumps of small red berries fell scattered around a shrub with feather-like leaves running opposite of each other along its branches.

Abigail sucked in a breath, the heaviness in her chest taking flight. "The red berries!"

"Now, that didn't take too long, did it?" Garrett gave her a satisfied grin before he took the shovel to the dirt at the base of the plant.

With both joy and relief filling her heart, she couldn't hold back from laughing. "Oh, thank you, Garrett. I have to say, I'm so relieved. I'm not sure what I would've done to bring down Mr. Bates fever. I know Mrs. Bates would've been worried. He'll at least have a little comfort once I get this to him."

Garrett's smile softened. "I'm glad I could do some good for you, Abigail. Hopefully, for Mr. Bates too. This should be enough for him until the apothecary has time to get more this week." He tucked the plant under his arm." I'll help you get it to the hospital. It's getting late and I don't want you walking back on your own."

Between focusing on their task and the conflict of their ambitions, Abigail hadn't noticed the sun had begun its descent. Having only visited the camp, Mrs. Schreier's house and the market square, she wasn't confident she'd make it back before dark, especially without a map. Still. "Garrett, are you sure? The hospital is only down the street from the estate George Washington is staying. Not to mention we have several patients from the continental camp there and the guard always outside. You'd be walking into enemy territory."

"I thought I was already walking in enemy territory? Cambridge is after all, fortified by Washington, isn't it?"

She gave him a sideways look. "You know what I mean."

"It'll be fine. No one knows who I am without my uniform. To them I'm just a town resident escorting a young woman back to camp. Really, you'd be doing me a favor. I'm not quite ready to return to the walls of the Schreier estate just yet no matter how welcoming they are. I'd give me an excuse not to. Call it a friendly request."

Abigail peered into his eyes, realizing there was a part of her that wanted that if it weren't for the past standing tall between them. "We're friends now?"

"Maybe not, but you're the closest to one I have and will probably ever get while I'm here."

The satisfied look on his face was enough to fool a stranger, but somehow Abigail had become more than that through her time with Garrett. She recognized the tightening of his neck behind it from both times he mentioned his father and his current separation from Nicholas. Behind the jest she could read the truth. How lonely it must be to feel isolated like he did, apart from those one cared about.

Abigail had come to Cambridge with Abraham but saw her brother less these days than a distant cousin who lived states away. Even as thankful as she was for Mrs. Bates, her letters from Charlotte were what she cared for the most. They were her lifeline to her mother, father, her sisters, and Henry. What happened if one day she woke up with it suddenly taken from her like his had been? Her heart stirred enough to make a move. "What if I offered to take your letters for Nicholas to the courier?"

Garrett looked at her, wide-eyed and shook his head. "Abigail, I wasn't trying to force your hand. I'm a prisoner. I'm not supposed to have any friends and I'd be foolish to expect your friendship after all I've done to you."

"It's not about that."

"Oh? Then what's it about?"

The polarity of her two siblings came to mind again. Abraham, who she arrived in the same town with yet never heard a word from and Charlotte away in Portsmouth who kept her connection alive and frequent through her letters.

"I just know what it's like to feel disconnected from someone while also connected to another. I'd much rather choose the latter option of the two and I'd like to extend that opportunity to you." She gave him a pointed look. "But only if you can follow my condition."

Garrett pulled back giving her a smile she took pride in. "Why, Miss

Thatcher, talk more like that, and you're in danger of becoming a captain yourself. All right, I'll bite. What's the condition?"

"There can't be any malintent in your correspondence." She eyed him again, daring him to do otherwise. "You can't compromise Washington in any way or plan an escape or anything else having to do with your side's advantage in this war. Can you promise me that?"

His smile came easy. "I can."

"Good."

The two of them walked on until they reached the steps of the Vassall estate. Mr. Douglas was on duty as usual.

Abigail stopped them there. Even as confident as Garrett seemed and the dark that now surrounded them, she decided the less contact Garrett made in camp, the better. With his boundaries now extended, it was only a matter of time before word got out of the face of the Royal Navy prisoner. "Most of our smallpox patients are next door. That's where Mr. Bates is too. I'll go there and get the tea ready for him. Thank you, again, Garrett."

"Thank you too, Abigail." His eyes met hers, looking into them in a way that made her heart jump and her throat a little constricted. She was thankful the moment didn't require her to say anything. "Not just for the distraction from going back to the Schreier house, but for today. I enjoyed it." That rogue-like grin she'd seen before expressed itself again, the seriousness of the moment all but gone. "Oh, before I forget, make sure to tell Mrs. Bates I said 'hello.'"

***

"Mrs. Bates?" Abigail knocked gently at the upstairs door with the sumac root tea in hand. Her focus was primarily on their new patient, but part of her still felt a little stunned by Garrett's comment regarding the poor man's wife. 'Tell Mrs. Bates I said hello?'

"Abigail, you're back." A relieved smile welcomed her in as Mrs. Bates

208

closed the door behind her. "You were able to get what you needed?"

She nodded, then remembered the sumac was actually the substitute for the lemon balm she originally intended to purchase. "It should be." She thought of Garrett's idea to suggest it, still impressed by his quick knowledge of it. "They were out of what I needed, but this was suggested as an alternative and the apothecary agreed."

"Agreed?" Mrs. Bates' frowned. "Was it someone else other than the apothecary that made the recommendation?"

"Yes, another person happened to be in the shop who's had prior experience with the plant."

"Well, I'm certainly glad they were there. I'll have to thank them. Who did you say it was, dear?"

Abigail paused but, in the end, decided to give credit to where it was due. "His name is Garrett Ward."

The older woman gave a startle and put a hand to her chest. "Mr. Ward?"

Her instant recognition of the name only heightened Abigail's interest with how they clearly knew each other especially in light with what Garrett had parted her with. "You know him?"

Mrs. Bates nodded; her eyes now bright. "I met him earlier today in the market. He helped supply the cost for the rest of the bread for tomorrow's breakfast."

"He paid for the army?" Despite her effort, cynicism encroached in Abigail's tone.

Mrs. Bates gave her a marked glance mixed with disproval and surprise. "Yes, and saved me more than a bit of trouble from Haywood I gather. I hoped you two might cross paths."

Abigail suppressed a smile. How many paths had she and Garrett Ward already crossed?

"It's not every day you come across a man like that, especially so handsome, dear."

A heat in Abigail's cheeks flushed understanding clearly what the woman was getting at. "Mrs. Bates, I hardly think being in the middle of a war is the best time for such things."

"And why not? I don't see anything wrong with finding a little hopeful distraction in a place so grim and conflicted as our camp."

If only her friend knew just how conflicted her life and Garrett's were. Abigail shook her head. "I think for now we'll focus our attention here." She went over to Mr. Bates, glad to see his condition hadn't changed for the worse, though he still looked frightfully ill even in his sleep. "Rest is always good." She put the tea on a single nightstand next to the bed. "I'll set it down here for now, but as soon as he wakes, make sure to give it to him. It should bring his temperature down. I'll inform Dr. Adams of how he's doing." She turned for the door.

"Oh, Abby, before I forget." Mrs. Bates pulled out a letter from her apron pocket. "The carrier came by today during dinner. He said this was for you."

Abigail took the paper, instantly recognizing Charlotte's handwriting. Her heart began to swell at another fulfilled longing. She ached to hear an update on her family and about the parties her sister might be attending as her aunt's way for Charlotte to come out in the world. That was, until everything came crashing down.

Chapter 18

Garrett finished at the drapers, buying a broadcloth in a similar olive green he'd seen back at the tailor's store. He dropped the fabric off with the guarantee by Mr. Hart his coat and breeches would be ready by the end of the week. His boots, however, were another story. Since he'd made the purchase for Mrs. Bates, he didn't have enough coin left over to buy anything from the cobbler. He would just have to make do and hope Mr. Hart's eye for his shoes were more due to his professional opinion than other's casual observances.

He patted the left side of his chest, feeling for the square fold beneath it. That was his next task for today's agenda. The map of Cambridge would come to test whether Mr. Hart's theory was true and crossing over the Great Bridge was his only way to get into Boston. If so, he had quite the challenge on his plate with the route just to get to the river alone stationed by rebels. So far, Garrett's overall assessment of the group wasn't high, but he wasn't willing to take that chance especially with his new, even if still bound, freedom to get this far. He'd rather be more cautious to do his homework and hope for the best.

Once Garrett had made his exit from the market, he found a place more private and took out the map from the coat he still borrowed from Mr. Schreier. He'd yet to meet the man, but already felt like he owed him so much. Garrett doubted the shopkeepers would be as friendly if he'd worn his navy one and he surmised the suspicious glances of everyone around would be on him, making it nearly impossible to carry out the very mission he needed to accomplish.

He unfolded the paper to its full size and began to glance over it in search of another route or a narrow ford in the river. But his research came to an end almost as swiftly as it began. It was the accent so thick of Scottish tone that caught his attention and made his ears stand on end. Garrett looked up in time enough only to see the back of a man's head walking, or rather limping, northeast towards the Commons. For him, there was no question between the combination of that physical malady and the Monmouth cap he'd seen back in Falmouth.

With no indication the man recognized him, Garrett let some distance draw between them before hastily packing the map back into his pocket to engage better in his pursuit. He remembered the conversation he'd had with Nicholas that followed their encounter on land the morning after the attack. Perhaps it was nothing, but with Nicholas and him in agreement something was off, that was enough to tell Garrett he needed to see it through.

And then there was Abigail's involvement with the man. Though what that was exactly Garrett couldn't be sure only that he wasn't entirely convinced this so-called Samuel was truly her uncle. She still claimed him to be when he last asked, but even then, her guard was at full defense, telling him he might as well forfeit any knowledge he hoped to gain. Now, however, she might be more inclined to the subject if he brought it up again. But maybe he didn't have to with his heels right on the very subject himself. Maybe those questions were about to get answered and maybe then Garrett could clear up whatever they couldn't quite pin the man on. For Abigail's case, he hoped it was nothing.

Still in sight and moving at a leisurely pace, Garrett watched Samuel, or whoever the man truly was, make an unexpected turn. It caused him to veer off course from the Commons Garrett suspected he might be going. The maneuver was easy enough to follow and with Garrett's eyes still locked on the back of the man's head, they continued, passing by a local tavern and down another street.

Ready to shorten the space between them so Garrett could eventually make his challenge and confront the man straight on, he was about to increase his stride when something changed. The limp in the older man's leg became exaggerated as his pace picked up speed. He looked back over his shoulder a single time, and Garrett was able to see the mixture of recognition and dread in the white of the man's eyes.

The strain in Samuel's gait was evident, his bad leg wobbling like a stiff cane he had to shift his weight under to keep balance. It was an advantage for Garrett who was still young and able. Garrett closed the space between them further, his heart mimicking his stride.

When he'd found himself in a crowd again, Garrett perceived they'd passed the draper's and were back at the market square. If the town wasn't set up as somewhat of a grid, he'd say they'd come nearly full circle. It was a smart endeavor on Samuel's part. Not only did the crowd slow down their chase, but it gave the older man opportunity to hide within.

Garrett's gaze remained keen, his body whipping in and out, this and that way, but always proceeding forward towards his target. When they seemed to have cleared the cluster of people, they took a left on Mount Auburn Street and headed north. With the lack of obstacle, the gap against them began to narrow, Garrett closing in while the older man's hobbled trot seemed to slow down.

Samuel's eyes shot towards him the slightest sign of defeat laced within them. Both men knew what was next. The Scotsman went ahead at a staggering walk, more pronounced than before their game of cat and mouse began though Garrett couldn't help noticing resolve speckled in his expression. As Garrett closed in, his heart pounded with questions at the ready until it registered exactly what building the man was going into. Christ Church.

A hurricane of emotion swirled around him, his father's death hitting him hard like the awful storm that worked to pull him under. Garrett had been to a building like this one in his youth more times than he could count, but a hesitancy rang loud within to continue forward. How many times had his father attended? How many times had he prayed or had tithed from the little they had? The building and what it represented only brought up thoughts of Garrett's loss he'd managed to suppress, feelings he preferred to stay buried. He didn't want to go in and would've called off the chase right there if it weren't for that nagging voice of the captain telling Nicholas and him to finish whatever they started.

With heart hammering despite having caught his breath, Garrett managed to step inside. Rows of pews stood erect. An aisle in the middle divided them and led to the pulpit. To his chagrin, the church was vacant, Samuel nowhere in sight. Now it seemed like he'd come inside for nothing. With his lead gone, Garrett dropped begrudgingly down onto one of the empty pews and rubbed his eyes with aggravation. If he hadn't hesitated, he'd be getting his answers by now. He didn't have to look at his map to recall just how close the church was to the Commons—merely a street away. Samuel was probably there in the safety of it and Garrett with no desire to enter the rebel camp.

"Would you like me to pray with you?" Startled, Garrett shot his eyes up and open to find a man dressed in what looked like a black robe. A kind smile brightened his face, but Garrett wasn't in the mood for company or praying for that matter. How had he missed the stranger upon entry was beyond him. Was he losing his edge?

"No." He cleared his throat; his tone coming out harsher than he intended it. "Sorry, what I mean is, I just don't find any use in praying. It hasn't exactly worked out for me in the past."

The priest nodded, showing no indication he was surprised at all by that explanation nor offense to it. "Yes, it certainly feels that way sometimes, doesn't it? I often pray for the Lord to reopen these doors, but he hasn't so far."

Garrett frowned. "You mean the church is closed?"

"For now, yes but thankfully it's only a building." The man gave a benevolent smile.

Garrett shifted his body, still feeling like he'd broken a rule. "Again, I'm sorry. I didn't realize no one was supposed to be in here."

"Don't be. Even if Congress has shut us down, the doors are always open. Besides, it's good to come across another soul looking for direction when things are so unknown in this war."

Garrett shook his head. "I wouldn't say I'm looking for direction—" He thought about telling the man he'd been chasing someone in here, but something about that didn't sound great in his mind. "—Just a person."

"I take it you don't mean Jesus?" The man gave a squared expression that made it hard for Garrett to suppress a smile.

"No, I don't mean Jesus."

The priest shrugged. "Well, I haven't seen anybody else here except for you."

Garrett nodded not entirely surprised, though still disappointed. "He's probably already gone."

"You're welcome to stay as long as you like. I'm just going to finish praying around these pews before I leave. Hopefully sooner than later someone will find their way in one."

Garrett knew the man referred to the church's closed doors and congregation, yet something deeper lay behind his meaning as if the statement were meant for him. For the briefest moment, it made him wonder if more had brought him here than just his own ambition to catch Samuel. But if that were true, then that meant someone cared for him, and experience told him no one was out there other than the captain and Nicholas.

"You can hide from me Garrett, but you can never hide from God." The words of his father echoed in his ear. He shut his eyes tight with frustration but reopened them again just as quickly not wanting to give another false impression he'd been praying. He didn't need the man to come around again, but he did need to get out of here. Doing just that, Garrett looked for the priest to say goodbye, but the godly man was gone.

With stomach unsettled, Garrett walked back towards the Schreier estate. His errands for the day were done. It was something in the current moment he found the slightest victory in, ready to get as far away from the church as he could and away from the painful memory of his father. His heart only lightened at the possibility of who he might see back at the house, noting his stride lengthened a degree more.

Abigail. How the woman had a way of calming him he hadn't the faintest idea, only that it had nothing to do with any of the herbs she could purchase from the apothecary. For him, she was all the medicine he needed.

He thought back about her saying she would have to pray for direction in what she would do with her future. He hadn't meant to make an objection, but he could see in her eyes he had even when she didn't say anything. He just hoped she wouldn't put all her cards in one pile in the chance she didn't get an answer like he had when he tried to do the same for his father's murder. He found out then, no one was listening.

"Mr. Ward, please come in."

Garrett had just enough time to remove Mr. Schreier's coat that had become a little damp from the cold mist, its effect deepened by his impromptu run that afternoon. He placed the coat on the hall tree before he followed the sound of Mrs. Schreier's voice to the parlor. Upon entry he saw Abigail. His chest lifted then fell again, noting something was clearly wrong. She looked at him and gave him a weak smile before her own melancholy returned.

"Abigail." Mrs. Schreier turned her attention away from Garrett and back to the woman that held their concern. She gently pressed her to go on as if the two ladies had been in the midst of a delicate conversation. "As you were saying."

"It's my mother, ma'am. She's very ill to the point my sister isn't certain how long she has. I've made arrangements to go to Portsmouth this very night. I'm not sure how long I'll be gone."

A folded piece of paper lay gripped between Abigail's fingers. Garrett wondered if that was the bearer of the bad news.

The lady's eyes softened. "I'm sorry to hear that, Abigail, for your mother and for you. But of course, I understand. Though, we'll also miss you while you're gone."

"Thank you, ma'am."

"Are you coming back?"

Abigail turned to him, her eyes slitted with stunned confusion. "I'm not certain." She turned back to Mrs. Schreier who teetered on the chaise, the woman's belly now fully visible. "But Dr. Adams will continue to make his visits on your behalf. I hope to be back before the baby comes but it all just depends on my mother." She gave a depleted sigh. "Please excuse me, there are few more arrangements I need to take care of before I leave town." She pulled out a small bottle from her apron pocket. A pleasant smell of peppermint brushed under Garrett's nose. "This should be enough until the baby gets here. Hopefully then, your symptoms will improve." She handed it over to the lady of the house before excusing herself again.

Her eyes met Garrett's fleetingly as she brushed past him out the door, the ache something he recognized and giving him no alternative but to follow.

"Abigail, are you all right?" Even as the words came out, an instant regret to say them out loud invaded Garrett's heart. Of course, she wasn't all right. Everything in her countenance told him she wasn't.

She turned back towards him. Her eyes widened as if surprised to see him behind her. Garrett's stomach twisted realizing she hadn't expected his concern. Her lips parted just enough to let in another shaky breath, and he wondered what it would be like to embrace them with his own and take her in his arms.

"Truthfully, no I'm not, but I hope to be when I get to Portsmouth and by my mother's side. Charlotte isn't one to extend the truth of a matter. It speaks volumes she's sent for me to come to my aunt's."

He treaded closer to her carefully. "Do you think you'll come back?"

"I don't know. If my mother gets better, I would like to. The smallpox outbreak is still a problem and even with our newest recruit to take my place for the present time, Dr. Adams will need help. It would also be a special moment to see Mrs. Schreier's baby come. I would love to meet her."

Garrett's brow raised. "You think it's a girl?"

"I can't say for sure, but I have my suspicions. If not a girl, then for sure a boy." A weak smile formed, lighting the tears glistening in her green eyes. It took him everything not to pull her into him.

"I can't help noticing I didn't make it on your list. I'll try not to be too disheartened by that."

She gave him a sideways glance. Though not as pronounced as the one he'd seen in the field a week ago when their conversation had been easy instead of weighed down by what she was currently going through. "I'll be writing to Mrs. Schreier while I'm gone to keep me updated on how things are going. I'll make sure to include you in that agenda. Which reminds me. Haywood has provided a substitute in my stead to bring your meals."

Garrett had to hold back a grimace. If she only knew there was no substitute for Abigail Thatcher. "Thanks for thinking of me."

The side of her mouth raised slightly. "Who knows, you might not be here by the time I get back."

Only now, the thought of being traded didn't have the same appeal as it had before. Despite everything within him not wanting to let her go especially if that meant he'd never see her again, Garrett knew in that moment he had to do that very thing. "I know you said there are still some other things you have to do before you leave. I don't want to be the one holding you up from seeing your mother."

"Thanks. I appreciate that." She paused, her eyes shifting towards the ground as if expecting something to come forth from the cold, wet mud. Her gaze drifted up towards him again. "Garrett, could I ask you to do one thing for me while I'm gone?"

He blinked, the request unexpected, but welcomed. "Of course, name it."

"Could you pray for me, for my mother? I don't know what's going to happen, but I need all the strength I can get just in case it doesn't go the way I want it to."

Wishing not to disappoint her, he nodded before he watched her petite figure disappear past the sidewalk and down the street.

Chapter 19

Abigail sat on the edge of the bed in one of her aunt's bedrooms, feeling like she could hardly breathe. Her mother, Elizabeth, lay weakly under the wool covers accompanied by a glorious set of bed hangings, one of her aunt's many purchases from her travels to France a few years back. Her stomach wrenched. How much her mother had changed since she left for Cambridge, now almost two months ago. Her mother's eyes, even closed in slumber seemed swollen and the paleness about her complexion made her appear more fragile than Abigail remembered like she had aged ten years.

"I forget you haven't seen her lately. She tells us she looks worse than she really feels. You know Mother, she hardly complains about anything." Charlotte came in and plopped herself down on the side of the bed next to Abigail. "She'll be glad to see you when she wakes up. I know father and I are. Even as busy as Henry makes himself around here, he asks about you too."

The thought of her youngest brother made Abigail smile mildly. "He hasn't been bored then? I remember you were the last time we were here."

Charlotte shrugged, smoothing her skirt around her as if to make it lay neatly on the bed. "I was older than Henry is now and wanted to go to those parties you and Abraham went to. Henry doesn't care at all about that. It's not like home, but he does seem to enjoy it here. He likes to go to the barn out back and be with the animals. Sometimes I find him asleep in there when he's not anywhere in the house. It's started to become one of the first places I look now."

"He always did love the animals back home. I'm glad he's found some here." Abigail shook her head. The thought of Henry only helped to recall the momentary exchange she'd had with the youngest Thatcher since her arrival. "I can't believe how much Olivia has changed. She's already holding her head up so well."

Charlotte gave a faint laugh. "And filling out too. She's quite a talker in a baby sort of way. I forget how quickly they grow in that first year. I vaguely remember Henry being the same."

"And you? What have you been up to? Have you been to any parties like Abraham and I went to last year?

Charlotte nodded. "A few. We mostly go to the Lady Allewood's estate. She's a dear friend of Aunt Sylvia's. According to our aunt, she hosts most of the gatherings in town and by the look of her place, I wouldn't doubt it. She seems very wealthy and kind." Charlotte paused like she was searching for the right words, "In a sort of regal way. Aunt Sylvia says her late husband was a merchant who sold lumber for the British army. I believe she still does even though he's passed. There were a good number of British soldiers in attendance each time I've been over there."

"I'm glad to hear you've had the chance to venture out."

"How about you? What do they have you doing there in camp? From what you described in your letters it doesn't sound all that attractive especially compared to being here."

Abigail would've laughed, thinking how the damp and dirty cold of camp life couldn't be more opposite to the luxury and comfort of her aunt's home but under the circumstances she couldn't bring herself to do it. "It definitely lacks the appeal of Aunt Sylvia's touch, but it's not all that bad once you get over the smell."

Charlotte wrinkled her nose. "I don't even want to ask about that."

For the first time Abigail entered her aunt's home with heart heavy for her mother, she smiled. "Probably for the best."

"So, what do they have you doing there?"

Abigail shrugged. "Just odd jobs for whatever has to be done; washing and mending clothes, preparing food, things like that. When I first arrived that's mostly what I did and still do at times, but I mainly work at the hospital now."

Charlotte's eyes thinned with investigation. "The hospital? You mean you already have patients even when the camp hasn't had a battle?"

Abigail thought best not to mention the smallpox. "It's mostly due to camp conditions and lack of sanitary supplies. You'd be surprised by how many men don't seem to care enough to groom themselves even at the basic level."

Again, Charlotte made a face like she'd entered the camp herself. "You always seemed to have a stomach for such things. I can't forget how you helped Father with Agnus's birth. I couldn't watch you two pulling that calf out and Abraham looked like he might vomit even if he wouldn't admit to it. I bet that's just perfect for you."

"There is something rewarding about it."

"Have they got you doing anything else?"

Abigail hesitated; the thought of Margaret popped up before her image suddenly became clouded over by someone else. Garrett Ward.

Charlotte read her hesitation, her sister's eyes brightening with intrigue as she scooted closer to her on the bed. "What? Is it a secret?"

"No." Abigail offered the negative instantly to extinguish her sister's flames of enthusiasm before they became too hot. "Not at all. I'm helping

222

the camp doctor with a woman who is expecting and..." She winced, not certain on the best way to convey the next detail. "A prisoner she's housing."

"They have you helping a British soldier?" Charlotte pulled back, eyes wide as the new piece of information overshadowed her concern for the soon to be mother. She gave a cat-like smile, leaning in. "What's he like?"

Abigail pressed her lips into a fine line and gave her sister a sidelong glance.

"I can't help it, Abby. They might be parading around here in their uniforms, but you must admit, they look good doing it. A couple of them have even come to call and I might be so inclined to be escorted if it weren't for mother's condition and my needing to be here."

Guilt rang through Abigail like the clang of a gong vibrating every inch of her body. Had she made a mistake leaving in the first place?

Charlotte frowned. "Not that I mean anything by that. We've had tons of help here between Rachel, Aunt Sylvia, the doctor and me. Frankly, it sounds like they could use your help in Cambridge." A twinkle sparked in the corner of her eyes again, her voice tinged with teasing provocation. "I'm sure that prisoner doesn't mind your help either. Is he handsome?"

Abigail didn't answer.

The silence only encouraged Charlotte who took liberty to make what she could with her own decipher. She squealed softly. "I thought so. What a way to meet a man."

"It's not like that, Charlotte."

"The flush in your cheeks says differently."

Instinctively, Abigail's hand drew to her face in a failed attempt to hide the rosy color that warmed her fingertips. "Fine, yes," she conceded, if only to drop the subject than let her sister continue to feed off her discomfort. "I'll admit he's nice and handsome." And kind and generous, thinking back to what he did for Mrs. Bates to feed the soldiers and helping her find the sumac. Her gaze sharpened. "But he's also the enemy of the continental camp."

Charlotte straightened, crossing her arms. "Is there a rule about falling in love with someone from the opposing side? Besides, most of our family stands neutral on the war. It's only Abraham that has the passion of the so-called cause. You only joined the camp after our town was hit."

Abigail cringed, the casualness in her sister's tone making its own blow. "You make it sound like it wasn't that bad, like everything wasn't destroyed including our home."

"I don't mean to sound like what they did wasn't terrible. It was, but thankfully the Navy gave most of the people time to get out and there are already plans to rebuild. Father's been meeting with some of the town leaders. He's talking like we'll have most of our home standing sometime in the spring. It won't all be done, but we'll be able to go back." She gave an aggravated sigh. "Honestly Abby, you can't blame the man like he fired the canon himself."

Their eyes met, Abigail's unflinching.

Charlotte's mouth gaped open. "Don't tell me he did?"

Abigail shook her head looking down at the bed covers though not entirely sure. "No, at least I don't think he ignited the fuse. To be honest, I haven't had the courage to ask, but he is in the Royal Navy and he was on one of the ships that day."

Charlotte leaned back, blinking. "Well, for the first time I'm speechless."

"Good. I'd like to leave that subject alone if you don't mind."

Charlotte nodded, seeming to understand as much. "Okay, okay, what about Abe? You barely mentioned him in your letters."

Abigail shrank a little more inside. Normally, she would've been happy for the change in subject, but the topic of her older brother was one she felt just as uncomfortable with as the one they'd finished about Garrett. "Truthfully, I haven't seen him very much since we got to camp. I've been told he's all right, but that's all I know. I think Washington has him pretty busy with something, but I don't know what that is. The last time I saw Abraham, he barely said anything at all about it when I asked. I left a message for him about Mother with a mutual friend, but I don't even know for sure if he received it."

Charlotte pressed her lips before giving a gentle sigh. "I can't say I'm surprised. He was the one I always thought would dive headfirst into this rebellion. I just hope whatever Washington has him doing he's okay."

Abigail agreed. "Me too."

"Abigail?"

They both looked towards the headboard where the weakened voice of their mother came from. Charlotte smiled at her awakening before she rose from the bed. "I'll give you two some time to catch up."

When she left the room, Abigail turned back to her mother, carefully grasping her hand with her own. "I'm here, Mama. How are you feeling?"

Her mother breathed in a shallow breath, a hint of wheezing in her lungs. "Mostly tired, though I think I look worse than I feel."

Abigail noted all the symptoms she could: the wheezing breath, occasional cough, the swollen ankles and feet and the overall weakness she could clearly read in her mother's pale blue eyes, now a shade lighter than they had been when she left. Unable to come up with an answer, she wished desperately Dr. Adams was here. She hadn't seen anything like it in camp, only familiar with how to help relieve the cough with a ginger tea she'd prepared earlier. She went over to a fire that'd been put out recently, it's kindling still hot and the teacup in front of it still warm.

"Here, try this." Abigail passed the cup while she kept her hand steady behind her mother's in the chance fatigue might take over and cause her to drop the porcelain container. She took the cup back when her mother had taken what she wanted.

Her mother gave a languid smile, a half version of the one Abigail was normally used to. "You've been busy I see. What have they got you doing there in Cambridge?"

"I work a lot in the hospital."

The feeble smile grew a degree. "You like it."

Abigail could sense it wasn't a question, yet how could her mother read her so well even in her current state? "I do. I like helping people in that way. I feel useful."

"You're always useful, Abby." Her mother gave another gasped breath. "But I'm glad you found something you enjoy. It doesn't surprise me you found your way to the sick. You've always had the healing touch."

Abigail did her best to hide the frown. Part of that pained her. If she'd always had the healing touch, then why hadn't she been able to help her mother sooner, or even now? "It's been quite something learning from Dr. Adams. He's taught me so much." She considered her lack of knowledge regarding her own mother's condition and her chest constricted. "But there's still so much to learn. He's always teaching me something new. I'm going to miss learning about it all when we go home."

"Who says you have to stop?"

Abigail shifted uncomfortably, reminded of Dr. Adam's warning regarding the barriers ahead of her. "I just don't see a need to in Falmouth, not with being back on the farm."

Even with her eyes faded, Abigail could read her mother's scrutiny clearly. "That's fine if that's what you want, Abby, but I've known that look since you were a tot. It's the same one you used to give when you wanted to go down to the harbor by yourself to see the ships come in. We wouldn't let you, of course, because you were too young, but I knew you wanted to. Why not continue down this path when I can see that same desire in you?"

"I just don't know if Falmouth is ready for me to treat its townspeople, especially with the role being so dominantly male. Some of the doctors are even taking the traditional responsibilities of the midwives."

"Then I don't see why it can't work in the opposite direction too and you become a physician."

"It's not that simple, Mama. There's still so much I have to learn but I don't think I can get into a university. Women aren't allowed, at least not yet anyway."

"What about Dr. Jenkins, could he not teach you?"

Abigail shook her head. "He's not the teaching type and even if he was I get the feeling he wouldn't take on a woman apprentice."

Her mother seemed to consider that. "You may be right."

"But it's not just that." Abigail pressed on urgently. "I should be home with you and on the farm. That's where I belong. That's what great-grandfather wanted for us, isn't it?"

Her mother's mouth turned under. "Who told you that?"

"No one. I just always thought when you and father mentioned them coming to the colonies, it was to escape their old lives and make a new one here."

"Well, that is true in part."

Abigail slanted her head, searching in her mother's countenance for the part that remained disclosed. "What do you mean?"

A weak smile emerged, one that surrounded Abigail with love. "Your great-grandfather and great-grandmother came over to start a new life from the motherland, but not because they were trying to escape or run away from something. They came because there was a new land of possibilities and an adventure in doing it, including changing what tradition has passed down." She eyed Abigail. "Something you might be trying to do now if you let yourself. They would be proud of you for doing it, just like I am. It may be a good time to take advantage of that." Her mother coughed again and Abigail offered her the ginger tea. She took another sip, giving a less struggled breath afterwards.

"And the farm?"

"Will always be there for you if you decide not to. But enough of that for now." Her mother smiled again, a hint of the smirk she'd seen earlier in Charlotte's eyes. "Tell me about this man you're helping."

"You were listening?"

"I was in and out, but I caught some of it, enough to sense there's something you're not saying—not just out loud I take it either."

"Did you hear the part about him being there the day of the attack?"

Her mother closed her eyes and nodded. "I did and I know you're still angry about that day. There's nothing wrong with that, dear. Even Jesus was angry at times. We know that and he was the Son of God." A more pointed expression dimmed across her face, reminding Abigail of a time she'd been in trouble as a child. "What is wrong, however, is that your anger is being used as a hindrance to forgive someone. You have forgotten that Christ forgave you for your sins and how far gone you are without him." Her mother's expression softened. "Maybe this man isn't someone you want to spend the rest of your life with, but how much more should you forgive him for what wrong he did to you?"

Abigail's whole body went tense. The truth in her mother's correction stung. Her mother was right, yet how could she find it within herself to forgive, to let go of something she'd clung to just to get her through what she had lost? A great divide rose inside, struggling to pull between doing what she knew was right and what she thought she needed. If she let go of her anger, she'd let go of the one thing that kept Garrett Ward at a distance. What would happen if it was no longer there?

In the back-and-forth tug between the two, an overwhelming sensation to cry took hold. Before Abigail knew it, her cheeks became wet with tears she'd long suppressed. Like when she was a little girl, her mother held her arm open, inviting her into her loving embrace until the wet streams of water flowed freely into a restless sleep.

***

Abigail awoke with a startle then panicked at the sensation of a small impression upon her cheek. "Mother?"

"I'm right here, Abby." Her mother still lay beside her, though now it wasn't just the two of them. Olivia was among them, her legs and arms outstretched as if exploring her surroundings. Her mother's mouth tilted upward full of compassion. "There's something about a good cry that makes things a little better. How do you feel?"

Abigail's fingers went to the corners of her eyes and wiped away the dried residue from her tears. "Better," she admitted. She pulled herself up from the bed covers and gave her youngest sister a small peck on the forehead. "Can I do anything for you?"

Her mother seemed to consider her for a moment. "Actually yes, Abby, you can do something for me. You can go back."

Abigail had been in the middle of giving Olivia a raspberry on her cheek when she stopped abruptly. "Go back?" She could hardly think about going back. "But what about you?"

"I'm fine, dear."

Her concern mounted. "Forgive me Mother, but you don't look fine. I still have a lot to learn, granted, but I know what sick looks like. I don't need to be a doctor to know that."

Her mother's easy expression turned downward, and Abigail clenched eyes tight regretting the hurt feelings she'd caused. Her voice softened. "I'm sorry, Mama."

"It's okay, Abigail. I understand. It's hard for you to see me this way but try not to worry. Sylvia has the town's physician at my beck and call, and you know your aunt, she always splurges for the very best." Her smile took shape again. "I'm in good hands, my love." She reached out her hands to take hold of Abigail's tenderly. "And it sounds like yours are needed elsewhere."

Abigail shook her head. "I don't understand."

"Your father and I have been talking, and we think you should return to Cambridge. We've heard you're doing a lot of good there."

"You've heard? From who exactly?"

A gleam lit her mother's faint blue eyes. "From someone you need to catch up with. He's waiting for you down the hall. Don't be too hard on him."

Having scooped up Olivia in her arms, Abigail gave her mother a quick kiss on her forehead before she walked the hallway in anticipation.

"Abraham." Both frustration and relief whirled inside her to see him now after so many days leaving her uncertain about his well-being. She thought to question what he'd been up to, but remembered how that went the last time she'd tried. With their time so limited together she didn't want to waste it on arguing this time.

"Hey, don't look so happy to see me." Abraham pulled himself from a desk, a corner of his mouth tipped upward.

"I just didn't know the next time I would."

"I guess that's fair. It's been some time since we've seen each other." Abraham held a piece of paper with drawings, simple in their design, but containing a mix of letters, grids and dots she couldn't make out. He followed her eyes, tucking the strange picture casually aside like he'd been working on something of little importance.

Abigail leaned to one side, letting Olivia rest on her hip while the irritation towards her brother won out. "Some time? Abraham, it's been nearly a month. Taking into account we've been at the same camp, I'm not sure what to think of that"

"Don't think anything of it." Her brother's jaw tightened, before it relaxed again. "I know you're worried but I'm fine. Just know that."

"I get the impression that's all you're going to tell me whether I like it or not."

"It is."

She let her own soreness over the subject dissolve. Despite whatever secret lay between them she was glad he was here. "Well, whatever you're doing, thanks for coming. I'm sure it's very important but it means a great deal that you're here."

"You don't think I would've come?" His expression was wounded like she'd shot him in the stomach. "Even if I was in the middle of commanding a battle, Abby, I wouldn't hesitate to be here. This war is important, probably more important than we understand, but even so it's no contender to what really matters most."

She swallowed, beginning to see more of the brother she knew growing up with again. "It's good to hear that coming from you. I'm sorry."

Abraham shook his head and let the pieces of discord that formed between them fall to the ground, Abigail's heart filling with gratitude for it.

"How is she?"

The pressure in her chest from earlier built up again. "Honestly I don't know. She doesn't say much on it, only that she's fine."

"That sounds like her. She hardly complains about anything."

"She said you mentioned my work in Cambridge?"

He gave her a one-sided grin. "You were sleeping but we talked for a bit. I'm glad we did."

"And father too?"

The other side of his mouth rose to reveal a full smile and the truth. "You must've been tired. You barely stirred the whole time we were talking."

She gave him a sharp look. "What did she say?"

"She didn't say much, only that she was worried you might be closing a door you were meant to go through. From that and what I've heard at camp, I'm guessing she means your work there."

"Who have you heard anything from?" Abigail remembered, then, their mutual friend. "Cleo?"

Abraham smiled again. "No, but he's mentioned you too in a different regard. I ran into Dr. Adams one day. He speaks highly of you, Abby. I don't imagine he does that a lot. I also imagine he could use your help with what's still going on in camp."

Certain her brother meant the smallpox outbreak, she took a deep breath dipped in divided responsibility before she squared her shoulders. "I'll have to think about it."

He frowned but nodded. "Well, let me know. I'm leaving to go back tonight. You can ride with me if you decide you want to come back."

"You're already going back?"

"There's no more need for me to be here. Mother's doing fine, or so she says. And Charlotte tells me there's plenty of hands to help out. Henry seems taken by the animals and Olivia..." He gave the babe a warm smile and kiss on the cheek. She cooed with delight. "She seems okay." His face went serious, meeting her eyes again. "I need to get to my next assignment. I'll check with you later this evening. If you're coming, be ready."

When he closed the door Abigail stood in the hallway outside of it, Olivia still in her arms. "What should I do?"

Her baby sister cooed again in response filling her heart with love and reminding her of the baby still needing to be born back in Cambridge.

"It'll only be for a little while. I'll be back in the spring." She made the promise to her youngest sister before she knocked on her brother's door. His answer came swiftly. With the decision settled she inhaled a determined breath and let her misgivings out upon its release. "I don't need to think about it any longer. I'll be ready."

Chapter 20

Garrett wouldn't say Cambridge was becoming more like home, but it was certainly becoming less like a prison. It surprised him how he missed Abigail. She'd only been gone for less than a week's time, yet there was something about the lack of her presence that ached like a void in his chest. He was afraid of what that meant. It wasn't because they came from different worlds or different sides of the war for that matter. Those were mere obstructions compared to what made his stomach twist and turn like it did. The real obstacle and question he'd brewed over these past few days was whether her feelings were mutual.

The muscles in his back grew rigid, as the hollow in his heart dug in further. Not that it mattered at this point. Because another thing he was uncertain about was whether she was even coming back.

Garrett thought about what Abigail asked him to do for her. At that moment, he was willing to do anything until she said it. He hadn't expected that from her, not the part where she requested prayer, but the part where she asked him of all people to do it. Yet, he still wanted to help, to pray. He cared too much not to. It wasn't he believed somehow

God would hear him, or even that making his petitions would do any good, only that he'd come to esteem the woman who'd asked him to implore the heavens on her behalf and that's what she needed from him right now.

Garrett walked down Brattle Street towards the market, a discomfort in his hands from the last time he tried to put them together in an appeal to God over his father's death. He wasn't exactly sure how to do it anymore feeling like he failed the first time. Not to mention it being so long since the last time he tried. And what about God? It wasn't like they were on the best terms. He'd been so angry at God these past years. Was the Almighty even willing to listen? Had he burned a bridge he could never repair?

His hand reached inside his coat for the letter from Nicholas. The very fact he had one, made the stiffness in his back ease. Gratitude filled him towards Abigail for the arrangement until he thought about what the contents of his friend's message contained inside. Now that he knew the facts of Samuel, or should he say, Cleophes Lockhart, what was he going to do with the information? Garrett still didn't know what Abigail's relationship was to the man, only enough that she knew him, but what did that mean? Did she know his past? Did she know he was a pirate, a crook? And if she did, what did the man mean to her to protect him that day in Falmouth? He wanted to find out, but not as much as he wanted to know what he was about to do next.

Cleophes was here in Cambridge. With the missing pieces to the man's past in place, Garrett had a duty to see things through, to bring him in. The fact of his own captivity was only a benign detail. Once he wrote to Nicholas about his sighting of the fugitive, he was almost certain his freedom would be restored. So why did he hesitate this morning in writing it? He'd had the ink and quill ready in hand directly after reading Nicholas' account, yet he couldn't seem to bring the pen to the piece of paper.

A chill ran through Garrett's body, not certain if the cause was the draft attributed to his borrowed coat or something else. Then the answer dawned on him. It was a woman he continued to care about more each time he spent moments with her. If Falmouth hadn't stood between them, he'd make sure she knew it, courting her like she should be, like she deserved. As it was, the town continued to separate them. Maybe it wasn't like the solid brick wall it had been when he first arrived in Cambridge, but something still stood there. Some of the dense structure had fallen, but not all. And without knowing what Cleophes meant to Abigail, sending that letter might only strengthen the bricks and mortar that remained.

Garrett tucked the letter back into his pocket, feeling like somehow one of those bricks from the wall sunk into it.

"Mr. Ward, come in, sir."

The door clicked behind him. Mr. Hart was dressed in a coat and waistcoat this time instead of the robe Garrett had seen him in on his first visit to the tailor's shop. It was certainly plainer and more traditional in comparison, but the trimmings of the coat still had its embellishments. A clear sign of the work to the man's industry in both fashion and wealth.

"Your coat and breeches are ready over here." Hart took Garrett's clothes gently from a hanger that dangled on a small pole and brought them over to him. Garrett took off his coat, or rather the coat he still loaned from Mr. Schreier, and deposited it on the platform the man's apprentice was sitting on in front of the window. Like the time before, the young man had a thread and needle in his hand. But instead of the olive-green coat he'd worked on last time that'd inspired the one Garrett was now getting ready to try on, he'd sewed to secure a button onto a caramel-colored vest.

Hart helped Garrett slip on the coat and in an instant, Garrett felt a small strain lift from his shoulders. The piece felt good and fitted him perfectly, like a glove. As much as he loved his officer's coat, he had to admit the one he wore now fit still better. Not to mention the color was his favorite, reminding him always of those brilliant green eyes that continued to catch his breath.

"Much better wouldn't you say, Mr. Ward?" Hart brushed the shoulders of the coat and smiled in a way that told Garrett he already knew the answer.

"Yes, much."

"The color's a good match on you, too. You better be careful out there. You might just find yourself a lady and that might mess your plans up for going to Boston."

Garrett smiled to himself. The man was only two months late to that detail. At least the part about a lady. He was still intent on getting to Boston.

"Which reminds me." Hart's eyes pressed to the floor. "I can see you've chosen to keep your boots, but I would still encourage you to heed my advice when you decide to go."

Garrett had every intention to do so, but that was before he ran into Mrs. Bates and the woman's desperation that had pleaded at his heartstrings. He only had a little change left, but not enough for a pair of boots, especially when he didn't know what he might run into on his way into Boston. There were always robbers along routes and that was apart from what the tailor mentioned about Washington's soldiers along the way. He might need a little extra funds to ensure a safe passage. Who knew? His boots might even come handy in the chance he had to hand them over. At least if he made it into Boston, he could worry about having no shoes then while in the presence of his own comrades and Nicholas.

"Trust me, I've thought about it, but I'm afraid they'll have to stay for now."

Hart shrugged in a way that told Garrett he was making a mistake but cared little to the outcome of the decision. "Well, at least they look good with the coat. Just don't say I didn't warn you."

"I won't."

"Would you like to wear it out? I could dispose of these if you want." The tailor gave Garrett an encouraging glance that was little needed.

More than happy with his new clothes, Garrett accepted the advice, though turned down the offer to completely rid himself of his borrowed ensemble. "Thanks, but I'll take these with me." He folded Mr. Schreier's clothes over his arm, then paid the tailor the agreed amount before the door clicked behind him.

As he hit Brattle Street again, Garrett's attention was drawn by the young boy he'd met back at the Schreier estate. Thomas, was it? The lad sat on an uneven curb next to the cobblestone street and prodded the snow-dampened mud with a stick. The action was absentminded as he nearly missed the downward contact of a horse's trotted hoof that passed by. If he'd leaned in any further, he'd been hit for sure. Despite the boy's dislike of him, Garrett resolved to make his way over.

Garrett stood, his foot an inch from where Thomas sat. Thomas never wavered from his activity, his head glued to the pavement with an expression only known to the brick below him. He didn't want to be seen, at least, not his face and as a drop of water hit the pavement, Garrett instantly understood why.

Thomas had been crying, but the tears were far and few between as new emotions took shape, ones Garrett recognized: Anger, sadness, and frustration, all mingled together under an umbrella of sheer humiliation.

Garrett couldn't help but be reminded of the days after his father's murder when like Thomas, he was too young to experience death. It was bad enough he'd lost his father at the age of nine, the only family he had left. But to be mocked, ridiculed, called an orphan, and a stray by boys with both parents still very much alive, was unbearable. Seeing Thomas on the curb was like a reflection of himself years ago, alone, and deeply hurt, like no one else understood nor cared. But like the boy now, Garrett was wrong then too.

Back in England he'd been seated on a similar version of curb that Thomas slouched on now when Nicholas' father approached him, silently at first. The man stood at six feet and four inches, towering over his childhood frame like a giant. His face was unreadable, and Garrett thought for a moment he too considered him unwanted filth, about to kick him from the street despite the friendship shared with his father. But Garrett didn't move. He didn't flinch, just like what Thomas was doing now. He didn't care then what the captain said or did. He couldn't be brought down lower than he already was, so it surprised him when a man with such a hard and calloused reputation, never mind his high rank, stooped down to kneel beside him.

Garrett remembered being so caught off-guard by the man's action that he lifted his head while angry tears streamed down his cheeks. He wanted to turn away, but Nicholas' father stopped him with a small gesture that spoke volumes. The captain put his hand on his shoulder and looked him square in the eyes, Garrett still feeling the anticipation of the man's disproval. Now, he was thankful he'd been wrong.

At first, the captain said nothing. But then, with the release of one slow breath full of assurance, the words came. "You'll be all right, son. Let's go."

The length of the words didn't matter to Garrett that day because the meaning behind them was life changing. Let's. That small combination of words made all the difference. He was not going to be an orphan and he was not going to be alone.

Garrett wasn't like Nicholas' father, but nothing was clearer to him now than what he had to do next. "Better watch out there." His tone came out light as he tried for humor. "You wouldn't be the first I've seen to catch a hoof in the head."

Thomas gave only a slight turn in his direction, enough for Garrett to see the boy's disappointment and that he'd been right. Tears, though half-dried, were still present on Thomas' cheeks. Thomas turned away again without a word.

That was expected. The day Garrett lost his own father, there was no one he wanted to talk to, and the captain had been a family friend. But he, Garrett, was a stranger to Thomas who shared allegiance with the men responsible for his father's death. Still, Garrett wasn't through. He had to try. Garrett let his ill attempt at humor pass, the small smile he offered now gone. "Who are they?"

Thomas stiffened, then turned 'round to Garrett with a look of question in his eyes before he wiped a hint of snot from his nose. It was a reaction Garrett hoped to get. "How did you know, sir?"

Truthfully, he didn't. It had only been a guess based on his own experience. "I can't say I fully did. But the way you look now, with that bitter sorrow in your eyes reminds me of a day I long to forget of my own." Observing Thomas hadn't told him to get lost, at least not just yet. Garrett took another risk by taking a seat next to him on the curb. "I know I'm probably the last person you want to talk to or be seen with, so I won't stay long. I just want you to know I've been there. I get it."

A long pause hung in the air. Garrett took the boy's silence as a charge for him to move on. He was about to get up and leave when Thomas spoke again, his lip quivering. "They're boys from camp, older ones, but not that much older." Thomas gave a scowl. "Jacob and Eddy are the oldest. They're 16, but both Amos and Gus are my same age. They're just taller so they look older." The boy's agitation rose, his nostrils flaring. "I told them I was planning to be on the field and play the fife for the general, but they say I'm just a runt and would only get in the way of the other men fighting. They say I'm so small, the soldiers would trip over me, and I should join the lobsterba…" Thomas gave Garrett an apologetic glance. "Sorry. I mean the other side instead, to give Washington the advantage." The boy tightened his grip around the stick, digging further into the dirt, his jaw set. "I told them I knew I was small, but I'm fast too."

Garrett watched as Thomas' head fell, and he guessed the boy was reliving the moment again.

"They only laughed, saying that didn't mean anything. Mice are fast, but cats still catch 'em."

Like Nicholas' father that day, Garrett too let out a heavy breath and he wondered if the captain had thought the same thing. The tale was old as time; men belittling men and for reasons that were not always clear. And these men, boys rather, were on the same team.

"Maybe I should just go home," Thomas started again. "If it weren't for the coin, I have a mind to, but Mother really needs the money."

Garrett grimaced with the reminder of the boy's father. "I'm sorry about your father, Thomas."

A trace of suspicion held in Thomas' eye. "Miss Abby tell you?"

"She did. I hope that's okay."

Thomas stared at him for a moment and then nodded. "She wouldn't have told you if she thought I'd mind it. Miss Abby is real kind." His expression fell. "I do miss him, though. I know my mother does too. Before I left, I heard her crying almost every night." He paused and looked at Garrett with a new curiosity, then asked, "Is your father still alive, sir?"

Garrett's mouth went dry, but he managed a weak smile. "My father died when I was about your age. I miss him too." Another moment of understood silence held between them, "but," Garrett continued, "I often think about what my life would've been like if he hadn't died. Not to say I'm glad he did. Far from it, but after his death and with the help of others, I was able to join the Royal Navy. I've been able to see and do things I wouldn't have otherwise been able to do because of it and that, I don't regret."

"I joined the army after my father's death, too."

240

Garrett gave the boy a good-humored smirk. "And who knows just what that army will do one day."

Thomas gave a side grin and a light inside Garrett seemed to radiate. It felt good to help bring that smile to the boy's face. Maybe he couldn't do what Nicholas' father had done for him, taking him into his family, but Thomas already had a family. He just needed a friend to know he wasn't alone. He needed someone who understood, and Garrett hoped that's how Thomas saw him now. It was then the idea came.

"Would you like to come with me? I'm on my way back to the Schreier estate. I might be able to convince Rebekah to whip up some of her molasses cookies. They're quite a treat." God knew the boy needed it and not just in something to look forward to. He was rail thin.

Thomas' eyes brightened, then dimmed again. "I better not. I need to get back to the camp, anyway. Mr. Haywood might have a message for me to deliver and he doesn't like to be kept waiting."

The mention of Haywood brought pins to Garrett's forehead, but he nodded. He had no intention of getting Thomas into any trouble and he couldn't blame the young man for not wanting to be seen with him, if that's more of where his hesitation was placed. It wouldn't exactly help his situation if someone happened to recognize the navy prisoner alongside him. Garrett shuddered to think what Jacob and his friends might say with that kind of ammunition.

"I understand." Garrett rose from the pavement, bringing Thomas to his feet too. He looked him over for any signs of tears before he'd let him venture back into camp, but found they'd dissipated. "I won't keep you. Maybe another time then."

Thomas turned towards the Commons before pausing to turn back again. "You know, for one of them, you're not too bad, sir."

The remark brought an easy smile to Garrett's face. "Garrett," he added, "and thank you, Thomas. That means a great deal coming from you."

Chapter 21

Abigail stared at the outside door of the Schreier estate, her feet like anchors not wanting to move forward and her stomach a taut bundle of nerves. She'd purposely procrastinated coming here for as long as she could. She'd returned to the hospital to check on Mr. Bates and the other patients first before approaching Haywood in hopes he might have some other chore to help detain her arrival a little longer. Who knew the time she longed for an assignment was the day he wouldn't have one?

Abigail prayed for a clear direction to take, but nothing resounded more apparent than the words of her mother back in Portsmouth.

"Your anger is being used as a hindrance to forgive someone. You have forgotten that Christ forgave you for your sins and how far gone you are without him."

The conviction in Abigail's heart only proved that those words were true. As soon as she stepped through that front door, she would have to forgive Garrett for what had happened, to let go of the past that did well to divide them. But once she did, what would Garrett Ward mean to her from now on?

"Why, Miss Abby, you're back." Rebekah greeted her with a smile that instantly melted the cold from her body. "Come on in here and out of that cold. The lady will be glad to see you."

Abigail noticed a bundle in the woman's arms.

"Say, you mind takin' these upstairs for her?" Rebekah handed her a stack of freshly pressed linens Abigail consented to carry. "I got a pot goin' and I need to get to it before it starts boiling over. We been drinking more than our fair share of tea just to keep warm today. 'Seems like even the fires can't keep themselves lit with the outside air competin' with 'em."

As Rebekah traced her steps back towards the kitchen, Abigail set her sights above. She took the stairs up to Margaret's room, though not before she glanced down the hall to notice Garrett's door was closed shut. Her heart jumped a beat, nearly leaping into Margaret's chambers and out of a conversation she wasn't quite prepared to have. Though would she ever be?

Margaret sat reclined in the bed; the sheets drawn over her legs. The white linen of her shift lay uncovered and dipped from her chest before it rose into a large mount at her abdomen. Somehow in the two weeks she'd been gone the lady's stomach had managed to increase in size like she could have the baby any day.

"Abigail, you're back." Margaret looked up from the bed to meet Abigail's gaze with a gracious grin, though with less enthusiasm as she'd been accustomed to seeing her with. "I trust that means everyone in Portsmouth is doing okay?"

Abigail offered a faint smile, thinking of her mother. "They were when I left." She sat the pile of linens she'd received from Rebekah on the edge of the bed before she proceeded over to the mantle to prod at the red embers left from a fire that was on its way to dying out. She added another piece of firewood to the charred pile and some dry kindling, poking it once more until a bright orange and yellow flame began to grow again, the heat along with it. When she finished, her attention drew back to

Margaret and the stack of bedsheets Rebekah had handed her. "Why don't we get these taken care of. Here." Abigail went over to the bed to help Margaret prop herself up to her feet before bringing her to a nearby chair.

"Before you get started with the bedding, would you mind bringing that over here?" Margaret pointed to a footstool embroidered in red with gold trimmings.

Abigail brought the small furniture piece over and the soon-to-be mother propped her feet up on it as she gave an exasperated sigh. "I knew my midsection would grow large, but honestly, I had no idea how swollen my feet could get."

It wasn't surprising. The added portion to her abdomen shortened the length of her shift to reveal a pair of fair ankles, or at least what would've been ankles if the weight of carrying a child hadn't rested on them. Abigail remembered her own mother's feet had looked just as swollen while she carried her brother Henry and again with Olivia. "That's normal with how close you're getting, but I'll let Dr. Adams know just to be on the safe side. Anything else that you're noticing?"

"You mean other than feeling like a whale flopped on my back? No, not anything worth mentioning." Margaret's face lit with a dry smile.

"I'm sure after learning a new language in just six weeks this is easy."

Margaret laughed. "I'm not so certain of that. Growing a miracle inside my body offers its own challenges and on a whole new level to them."

"Still, six weeks, that's impressive and your accent is hardly discernable."

The side of her mouth tipped. "That just means you haven't seen me mad. Rebekah says I sound like an angry dog, barking out German words she can't understand." Both women laughed. "Besides, I wasn't so impressive while we were in France. Actually, I was a bit of a laughingstock there."

"You were in France?" Abigail's stopped just as she was about to strip the sheets. How Charlotte would've swooned for another account besides their aunt's French culture. She'd always wanted to visit Paris and Abigail had to admit, seeing more of the world outside their farm did have a certain appeal to it. Though, she couldn't imagine anyone with a thought less than high of Mrs. Margarethe Schreier. The woman was not to be trifled with.

Margaret nodded. "My husband and I were for a short time on our way here to the colonies, yes. Overall, we had a pleasant stay and were welcomed wherever we went, but I could tell I wasn't fitting the French mold. Most of the women let me know it, sometimes even directly."

"How do you mean?"

"Since Alex and I had plans to settle here and not there, my agenda was focused on the life of an English woman and not so much of the French one I knew was temporary. It was during our travels I learned the language, though my German accent was much more prevalent then. It was also when I acquired many of my English garments which the French women made their disapproval frank. Some of the men too. I had to sell nearly all the antiques we owned and brought with us to get the money to purchase those garments and help us complete our journey to the colonies." She gave a gentle shrug. "There simply wasn't enough for enjoying the French fashions and culture like we would've liked, but that wasn't our end goal. Even as uncomfortable as it was at times, we had to keep that in mind."

Abigail listened, marveling at the woman's account. She thought of Margaret in English fashions amongst a place so well known for different ones. How challenging it must've been for her to go through that time in France, never mind leaving her home country and the comforts of it to learn something entirely different here in the colonies. The pain of conviction from her own situation to leave the comforts of her family's farm pinched at her side.

"I am glad you're back, though." Margaret sank further into the seat; her face composed as if the struggle she encountered was but a trifle nuisance. "Despite our newcomer, the house has been a little more on the lonesome side these past weeks. Whatever Mr. Ward is doing, he's keeping himself busy with it."

"He's not here then?"

"I don't think so. Rebekah said she saw him leave earlier, but neither one of us have seen him come back just yet."

Abigail tried not to let her relief show too much. She managed to hold back a telling breath that desperately wanted to work itself out. It looked like she wouldn't have to worry about facing Garrett today. Yet, curiosity flourished. What was Garrett up to that had him out of the house so much? She remembered his concern over the extension of his boundaries and how pleased he'd been when that had happened. Maybe that's all it was, time spent away from the house. She couldn't say she wouldn't do the same if that's where she woke up one day to find herself imprisoned. A cage was still a cage no matter how dressed up it could be.

Remembering the coverings again, Abigail went back over to the bedside. She removed the first layer before her breath stopped cold. A faint, but noticeable enough patch of crimson tarnished the bright white sheets right where Margaret had laid. Abigail looked to Margaret for answers but found no trace of knowledge to her recent discovery within the woman's face.

Willing herself to remain calm, Abigail suppressed the alarm upon her own countenance as to avoid upsetting her pregnant friend. In an even tone as she could muster, she went over towards the chair. "Margaret, let me help you up from there. I need to see something."

The confusion in the lady's expression only confirmed her ignorance to what Abigail had seen, but she took the hand again to rise. As she did, a bright, red spot that matched the one on the bed stained through the lower back portion of her shift. Blood. Again, the alarm bells rang as Abigail struggled to keep her composure.

"What is it?" Margaret's eyes caught sight of hers, searching them. When that failed, she turned them to the bed, half stumbling backwards at what she found. "Is that blood?"

"Yes, it is." The answer came stammering out as Abigail worked to remain collected. "I better get Dr. Adams." She looked at Margaret who now stood vulnerable as a pregnant woman in her undergarments could get. For the first time she saw fear strike in her eyes, but Abigail guessed it wasn't for her own life. "Don't think that way." Abigail grasped Margaret's hands into her own and gave them a firm squeeze. "We don't know anything yet. Can you feel the baby move?"

Margaret's frown weighed further down while her other hand rose to her stomach. "Not recently but I usually don't. I think the baby sleeps this time of day."

Abigail nodded, trying to appear confident and reassuring. "That's fine. Until we know further, let's keep that in mind. Stay here. I'll leave now and be back as soon as I can."

Margaret shot her a disapproving glance, somehow rallying herself again. "Oh, no you don't. There's no way I'm letting you go on foot especially with me like this, not knowing. Get Nikolai. He'll take you back in the carriage."

Abigail had no desire to argue. She hurried down the stairs and told Rebekah the quickest version she could think of over what happened before she made it outside to the barn to find Nikolai. When she got there, however, she was a little flustered to discover not only the man she searched for but also the one she'd hoped to avoid at present.

"Abigail, you're back." His tone was warm, matching the smile on his face. She could hear the pleasure in his voice and felt an unexpected pleasure of her own to sense his satisfaction in seeing her. His smile turned. "But is everything all right?"

"I don't know," she said, suddenly reminded everything was not all right. "What I mean is I hope so, but I need to get to the hospital. Dr. Adams should be there."

"Is something wrong with the lady, Miss Abby?" Nikolai had finished feeding one of the mares before he stepped up beside Garrett."

"I don't know. It could be nothing, but that's why I need the carriage. I think Dr. Adams needs to see her. Will it take long to get it ready?"

"Not too long." Nikolai scratched some gray whiskers on his chin. "I just need to bridle the horses and hitch it. Shouldn't take but a few minutes and it'd still be faster than walkin'."

"Why don't I take you on horseback? That'll be even faster."

Abigail shook her head, her eyes meeting Garrett's fleetingly. "Because I need a way to get the doctor back here and last time I checked, a horse's back isn't built for three."

Garrett frowned. "We could take Greta for Dr. Adams. Even with another horse in toe, it would still be faster than the carriage."

"Maybe, but I'm not sure how Dr. Adams is on a horse, and I don't want to waste time finding out he can't reign one." In truth, the thought of finding herself so close in proximity to Garrett Ward on the back of a horse left Abigail's stomach a little uneasy and not in the sick kind of way. She had to keep focused.

Garrett frowned again, letting her know he didn't agree. "Fine. Well, at least let me help. I'll get Athala while Nikolai gets Greta ready."

***

"I thought by helping, you just meant you would bridle the horses." At Abigail's surprise and chagrin, Garrett stepped into the carriage after her, taking a seat directly across from her own. He gave her a roguish smile; one she was beginning to like the more she saw him.

"I did, at first anyway. Then, I thought it might be a chance to talk."

"For a quick conversation, I hope. The Vassall estate is only a mile and we're in a hurry remember?"

His grin faded into a side smile at her jest. "A little time is still better than nothing. Besides, I wanted to see how you were doing and if that look I saw in the barn earlier was meant only for Mrs. Schreier or something more too. How was your trip to your aunt's?"

The concern in his voice touched her heart at the unspoken question regarding her mother. "Right now, I think she's okay." Abigail averted her eyes out the window. She needed a minute to get over the image of her mother in her aunt's bed. When the moment became too long, she returned her gaze to Garrett again. "It's just more of an unknown of whether she's going to get better or not."

His expression softened further. "I'm sorry to hear that. I'm also a little surprised you're back, then."

"She's actually the reason I'm back."

"Oh?"

"She thinks there's more for me to do here, that I'm needed. Apparently, my brother thinks so too."

He leaned back in the carriage seat. "You have a brother here?"

"Yes, his name is Abraham." She gave him a knowing smile. "You've met him actually."

Garrett scrunched his brow as if trying to recall before the thick, dark hair above his eyes arched again showing her the recognition was clear enough. "Oh, that brother."

Despite herself, she laughed.

"Well, it seems this time your brother and I agree, along with your mother. You're still needed here and I'm glad you're back. I've missed you, Abigail."

"I've missed you too." The words came out easily but surprised her not only because she'd said them but that she meant them too. She thought of her mother's words again and what she still needed to do. "Garrett, there's something I need to say."

Concern lined his face and replaced the smile he wore just seconds ago. "So, there is something more? Is the rest of your family all right?"

"No, nothing like that. It's just something I need to tell you to, to sort of clear the air between us."

His black brow arched high again. "Clear the air?"

"So to speak, yes." She took a breath in. She wasn't even to the hard part, but the start was not off to a good one. "I wanted to tell you that I'm sorry."

He blinked. "You're sorry?"

"Yes, I am. I'm sure you're well aware I haven't exactly treated you with kindness. I've been angry from what happened back in October and for whatever reason, I needed to blame you for it."

"You mean the attack." A darkness overshadowed his eyes. "Abigail, I was there. As far as you know, I was the one that gave the order for the men to fire on your town."

She shook her head. "I don't think you did, but even if that's true, you only followed orders. It's not fair for me to hold that against you. I'm sorry I have for this long."

He leaned back into his seat again, seeming to consider her for a moment—a long moment.

She wanted to shift in her own, the discomfort mounting, but managed to keep still.

Finally, he spoke, his eyes bright. "Well, that's certainly surprising. I helped attack your town, and you're the one apologizing to me. I can't say that's happened to me before. Is that something you picked up in Portsmouth on your visit?"

"From my mother, actually." She wanted to say from Jesus, remembering the conversation with her mother, but something told her Garrett might not be ready to hear that just yet.

"Your mother sounds like a wise woman, and someone I'd like to meet."

Abigail managed a smile, recalling again her mother's frail state. "Thanks. She is. And she'd probably like you too."

When they pulled up to the Vassall house, Garrett left the carriage first, helping her on her own descent. Agreeing he'd wait while she went in for Dr. Adams, Abigail bounded up the front steps. As she did, she couldn't help to notice the pain in her chest she'd been feeling over the loss of her home was a little more diminished, and the weight of the burden it carried a little lighter.

Chapter 22

Abigail awoke. The sweet smell of salted bacon tantalized her nostrils. She breathed in again the fragrant aroma of the cooked meat, trying to remember the last time she'd had it. Meat of any kind had already become sparse at the camp with rations so limited that the smell of it now was a luxury. She quickly dressed, securing her stays, pockets and petticoat before tying her apron and following the scent down the staircase.

"Well, good mornin', Abby." It was Rebekah who greeted her with a warm smile and without need of further inspection, the very woman responsible for the delicious perfume that caused her mouth to water. Abigail sucked in a deep breath again and closed her eyes, letting Rebekah know she enjoyed her skill in the kitchen.

"Oh, Rebekah, it smells delicious in here! Where did you learn to cook like that?"

The woman grinned. "From my mother, of course. Didn't your own teach you the same?"

Abigail closed her eyes again, shaking her head. Her own mother had taught her to cook, but as good as those meals were and as thorough a teacher she'd been, something about Rebekah's cooking was just far better.

"She did," Abigail confirmed, "but not like that." She pointed to the smoked bacon warming over the stove and the perfectly buttered cornbread cooking in the cast iron.

Rebekah laughed. "As I said, Miss Abby, the cornbread I learned from my mama, but the bacon…well, that's a little trick I learned from my uncle while still workin' for a family in Georgia. He was one of the men in charge of the family's smokehouse and could always get the best flavor." She tested the cornbread to make sure it was done before she removed it from the stove. "The wood is the trick," she said, turning back. "Different woods give different flavors. This one's hickory, strong and sweet. Help youself."

Already too tempted not to, Abigail grabbed two pieces of bacon for herself and a piece of cornbread. The breakfast was completely satisfying.

"Rebekah, do you think there'd be enough if I took a few more pieces, for later I mean?"

"Oh sure. 'Should have plenty. The lady doesn't seem to care for the meat these days, though I take that's more due to the baby than my cookin' and there's still more than enough for Mr. Ward if he chooses to have it this mornin'."

With the woman's blessing, Abigail laid aside the extra pieces of bacon she would later distribute to Thomas, certain the boy wouldn't mind the surprise.

It was just yesterday when she and Garrett went for Dr. Adams on Margaret's behalf. To everyone's relief, as far as the doctor could tell, both mother and baby were fine. But the remainder of the pregnancy was to be met with caution. As such, Dr. Adams advised Margaret to bedrest until the baby arrived. The mother, despite Rebekah already taking great care, requested Abigail be "readily available" in the chance anything might happen again.

Per the doctor's consent and Haywood's reluctant approval, it was quickly decided Abigail would stay at the Schreier residence at least until Baby Schreier was born.

Abigail couldn't say she altogether disliked the change. Her new quarters were a far cry from the crowded tent she shared back at the Commons and her walk to the hospital was closer from Margaret's house than from the campus. Yet, she couldn't help but think of Mrs. Bates and all the others in camp. No doubt they too longed for the comfort of a soft bed to the cold ground or cot and the satisfying taste of bacon on their tongue instead of the usual hardtack bread and dry beans. She thanked God silently for the sweet and salty provision.

There was however, one thing that made her recent move prove a little more difficult. Haywood might have agreed she'd stay to keep a closer eye on Margaret, but he made it clear Abigail's duties to the camp, as far as her workload was concerned, remained intact. At least when she was sleeping in the commons, she was on site to take care of her responsibilities. Now, she'd lose time just trying to get back to the camp to start them.

She watched as Rebekah pulled an iron kettle from near the fireplace and poured the hot, dark liquid into a cup before adding a small amount of cream to it.

"Would you like a cup of coffee, Miss Abby? I introduced the stuff to Margaret in Pennsylvania, and I'd never seen anyone take to it like she did. She likes hers with a bit of Lisbon sugar for some sweetness. I can add it for you too if you like."

Abigail had certainly had coffee before. It was easily obtainable prior to, but especially after, the Boston Tea Party. Following the tax put on English tea, the event in Boston's harbor people were still talking about from two years ago, and her brother's zeal for the cause, her family had no choice but to partake of an alternative beverage even if it wasn't her favorite.

"No, thank you," she politely declined, "but that does remind me of a question I have, if you don't mind me asking."

"A question you must think I can answer. Sure, Miss Abby, go on."

"You mentioned earlier you lived in Georgia. How did you end up in Pennsylvania and come across the Schreier's?" Rebekah took a sip of coffee before placing the mug slowly and gently on a small table. The look Abigail read on the woman's face made her sorry she'd asked the question.

"That's a part of my story I wish I could erase sometimes, but I suppose everybody's story has a little ugly in it. Thankfully, mine has a little good to go in too." She gave a gentle smile before going on. "My family, that is my mother and father, brothers and sisters and my uncle I already mentioned, were bought by a wealthy cotton owner in Georgia. That was uncommon seein' most of the families were torn from each other and sold separately. I was in the fields for six years before workin' in the main house when my mother went home to be with Jesus. I stayed workin' there for another stretch of time, enough to see the man's children grown and start families of their own and to see my father and uncle move on to the next life. One day the man came to me in my room to say it was time to go before takin' me to board a ship headed for Pennsylvania. When I asked why, that I'd done everythin' to the best of my God-given ability for as long as I could remember, he told me it was 'cause I was getting too old for the head lady of the house."

Rebekah closed her eyes and pulled in a long breath like she was reliving an all too painful memory.

"They unloaded us in Pennsylvania and auctioned us off like cattle. I can still feel the grip of those iron shackles pushin' their way into my wrists while onlookers placed bids on us, stared, or passed by like our own lives only amounted to the cost someone'd pay for us. That was the day I met Margaret and also when the ugly to my story turned into a little good. For whatever reason, when it came to my turn for biddin', Margaret won the bid." Rebekah shook her head. "I spoke later to her about it, and she admitted she'd was just walkin' by but was caught by the spectacle, amazed in the wrong kind of way to see an auction' of human souls treated worse than the animals she knew they kept in their barns. After she paid the auctioneer, she took me aside from the crowd and told me I could go live my own life before handin' me the same amount of money she'd bought me with. I almost did 'til it dawned on me I hadn't lived my own life in so long I forgot how, not to mention I was scared someone would see me without a master and just auction me off again. I told her I'd like to stay until I felt more ready to go and had a plan in mind for it. I also figured a woman who paid for my life just to let me go to live it, couldn't be all that bad."

Rebekah gave a long, drawn-out sigh. "That time for me to leave never came, though. My life out there holds no guarantees, but while I stay part of the Schreier household, I know I'm safe and free. Not to mention, I kind of like the lady. We've developed a sort of kinship over the years, much different than the forced one I had to manage with my owner's wife back in Georgia."

"What about the rest of your family: your brothers and sisters? Don't you wonder about them?"

"My heart would be stone-cold if I didn't. I do think about goin' back to see them, but then I don't know what I would do when I'd get there. The day I was shipped off, I didn't get a chance to say goodbye. I don't even know if they're still there or if they were sold too. We've even tried since I told Margaret about them. She's been writin' to my former master on my behalf, but we haven't heard a word. That's been a little over two years now."

Abigail's words felt empty. What could she say to this woman who had lived under such oppression? Yet, she wanted to say something. "I'm sorry, Rebekah. That must be really hard not knowing."

"It is, but I keep prayin' they're all right and if I don't see them again in this life, I'll see them in Heaven."

Rebekah's eye was caught by something out the kitchen window. Abigail followed her gaze, revealing the dark figure of Nikolai carrying a shovel on the back of his shoulder blade and headed to the barn. A piece of straw hung from the corner of his mouth as he whistled a tune Abigail didn't recognize. He didn't appear to notice them eyeing him, but Abigail could tell by the interest in Rebekah's stare out the window there was more between them than just her passing glance.

"And what about you and Nikolai?"

Rebekah shot her eyes back at Abigail, a fine, arched brow lifted. "What about me and Nikolai?"

Abigail's heart began to pound. After the account she'd just heard from Rebekah of which she'd been so vulnerable about, she wondered if her further curiosity had taken it too far. She wanted to back step, but felt it was too late.

"I just wondered if there was something more between you two than friends."

The corners of Rebekah's lips turned upwards into a sly smile that allowed Abigail's heart to slow down.

"As much as there is between you and Mr. Ward."

"I'm not sure what you mean."

"You don't mean to tell me you can't see the man has eyes for you?" She gave Abigail a doubtful look then shook her head and laughed. "I've seen him in the market, Miss Abby, those gentlewomen gawking at him, but he doesn't seem to notice them. I've seen him too here with you and trust me when I say you have the man's *full* attention."

"Good morning, Rebekah, Abigail." The smooth, rich voice and familiar scent of sea salt and sage sent an icy jolt up Abigail's spine despite the ongoing fire now arranged with an assortment of pots and pans in the flames Rebekah used for cooking.

Rebekah beamed, sharing a knowing glance with Abigail, who'd managed to calm down her fluster of nerves upon his arrival. "Good mornin', Mr. Ward. Cup of coffee?" Garrett accepted Rebekah's offer, though refused the cream and sugar.

"You're up early." He looked to Abigail. "I hope your first night went well."

"I was more than comfortable, thank you."

Abigail couldn't blame the soft, warm bed heated by the bedpan Rebekah suggested she try or the delicate, smooth covers she sunk into beneath the canopy for her interrupted slumber. Thoughts swirled around her mind haphazardly. One minute she thought about her mother along with their conversation, next it went to her responsibilities at camp to keep Haywood at bay, then to her work with the hospital and the smallpox cases that only seemed to grow in number. Finally, it jumped to Abraham and her continued ignorance as to what he was doing for the army. Put the fact her new room was just footsteps down the hall from the man who somehow seemed to drive her pulse up a notch each time she saw him, and the combination made for one restless night.

"Anythin' new for today, Mr. Ward?" Rebekah casually slid a full plate in front of him. His eyes showed a hearty appreciation for the meal along with an expectation for it.

Abigail eyed him with accusation. "And just how long has Rebekah cooked for you?"

Garrett might have answered if Abigail would've let him, but that rogue-like grin was more than telling.

Her own eyes shot wide. "Garrett Ward! You mean to tell me I've been bringing your meals for naught? That wasn't part of the agreement for you to stay here. You can't just eat from Mrs. Schreier's pantry and..."

"S'alright, Miss Abby." Rebekah came to his rescue. "Don't get youself all worked up for somethin' that's really nothin' at all. The lady knows of it and is glad to partake 'specially as much as Mr. Ward has been helpin' out since Mr. Schreier's absence. Our fire stays nice and toasty because of Mr. Ward here, and Nikolai doesn't mind the extra hand since he likes to be with the horses." Rebekah put her hands to her hips, a twinkle in her eye. "Besides, ma'am, you can't blame the man for takin' a piece of steak over a bowl of porridge or whatever you all are servin' those men out there."

Abigail relented. She really couldn't blame Garrett for that.

Rebekah gave her a pointed look that only did further to silence her while her conversation aimed back over to Garrett.

"Now, as I was sayin', what are you up to today, Mr. Ward?"

Garrett snuck Abigail a truce-like expression, but she could only manage to bite her tongue. His attention went back to Rebekah and her question.

"I thought I might go into town after seeing if Nikolai needs some help out back."

"Another trip into town, sir? Are you getting youself set for another coat down at Mr. Hart's place again?"

It was then Abigail noticed Garrett wasn't wearing his navy-blue uniform or the clothes that belonged to Mr. Schreier. A different coat completely adorned his shoulders with a new set of breeches to compliment it. Her mind raced back to the day before in the carriage on the way to retrieve Dr. Adams. He'd had it on then too, but she'd been so preoccupied between Margaret and her apology, she'd missed the change entirely.

She'd always considered him handsome in his uniform, even while she'd been angry, but something about the less decorated jacket, even in its beautiful olive green against his dark hair was striking. Not just because it was tailored perfectly for him, but that it also helped her see more of Garrett Ward and less of Lieutenant Ward.

"No, just seeing if I can explore some more of the area and talk to some people." Garrett continued, taking a hearty bite of bacon.

"So, you've managed to make some friends in town after all? Glad to hear it." Rebekah smiled as she poured another cup of coffee and set it on a tray with a readied plate. "I'm going to take this up to the lady's room. She should be stirrin' right about now, or soon."

Once she left, Garrett turned his attention back on Abigail.

"What about you?" He gave a kind-hearted smile full of interest that caused her irritation from earlier to fade. "Any big plans for today?"

A breath drew upwards from her lips, blowing a strand of hair away from her face. "Just the usual. I thought I'd start checking in with Margaret, then go to the hospital to see how Mr. Bates and the rest of the patients are doing. Then, I'll head towards the campground."

"Sounds like a big day to me." He took a bite of cornbread along with another piece of bacon before washing it down with a sip of coffee.

"And you? What is it that you're doing in town if it's not getting another coat and set of breeches?"

"Actually, I'm looking for an alternate route to get back to Boston where I'm hoping I won't run into any of your rebel friends along the way."

Abigail blinked and wondered if she heard rightly. "Well, I didn't expect that."

Garrett laughed, the sound of it both smooth and inviting. "What did you expect?"

"I don't know. I thought you might say you were just walking around, getting some space away from the house in case you felt too closed in."

"Closed in?" He shook his head. "I'm used to having six feet of a square room on the ship, remember? What would make you think that?"

The sting of embarrassment filled her cheeks. Maybe she couldn't read this man as easily as she thought. She recalled Rebekah's comment from earlier this morning of Garrett's attention towards her. Now, she wanted anything but, ready to get this conversation over with as soon as possible.

"I just thought you might feel a certain confinement to the place, since you're still a prisoner." Her eyes searched his and looked for any sign of agreement. Though she saw a gentleness about them, she found nothing that told her she was even close.

"No, but I can see what you mean, and I did feel that way at the beginning even if I don't now."

She gave him a weak smile, appreciating his soft attempt to rescue her from her own mistake.

"I see, well, clearly I was wrong. Still Garrett," she eyed him, her embarrassment quickly fading, "I'm surprised you would tell me something like that."

"Why not?"

"Well, for one very obvious reason that it seems like you've forgotten, I'm part of the army you're still a prisoner of."

He shrugged, taking a final sip of coffee before setting the empty mug aside.

"I'm not a man who likes to beat around the bush. I like to be honest, especially with you."

"Trusting apparently, too."

He laughed. "Apparently."

She shook her head, still not entirely over the fact he was so transparent about his intentions to escape. "Part of me thought things in town might be a little bit more exciting for you too, even if it's nothing compared to that of the sea life you're used to. I'm sure a small town like Cambridge is quite mundane compared to the possibilities of an ocean and a means that can take you anywhere." Her words echoed that of Charlotte's back on the farm on the morning of the attack.

"I have my mundane moments too."

"Really?"

"Really. More often than not there's nothing but calm water, miles upon miles of it with no ship or land in sight. Even as it hits against the hull and the motion of the vessel feels like you're being carried forward, you still sometimes doubt if you are with nothing behind you to measure the distance you have gone and nothing in front of you for the distance that remains ahead. It's all pretty routine until out of nowhere and often without warning, a swell hits to leave you and everyone else on board scattered. No matter how much you've done the exercise you're wondering if this is the time the ship doesn't make it through."

He took a breath and exhaled it slowly. "But then, when you do manage to pull from it, to finally step foot on dry land again, you're able to discover that land and those people. You can appreciate the similarities and even more," he caught her eye, his smile resurfacing again, "the differences between you." He paused, firming his lips before beginning again. "Do you remember the story I told you, when Nicholas was sick and the tribe helped him?"

She nodded, thinking back to when Mr. Bates was first ill. "Yes, the sumac. How could I forget?"

A kind smile touched his lips. "Right. Well, those people taught us something new and different, it may have saved my friend's life."

"And something you were able to share with me to help others. We got enough that day not only for Mr. Bates but the other patients too." She could see the satisfaction in his expression filter through.

"It's one of my favorite parts other than the time I'm gone on the water. The more I get to see and know, the more I begin to grasp there's still so much I don't know."

She laughed. "You don't seem discouraged by that."

He shrugged. "No. I think I'm more amazed by it than anything. There's always more to learn."

She couldn't disagree with that. Between the army camp, her work with Dr. Adams and here at the estate, every day was a new area of discovery. But encountering a foreign land when the safety net of Falmouth held secure, seemed both appealing and downright unnerving at the same time.

"It's hard for me to imagine. I've never been anywhere outside the colonies and not even all the provinces."

"Well, you never know. You might just find yourself on a ship one day."

"I'm not so sure, Garrett." She gave him a doubtful look, but could tell he didn't buy it.

All humor faded in his expression. "Did you ever think you'd join the army or work alongside a physician to treat a part of it undergoing a crucial illness?" He locked eyes with hers and she knew she was in trouble. "Or how about a friendly conversation with a man who watched your town get blown up from the safety of the ship that fired upon it? I'm just saying, Abigail, you never know where things might lead. Trust me, I know."

He did, didn't he? She doubted he'd thought about ending up here, captive, with only a handful of miles from the freedom of his own comrades back in Boston. Yet, it was just far enough from touching the city's borders.

"I know," she said softly. "Thanks for the advice." The bright, orange rays of the sun had started to fade into their golden yellow as it ascended higher in the sky. The morning had grown later than she intended. Abigail quickly rose from the table. "I better go see how Margaret's doing this morning." She was about to excuse herself when the troubled expression on Garrett's face made her reconsider.

***

Garrett had been weighing his options back and forth even as she stood up to go, but her look of consternation told him she could sense something was on his mind. Now, there was no turning back. He told her he wanted to be honest with her, and he meant it. He just wasn't sure how much his honesty would cost him this time.

He motioned for her to take a seat again, already regretting what he was about to say. She had enough to worry about. Yet, to hide it didn't seem right either. When she declined his gesture, he took a deep breath before he forced the air out and prayed if there was a God, He'd help him find the words.

"I know you need to get started with things for the day, but there's something I do need to tell you. I planned to tell you yesterday when you came by the barn, but that was before the news about Mrs. Schreier. As I mentioned before, I like to be honest with you." He swallowed, not sure if there was a better way to put his next words together. Instead, he just them flow freely. "I ran into Cleophes Lockhart while you were in Portsmouth. I know he's in town. He's also one of the reasons I go to town. I'm trying to find him or get any leads as to how I can."

She pressed her lips together, before letting out a sigh. "I'm sorry I told you he was my uncle. I'm sure if you've found out his real name then you know he's not." Her jaw tightened again. "But any leads? Why is he so important to you? He's just a kind man, working to move on with his life."

A sarcastic chuckle from his own mouth took Garrett by surprise, but it was too late to back step. "I'm sure he *is* trying to move on, but he has to be held accountable for what he's done. I wanted you to know when I'm no longer a prisoner of war, I plan to arrest him and bring him in."

Abigail's eyes widened, then narrowed. "Garrett, the man has barely done anything deserving of a crime. Surely, you can't convict him of going through unclaimed materials left from the bombing."

"I'm not talking about his theft in Falmouth, Abigail. The man is guilty of some things I can see you're clearly unaware of. He needs to be brought to justice."

A feminine eyebrow peaked with objection. "I have a hard time believing he's capable of anything vile beyond that. He can hardly get around on his own and his means are limited. You saw him yourself that day. Tell me otherwise, Garrett," she demanded, those green eyes daring him to do so.

"So, he hasn't told you how he acquired that limp? I must say that sounds rather convenient. And as for means, something tells me he's able to get by." He could hear his tone was saturated with sarcasm, but he didn't care. Maybe this wasn't going the way he hoped but she needed to understand. If he had to be the one to make her, so be it. "Please, Abigail, allow me to clear any misconceptions you have of the man by telling you of his crimes. Perhaps then you will feel less of a burden to keep his whereabouts hidden so I can bring him to justice."

She hesitated, but soon recovered.

"No." she said decidedly.

Garrett straightened in disbelief. Why protect him?

"Even if it was murder?" He saw her flinch, but was disappointed, though not entirely when she held her ground. She shook her head.

"I don't care what he did, then. It doesn't matter now."

"I'm not so sure His Majesty would agree with you," he scoffed.

"I'm not so sure you agree with me, but I don't care. I never met the Cleophes you speak of. I only know of the man who warned my family to flee Falmouth long enough before..." She hesitated again and looked into his eyes with a pain he recognized, a wound that might have been healing until he'd reopened again.

He knew what her next words would be as the weight wrenched itself into his own heart. The anger he felt climbing, faltered, his voice along with it. "We attacked."

She didn't say anything, but he could read the confirmation in those grief-stricken green eyes. So that was it. He, an officer of the most respected naval fleet in the world, was responsible for her town's downfall while this criminal had saved her in the midst of it. Garrett leaned back; the blow she hadn't intended to give hit harder than the day he'd received his black eye.

"I see. I understand better what the man means to you now, but I still have a duty to bring him before the king." He tried to let the words come out gently, though still firm to let her know his intention was unwavering. "I have a strong feeling you know where he is, but I won't ask that of you. You should know, though, it's only a matter of time before I do find him, Abigail."

She met his gaze again, her own stare as steadfast as his own. Her silence told him more of what she thought than if she spoke it outright. Without another word, he watched her go, her silence only confirming what he feared. They may have taken a few steps forward towards reconciliation these past weeks, but this recent news just sent them back twenty more.

Chapter 23

"Okay Mr. Davis, you're clear to go." Abigail finished her last assessment of Mr. Davis's body. The last scab had finally fallen off.

"Thank you, Miss Abigail. I never thought I'd say this, but I look forward to my pallet back at the camp. Don't get me wrong, miss. I'm thankful to be under you and the doctor's care, but I'll certainly be happy to find myself resuming life again."

Abigail smiled. "Don't worry about that. Dr. Adams and I don't take your desire to move on from here personally. In fact, we're glad to see you leave in good health."

She took a quick glance around the rest of the room and wilted slightly. Even between the Vassall estate and the house next door, the bedding had become scarce. Every makeshift bed stuffed with hay they'd managed to put together possessed a soul upon it. Anymore who came into the door might have to find a place somewhere on the floor. No one could deny that despite their efforts to keep the disease contained, it still spread with a vengeance.

At least her last visit to the apothecary's was promising with the supplies somewhat recovered. It was enough to take care of their need for the time being, though how much longer that would last at the rate men and women came in with complaints of symptoms, Abigail wasn't optimistic. Twenty-one days. The number of days Dr. Adams recorded in a small journal he carried in his medical bag. If these patients remained contagious for that long, she was certain even with the apothecary's new stock of supplies, it wouldn't last long enough.

Dr. Adams entered through the front door and ran into Mr. Davis who was on his way out. The two seemed to chat for a brief moment, both giving a friendly nod before they parted ways.

"How is Mr. Walker doing?" Abigail worked to divert her concern over the disease they fought in hopes to find a better outcome to an entirely different case. "I know you said he complained about some pain in his mouth."

"Oh, he's fine now. I just gave the guilty tooth a good yank and applied a cold compress after. He seemed in much better spirits when I left compared to when I first arrived." Dr. Adams placed his medical bag and bicorn hat on the desk in his office then came up beside her. "It looks like our first smallpox patient has recovered, though we still have plenty of others to keep us busy for a time yet." His eyes seemed to circle the room while his mouth tipped downward. "I hoped keeping our first cases away from the camp might've done better to slow the spread, but I'm afraid it hasn't proved effective enough. Mr. Davis was lucky, but as you know, not everyone is, especially as we run out of resources for them. I only hope if the general finds himself in the same predicament again, he'll be more likely to consider my recommendation with more willingness."

"Your recommendation, sir?"

Dr. Adams nodded. "Inoculation, that is, cutting into the skin to expose a small amount of the illness will serve to build up better immunity to it. The sickness would still take place, but it's not as severe as what we're seeing here."

Abigail signaled she understood then shuddered. It wasn't the method Dr. Adams described that made her body weak, but the ones they'd already lost—those who hadn't lasted a week past the fever. She couldn't even mourn their deaths as new patients came in to replace the beds they once occupied. The cold under her skin only dropped further as she thought of Washington having not only this one, but another outbreak on his hands, all the while the British stood on his heels in Boston. Talk about vulnerable.

"I wouldn't want to be in his shoes. That seems like a hard decision to make, purposely leaving so many of the men sick while the British are at our doorstep. Just think what would happen if word got out."

"I'm glad I don't have to." Dr. Adams straightened with jaw tightened. "There, now. General Washington has his responsibilities, while we have ours and right now, that's just focusing on the current disease." He looked to her with friendly concern. "How is your friend, Mr. Bates getting along with it?"

"He's managed all right under the circumstances. The bumps have started and are growing in number. He's very uncomfortable, but Mrs. Bates comes in often for his care, including his meals and she applies the ointment and cold compresses. I haven't done much for him on my own accord except provide the laudanum he may need from time to time."

"That's good. With the number of men and women coming in, one less person to take care of will help a great deal." His face fell. "Though, we may need to come up with another plan soon. We could use another hand here if things don't calm down and more beds if we can make room."

"I think we'll have room, but I'll check with Mr. Haywood about the bedding. As for help," Abigail sighed in foreseen disappointment, "I doubt he'll suggest a solution. With some of the camp followers sick here, there's fewer hands available to help out in the commons."

Dr. Adams put his hand to his chin and nodded. "Yes, I can understand that might be a problem. I'll try to speak with him on the issue, but even so I'm not so sure he'll budge given his own decline in resources. If that's the case, we'll have to make do and come up with another plan, but let's save that for a different day--one that doesn't involve the celebration of our Savior and the new year." He glanced towards the mantel at a small clock embellished in gold detail. "For now, isn't there somewhere you need to be soon?"

She mirrored his gesture, following his gaze. The hour and minute hands confirmed his inquisition. She'd need to get back to the Schreier estate soon if she was going to get ready in time for the service that evening. Everyone was talking about it, that is, everyone who didn't have smallpox in mind or body to deal with: the reopening of Christ's Church. The excitement she felt running through her veins in anticipation of tonight dimmed at the amount of people who'd be missing it, both gone from this life or sick in the hospital.

Abigail turned back to Dr. Adams. "Yes, but are you sure? I've checked in with most everyone here and given the appropriate medicines required, but I haven't made it to the other house yet."

"That'll be fine. I'll finish up there before making my own way to the service. Other than what you mentioned there's not much else I can do for them as they go through the process. I should have enough time between now and when the service begins to finish what I need to." He looked at her pointedly. His expression reminded her more of her father's gentle sternness than the times she'd found herself across from Officer Haywood. "You on the other hand better get on if you're going to help a woman prescribed bedrest get ready and loaded in time."

Her lips turned upwards in a smile. "Thank you for that, by the way, your approval of it."

"I never said I approved. It was more like I didn't want to get in the way of that woman and her determination to be in the house of God again. The way I see it, she should be in as good hands as any with the Lord present. Still, better get her back home soon after the service for caution's sake."

Upon giving her word she would, Abigail left the hospital to make the short walk back to the Schreier estate. The wind bit at her ears as she pulled her cloak hood over them. Her ears thanked her, the sharp sting lessening while her hands began to take over the protest, pain from the cold running over her fingers. She put them into her apron pockets but gained little relief. How she'd managed to forget to pack her wool mitts on the onset of winter she wanted to scold herself for. Now, as it was, her hands did it for her, protesting bitterly at her forgetfulness.

Despite her numbing fingers, she pulled out the brooch she'd acquired back from the goldsmith, both pin and clasp now fixed. The craftsman had even polished the piece of jewelry to reveal its true beauty. She hadn't spoken to Garrett for almost a full week, not since he told her about his plans for Cleo once Garrett's freedom was returned to him. But it hadn't been any challenge to avoid him, as Abigail found herself constantly drawn now more between Mrs. Schreier's health and the smallpox patients.

Yet, she'd needed the time. There was nothing good to say that day in the kitchen and so she didn't. Now, she reflected on what Cleophes had done for her and for the rest of her family. The pain she thought she'd started saying goodbye to reared its ugly head again and gave caution. She hadn't completely let go of the past.

Even as the days passed, an odd kind of thought surfaced. She actually missed Garrett, even uplifted at the prospect she'd see him tonight at the service. Part of her wondered if the alignment of her heart and the very occasions they were celebrating were more than just coincidence. The truth spoke into it warm and full of grace. God had given the gift of forgiveness, starting with the birth of a Baby in Bethlehem. Now, it was her turn to follow His example to forgive. She gave the brooch one last appreciative look before returning it to her apron, clutching her arms and cloak around her for the last few steps up the Schreier walkway.

It didn't surprise her to find Garrett in the parlor by himself while Rebekah and Margaret were sure to be upstairs and getting ready. The front door thudded on her entry and grabbed his attention. He offered a conciliatory smile, one without any hint as to whether he felt some anger of his own over their past disagreement, he and stood up as she entered. Abigail picked the chaise lounge he occupied before Garrett took his seat again, though allowing a comfortable space between them. She could see by the slightest curve of his mouth that he was pleased by her decision.

"Merry Christmas, Abigail." The kindness in his tone moved her and she felt further convinced this was the time to let it all go.

"Merry Christmas, Garrett, and I suppose I should say Happy New Year too." She smiled and he mirrored one back. "About our last conversation…"

He shook his head gently, stopping her. "I don't want to talk about that right now. Not that I mean we shouldn't, just not tonight."

Abigail nodded. She had another way she could make amends. "All right, well, I have something for you." She pulled out the brooch from her pocket and handed it to him. "I'm sorry it's not wrapped."

He leaned over it; his eyes transfixed on the piece of jewelry. "I thought I'd lost it. Thank you, Abigail. This means more to me than you know."

"I found it the day you arrived in Cambridge. The clasp was broken, but it's repaired now. I hope you don't mind, especially since it's taken this long for me to get it back to you. It should be good as new."

He turned it over in his hand looking at it twice over before his eyes went to hers again and grinned. "I actually have something for you too. Hold on just a minute."

Garrett rose from the chaise and went into the library before he returned, closing the distance between them on the lounge. He produced a box wrapped neatly in newspaper and tied with a piece of twine.

Abigail opened it to reveal a chocolate colored, leather-bound notebook full of blank, white pages. It was small enough to keep in her personal satchel.

"I've seen some of the doctors on board with journals like these. They use them to take notes on the cases they've seen. I thought maybe with your work in the hospital and whatever comes your way after Cambridge, you could use it to do the same." He gave her a smirk. "Either that or record all the accounts of the adventures you'll be having across the ocean."

She returned his suggestion with a sideways glance, then smiled as her fingers grazed with admiration over the woven detail on the cover of her gift. "Thank you, Garrett. This means so much to me. It's really perfect."

What seemed like a moment later, Abigail flinched by yet another gift at the entryway of the parlor. The new figure caught her eye. "Thomas?"

The blonde boy, now starting to resemble less of one, stood in a new waistcoat and clean breeches.

He gave her a bashful grin. "Yes, Miss Abby, it's me. Nikolai told me I could come in the back. I'm all ready for the service this evening."

"I can see you are. You look very handsome." Abigail looked back at Garrett, appealing to him for answers.

He laughed. "Thomas is joining us tonight for the service and the dinner party afterwards."

Her eyes returned to Thomas' new wardrobe. Every pence Thomas made from the army, which currently was naught, went back home to his mother. So, who'd made the generous contribution? Abigail eyed Garrett again, and he understood.

"Don't look at me, I just offered the invitation." He feigned an agitated sigh. "One that was only accepted after I mentioned you'd be in

273

attendance too. The credit goes all to Mrs. Schreier for the rest. If you want to scold someone for benevolence, take your complaints to her."

"Miss Abby, I don't see why I have to wear this while you're going in that." Thomas fidgeted the buttons of his waistcoat. The comment made Abigail suddenly attentive of her own wardrobe and the fact she still needed to get ready before helping Rebekah with Mrs. Schreier.

"He's right. We'll be leaving here in about twenty minutes to get to the church, and I doubt Mrs. Schreier will be happy to see you've chosen your work clothes for the service. You better get ready too."

Finding herself in full agreement with Garrett's warning, Abigail made haste, bounding straight up the stairs.

***

It was about an hour later when Garrett found himself in one of the back pews of Christ Church. Abigail sat comfortably next to him despite the occasional glances in their direction. He wondered if word was getting out about his identity. Or, maybe their stares had more to do with Mrs. Schreier, one of the few, if only, loyalists besides himself attending a service mostly comprised of rebel citizens. For the sake of Abigail and Thomas who sat just on the other side of her, he hoped not.

"Do you see that couple over there?" Abigail pointed past Mrs. Schreier and Rebekah in the pew in front of them to the very first, center row of the church.

All he could see was the back of a man's head, hair powdered and tied back, next to a woman whose hair was a faded brown but equally fashioned as the man beside her. What did take Garrett's notice, however, was the man's tall frame and broad shoulders underneath a long, but pleasant face comprised of a straight nose and determined chin. They were characteristics he'd heard in mention before of the man who'd be leading the rebel army.

"It's General Washington and his wife, Martha," Abigail whispered.

"I've never seen her in town before. She must be here to celebrate the occasions."

Garrett considered the two, companionable with each other while each was drawn to different conversations as others approached them from both sides. Occasionally, he noticed an affectionate glance from George towards Martha who offered the same in return. The picture made him acutely aware of one thing: that he wanted that, the bond they shared, but with Abigail as his own. He imagined what life might be like with her by his side for more than just a fleeting moment in a church service.

Before Garrett could respond to Abigail, the priest took the pulpit, and everyone went silent. Garrett recognized the man on stage from the day he'd come close to catching Cleophes Lockhart. The same black gown and black cap covered his body. The congregation all listened as he welcomed everyone in, the joy ringing in his tone at the reopening of the church's doors before he motioned a time of prayer.

Uncomfortable, Garrett followed the lead of everyone else within the church and bowed his head. The gesture seemed so foreign to him with the years between now and the last time he prayed soon after his father's death. He peeked over towards Abigail, who held her own shut, seeming caught within the prayer and hands clasped lightly together in her lap.

"Thank you, Father, for allowing us to open our doors of this building to gather here tonight and worship you." The priest's eyes were also closed, his head towards the floor. "We thank you for the men and women of this army and the leader you have placed at its head. We thank you for your provision during this long, cold season where our resources are limited, reminding us of the humble means you sent our Savior, Jesus, into the world. We pray, too, for our opponents just neighboring us in Boston. Though we may not see things the same way or agree with each other, we also recognize they, too, are Your children. Because of that we pray for quick resolution, one with the least bloodshed if possible. But in all this we pray not for our own wills, Lord, but for Your will to be done."

As if on cue again, everyone's heads raised as the man finished, including Garrett's. They took minutes to sing a few traditional hymns, the first he didn't recognize, but the next one nearly stopped his heart. He closed his eyes, the melody of *Our God, Our Help In Ages Past* in his father's voice bellowing through:

O God, our help in ages past,
Our hope for years to come,
Our shelter from the stormy blast,
And our eternal home:

Under the shadow of thy throne
Thy saints have dwelt secure;
Sufficient is thine arm alone,
And our defense is sure.

Before the hills in order stood,
Or earth received her frame,
From everlasting thou art God,
To endless years the same.

A thousand ages in thy sight
Are like an evening gone,
Short as the watch that ends the night
Before the rising sun.

Time, like an ever-rolling stream,
Bears all its sons away;
They fly forgotten, as a dream
Dies at the opening day.

O God, our help in ages past,
Our hope for years to come,

Be thou our guard while troubles last,
And our eternal home.

The light touch of a hand on his own caused Garrett's eyes to open with a startle. Abigail gave him a soft smile as if she recognized what he was feeling even if he wasn't before returning her hand to her lap again. When the hymns had stopped, the priest began his message. It was good, centered on Christ's birth as to be expected during the time of year, but didn't move him as much as the hymn did. Nevertheless, Garrett didn't mind the extra time to sit next to Abigail, even if her full attention was now forward. Like the night of the dinner party, she'd worn her hair in a similar fashion, adorning an even more modest dress that still had a way of leaving him a little tongue-tied.

When the service ended, the Washingtons were excused first. Martha took her husband's arm as they proceeded past the inquisitive and admiring eyes on them down the aisle. The general's expression was happy, though not over joyous as he gave a faint smile to everyone they passed and spoke with on their way out. Garrett looked for signs in the man's countenance to see whether the general recognized him as one of his prisoners, but it was wanting. Washington didn't even give him a second glance, if even a first. To the general, he was just another face in the crowd.

When they'd exited out of Christ Church, Garrett offered to go with Nikolai to bring the carriage round. On their way over, the back of his neck went stiff. Haywood stood in his path and held what appeared to be anything but good will towards him. Garrett would have just walked past, ignoring whatever challenge the officer had up his cuff but the expression on his face was evident. He wanted to talk.

Garrett motioned for Nikolai to go ahead without him then approached Haywood head on. "I get the feeling you're not here to wish me Merry Christmas or a Happy New Year."

Haywood frowned, letting Garrett know he didn't find the humor in his comment. "I'm here as a courtesy, believe it or not."

"As a courtesy? You're right, I don't believe it."

The rebel officer's mouth deepened into a customary scowl. "Let's get this straight, Mr. Ward. I don't like you for the mere fact you're on the side fighting against us, but there is a code I stand by: fairness. And to be fair, I'm giving you this one and only warning. Be careful of what you're trying to do while on your errands to town. You might find an alternate route out of Cambridge, but you may not be alive to take it. I'm going to have enough blood on my hands if we see the day these armies attack each other here in Massachusetts. I don't want to shed more than I have to."

Haywood didn't wait for a response but walked on. Not that Garrett had one to give him. If he'd had suspicions about his recent activity being found out they were answered with a resounding yes. Garrett eased his shoulders, now more than a little stiffened before he joined Nikolai at the carriage.

Nikolai was already sitting on top of the driver's seat. "Officer Haywood givin' you some trouble, Mr. Ward?"

Garrett looked back towards the direction the rebel officer had taken. He was gone. "Not any that I can't handle."

"I don't doubt that. Just don't let that man get to you. Every time I see him he looks like there's always somethin' troubling his mind. Besides, he's not the one that'll be sittin' next to Miss Thatcher tonight at dinner." Nikolai revealed a white smile. "Speaking of, we should get goin'. Don't want to keep the ladies waitin' especially now that Mrs. Schreier is all but ready to have her baby here in the winter snow. Rebekah wouldn't let me hear the end of it if I was to blame for that."

The image giving no need of further prompting, Garrett hopped up beside Nikolai, heartened by who and what awaited him this evening.

Chapter 24

Another dead end. Garrett gripped the reigns of Athala more tightly than he meant to before he gave her ribcage a squeeze with his legs. He did his best to make sure the cue for her to go came out gently. It wasn't the horse's fault he wanted to kick the ground in defiance as in the days of his youth.

None of his leads were pairing out, not with Cleo and now not with the locations he'd marked as possible escape points to Boston. Both his respect and irritation for Washington went up a few notches, though irritation clearly won out between the two. Every route he'd managed to find was either impossible since he didn't have a boat or was guarded by a group of men he had no trouble identifying as part of Washington's army. Garrett hadn't let himself get close enough for those men to see him apart from one exception that had been a mistake. It was the briefest glance, but there was no doubt as to the man's scowled recognition. Garrett's identity was known, if not to everyone at least within the group of guards, and unwelcomed.

Garrett pulled one side of the reins, signaling Athala to slow into a walk. He took out the map from his breastcoat pocket just to make sure. Again, his hopes plummeted. That was the last route on his map he'd marked. Now, he wasn't sure how he was going to get to Boston.

Before he reached the main part of Cambridge, Garrett returned the map into his pocket. Even if the guards along the routes knew he was a British prisoner, the rest of the town might still prove ignorant. Most of the townspeople treated him with the same regard as any of their own, however, his conversation with Haywood on New Year's Eve made him all too keen someone was watching him, even if he didn't know who. But the who in a town hosting rebels wasn't as important, only that he needed to be more careful and alert. He didn't like the idea of finding himself staring into the barrel of a gun. His throat tightened at the other possibility he hadn't considered: his neck in the middle of a noose. Not that it mattered, now. His leads had gone nowhere. Now what?

The rebel army's vulnerability with the smallpox disease could be to his advantage. Garrett played the scenario over in his head. It was a perfect time to come in and take things over. A full-on attack wasn't even necessary. More lives could be spared. There'd be little bloodshed if any, though plenty of prisoners. Having been a prisoner himself, he could help with that part except—he tried to breathe in deep, but it felt like a horse stood on his chest. No one seemed to want him back.

They were already into the next year, 1776. That meant a little over two months had passed since the capture of the HMS *Piper* and he'd been taken here to Cambridge. Two months and no word from anybody in Boston. Even Nicholas managed to evade on the issue when he'd inquired about the delay. Garrett wanted to read his friend's silence as a way of telling him something was in the works that was too risky to put in writing in case their letters were intercepted. Though with the continued delay, Garrett's resolve for his rescue lost its strength. He wanted to yell, though he figured he was doing enough of that on the inside and was sure the sudden outburst to any onlookers would be one to remember.

Haywood's words came to mind the day he'd received his extension to go beyond the Schreier estate borders. "I wouldn't count on a trade if I were you."

The smug expression on the officer's face still rubbed Garrett raw. He wondered if the man was smiling ear to ear every time he thought of it.

Athala stomped along the cobbled streets. Garrett had to give her little instruction on the way back to the Schreier estate, as if she too could sense their adventure for the day was over. A large burst of laughter rang forth from a nearby building and caught his attention. He looked up to see a sign that read Blue Anchor Tavern. His stomach growled at the mention of it in his mind. No doubt there was ale to be had, but even better, food. He looked in the direction of the Schreier house again. He wasn't ready to go back like this, not when his mood was more than a little unhinged and not when he might have to face Abigail with it while she still stayed at the house. He wasn't so sure he wanted her to see him like this: angry and bitter, but mostly hurt. Another bout of cheerful howls escaped through the door as a man walked out. Garrett took it as a sign. After all, he could use a little laughter in his life right about now.

Garrett took a seat by himself in the corner to draw as little attention as possible. Even out of his uniform, he still didn't want to risk being noticed, especially after his conversation with Haywood and the rebel guards that recognized him.

A brunette came by and sat down a mug of punch. The smile on her face lingered. Garrett politely smiled back, but when he looked at the woman another came to mind.

"I'll just have whatever the special is today." He pointed to a plate on another table. Remnants of some kind of roast and a few scattered peas still lay on it. He was about to return the drink having no means to pay for both it and the meal, but her smirk told him that wasn't a problem.

"That'll be the English roast and potatoes. As for the drink, it's on the house." He could hear the flirtation in her voice. "We're making more than enough this morning alone to cover it."

She moved on and filled a glass for another customer before disappearing into the back and returning with a plate in each hand for another table. Her foot caught a piece of paper that eventually slid its way over to his chair. Garrett picked it up. It wasn't just a piece of paper. It was a pamphlet. *Common Sense*. The author was not mentioned, but the title drew his curiosity, and he began to read the first few pages. As his eyes moved from one line to another, he could feel his jaw clench stiff, his fists along with it. He had to steady himself from showing a reaction, never mind the wrong reaction, in a tavern full of rebels. It was bound to get noticed.

Common Sense. It was the worst thing that could happen since the beginning of this war, at least, from his point of view anyway. From what he read thus far it was an opinion, or rather argument, pushing the colonists for independence. And though Garrett hated to admit the argument was good, compelling even, it was fuel added to the fire of liberation that was already burning. *Common Sense* was in favor of a government, but one without a king, without a monarchy. It argued to have such was to concede to have one person, cut off, independently, from the rest of their people, yet expecting them to act in cases where the highest judgement and knowledge was required. Like an island ruling over a continent, it made no sense, and Garrett suspected others would agree.

The British army carried the expertise and training a king could afford. Those loyal to the Crown had no doubt recognized that, too, along with their devotion to the country from which they came. But this document could serve to break that loyalty, questioning a mother country's rule on a separate land. The lack of support would be crippling.

Garrett began to take notice of the boisterous chatter around the

282

room, the fever for those already rebelling against the Crown had grown rapid. Cambridge consisted primarily of revolutionaries now, but what about those cities that were more divided? Philadelphia, New York and even Boston? He imagined riots breaking loose, more so than already and his comrades pressed to maintain order. The thought sparked another that sent his mood spiraling even further downward. Graves would be too busy working to combat chaos. Negotiating prisoners would not be a high priority.

Garrett let out a silent sigh of aggravation before placing the wretched pamphlet on his table and taking a hearty swig from the punch the waitress had provided. The burn felt good to his throat, and he slurped back a few more gulps to finish the mug off. The waitress brought over his plate along with a pitcher. When she looked like she might pour him another mug, he declined.

His stomach now suddenly less than hungry, Garrett managed to take a few bites just to be polite. He couldn't hear another mention of liberation, independence, and freedom repeated time and again as the conversation over the pamphlet seemed to crescendo. So much for lifting his spirits. He needed to get out of here. He left a tip and was about to leave right then and there when a different sort of conversation struck his ears.

"I tell you, Linus, this is the last straw. If that Cleo doesn't have my shipment this time, then he better not come back here if he knows what's good for him." A large, robust man made his complaint to a much shorter, much rounder one.

"Why don't you just go to Washington? He seems like a man who's sure to have a debt settled."

"Linus, you nitwit, you know very well why I can't go to the General."

The man called Linus scratched his head. "Just because he doesn't like your methods, Jasper?"

"*Exactly* because he doesn't like my methods." Jasper's tone grew more irritated. "The man won't stand for plundering or robbery by his own men, but what about when those redcoats come and do it then? They act like they're here to restore order, but they've pillaged their own fair share of destruction." He eyed his companion. "Remember Falmouth?"

Garrett's ears perked at the mention of the town. The weight of regret was like a millstone around his neck.

"I tell you, Linus, the way I see it, I'm just helping to level out the playing field."

"What are you going to do, then?"

Jasper gave an almost sardonic smile. "Let's just say if ole Cleo doesn't show tonight, the next time I see him will be the last time anyone sees him."

Linus scooted forward in his seat and leaned in. "Did you want me to come along, you know, in the case Cleo has something up his sleeve? You remember hearing how he backstabbed King George, don't you? How in the world the man managed to keep 40 live hogs and all that porter hidden from the king's men continues to confound me. If a man can do that and not get caught, what else is he capable of?"

"Precisely the very reason I hired him." Aggravation pierced the larger man's tone before it softened again. "But you have a good point, Linus. Yes, meet me at Gallows Hill at half past nine. We'll see if the man shows."

That had been all Garrett needed to hear. He'd make sure he'd see Cleophes tonight.

***

Garrett dismounted Athala and gave her a drink of water before situating the mare back in the barn.

"How was the ride into town today?" Nikolai sat a pile of hay in front of Greta, then added one to Athala's stall. The second horse devoured it. "And wat have you been doin' with my horse? She's worked up a hunger

284

I haven't seen in a while."

Garrett had taken Athala further than he planned trying to cover all the points on his map along with the ride into and out of town. "Sorry, I should have paced her better. We went further than I expected."

Nikolai gave an easy chuckle. "Don't worry about it, sir. The exercise is good for her. Keeps her young." He gave her a gentle nuzzle, the horse seeming to return the affection. "So does that mean today was good?"

"It was okay." Garrett considered the dead-ends he faced this morning and the *Common Sense* pamphlet along with the conversation he'd overheard between Linus and Jasper. "It had its good moments as well as the bad ones."

"That grimace across your face makes me believe the bad ones won out. Care to talk about it?"

Garrett gave Athala a pat. Did he want to talk about? Other than his inquiries about his trade status, he hadn't voiced a word about how he felt to Nicholas, his best friend. Then again, paper and quill just didn't seem fitting enough to express the feelings that overwhelmed him.

Nikolai tilted his chin, seeming to read his hesitation. "It's all right. I won't take any offense if you don't want to talk with me, but I think you might need to speak with somebody. It's not good for a man to hold whatever you have inside for too long. I've learned feelins have a way of findin' a way out eventually." His eyebrows raised. "It's up to you how that happens."

Garrett only offered a weak, one-sided smile. "Thanks, Nikolai. That's good advice. I just don't know if there is a right person to talk with at this time about it."

Nikolai shrugged without a hint of surprise in his expression. "Maybe not one of us walkin' around here in Cambridge, but there is someone you can always talk to who's just as willin' to listen."

Garrett's interest peaked. "Who?"

"Jesus Christ."

Garrett had to choke back a scoff at the answer. How did he not see that coming? He wasn't so sure a man he couldn't even look in the eye and who walked the earth nearly 1800 years ago could help him.

Nikolai nodded, his look one of regret. "I can see that doubt swirlin' around in your mind like Rebekah stirring a pot of pork stew over the fire. I'll be prayin' for you, Mr. Ward, seein' that's a hard thing to overcome. In the meantime, you need to know whatever's in that heart and mind of yours, it's never too big for the God who created the heavens and this beautiful world we live in. Trust me, He can take it."

The steel conviction in the man's dark brown eyes never wavered. Garrett couldn't imagine what Nikolai had been through before he made his way here to Cambridge to the Schreier homestead. What had it cost him to finally get his papers signed—papers that were really rubbish when Garrett thought about it, stating a man was free when he should've been free in the first place. If Garrett didn't think this man knew pain, he was a fool.

"Thanks again, Nikolai. I'll consider it."

The intensity in Nikolai's stare relented into an easy smile. "I hope you do, Mr. Ward."

Chapter 25

"How's that load coming along, dear?" Mrs. Bates was in the process of hanging a pair of worn breeches from their first load to dry when she looked over at Abigail from the clothesline.

"Almost finished. I'll get these over to the rinse tub in just a minute." Abigail continued agitating the garments with a stick along with the boiled soap before she placed them in the rinse tub.

"Oh, thank you, Abby. Maybe at this rate we'll finish with enough time for a break before the men will be wanting their supper." Mrs. Bates shook her head and let a small sigh hinted with disapproval come forth. "But I still can't believe officer Haywood has you here instead of at the hospital with everything going on up there. Doesn't he know nearly half of the camp is running rampant with smallpox?"

A tiny smile turned Abigail's lips upward while she wrung the clothes from the rinse tub out. "Oh, he knows, which is precisely why I'm here. A lot of the cases we're seeing are the camp followers. There's only a few to manage the camp now. It's all right, though. I was there this morning and made sure everyone was as situated as they could be before I came

287

here. Once we're finished, I'll head back over to check on things. Besides, Dr. Adams is there."

"Were you able to get more help? I spoke with Mr. Haywood about volunteering since I'm already over there for Mr. Bates but I'm sorry, dear." She frowned. "I'm afraid he declined. I wish I could do more for you."

Abigail shook her head. A sense of gratitude filled her for the woman's willingness to try. "You are, Mrs. Bates. Taking care of your husband is a great help and, I'm sure he'd rather have you by his side than anyone else."

Mrs. Bates laughed, her eyes smiling. "For fifty-one years now."

The older woman's joy was contagious, Abigail again feeling her own smile lift higher. It certainly would be something to be with someone so long. She imagined all that time would bring about some challenges, ones that no doubt had brought Mr. and Mrs. Bates together, only strengthening the bond they clearly had.

"Have you seen him today?" Abigail didn't recall having spotted Mrs. Bates at the hospital this morning, though that didn't necessarily mean anything. She'd made her own rounds quickly to make it in time for the washing.

Mrs. Bates shook her head and sighed. "Not yet. I had to get things ready here, but I hope to find some time before it gets too late this evening."

Abigail looked towards the sky. The sun was already near its peak. They'd been at work for five hours and that wasn't counting Mrs. Bates' time for set-up. She glanced at the heap of clothing that still lay unwashed and frowned. There was plenty left and with only the two of them to do it. She caught Mrs. Bates give pause to stretch her back, a product of bending over time and again to remove the clothes from the basins. A heaviness pressed down on Abigail's chest.

How many nights now had she'd spent at the Schreier estate upon the soft sheets of the bed while Mrs. Bates still slept on the hard floor? Even if it was part of her orders to stay at the house until the baby arrived, there was something wrong about the whole ordeal. She at least wanted to get some hay and tick for the woman to lay on while she stayed by her husband's bedside each night. But even that was hard to come by as the winter season continued to drag on, the hay becoming scarce enough to feed the demands of the horses from both locals and army alike.

Other options seemed just as dismal. Wool was coveted for warmth this time of year, and cotton, well, she hadn't seen much of that as the ships in Boston continued to be searched and coveted by the British in the city. Part of her even wondered how they were getting any supplies at all.

Again, Abigail's ears captured Mrs. Bates give a quiet, strained breath as the older woman put another pile of dirty clothes into the soap bin. The uncomplaining nature of her friend captured Abigail's heartstrings. Maybe she couldn't do anything about the bedding, but she could do something now.

"Mrs. Bates, I would be more than happy to finish the job on my own. There's only a few more loads to get done before I need to get back to the hospital. That should give you a good bit of time to see Mr. Bates before supper."

The woman's voice came out sweet but firm. "Oh, no, dear. I couldn't let you do that, not when I'm an able-bodied woman still yet. I'm not about to leave you to do all this yourself. It'll be faster if we both lend a hand. We started this together and we can end it that way too."

Deep appreciation at her friend's sheer willingness and determination to help touched Abigail's heart even if the argument wasn't necessarily true. Abigail was twice as fast at the task.

"Besides, dear, what about Mr. Ward? You still have to take the man's supper, too, later, don't you? I can't see you doing that with all of this left to do."

Abigail shook her head. The morning she caught Garrett in the act of eating Rebekah's bacon and cornbread and learned it hadn't been the first time resurfaced. "I wouldn't worry about Mr. Ward. He's taken a liking to Rebekah's cooking. No one will be expecting me until later this evening."

Mrs. Bates shook her head too, though a small grin held on her face. "I still can't believe that man's the camp prisoner, especially when I think about that day in the market."

Abigail smiled too, for both Mrs. Bates' surprise on the day she finally revealed Garrett's involvement in the army and for her own amazement to hear he'd helped pay for the food to feed the soldiers. Even if she hadn't altogether liked him then, the act still spoke volumes.

"A man who helps feed his enemy is certainly one to take notice of." Mrs. Bates continued working on the wash, her eyes focused on the task, yet Abigail could hear the keenness in her tone.

The woman didn't have to worry. Whether Abigail liked it or not, Garrett Ward had certainly captured her notice.

Mrs. Bates rubbed her back again, before she moved her hand up to her neck to massage it. Abigail made the decision to convince Mrs. Bates to leave the laundry to her, standing firm this time.

"I can assure you Mr. Ward is getting plenty of attention, probably more than officer Haywood would like even, but you, Mrs. Bates, could use a little care of your own. Really, ma'am, I insist." Abigail considered prodding the woman's own feelings, hoping it might do the trick. "Even Jesus took a break now and then."

To her delight, Mrs. Bates laughed, her eyes grinning. "I suppose I can't argue against the Son of God, now, can I?"

Abigail let out a breath, feeling the sense of victory. "No, ma'am. You are a woman skilled at many things but arguing against the Almighty is not something any one of us can do and win." She was beginning to understand that firsthand.

"Thank you, Abby. I'll leave you to it then, but if you change your mind, I'll be over at the hospital."

Abigail nodded. "Tell Mr. Bates hello for me."

***

A few hours later with three loads washed and hanged to dry, Abigail found herself gathering the rest of the firewood to heat the kettle again. There were just two more loads to finish, but her kindling was running out. She lowered herself to arrange the wood accordingly before igniting the flame. Now, as she stood again, she was more than ready to be finished with the day's task. That's when she saw him.

"Garrett? What are you doing here?" Part of her wanted to laugh in disbelief, seeing the man she never thought would step right in the middle of what he called a "rebel camp" do just that. The other part of her felt the rhythmic beating of her chest take flight. She'd been touched by his regard for Thomas to invite him to their Christmas dinner. She judged too by the boy's beaming expression throughout the evening, it had meant more to him than Garrett would ever know. But what had happened to change things between them? The last thing she recalled was Thomas' suspicious glances of the Royal Navy lieutenant at their first meeting. Whatever had occurred since then, it was plain enough he looked at Garrett with different eyes now.

"Garrett, you really shouldn't be in the camp. If someone recognizes who you are..." Her words fell at his pained gaze. "Garrett, what's wrong?"

"Abigail, it's Mrs. Schreier. The baby is...coming."

The firewood dropped to her feet. It was only a matter of time, but now that the time had finally come, she couldn't help but feel a little frozen in it.

"Abby, did you hear me? Mrs. Schreier..." Garrett broke the spell that allowed her to think of what to do. It quickly came. With one swift motion, she doused the fire and took hold of him, putting her arm

291

through his to bring him alongside. They took on a brisk walk through the grounds.

"We'll need to get Dr. Adams, but he's not here in the commons. At least I don't think he would be. Our best chance is the Vassall house where the other patients are." Abigail noticed some of the soldiers eyed her and Garrett with looks that only made her determined to get him out of the area as soon as possible. The last thing they needed now was someone trying to start a fight. "Remind me, how did you manage to get through the camp without so much as a confrontation?"

"Well, for one thing I wasn't arm-in-arm with one of the female camp followers, not to mention one of the more attractive ones."

Her cheeks went hot, and she instantly drew her arm away from his. Garrett frowned.

"Something tells me there's more on their mind than our close proximity," she said, giving him a pointed look. "But never mind that. The Vassall house is still about a mile from here. We'll need to be quick."

"Then leave that to me." As if changing their roles, Garrett took her arm into his again and led her through the rest of commons until they reached the outside of camp where a chestnut mare was waiting.

"Athala." Abigail couldn't help but give the animal a gentle scratch on her neck as Garrett untied her and took his mount. When he extended his arm out towards her, Abigail took it with some hesitation.

"You all right?" He gave her a puzzled expression. "I thought you said you've been on a horse before?"

She nodded as she shifted her weight. "Yes, I'm fine. And yes, I've been on a horse before." It was just that being on a horse was one thing but being on a horse so close to Garrett Ward was an entirely different story. The urgency in his eyes reminded her again of what was at stake and won out. She accepted his hand, taking the place behind him on the mare.

As they rode past the square and towards the hospital, Abigail caught the scent of sea salt and sage mixed with leather. With Margaret's current condition somehow not being enough to distract her from their close proximity to each other, Abigail threw out the first thing she could think of to keep her head clear.

"I believe the estate used to belong to a man by the name of Henry Vassall, a wealthy plantation owner."

Garrett gave a slight turn of his head back towards her. "Used to belong?" The one eyebrow she could see lifted. "Let me guess, he supported the Crown like Mrs. Schreier?"

"Well, I've been told by Dr. Adams he actually died a few years ago, but yes, his wife did leave with many others. Since then, the army has used it as a sort of hospital. Before Dr. Adams started treating patients there, a man by the name of Benjamin Church occupied it and was the director of medical service for the army."

"What happened to him?"

"I don't know all the story, only that he was expelled for treason."

"I bet that didn't go over well."

"I can't imagine it did, but I don't know much more than that."

Not long after she'd offered her small piece of information about the Vassall estate they reached the homestead itself.

Garrett dismounted before helping her down.

Abigail let out a quiet breath she hadn't perceived she'd been holding as the space between she and Garrett grew again off the horse. "We better get inside. Dr. Adams was here earlier this morning, but that's been hours ago since I've last seen him. I only hope he hasn't moved on to other patients in town."

When they got up to the door, Mr. Douglas was standing outside of it as usual.

"Miss Thatcher." Douglas greeted her with a stale grin, an expression that always made her feel she was an interruption to whatever his thoughts entertained in the moment. His contorted smile only grew sourer when Garrett stepped beside her. "Who's your friend?" There was a cordial malice in his tone that made it evident he didn't approve of her companion and perhaps even knew who Garrett was.

Abigail gave a brief glance over; thankful Garrett hadn't returned the man's challenge. Already short on time, she straightened and squared her shoulders. She hoped it would be enough to let both men understand she wasn't in the mood for contests of bravado. "Do you know if Dr. Adams is still here?"

Douglas seemed to soften his glare as his eyes jumped from Garrett's to hers again. "He is, miss. You can go on in if you like, but I have strict orders from the general to keep those without permission out, and this man here…" He gave a cynical scoff, eyeing Garrett once again. "I highly doubt he has permission. He'll have to wait outside."

"Of course, Mr. Douglas. As you know, I'm already well-informed of your orders." Abigail looked at Garrett and gave him a reassuring smile. "I'll be right back," she promised as the guard shifted to allow to her to enter the doorway.

"And I'll be all right." Garrett made a nod of his head as if nudging her forward before she let herself disappear from his view.

Upon her return she was both thankful to have found Dr. Adams just as Mr. Douglas had stated and to observe the only thing that seemed to occur between the two men waiting outside were a few sideways glances. Abigail gave Garrett a disapproving look to let him know she was on to him. He threw his hands up as if innocent and she had to hold back her laughter.

"Dr. Adams is readying a horse and will meet us there," she announced, putting her focus on their task again.

One of the corners of Garrett's mouth raised into a wry smile. "So, the doc does know how to ride a horse after all?"

"I guess so. He's having to borrow one, though." She gave him a chiding grin. "You may be right about his ability to ride, but it turns out he doesn't like the idea of trying to fit three on one horse."

"It sounds like we were both a little right then."

Her smile came easily, his own grin seeming to grow on her more and more. "Sounds like it."

"We better get going." Garrett mounted Athala before he offered his hand to Abigail again. "Let's see if we can beat the doctor back. I don't know much about babies, but I do know I don't want to keep Mrs. Schreier waiting, especially right now."

The two of them rode in silence on the way to the house, but Abigail didn't mind. Her thoughts were less concerned with Garrett Ward and on full alert about Margaret and what role she'd have to play in the very near future. She thought about her mother still working to recover from Olivia's birth, one that had come later in her life just like Margaret's. Dr. Adams had already given the strictest advice for her to keep to the bed as much as possible, but was that all or was there something more they'd find out today? Was the baby really okay? Would Margaret end up like her mother now, still so weak?

Abigail tried to focus on the sound of Athala's hooves clapping over the cobblestone, getting away from the silence that had somehow become so deafening. She let herself sink into the rhythmic beat. Her arms reached out in front of her for something to keep her from being pushed over.

It was when Garrett reined the mare in, coming to a stop in front of the house when she realized she still had her arms wrapped around him and more tightly than necessary. Her cheeks burned, and she was thankful he couldn't see her in that moment, still behind him and now protected by the evening darkness. Instantly letting go, she waited for him to dismount, then help her do the same.

"I think Dr. Adams beat us, but they'll be needing you in there." The tenderness in his voice was all she could detect. "I'll take Athala to the

295

barn and see you inside." Garrett motioned his head towards the house and with nothing really to say, Abigail nodded before beginning her ascent to the door. It was then she felt a slight jolt that stopped her progress and led her to turn back. Garrett had taken hold of her hand. His touch caused her to turn almost feverish, and part of her wished she could read his face then.

"Abigail," he started, his voice softened, and the very mention of her name coming from him stirred both a warmth and a calmness inside her. "It's going to be all right. You can do this." She wanted to believe him.

Garrett let go of her hand and drew his attention back to the horse. She watched as he proceeded to lead Athala in the direction of the barn before finally opening the door to a challenge she was only half willing to accept.

Chapter 26

Abigail could almost hear the cracking of the bones in her hand as Margaret squeezed it with what felt like all the strength the woman had.

Hand throbbing, Abigail turned to the doctor who stood at the foot of the bed to take an examination of his patient. "Dr. Adams, do you think we could give her something for the pain?"

The man looked up through his round-rimmed spectacles seeming to observe both her and Margaret's tense state and nodded.

Having his consent, Abigail gently released her hand from the lady's grip and went over to the dresser where a bottle of whiskey stood at the ready. She took the bottle back over to the bed along with a damp cloth she'd retrieved from the washbasin. Abigail proceeded to give Margaret a drink while she wiped the beads of sweat from her friend's face. Margaret only groaned in response and took in a series of heavy breaths.

Abigail still couldn't believe she was here, that Dr. Adams thought her suitable enough for the task. Though what task that was, she wasn't entirely certain. Dr. Adams had yet to reveal the state of Margaret's complications, but he did mention there was a chance the delivery might be a special case. She swallowed hard, trying to force down her nerves. Thoughts continued weighing at her confidence. Thankfully her current responsibilities for Margaret had left her little opportunity to dwell on them for too long.

"You've witnessed two of your mother's births, Abigail? Is that correct?" Dr. Adams peered over the top of his eyeglasses towards her.

"Yes, sir, but I was barely involved. The midwife did nearly all of the work on both accounts, other than my mother of course."

"Yes, well, that'll do fine. It's more experience than anyone else seems to have in camp and not much less than my own, having only conducted a handful."

"A handful?" Hesitation choked the rest of her words, "of deliveries, sir?"

"Why yes." The doctor's relaxed state portrayed the information like it was common knowledge. "I may be a doctor, but childbirth is not one avenue I've had much experience in either. Most births here in the colonies are done primarily through the midwives. My encounters on such have only occurred by chance when the town's midwife was otherwise occupied." He gave a sigh, his tone tinged with agitation. "And more recently, at the camp where I've had to intervene thrice, now because not one of the women residing within the grounds claims to have knowledge of it."

Abigail considered the man's explanation. Midwives in Falmouth were solely relied upon for such cases. There were no doctors there at all. She imagined Cambridge, a place so close to an expanding city like Boston and where doctors were more available, might be different. A shot of pain carried through her fingers again, Margaret's hold only growing tighter as the tormented woman gave another groan.

A little more than confident her friend was too distracted to mind her next question, Abigail inquired further. "Dr. Adams, you mentioned Mrs.

Schreier's condition was a complicated one. I can't pretend to know what that might mean. Can you at least help me understand why the situation calls for such caution?"

The doctor pressed his lips and gave her a weak smile. "Yes, Abigail, I believe I can. You see, the placenta, a structure we in the field know to provide sustenance along with other functions for the infant, has blocked the path of the journey the babe needs to take to get out of its mother's womb. I hoped as Mrs. Schreier progressed in her medical state the issue would resolve itself. In most cases I'm familiar with, it has, but I'm afraid this time it has not and the child is ready to enter our world."

Abigail scrunched her brow, trying her best to understand a field she was just at the cusp of learning. If the child could not get out, what could be done? The child had to come out. There was no other place to go.

"Dr. Adams, you said the baby is ready, but if it can't get out..." Abigail gulped a heavy breath full of emotion. "Then will the child not..."

"The child will come out, Abigail, but now it's more a matter of how that's going to happen." The doctor took in a slow breath of his own and removed a handkerchief from his waistcoat. He patted the sweat from his forehead, not giving her the assurance she hoped for. "There is a procedure I've read about and has been performed successfully by a group of indigenous people in Africa. I thought it might be worth studying in the chance the obstruction did not move and in this case, it hasn't. But we'll need Mrs. Schreier to comply, to be calm." He looked over to his patient, whose already pale complexion was faded. Her moans had escalated another degree along with her strength.

Abigail felt another crack and she was certain her fingers, at the very least, were broken. She closed her eyes, thanking God she couldn't feel the pain. Her hand had long since grown numb, and her body's nerves grew more agitated the more she learned of Margaret's condition.

Dr. Adams shook his head. "In this case she is in no condition to do so. I'll have to give her something for the pain."

"Should I give her some more?" Abigail started to reach for the whiskey again, but Dr. Adams stopped her, gently pulling her arm back.

"No, we'll give her something stronger, but I don't like to mix the two. I've seen some bad effects of doing that. Thankfully, she hasn't had too much of the whiskey, but let's not give her anymore."

Abigail nodded and retracted her arm. She watched as Dr. Adams pulled out the vile of laudanum she'd been so accustomed to seeing these past few months and give a small dose to Margaret.

It took about half an hour for the drug to take hold, as both doctor and assistant saw the woman begin to relax. Her grip on Abigail's hand loosened and her breath slowed to a more normal state. With his patient now in a condition of compliance, Dr. Adams began his procedure.

Abigail watched both with intriguing awe and sheer horror as the doctor grabbed the bottle of whiskey, using it to cleanse his hands before proceeding to cut into Margaret's abdomen with his knife. It was not the first time she'd seen blood, so she didn't understand why she began to feel light-headed then, but she did. Perhaps it was because she'd never seen a birth done in such a way. Thinking of Margaret undergoing such an operation and more so the thought of the fragile infant so close in proximity to such a sharp blade, made her head spin.

Averting her gaze from the doctor's hands, now inside the lady's womb, Abigail looked to their patient and was thankful she seemed ignorant of what was being done. Margaret was laid back, more comfortable now and breathing easy. Only a few minor twitches here and there were a reminder their patient wasn't completely pain-free while doing better to assure them she was also very much alive.

Satisfied by the desired effect of the opium, Abigail left the woman's side for the washbasin. She soaked a cloth in the untainted water before applying it again to Margaret's forehead.

"Abigail." Dr. Adams addressed her, his mouth firm, more so than she'd seen just a moment ago. Perceiving the man's troubled expression, her own chest galloped like the pounding of Athala's hooves on the ride over. She said nothing, ready to comply as quickly as she could. "Bring me that cloth, please."

She did as Dr. Adams asked. Though his current position hovering over the lady's midsection prevented Abigail from seeing more, what was in plain view from any angle was the crimson color of blood spilling from the opening he'd just made.

Abigail sucked in a breath, a knot forming in her throat to make it hard for her to swallow. She wanted to ask Dr. Adams about the babe but the fear of what answer she'd receive silenced her. And not only that, to risk throwing off the man's concentration when it seemed like every ounce of it was crucial now was not something she wanted to be responsible for.

"Abigail" the doctor bellowed again. His critical tone released her from her stupor. "We'll need more cloth. Please be quick if you can." He didn't change his gaze, still concentrated on his patient, but Abigail didn't mind. She took the order willingly, not only to be of help, but as a welcomed reprieve from the horrible scene before her.

With haste, she took the staircase down to the kitchen. It was empty, but that didn't surprise her. It was well past the dinner hour, though she wondered if Rebekah had served a meal at all with the excitement of Mrs. Schreier underway.

Springing for the cupboard, Abigail collected most of the cloth she could, hoping it wouldn't be needed, yet not wanting to risk the extra time in having to return in the chance that it was. With items in hand, she was about to bound back up the stairs when she came face-to-face, nearly colliding, with Garrett.

"Everything all right?" He looked down at her hands and eyed the cloth in her arms.

"Yes." The response came out a little too quickly. "I was just getting some fresh cloth for Dr. Adams."

Garrett shook his head. He put his hand on her shoulder and she welcomed it. Again, his very touch seemed to calm her in a time when she needed it.

"No," he said, looking her straight in the eyes with a concern she read as genuine. "What I mean is, are you all right?"

"I'm fine" she managed, though not certain if she spoke truthfully. Garrett seemed to search her, looking only half convinced, and she couldn't blame him. The brief trip she'd taken downstairs had provided her some relief from the intense moment, but just thinking of what she might find upon her return sent a nervous chill up her spine. She silently prayed it would be a healthy baby and a resting mother.

A growing tension inside her told her she'd already been gone too long. She gently broke his touch, despite a part of her not wanting to. "I need to get these upstairs," she said, hearing a shakiness in her own voice. She forced a weak smile. "But I'll be back as soon as I can with some news." She swallowed, not sure what kind of news to expect, then leaving Garrett in the hall, made her ascent.

When Abigail reached the threshold of Margaret's bedroom again, she wasn't sure what she'd find on the other side of it. She braced herself and prayed for the two lives at stake as she opened the door.

Dr. Adams nodded as he eyed the cloth in her arms. She saw from his unchanged position and the continued strain in his brow the situation had not changed.

"Quickly, bring those over." He pressed the order and she readily obeyed, while also trying to get a better view of Margaret's abdomen. With no knowledge of the procedure the doctor was taking, Abigail wasn't sure what she should look for, except for perhaps movement. Not that it seemed to matter, however, for their patient's midsection had not changed either, still hidden underneath the layer of blood. Seeing the doctor had used the original cloth to manage some of it, Abigail brought the others and imitated the man's actions as they both worked to soak up more of the red liquid.

"There, I can see better." Dr. Adams wiped his face with a separate rag before he pushed his shifted spectacles back up his nose. "Thank you, Abigail. It should only be a moment, now," he said with a more optimistic tone.

Already tense, Abigail watched with weighty expectation as Dr. Adams continued his task and removed the babe from its mother's womb. Her own breath stilled at the awe of new life before her, the beat of her heart climbing with anticipation until it all came to an agonizing halt.

At first, nothing. In the place where a crying child should've been heard, only the crushing sound of desperate silence enveloped the room. Cold chills ran throughout as Abigail's body went nearly limp, feeling like her heart might be ripped in two. She couldn't make herself look at the doctor, not when doing so might confirm what she was afraid she already knew.

Instead, she glanced at Margaret, still reclined and oblivious under the laudanum's spell. Purposely avoiding Dr. Adam's gaze and leaving the infant in his arms, Abigail went over to the babe's mother, who still lay unbeknownst to the fate of her poor child. Tears formed, then rushed down her cheeks as she did the only thing she could think to do. She took her friend's hand gently into her own, her heart becoming still heavier before she dropped to her knees and prayed more fervently than she had ever done in her life.

The time she'd been praying was unknown. A minute? An hour? Abigail didn't care. As her heart lay broken for this family; this woman, this child, and the father it would never know, she knew not what else to do. It was after making her petitions when she realized she'd left Dr. Adams alone to not only a heavy burden, but to finish the work on his patient while carrying it. With eyes still blurry, Abigail stood, about to ask for the doctor's next order, when she heard it. Her breath caught.

The sweet sound of a crying infant filled the room and Abigail's heart soared. The miracle gave her courage to look at Dr. Adams, his eyes red. He let out a joyful shout before handing the child over to her. Instinct took over. She cleaned the babe using the water left in the basin before she wrapped the child in linen. The normal custom would've been to hand the infant over to the mother, but Dr. Adams was not finished with his patient who had yet to fully come to. Instead, Abigail simply continued to hold the babe with sheer elation as she watched the doctor pin the wound and dress it with a paste.

"The indigenous people of the procedure I studied used a mixture prepared from roots. This is of a similar type." Triumph now illuminated both Dr. Adam's tone and expression. He wiped his brow one last time with his forearm before washing the blood from his hands. "The study said the patient recovered well. We'll hope for the same for Mrs. Schreier." He smiled and the very action was like a breath of fresh air that Abigail breathed in deeply.

It was some time before Margaret was well enough and recovered from the laudanum to receive her child, but when she finally did, she wept. Tears of joy flowed as she took hold of her daughter for the first time and Abigail, still feeling a surge of emotions by the whole evening, couldn't help but mirror the woman's reaction before she left mother and child to rest.

With the washbasin in one arm, and several towels in the other, Abigail again descended the stairway, but this time with a lightness in her step. As she did, she silently thanked God for the doctor he provided and the lives that had been spared.

It was when she reached the foot of the stairs when she saw them. Garrett, and now Rebekah, coming to meet her. Rebekah's dark eyes were wide with what Abigail could only decipher as alarm. Water began to stream down the woman's cheeks, but something told Abigail they weren't tears of joy. Confused, Abigail looked to Garrett for answers, but he too seemed disturbed, his expression grim.

"Abigail," he started, his tone laced with melancholy, "Is everything...," she saw him swallow hard as if he didn't want to continue, but he did, "all right?" She scrunched her brow, still uncertain behind the reason for his downcast state.

"Yes, everything is very good, actually."

Garrett's eyes narrowed. "Are you sure?" The disbelief in his tone told her he wasn't convinced. In need of an explanation and bothered by their reactions when she just witnessed something so wonderful, she felt a slight irritation.

"Yes, I'm sure," she said, her tone firm and insisting. "Is there something going on that I don't know about?" She looked between them again for answers, they both seeming paralyzed and speechless, the opposite reaction of what she envisioned for the birth of Margaret's child.

Garrett cleared his throat and gave a sigh, then pointed directly to her. She put her hands to her hips and her lips flattened, but let her eyes drift downward. That's when she knew.

The bodice of her dress and the top portion of her apron were stained with smears of blood. Her eyes moved over to the washbasin she'd been carrying. It too tainted with the crimson color along with the used cloth in her other arm. Abigail froze and imagined what the sight would've been like from another's perspective and shuddered.

"Trust me." Abigail dropped her hands from her waist, retracting her sharp tone for a more reassuring one. "Everything is all right and everyone too." She tried to offer a heartened smile as she explained what happened. "Dr. Adams had to perform a special kind of delivery but believe me when I say both mother and child are doing fine now. Mrs. Schreier was holding her daughter when I left them." Having only experienced it moments ago, she recognized the relief she now saw in both Garrett and Rebekah take effect, though sorry they'd experienced the turmoil at all.

Once Rebekah had fully recovered, she went to the kitchen promising cordials to celebrate the night's event and the new blessing to the Schreier household.

Garrett approached Abigail, a warm smile touching his cheek. "You really had us worried, you know."

She frowned. "I'm sure I did, especially once I thought about what you and Rebekah must've been thinking to see me like this." She pointed her eyes down to her stained clothing again. "I'm sorry for that."

"It's okay. We just didn't know what to think. You were up there a long time, and Rebekah worried when she didn't hear any noise coming from Margaret. I'm told there's supposed to be more groaning and screaming involved."

"We had to give her some laudanum for the procedure to help her stay still and relaxed. I should have mentioned it when I came down here earlier."

"It's okay. You looked like you had a lot on your mind."

She nodded, though somewhat reluctantly. "I did."

"Are you fine, now?" Again, that gentleness she'd heard earlier in his tone seemed to make her shoulders relax. She hadn't realized she was still tense.

"Yes, much better." The calm she now felt with him gave way to an easy smile. He seemed to look her over again, but this time as if to survey her. He crossed his arms, his shoulders drawing backward.

"Blood-stained and sweaty garments with a set of towels to match." Garrett nodded with approval in his eyes as he glanced at the linens she still held onto. "Yes, you certainly look the part now." The unexpected comment gave way to a small laugh. "You sure you don't want to go down that road further? It takes a lot for someone to be in that room like you were tonight. There was a reason I was down here."

"I don't know, maybe." She shrugged. "As scared as I was during the whole thing, I was also excited about it, too. I wonder if that's how Dr. Adams felt."

"You should ask him when you get the chance."

Abigail nodded, already planning to. "I will, but for now I'm going to get changed before Rebekah gets back with the cordials. I'll see you back in the parlor."

Garrett gave a slight bend to his head. "See you there."

Abigail headed to her room to slip on a plain blue dress and wash the remnants of the prior hours away in the washbasin. When she'd finished, she pulled at the nightstand drawer to take out the leather-bound journal Garrett had given her and jotted a few notes down on the first page. She wasn't sure if she'd make it a habit, but began with the date, more so for personal reasons than for information to learn. January 12, 1776. She wanted to make sure she'd always remember the date, not just for the miracle of the baby girl safely in her mother's arms, but also for the man downstairs who looked at her with a pride she hadn't missed. Her heart leapt with both celebration and courage. Whether it was God-ordained or not, Garrett Ward seemed to be the push for her to do what she thought was impossible.

Chapter 27

Garrett tied Athala off at the Blue Anchor Tavern, not entirely looking forward to entering the place a second time. He didn't exactly like the reminder it held of the day he heard of and read the *Common Sense* pamphlet, but the visit today was a necessity nonetheless. He still didn't have any more leads on Cleophes Lockhart since his no-show with Linus and Jasper, but maybe they'd connect again eventually. It was a long shot for the men to be here, never mind discussing Cleophes as their topic again, but there wasn't much else to go on. The fact was, he had nothing.

Garrett hadn't seen Cleo since their run-in when he lost him at the church, and, with his escape routes leading nowhere, there wasn't much else he could do. Still, there was one positive he managed to see, even if no leads turned up on his intended man. The Blue Anchor Tavern was a place where people talked, a place of current knowledge. *Common Sense* told him that much on the day it appeared. If he was going to keep up with this war and learn anything else from the rebels, this was the place to be.

Since the table in the back corner he'd sat at last time was occupied, Garrett picked a spot at the counter. He left his back exposed to the crowd while it allowed him a view of most of those who came through the door.

"I thought I recognized a face from the New Year service."

Garrett jumped, realizing the comment was directed to him. So much for not being noticed. He turned to face a man dressed in a plain brown coat and waistcoat with matching breeches before his head pulled back.

"Father?" The title felt foreign on his tongue, particularly because it wasn't his own father he was talking to.

The holy man gave a small chuckle, his eyes bright with warmth. "It's all right, you can call me Isaac."

"Isaac?" Garrett wasn't expecting such informality with a priest. "What happened to your robes? I thought you were supposed to wear those all the time?"

Isaac nodded like the question wasn't a new one for him. "I do most days, but I've also found the robes seem to intimidate people more than invite them, especially in here."

Garrett took a quick survey of the room. The tops of a few tables already had pints of ale on them or whatever punch the house was serving that day. Two men in the back were in the middle of a wager over a card game, but no one seemed to notice the priest. "That begs another question. What are you doing here? I would've thought you'd be at the church or somewhere more religious, not in a tavern."

Isaac shrugged mildly like the place he found himself at was of little consequence. "I think it's good to try and meet people where they are. Sometimes that's in a church and other times it's in a tavern like this one." The corner of his mouth tipped upward. "That and I came for the fish cakes they serve on Fridays."

Garrett's once clouded expression cleared into a smile. "That good, huh?"

Isaac nodded, the other side of his mouth bending to match the other.

"That good."

The brunette Garrett recognized from his last time at the tavern came over. She gave him a quick smile before giving her full attention to the priest.

"The usual, Father?"

Isaac nodded, the same warmth he'd greeted Garrett with now extended to her. "Yes, Anne, that will do just fine."

As the waitress left, Garrett caught the priest eyeing an empty table in the middle of the room with a checkerboard on it.

Isaac made a gesture over at the game table. "You care to play?"

"Sure, why not? I'll even let you have the first move."

"I should warn you; I tend to play a fairly decent game. I may be a religious man, but that doesn't mean I'll go easy on you."

Having played more than a handful of games himself while at sea when boredom struck, Garrett did well enough not to think much of it. "Thanks for the warning. I'll take my chances."

Isaac started the game by moving his first checker piece diagonally forward.

Garrett mirrored the move on his own side. They each moved a few more pieces forward with little activity otherwise. "How are things going since the church reopened its doors?"

Isaac used one of his checkers to jump one of Garrett's pieces, taking it as a souvenir. "It's been a prayer answered. What did you think of the New Year service?"

Garrett recalled the hymn that reminded him so much of his father and had been the only part of the service that truly moved him. "I thought it was well-suited for reopening the church, but truthfully I enjoyed the music a little more."

The priest gave an amiable smile that instantly brought Garrett to ease. It was good to know the man could handle the hard stuff.

"I appreciate your opinion. Any song you enjoyed in particular, if I may ask?"

"Actually, yes. *Our God, Our Help In Ages Past.* It reminds me of someone."

Isaac nodded. He closed his eyes as he began to hum the first few lines. "That's a good one. I enjoy it myself." He jumped two more of Garrett's pieces. "Did you ever find the man you were looking for?"

Garrett couldn't help but frown, not because he was currently being out-skilled by a holy man, but because the thought of being so close to catching Cleophes Lockhart before losing him in the church still got to him.

Garrett shook his head, changing his game tactic into a defensive one rather than taking offense on the checkerboard. "No, I haven't seen him since. You don't happen to know a Cleophes Lockhart by chance? He's an older fellow with a limp and usually wears a sailor's cap."

Isaac paused with an expression that told Garrett he was genuinely trying to recall but in the end came up empty. "Sorry, no. I don't know that name, but if he's part of the army, there are many in the camp I still have yet to meet." Isaac claimed another two of Garrett's pieces. "The description you gave, however, does remind me of a Mr. Tully I've had the pleasure of talking with. He's visited me at the church a few times here lately. Poor man. He has a lot of guilt."

Garrett bit the inside of his cheek. He was sure the man whom the priest spoke of was Cleophes under a false name. Garrett wanted to ask Isaac more, but he could sense a certain regard coming from him concerning this so-called Tully, and something told him not to push it. Besides, Garrett needed to focus on the game in front of him. He was currently getting his you know what handed to him.

"You weren't kidding about being good."

The priest gave a hearty laugh. "I've had a lot of practice."

"I'm counting on the notion lying isn't a virtue in your industry, so I'll accept that excuse gladly." Catching he was about to lose another checker piece; Garrett moved the one about to be taken out of danger's way. In response, Isaac made one of his own to Garrett's side of the checkerboard with the expectation of promotion, except Garrett had yet to acquire anything to crown the new king. Maybe focusing on the game was a bad idea after all.

"How has the attendance been since you opened the doors of the church again?"

"It hasn't been as packed as it was for the New Year's service, but still full. I think people are trying to look for answers between the war and the smallpox that's invaded the camp." Isaac's eyes gleamed. "By your question, I can only deduce you haven't been among the attendees?"

Garrett gave a rueful smile, not realizing he'd given himself up but also thankful not to hear any judgment or condescension in the man's tone.

"I was surprised to see the lady Schreier's absence until I heard she was in a critical state. I thought perhaps her time had come with the child until I noticed a young lady in the crowd she'd attended with on New Year's."

"Abigail was there?" Garrett had to bury his emotion. Of course, she was. Why should he be surprised by that?

"I thought maybe you knew the young woman, having also been a part of the group on that particular service."

"Oh, I know her, but the church thing isn't really my deal. In fact, I'm not so sure God wants anything to do with me at all based on how things have gone."

"You mean the fact you're a prisoner of a new army?"

Garrett's focus moved from the checkerboard to Isaac, stunned. "How long have you known?"

"The first time you stepped into the church. I like to keep tabs of who all find themselves there to keep up with how they're doing." He gave Garrett a stern look. "You're no exception, Mr. Ward. I'm guessing things aren't going well by your previous comment?"

Once Garrett got over his surprise, he wasn't sure what expression took over, but he imagined it was a sarcastic one. "Not the way I planned them, no. But even before that I never really felt like God was One to smile down on me."

"You mean to tell me that being captured wasn't a part of your plan?" The priest gave him a droll look Garrett wasn't quite sure was condoned in the man's line of work. Between that and his crushing defeat on the checkerboard, a trip to the church wasn't getting any higher on his priority list.

"You know for a priest you don't exactly make me feel better."

The man shrugged, a slight smile still covering his expression. "I'm not that kind of a priest."

"Then what kind are you?"

Isaac completed a series of jumps that at Garrett's awe and dismay, ended the game before giving Garrett a hard look that demanded his attention. "The kind that speaks the truth, God willing. And the truth is Mr. Ward, God does care about you. It's easy to think He doesn't when life doesn't go on our own terms, but He does have a plan for you even if it isn't your plan. I think in time you'll start to see He cares about you more than you think, which I gather at present isn't a very much. Just consider you might be here for a purpose you don't know about yet."

The waitress came over with two sacks in hand. The smell of fried fish told Garrett the man's lunch was inside. She gave one to the priest and to Garrett's continued bewilderment, the other to him. He looked at the waitress whose eyes only pointed back to the holy man.

"What's this? I didn't order anything."

"It's my treat. Thanks for the game, Mr. Ward, and the conversation. I look forward to our next one." Isaac thanked the waitress and pronounced the rest of his salutations. Garrett watched him go out the front door wondering, if he, too should just call it a day and leave with his unforeseen lunch in tow.

Looking down at the checkerboard again, his mind was set on doing just that when a whisper caught his attention, the message containing anything but the expected in a tavern full of rebels.

"God save the King."

Instantly Garrett's ear drew towards it to find another surprise. "Mr. Hart?"

"Still have those boots I see." Hart came over and took a seat. He glanced at the checkerboard on the table. "Want to go a round?"

Garrett grimaced. He didn't know what Hart's skill was at the game, but he wasn't in the mood to lose a second time just in case. "No, I think I'd rather not. I will say, though, I'm surprised. I even had my suspicions you were the one that disclosed my plans to Haywood."

Hart furrowed his brow, shaking his head. "I don't know anything about that, but your plans to leave are actually the reason I came over. Washington's men are at all the main points, but there's one place they won't be suspecting: the Great Bridge."

Garrett scoffed. "You mean the main crossing over to get to Boston? I'm not sure what your intentions are, Mr. Hart, but you might as well get the noose ready for me. Washington's men will no doubt be all over that route."

"He has men there, but it's not as bad as you think. Many are down with the pox, leaving them a little scattered trying to guard the routes to and from Boston. Besides, if you go along with someone well-known in the community, it'll be less suspicious."

Garrett's eyebrow gave a distinctive raise. "Someone like yourself?"

Hart leaned in, his voice low. "As I mentioned while you were in my shop, I have family in Boston I'd like to see. I don't expect Washington's men to give me any trouble getting out of Cambridge, but I don't know about your comrades on letting me in. Even if I am a loyalist, coming from Cambridge where the opposition rests raises many alarms."

Garrett nodded, understanding perfectly. "And I could be your way in."

"I hoped we might help each other."

Garrett rubbed the side of his jaw. "That doesn't sound too bad, but there's still an issue. I saw the men on guard at one of the routes I marked, and I've been in the camp. More of the men know who I am. If they recognize me with you, resident or not, you'll go down, too."

Hart nodded. "I've thought of that. But don't forget, Mr. Ward, I am a tailor. I'll come up with something they'll be less likely to distinguish you by. Leave that part to me." Hart looked at him with confident expectation. "Otherwise, do you believe you'll consider my offer?"

With his other options having come to a standstill, Garrett wasn't sure if he'd find another way back to Boston any time soon. This might be his only opportunity and part of him wanted to reach out and take it with both hands.

"Yes, Mr. Hart. I've considered it. I'm in."

***

After Garrett had situated Athala in the barn, he went through the back door and made his way towards the front of the house. He smiled when he arrived at the parlor, the woman he recognized easily even from her back sat in the chaise lounge with a child in her arms. Not wanting to scare her or disturb the infant she oversaw, he softened his footsteps as he went around to meet her. Abigail glanced up from gazing into the child's closed eyes, but met his own with a startle. So much for keeping things calm.

"I didn't mean to scare you. I'm sorry." Garrett took a seat next to Abigail and allowed just enough room between them to be considered appropriate in public company despite wanting to be closer.

315

"It's all right." Her cheeks turned a lovely shade of pink. "I just didn't think anyone was there."

"No, you seemed caught in the moment," he admitted. "I didn't want to disturb you." Garrett's attention turned to the infant girl, nestled in her embrace. Mrs. Schreier had named the young babe Sophie after her grandmother. "She seems to have taken to you."

Abigail gave a tired smile. "I've had some practice. I held both my brother and sister when they were this young."

"Well, you better be careful, or Mrs. Schreier might have you staying longer than you intended." He gave her a smirk and she stifled a laugh, hoping to avoid waking the infant.

"Is my stay here wearing on you, already, Mr. Ward?"

Garrett could easily sense the teasing in her tone and was delighted by it. "Not at all. I for one consider it an improvement on the confines of my imprisonment here."

She gave him a droll look. "You mean your soft bed and Rebekah's impeccable cooking I'm now aware of you've been eating? I can see that all would be a rough way to be held captive."

He laughed then drew his attention to the two fingers wrapped in a small bandage. "How's the hand?"

"Better today, I think." Abigail glanced down at the injured appendage. "Although I'm not sure without moving it. Dr. Adams says one of the fingers is broken." She worked to wiggle it, but Garrett's hand gently stopped her.

He shook his head. "Not until the doctor says so. With everything you're doing around here, you'll need all ten fingers to do it. Better not chance having to handle with nine for longer than you have to."

Sophie gave the tiniest whimper that caused both sets of adult eyes to draw on her while her own remained closed in what appeared to be a deep and blissful sleep.

"Speaking of," Garrett continued, "how is our new mother doing?"

"She seems to be healing well. I haven't seen any signs of infection, but both Dr. Adams and I are keeping a close eye. It was a lot for her. I know she's growing tired of her bed, but she's going to need some more time to heal. While she does, Rebekah and I agreed to take care of this little peanut, other than her food of course." Abigail gave Sophie a tender smile before her mouth turned downward and more tense. "After that, I'll need to get back to camp. Dr. Adams and I are doing our best to trade off, but between here and the hospital and the other calls we make around town, things are a little stretched. Sometimes I wish the days were longer just to get everything done."

"I take it things haven't slowed down with the outbreak?"

She shook her head, a somberness in her expression. "No, in fact, we're running out of beds for the people coming in. I've approached Officer Haywood about the problem and requested some hay to use for bedding, but with little luck. Most of it's already set aside for the horses and that's already in short supply."

"That's not surprising, especially with winter on us. Still, there has to be something that can be done to help."

"Well, if you think of something, let me know. I'm open to ideas. I doubt anyone would have anything negative to say about it if they found out one of the King's men helped treat the smallpox endeavor and got Washington's troops up and running again." She smiled before a yawn beckoned.

Garrett looked again towards the infant, still snuggled in Abigail's lap. "Why don't you get some rest." It had been more of a suggestion than a question. "If Sophie wakes up, I'll have Rebekah take her to her mother." Before she could refuse, he took the child gingerly in his arms. Her brow compressed as if to convey her confusion before the eyes beneath them began to glisten in response to his offer.

"Thank you," she said. The depth of the appreciation in her tone only made his desire rise to carry out the task. He watched her climb the stairs before turning his attention back towards Sophie, now cradled in his own arms. Taking a deep breath, Garrett knew exactly what he needed to do.

Chapter 28

Abigail awoke from the most refreshing sleep she could remember. The warm bed, with its soft, linen sheets heated by the hot coals of the warming pan were beyond commendation. Not just compared to the barracks of the continental camp, but because the dire need for sleep she yearned for the past two weeks had finally been met.

She didn't mind helping tend to Mrs. Schreier and she found she rather enjoyed taking care of baby Sophie. She'd aided her mother with Henry and Olivia, but she hadn't comprehended how tired she'd become or what little rest she would obtain between here at the estate and her responsibilities back at the camp. If she'd been busy before, now she was pushed more than ever. Or at least she had been.

Abigail closed her eyes, taking in a deep breath and savored the sweet moment. Garrett. He had surprised her too. Without realizing it, she was certain, he had been there for her, in a way she needed someone the most. He'd given her the opportunity to step away, literally taking one of those responsibilities out of her hands, and for that she was truly thankful. She stretched, then veered her gaze towards the bedroom window and gasped.

The sun was at its peak. Half the day was already gone. How long had she slept? Hours? Days? She quickly readied herself to fasten her corset and working dress before pinning her hair back and out of the way. With hurried steps down the stairs, she wondered if Garrett had been tending to Sophie all the while she'd been asleep.

"Well, good afternoon, sleepy head." The youthful greeting had come from a voice she recognized well, but not one she'd expected to hear in the Schreier estate.

"Charlotte?" The younger Miss Thatcher was propped in the chaise where she had left Garrett, though Abigail knew not how long ago. And as if unchanged, Sophie was sleeping soundly on her lap.

"In the flesh."

"How? When?" Abigail considered pinching herself to see if she was still dreaming.

"I've been here since the morning, but as far as the how, well that's a little more interesting." A smile curled Charlotte's lips." It seems you have a guardian angel here in Cambridge."

It didn't take long for an image to come to mind.

"Garrett." Abigail whispered his name under her breath but could see Charlotte was waiting for the confirmation.

Her sister's smile deepened. "I received word from him by the courier. He cares for you, Abby. That's plain enough."

"He's been a good friend."

"He's become more than a friend, if you want my opinion."

Abigail hesitated. It wasn't that she didn't want to tell Charlotte how she was beginning to feel about Garrett, but more that she didn't quite know what to do about it. It wasn't that long ago when she'd held him responsible for the destruction of her town. She understood now how unfair that was. He'd only been following orders. Orders that had been given by someone else. Now, she was beginning to see a new side of him.

She pushed that thought aside for another. Or could it be that side had always been there, but she had been so caught up in her own pain that she hadn't seen it? When she didn't answer, Charlotte took it upon herself to interpret.

"Oh, come on, Abby," she sneered. "I'm your sister. I know what that expression means. You care for him, too."

She did. Abigail couldn't argue with that. Not that Charlotte would have believed her if she tried, but there was an obstacle between them she didn't quite know what to do with.

"I do care for him," Abigail admitted. "But even so, I'm not so sure it matters. We're on different sides of this war, remember?" Even if her reason for joining the army camp was no longer out of anger, she was still serving the cause, a cause she didn't necessarily refute, either. And Garrett, too, had made himself clear. He wanted to make captain more than anything. She wanted that for him, even knowing she may never see him again. All that she did know was one day Garrett wouldn't be a prisoner anymore. He would return to the Royal Navy and, as if they had never met at all, each of them would go about his or her own way. It was a thought that crushed her inside more than she realized.

Charlotte gave her a probing eye. "That may be, but right now you're not. From where I'm standing, he's not even in it, but more on the sidelines, really."

"He'll eventually go back, Charlotte. What would I do then?"

"Well, for gosh sakes, Abby, it's not like you have to marry the man."

Abigail blinked. "Marry?" The very mention of the word made her falter, but then she began to think of what life would be like married to Garrett Ward. He was a man she respected more than she thought possible and had somehow managed to soften her heart towards him despite thinking it could never happen. The idea of it was certainly more than appealing.

Charlotte shook her head, concern lighting her features. "I was just kidding, Abby." The smile faded a degree. "The truth is, I'm not sure about all that, but I do know you like him. That means a lot considering you haven't given any of the men back home a chance to court you." She let a deep breath pass in and out again. "Besides, I'm not completely convinced he's as hard-pressed to go back as you think, at least not in light of what he's done."

"What do you mean? What has he done?"

"I'll let him tell you himself, but I think you'll appreciate it." Charlotte gave a heartfelt smile that somehow made Abigail feel a little better despite the questions that still lingered in her mind. The moment passed, however, realizing if her sister was here, what did that mean for things back home?

"What about Mother? How is she?"

"She's actually doing well, even better than during your visit. I'm glad I can tell you that."

Abigail's heart stirred with relief, now ready to feel the full joy of having her sister nearby. "Me too, and I'm so glad you're here. How long are you staying?"

Charlotte shrugged. "That depends on Mrs. Schreier. I've had the liberty of meeting her already, and she wants me to stay at least until she's well enough to host another dinner party. She seems insistent to it. But honestly, Abby, I don't think I can tell that woman no after she's been through so much. I suppose with Mother's doing all right, a little longer wouldn't hurt."

Abigail stole a glance at Sophie, amazed the new infant seemed to have already changed so much. She still slept soundly and still needed to be handled with much care, but she also seemed less fragile than the first day she drew breath.

"I can take her if you like," Abigail offered, gesturing her hands out to receive the babe.

Charlotte gave an adamant shake of her head. "Not today. I'm under strict orders not to relinquish Sophie to you for the next few hours. If you have a problem with that, you can take it up with my superior." A mischievous grin broke through.

The older of the two crossed her arms. "And where might I find your superior?"

Charlotte's eyes shifted to the corner and upwards in the direction of the stairs. "He should still be in his room. When I spoke with him earlier, he said for you just to knock when you woke up."

"I'll do that. Making good on her word, Abigail ascended the stairway. She had a good idea in mind of just who Charlotte's superior was.

What had Garrett been up to? Yet, she couldn't help but feel grateful for what she'd already known he'd done. The joy beat rapidly in her chest, now fathoming just how much she'd longed to see Charlotte until her sister was right there in the parlor in front of her. But Charlotte hinted there was more.

When she arrived at the designated room, she gave the door two light taps. A moment later, Garrett stood before her underneath the entryway.

"Garrett Ward, why, I have half the mind to..." She held his gaze, unflinching before letting out a breath. She let her gratitude show. "Thank you." The alarm starting to cross his face, receded into that rogue-like grin she was starting to like more each time.

"You had me. I was beginning to think I'd made a mistake writing to Charlotte to come."

"No, actually I'm grateful she's here. I've really missed her. Thank you for doing that and for taking Sophie last night, too."

"You're welcome. Come on in if you like." He moved over to allow her to pass through, leaving the door open. "There's just one thing I need to finish up."

She watched him walk over to a small secretary. There he gathered a few sheets of paper before folding them together and sealing them with the wax she'd recognized from previous trips to the courier.

"Is that a letter for Nicholas?"

He nodded. "It is, actually. Would you mind taking it?"

"No, I don't mind. I did have one set aside for Charlotte I was going to take, but that's no longer a priority it seems." She was about to grab the small bundle when a piece of paper once covered by Nicholas' letter on the desk, now lay open in full view. The markings were what drew her attention, not completely identical, but too close in comparison to another she'd seen in Portsmouth when she'd spoken to Abraham. With her appreciation suddenly deflating, she pointed to the table. "Garrett, what's that?"

Garrett's eyes followed her finger at what she could only guess to be a tool in correspondence. Without wanting to, her mind drew quick conclusions for its use and why she'd seen her brother and Garrett, both soldiers of an army, with it.

"That's a cipher key. I use it for my letters with Nicholas." He went over to the desk and grabbed the sheet in hand. "Here, I'll show you how it works." He drew a set of symbols across the page that to her looked more like Henry's doodling back home than a means of exchanging information. "You have to have the key to know what to look for and figure out the message, otherwise it means nothing." He placed the paper containing the key below the drawings and pointed to the letters that went with the corresponding symbols. Once he showed her, she got it.

"X MARKS THE SPOT"

She would have laughed if it weren't for one thing. "That's clever, but why would you need a cipher?"

The realization of what she was asking shot across his face. "Now, hold on, Abigail." Garrett held up a hand as if trying to block her thoughts from going down a one-way path. "Before you decide I went against our agreement and have been telling Nicholas about the state of Washington's army, let me explain. Nicholas and I aren't exchanging that kind of information. We're only trying to be careful. We may not be passing critical knowledge back and forth, but you never know what someone can make out of the bits and pieces even if you think it's nothing. When it comes to war, information is critical. You might be willing to take the letters to the courier for me, of which I'm grateful, but I wouldn't be surprised if Washington has someone intercepting them. I'd expect the same for when Nicholas receives mine. It's just part of how things play out." His eyes locked onto hers. "But believe me, Abigail. I am a man of my word, and I promise I haven't gone outside of it."

"Fine." Abigail took the intended letter for Nicholas and placed it in her apron pocket. "I believe you. I just don't know what to do with what you told me about that." She gestured over to the cipher key. "I saw my brother, Abraham, with one on my visit to my aunt's. What would he be doing with it?"

"It's hard to say for sure. As I mentioned earlier, you just never know whom to trust when it comes to war. Being cautious becomes essential. He could just be doing the same thing as Nicholas and I are doing, or…"

"Or what?"

Garrett scratched the faint whiskers of his chin. "Or he could be a spy."

Abigail half stumbled backward. "A spy? For Washington's army, you mean?"

Garrett shrugged as if the alarms that sounded in her had somehow been triggered by mistake.

"That's another reason that comes to mind, but if Washington is using spies, they'll be people he trusts, and it sounds as if he didn't even meet your brother until a few months ago. It would be hard to build trust in that amount of time."

"We've known each other that long." Her face went warm, but she felt what she had to say was necessary for argument's sake. "I think it's possible."

Garrett smiled. "It's good to hear you say that in light of what we just discussed earlier, and I agree, it's possible. But we've been in contact nearly every day and have spent more than just a few minutes with each other even on occasion. Washington, on the other hand, is the head of an army. He sees more than a handful of faces each day, and the ones he encounters the most, besides his wife if she's in town, are his officers. Since your brother is neither, I would guess he hasn't had much time with the continental general." His eyes filled with compassion. "I'm sorry I mentioned it. The truth is we don't know anything for sure. Try not to get too worried about it just yet especially since I might have an idea to help with what's going on at the hospital."

Abigail's concern for her brother lessened somewhat by both Garrett's explanation and her intrigue.

"You have an idea?"

He nodded. "But it's going to have to be a team effort. I was thinking of how we sleep on the ship while on the water. For most of the crew, we just sleep on hammocks hung from beams above us and take them down in the mornings to get them out of the way. I imagine getting hold of sailcloth would be easier in Boston by the ports and I doubt the Vassall house has any places to hang the canvas, but the idea got me thinking. If Nikolai and I built the frames underneath, fabric could be stretched over it like a cot. It wouldn't be as comfortable as a straw stuffed mattress, but better than the floor." His eyes wandered over hers with anticipation.

"What about the material? Wood could be used for the platform, but where can we get the cloth?"

"I have an idea on that too. Just let me worry about that and the structures. What I don't know how to do is sew, at least nothing more than a button and not particularly well. If you could work on the cloth, we could get the job done. I'm sure of it. We wouldn't be alone in the work either. I've enlisted some help already if you think it's a good plan."

Abigail's heart stilled, overwhelmed. "A good plan? Garrett, that's just what we need. How fast can you get the material?"

His smile resurfaced again. "I'll go now if you want."

"Good, I'll come with you. Since Charlotte is watching Sophie, I have a little time before I need to get to the hospital."

He raised a thick, black eyebrow. "Are you sure? I thought maybe you'd like some time to relax?"

"Garrett, I've already had more time to rest this morning since I've arrived here in camp. I'm coming too."

He laughed and the sound of it made her heart lift. "All right then. Let's get going."

***

When they arrived at the cobbler's, Abigail's understanding of how they would obtain the material they needed was all but clear. She guessed Garrett could read her uncertain expression when he gently urged her to go in the store, giving her the comforting smile she now knew she could trust. Still, she had to ask.

"The shoemaker's?"

He tipped his head to signal she'd spoken rightly. "We'll get the fabric, but I need to make a stop here first." He put his arm through hers like they'd done in camp on the day of Sophie's birth and guided her the rest of the way.

Abigail stood in the back of the shop while Garrett went over to the man she'd guessed to be in charge seeing he was the only one in the store. Garrett kept his voice soft as both sets of eyes drew downward towards Garrett's boots before returning upwards again. She couldn't gather much from their conversation as far as dialogue went, but she read an earnest determination in Garrett's features as he waited for the response of the cobbler. After what seemed like some brief deliberation on the tradesmen's part, the man seemed willing to agree with whatever had transpired between them. The cobbler motioned for Garrett to follow him out of her sight. Within a few minutes the two men returned as they had left with one exception Abigail clearly noted.

"Garrett, you traded your boots?" She'd waited until they were out of the store, but now that they had, she couldn't continue to keep her shock at bay.

An easy smile without regret brightened his features. "I ran out of funds a while back, so I got us some cash for the fabric. I hope it'll be enough."

Abigail glanced at the shoes that had managed to replace Garrett's King ordered, Naval-grade leather boots. They were worn and ragged from use, barely put together, and did little good for the purposes of protecting one's feet.

"I can't believe the cobbler even had a pair like that. They look as if they need to be stripped for parts and thrown away rather than repaired."

He laughed. "Actually, they were thrown away."

Her eyes shot wide. "Garrett, you can't wear those. They barely have soles attached and even one of those has a hole in it."

"I'll manage. Besides, it's for a good cause."

"A cause you don't believe in," she reminded.

"I never said I didn't believe in human life." He revealed a handsome grin full of compassion. "Now, let's get to the drapers. We have a lot of work to do."

Chapter 29

Abigail sat in one of the wingback chairs of the parlor while she stitched a piece of linen fabric the draper sold them from Garrett's shoe money. A smile crept on her face for both the tragedy of the boots he now wore and the triumph she now felt in her chest for what he had done to help the hospital patients. She quickly corrected herself. What he was still doing.

As she worked on the cot sheets, Garrett was out back, building the structures to hold the fabric in place. She was just glad he wasn't alone in the task. He'd asked Nikolai and Thomas to join in, an invitation Thomas was more than a little excited to be a part of.

She'd appreciated that too, how Garrett had taken Thomas under his wing when things fell short with Mr. Bates. Not that it was the older man's fault for getting sick as he had, but Abigail could see there was a connection between them she wasn't so sure she could fully understand. It was something that went farther than a relationship between two males, something she'd never experienced, the loss of a father.

"You're sure smilin' about somethin' over there, Miss Abby."

Rebekah sat across from her in the chaise lounge sewing her own piece of fabric.

"I have a feeling I know just what that might be about." Charlotte finished tying off a piece of thread before she gave Abigail a knowing glance from the other wingback.

"Can't say I blame you. In time a person is bound to show his true colors, and I believe Mr. Ward has shown his on more than one occasion. Seems there's more to the man than just that navy blue he dragged in here with on his first day on the estate." Rebekah worked another stitch, moving through the material slow and meticulously.

Abigail stiffened. Had Garrett picked up on her feelings as easily as these two women did? "Believe it or not, ladies, I'm thinking of how much this is going to help the patients." And she was. Unfortunately, the smallpox cases still came in. She already had to put some of the patients on the floor temporarily, but at the rate they were going on the cots, she hoped to get them a bed by tonight, if not sooner. "They're so uncomfortable with their symptoms, the least I can do for them is get a suitable place to rest while they bare it."

"I assume that means the sickness is still spreading?"

Abigail nodded, confirming Charlotte's suspicion. "It is, but thankfully more mildly now. People are still coming in, but we've also had a few return to the camp. It's steady, but we're managing it. If things continue to slow down, Dr. Adams has allowed me to go with him on more visits, but that could be for some time yet." She shrugged. "I don't know. We'll see."

"Sounds like the good doctor has some plans." Charlotte gave an encouraging smile.

"He wants me to see all I can while he's still here."

Rebekah's careful pin and pricking of the thread ceased abruptly. "You mean he's leavin' us?"

"Not yet, but he's voiced his intention to in the spring." Abigail shifted, remembering that wasn't completely true. "Or when Washington moves on from Cambridge. Whichever comes first."

"Does that mean you'll be leavin' us too, Miss Abby?" Rebekah waited patiently for an answer Abigail didn't quite know the response to give. In truth, her plans for what she'd do after Cambridge were a little foggy. Part of her hoped Dr. Adams might have asked her to continue her studies learning from him, but he hadn't, while another part of her still yearned to be with her mother wherever that may be, to make sure she was truly all right. She knew Charlotte wouldn't still be here if that weren't the case, regardless of Margaret's feelings, but there was something about seeing a loved one in person rather than just hearing of them that deepened, her desire to see her mother. Voicing the truth, she admitted the only thing she did know.

"I'm not certain where I'm going when the time comes, but I will be leaving Cambridge. Whether that's to go back home or continue with the army, I haven't decided just yet."

"You don't know if you'll come home?"

Abigail met Charlotte's frown with a gentle smile. "Part of me does, but I also believe I'm doing a good thing here, too. Our mother and Abraham tried to help me see that back in Portsmouth and now I'm starting to."

Charlotte's downward expression curbed into a smirk. "Cambridge has changed you."

Abigail gave a slight tilt of her head. "For the better or worse?"

"I can't decide yet, but I'm leaning towards better. I remember the day of the attack when we were in the garden thinking you would never leave the farm. Nothing wrong with that, but I always thought you were capable of more. Now look at you. It's like you've spread your wings."

Abigail recalled their conversation that day and how willing Charlotte was to leave and discover more of the world. Pride bellowed out of her heart for her sister's own sacrifice to stay behind with their mother, knowing full-well Charlotte's own sense of adventure was surely calling.

"I think this war has changed all of us in some way." Abigail looked again at Charlotte, now seeing less of the girl they'd left back in Falmouth and more of the woman she'd become. "Thank you for staying with Mother and the rest of our family in Portsmouth while Abraham and I have been here. I know that's not exactly what you wanted to do, but it's been a great help." She let out a breath mixed with confidence and anticipation for the unseen future. "But something tells me you, too, won't be far behind and given the chance to spread your own wings."

***

Despite the coolness in the air, Garrett wiped the sweat from his brow before he counted the finished structures. With the help of Nikolai and Thomas, the three of them were able to cut, smooth and put together seven frames that could be used for the cots with one more on the way. It was a good start, and it was only because he'd had the teamwork of his companions to do it, though he had to admit his shortsightedness. He'd felt confident with Nikolai having seen him work around the estate and stables, but he wasn't sure what to expect from Thomas. What he discovered now, however, was the error of his judgment.

Thomas was an asset. He worked harder than some of the crew Garrett had been on board the *Piper* whom he'd watched rigging the sails over and again. The boy could smooth away the rough work of the chopped wood he and Nikolai produced more than decently. It was no wonder his mother missed him as much as she did.

"Garrett, sir." Nikolai took an old rag, wiping his forehead and neck with it. The winter air had failed to keep him cool. "It looks like we'll be needin' some more pegs for the headboard and nails, too, when we're ready to secure the fabric. I think I got some left in the shed. I'll be back in just a minute."

Garrett nodded. "Thomas, why don't we take a break, too."

Without need for coercion, Thomas yielded the smoothing plane in his hand and accepted the flask Garrett offered him with an over eagerness Garrett remembered in his own youth.

"Don't get too excited. It's just water, but feel free to have as much as you want."

Though wearing a look of disappointment, the boy still drank heartedly. "Thank you, sir." Thomas held the flask out for Garrett to take. "Where'd you get that?"

Garrett understood the question to be asking if the flask was a gift or memento of some kind from someone loved but gone. He wished he could say it was from his father, but in truth he'd received it from the captain soon after he joined the Navy. It did, however, still come with some fatherly advice. Garrett returned the now mostly emptied vessel back to his coat pocket.

"I received it as a gift when I graduated from landsman to seaman. I was told to always keep it full." It was the captain's way of telling him to always have a plan. Garrett gave a side grin. "You know, on a ship at sea we're surrounded by water on all sides, but there's not one drop of it I can drink."

The light in Thomas' eyes showed Garrett he'd comprehended the message. "You have to be prepared."

"It's a pretty good life lesson." Garrett admitted.

"Thank you for the water, sir."

"You're welcome. Thanks for helping. You're quite the worker, Thomas. I'm sure your mother misses that work ethic at home especially with your six siblings afoot."

Thomas let out a small laugh. "She does, but she also knows it's important to me to be here, even if we haven't received our wages yet."

Garrett had heard about that. Apparently, the rebel Congress had delayed the requested funds for its troops, though he didn't know why.

He wasn't jealous of Washington having to deal with that, but he hoped the delay might have been enough to send Thomas back home to safety. Still, he knew from experience the pain of losing one's father was strong. Garrett could understand Thomas' determination to find restitution for his death, but he liked the idea of seeing Thomas on the battlefield about as much as he liked imagining Abigail Thatcher on it.

"So, I take it you're not going home any time soon?"

"Go home?" Thomas shook his head with a youthful vengeance. "I can't go home now, not since I found out I'll be playing the fife to help lead the troops when Knox gets here with the guns and cannons."

Garrett's stomach did a somersault. The words "guns" and "cannons" deserved his attention. "I thought artillery supplies were low. What exactly does Knox have?"

Thomas hesitated, no doubt remembering Garrett's allegiance.

"Don't worry. Whatever you tell me won't get far. I made a promise I wouldn't say anything to jeopardize this army and whether I like it or not, I intend to keep it."

Thomas met his gaze, staring him straight through before he began again. "There's news General Henry Knox has over fifty cannons from Ticonderoga."

Garrett's jaw went slack. "That's over 300 miles from here, not to mention the snow and ice he'll have to cross."

"Some say he's had to use a combination of boat and ox-drawn sleigh to do it."

"And a whole lot of manpower, and I suspect it wouldn't take anything short of that."

Thomas gave an enthusiastic nod. "Yep! I'm told Knox should be arriving any day now."

"Any day?"

Thomas beamed, but Garrett couldn't bring himself to share in the excitement, not when his comrades sat unsuspecting in Boston. Any day now, Knox would be arriving with a large mass of artillery that would no doubt be pointed towards them and he couldn't do anything about it. At least, not if he kept his word to Abigail, something he was determined on doing. But, was it ever as tempting as it was now to break.

He wanted to warn his comrades, to warn Nicholas of what was coming. Graves needed to know he was about to get a problem bigger than *Common Sense*. Garrett inhaled sharply. He never felt so torn. Loyalty to his country and to the men he served with or to be a man of his word. He shook his head in frustration, though glad to see Thomas had made himself busy again, smoothing out the rest of the wood for the last frame.

"For I know the plans I have for you," declares the Lord, "plans to prosper you and not to harm you, plans to give you hope and a future."

That's certainly not what it was feeling like. Garrett wished he could talk with his father now to sort all this out. Maybe he could've helped explain why God was putting him through all this. Instead, his conversation with Isaac came to the forefront of his mind. "He does have a plan for you even if it isn't your plan."

Garrett could agree on that much. God's plan was definitely not his plan. What he still had trouble believing was God cared for him when Garrett felt like he had both hands tied behind his back.

Nikolai returned with the nails and pegs and instantly frowned when his eyes caught sight of Garrett. "Thomas, why don't you go inside and get somethin' to eat. Ask Miss Rebekah and tell her I sent you."

Without further probing and hunger apparently on the boy's mind, Thomas put his plane aside on the porch before he disappeared inside.

When he was gone, Nikolai gave Garrett a scrutinizing look. "What's wrong, Garrett? I've only been gone a few minutes, but I can tell somethin' has happened even in that time."

Garrett closed his eyes, the weight of the discouragement sinking in like an anchor that pulled him down to the ocean floor. He told Nikolai of Thomas' news.

Nikolai had a solemn expression, one Garrett appreciated in that moment. "I'm sorry, sir. I know that's a great word for many, but not so for youself."

"I'm just trying to understand it all."

"Have you prayed about it, sir? It may not give you all the answers, but I do find it helps. I'll pray with you if you want."

"Thanks, Nikolai. I appreciate that, but maybe another time. For now, I think I'll go check in to see how the fabric is coming along." Garrett paused, thinking it couldn't hurt, especially now. "But I would ask if you wouldn't mind praying for me."

The man gave a gracious grin. "Never stopped, sir."

When Garrett passed through the back door, he spotted Thomas in the kitchen, grabbing a bite to eat and Rebekah close by. He waved to them briefly, but went on, making his way to the parlor.

"How's it going in here?"

"We have six sheets finished." Abigail pointed to a pile of fabric laid out in rectangles neatly on the floor. "Charlotte and I are working on the other two, but we should be done soon."

"That's good. After Nikolai gets the last frame together, we'll have eight beds you can use. We'll see if that gives you a good start."

"Oh, it will." Garrett could see the brightness in her eyes waver as she met his own. "But why do I get the feeling I'm more excited about this when it was clearly your idea? You're not having second thoughts about helping the patients, are you?"

He shook his head. "No, not at all. I'm glad we're doing this."

Abigail tilted her chin and narrowed her sight further in on him. Her eyes looked into his with concern.

"You know, I believe I'll go check on Sophie. I would think Margaret is done feeding her by now." Charlotte put her work aside on the cushion of the wingback chair she'd occupied and passed him on the way to the stairs, but not before he caught her lingering eye letting him know her action was deliberate. Garrett went over to the chaise lounge and took a seat.

Abigail came over next to him. The closeness of her made him feel better instantly. "Garrett, what's wrong? Are you all right?" She waited with patient expectancy as he drew in a deep breath and breathed it out again.

"General Henry Knox is expected to be in Cambridge soon with a gift for Washington I'm sure the commander will be more than pleased to receive." Confusion crossed over her face and he went on. "I'm told the former bookkeeper has over fifty cannons with him, and I also have a pretty good idea of what's going to happen when he gets here."

"You think Washington will attack Boston?"

"I would."

Abigail pulled back. "You would?"

"If I were in his shoes, I mean. I doubt anyone in the city suspects a man traveled 300 miles over ice and snow lugging a battery of cannon. A single 12-pounder alone weighs over 1,000 pounds, let alone fifty of them, and that's not taking into account any larger ones he might have with him. Even if people happen to hear about it, I doubt they'd believe it."

She leaned in again, doubt flickering. "But what about the army? There are still a good many men sick with smallpox. Wouldn't he want to wait until those men recover to attack?"

"Not if he wants to risk losing the element of surprise. If he waits too long he just might. Besides, with the guns he'll have, he won't need everyone on the battlefield."

"I'm sorry, Garrett. I know you're worried about Nicholas." Abigail placed her hand on his like she had when they'd been in the church for the New Years' service, but instead of taking it away briefly after, she kept a steady hold on it. Her touch came both as a comfort and sent up a spike of emotions that made him want to do more.

He was never looking for a wife, even before he woke up to find himself in Cambridge as a prisoner of this army, an army he was beginning to respect a little more each day. His mind was always set on one thing: becoming a captain. But as he'd learned through the years and especially now, the best things you come across in life are sometimes found when you least expect them.

"For I know the plans I have for you," declares the Lord, "plans to prosper you and not to harm you, plans to give you hope and a future."

The stillness of their small embrace made him all the more aware of something he'd failed to recognize as he continued to ponder the works of God's plan to his life. He didn't know for sure, but he couldn't help but wonder if Abigail Thatcher was somehow part of his future.

Chapter 30

The next day, and after a restless night of sleep, Garrett managed to find some solace in his dilemma concerning General Knox and his heavy guns. With the onset of the unexpected news, he'd somehow forgotten his deal with Hart. But now as he thought of Nicholas and the uncertainty if the courier would be back to deliver his message in time, Garrett's thoughts could scarcely think of anything other than the tailor getting him to Boston as soon as he could. Well, anything else, but the one woman who'd captivated his attention whether she meant to or not.

Having checked in at Hart's and seen the man was as truly prepared as he claimed to be, Garrett began to feel more settled about tonight. He was looking forward to the dinner to welcome Mrs. Schreier out of her bedroom chambers and into the world again, even if his true eagerness stemmed from spending the evening with Abigail.

He picked up the pace back to the Schreier estate, the clock's hour vivid in his mind from when he looked at it in Hart's shop. The time for dinner was right on his heels. Things had taken longer than he thought, mostly due to the fact the tailor wasn't expecting to leave the next day.

After some thorough discussion, though, they were able to sort their plan out to both their satisfaction.

Garrett entered through the back door of the house and bolted up to his room to get ready before heading back down again. When he arrived at the dining room, all parties had already taken their seats, a clear sign he was a little more than late. Despite his tardiness, he smiled to see Mrs. Schreier was now occupied in her designated seat after receiving approval from Dr. Adams to venture from her bed. Charlotte had also made the attendance and he was pleased to see Thomas had too, sitting next to the younger Miss Thatcher. The boy beamed with an awkward grin that reminded Garrett of the first time he'd spoken with a girl in his own youth, though he had the impression Thomas' feelings for Charlotte weren't mutual. Abigail sat across from her sister, and her eyes lit up when they met his. The small gesture caused his heart to gallop faster than Athala could run.

"Mr. Ward, please join us." Mrs. Schreier spoke from the head of the table. "My apologies, but we have already made ourselves comfortable. As you can see, the doctor has allowed me to finally exit my chambers, but I'm afraid I'm still a little weak. I hope you understand." She smiled good-humoredly before she addressed him again. "You can take your seat next to Abigail."

Garrett did so, more than pleased by the lady's order. "No apologies are necessary, especially since it seems I'm the one who didn't get here in time. You are looking well, Mrs. Schreier. I'm glad to see Dr. Adams has allowed you away from the bed."

"To be sure, Mr. Ward, to be sure! One gets restless when confined for too long. My gratitude goes to Rebekah and Miss Abigail and now more recently Miss Charlotte here too." She switched her glance momentarily to the younger Miss Thatcher, an appreciative smile across her lips.

Garrett looked about the room, realizing it wasn't complete. "And where is our little one who has caused all this trouble?" A playful banter encompassed his tone.

"Rebekah is getting Sophie tucked in for the night as we speak, but she'll be down in a minute. I suspect that's when Nikolai will join us too." The satisfaction in her demeanor slowly faded. "In the meantime, I've heard we've received some troubling news for our side of the war?"

Garrett winced. He was hoping the evening would stray away from topics that made him feel useless. "Yes, Madame." No doubt she was referring to Henry Knox.

Mrs. Schreier gave a disappointed sigh, taking a small sip from her drinking glass. "I suppose this awful conflict is going to last longer than I thought after all, though Mr. Ward," she tipped her chin, her eyes to the floor then back up again at him, "I would advise a different pair of boots if you're planning to keep up with it. Alex would like your choice in German taste, but I'm afraid he would not approve, and myself likewise, of the state those Hessian boots are in."

Garrett half-choked on his own drink, but his gaze turned towards Abigail and couldn't help smiling. She was having her own difficulty holding back a laugh from the small secret they kept between them.

"Have you heard of any news from Mr. Schreier as of late?" Having recovered before he did, Abigail asked the question and Margaret's eyes brightened.

"Actually yes. I'm expecting him in a fortnight. He'll not only meet Sophie, but you all as well."

As promised, Rebekah came into the dining room with Nikolai, both carrying a plate in each hand. "Now that little Sophie is in the land of hushabye, I have our dinner for tonight." She set the two plates on the table, Nikolai following her lead. It was then Garrett realized there would be something else he'd miss other than Abigail Thatcher when he left for Boston in the morning: Rebekah's cooking. The chef gave a languid smile with a twinkle in her eye. "I hope you're hungry."

"Schweinebraten. Rebekah, my favorite." Mrs. Schreier beamed and Rebekah responded with a satisfied smile at the succulent pork roast on the table.

"Not like I'm gonna fix anythin' else but for your celebration out of that bed. It's about time." Rebekah's expression grew more attentive. "How you feelin' now that you've walked about some, Miss?"

"I'm a little sore from the whole ordeal, and I get tired easily, but I hope that changes the more I move about." Mrs. Schreier looked to Abigail as if for confirmation.

Abigail gave an easy nod. "Dr. Adams says you're healing well and as much as I can tell I have to agree. But yes, you'll start feeling more like yourself as you gain your strength."

"That's good news, Miss Abby. You've been doin' a lot of good around here, not just with Margaret, but with those patients too. You and Mr. Ward here sure to make a great team."

Garrett noticed a pink hue in Abigail's cheeks, but she managed a smile.

"Thank you, Rebekah, but it was actually Mr. Ward's idea and not only that, but a group effort as you might recall." Abigail glanced around the table, eyes filled with gratitude. "We couldn't have done it without all those involved. And because of you all, everyone at the hospital now has a bed."

"That's wonderful news, Abigail." Mrs. Schreier clasped both hands, an expression of delight at the announcement.

"Sure is! Let me go back to the kitchen to get the rest and we can celebrate that too." Rebekah motioned to Nikolai. "Come on, Nikolai. I could still use another set of hands."

"And Rebekah, remind me when you return to tell you some news you too might be interested in." The woman stopped to look back, a questioning brow peaking just above her dark brown eyes. "I hope it's news that won't spoil our joy for the current occasion."

"I'll let you make the decision on that." A wry smile curved Margaret's lips. Rebekah shook her head candidly as she left the room with Nikolai trailing close behind.

It was only a moment after she disappeared when they all heard the knock from the front door. A few minutes later, Rebekah came back to the dining room, but empty-handed of the food she'd promised. The jubilant demeanor they'd last seen her with was now stricken bleak.

"What is it, Rebekah?" Mrs. Schreier was the one to voice everyone's concern.

"Ma'am, Mr. Haywood is at the door. He says he has urgent news for Miss Abigail."

All eyes turned towards the young lady of interest who wore a similar expression in regard to the officer's untimely visit.

"All right then, we'll set a plate for him." Mrs. Schreier's tone perked with confidence, no doubt determined to keep their party in high spirits. "Perhaps Officer Haywood would like to join us in our celebration. I doubt he cares much for my own accomplishment, but I can't imagine he wouldn't be satisfied to know the needs of the camp hospital have been met."

"Yes, ma'am. I'll get another setting and send him in."

A moment later after Rebekah had gone, Haywood entered past the entryway to the dining room. He held his hat between his fingers with a look of melancholy in his features. It made him seem like he carried more of a heavy grievance than the lightweight accessory that normally adorned his head.

"Officer Haywood." Their hostess addressed him readily. "Why, you look as if the war is over and your side was not the one to claim victory. Pray, what is wrong, sir? Please come join us for dinner. We have much to be thankful for this evening, including the new cots at the camp hospital, the very idea coming from Mr. Ward here." She gestured over to Garrett who caught Haywood's jaw go firm as an involuntary glare went his direction. The officer scanned over to the seat next to him to Abigail, his eyes softening. He cleared his throat and resumed his initial countenance as his voice took a somber, yet official tone.

"Thank you, Madame, but I'm afraid I will have to decline this evening, and I'm sorry, but it seems I have to further interfere with your, uh, dinner party." The last words came out coarse like he'd taken a bite of burnt toast and needed to spit it out. "You see, General Washington has requested an audience with Miss Abigail Thatcher this very evening. I am to bring her without delay."

Garrett noticed from Abigail's puzzled expression she too was perplexed by the ordeal.

"Me, sir? Are you certain, for a meeting with Washington?"

Haywood nodded, though with marked irritability. "Yes, Miss Thatcher. Quite certain, and as I said, without delay."

She nodded, rising from her chair to follow the officer, but not before her eyes met Garrett's on the way out.

***

Hours later, Garrett sat alone in the parlor. The fire had long since died after he'd said goodnight to Thomas who'd hitched a ride with Nikolai back to camp and to the women who resided in the house. All three had given up on their waiting to hear of what news had been made known to Abigail, even assuming she'd decided to stay within the camp for the night. Garrett wondered, too, but tonight he couldn't sleep. There was far too much on his mind that wouldn't allow it.

The news of Knox still ate at him, and now he wondered about Abigail. He'd wanted to tell her his plans for leaving tomorrow after dinner tonight, hoping they'd have some time for just the two of them to talk, but that strategy fell through. What urgent reason would the commanding general of this army have for seeing her?

Garrett tried to sort out the possibilities, coming up short until an idea came to him and the hair on the back of his neck stood on end. Could he be the reason Washington had sent for her? Did the general know about the letters to Nicholas? Was she in trouble? Garrett certainly hadn't said anything to his friend that would've compromised the continental general, just as he promised. He let his mind race through the contents of their correspondence just to make certain. No, he didn't. He knew he didn't. Not when Abigail had already risked so much to help him in the first place. But even so, that didn't mean she couldn't be reprimanded for the act itself. And, if that was the case, what would a man like Washington do?

Garrett continued to go over other possibilities, trying to make sense of it when he heard the faint sound of voices just beyond the parlor window outside the house. The blackness of the night made it hard to see, but he could pick up the rigid murmur of Haywood through the windowpane. Even in his own dim candlelight, Garrett recognized that figure next to the camp officer from anywhere.

Haywood was talking to Abigail. He'd accompanied her home. Garrett wondered if they'd seen him through the parlor window, but if they had, they gave no indication of it. He sat still, unsure of whether he should greet them properly at the door or if that would be seen as an infringement. Feeling he had already intruded, even if his presence in the parlor had been innocent, he decided to wait. Though only a few minutes passed, the anticipation to see Abigail and learn what she'd discovered this evening seemed to make the hands of the grandfather clock crawl.

Garrett finally heard a single pair of footsteps enter the house. At first, they stepped past the parlor entryway as if bound for the stairs. He felt her panic through the wood flooring before they slowed and turned back a few paces.

"Garrett?" The unease of Abigail's voice made his gut knot tight. He thought she turned towards him, but he couldn't be sure. Even with the single flicker of candlelight that haloed around her, it was hard to see her in the hallway.

"Yes, it's me. What's happened? Is everything all right?" He'd heard the despair in her tone to know it wasn't. He wanted her to be the one to decide if she wanted to tell him or not in case the news was meant to be confidential, though every fiber of his being wanted to go to her and hold her tight. When she didn't answer, he thought she was deciding not to tell him until his ears caught the faint sobs and his restraint broke.

Garrett went over to the hallway and put his arms around her. She didn't resist and he was glad for it. As much as it pained him to see her so sad, it felt good to hold her like this. To be close to her. It felt right.

It wasn't long before he started to feel the dampness of her tears through his shirt, and he pulled her closer into him feeling her body tremble. Again, she didn't pull away. He still didn't know what had happened, but something told him words wouldn't be enough.

It was Abigail who was the first to pull away, though she allowed his arms to stay wrapped around her. He could see by the small flame's light the tears still running down her cheeks as she looked up to him, staring deep into his own eyes. A desire within him stirred, the urge to tilt her chin gently up towards his own was strong, but a reluctant restraint took hold to stop him. He wanted their first kiss to be remembered for what it was in its own right and not the time he'd recall her sadness over something else that clearly burdened her. He also wanted to keep holding her, but something told him if he did, he might have trouble controlling himself. He gave a hard swallow before releasing her completely.

"Abigail." Garrett leveled his gaze on hers, the drops from her eyes continuing to glisten even as they slowed their trail down her cheeks. He'd wanted to tell her about Boston and his plan to find her when the city was no longer fortified but could sense this wasn't the right time. "I don't know what's happened, and I understand what Washington may have told you may be confidential and that's fine. I can live with that. What I can't live with is seeing you so sad." He paused, keeping his touch light as he wiped a tear away from her eye. "I want you to know I'm here if you need me. No questions asked." He wasn't sure how well she could see him in the darkness surrounding them, but he smiled just the same.

"Thank you, Garrett." Her voice quivered. "That means so much coming from you." She paused momentarily, and he wondered if she might cry again, but she didn't. Instead, she took a deep breath. "I'm afraid the news of this evening has proved to be more difficult than anything I could have anticipated." Again, her voice broke. The heaviness of whatever burden she carried made his chest ache, and he wished he could lift it from her. Her lips trembled as she spoke again. "It's Abraham."

Chapter 31

"Captured! What do you mean, captured?" Charlotte made the exclamation while she paced back-and-forth in the parlor. "You must be joking, Abby."

Abigail fell silent. She wished more than ever she was joking.

Charlotte gave a gasp, evidently reading the expression on her older sister's face. "But, he hasn't been in any battles. How could Abraham be captured if he hasn't fought in any battles?"

Again, Abigail hesitated, struggling by both the question she'd asked herself over and again when she'd first heard the awful news and the restless night she'd endured from its aftermath. It took all her strength just to drag herself from the bed this morning, knowing she would have to relay the information not only to her sister, but to her mother and father as well.

"He wasn't fighting, that's true." Abigail's hands began to shake. She still had trouble believing the truth herself. "But he's been a spy for the continental army, for Washington. That's just as bad."

"My dear," Margaret interjected from the chaise with Sophie in her lap and clear trepidation written on her brow. "That's treason. Your poor brother will be hanged for that."

"What?" Alarm deepened Charlotte's already clouded expression and Abigail knew just how she felt. "Abraham will be hanged?"

"We don't know that for sure, not from what I heard last night." Abigail rose quickly from one of the wingbacks, putting a gentle hand on her sister's shoulder as if preventing her thoughts from spiraling down a dangerous path that would do no good.

"What exactly did you hear last night, Abby?" Charlotte's eyes implored her own with an expectation she'd have to deliver and the events from the night before came back at her all too suddenly.

***

Haywood had barely said a word in the carriage on the way over to the Longfellow estate. It wasn't out of character for the officer and wouldn't have bothered her otherwise if it weren't for his grim expression back in the dining room of the Schreier residence when he'd come to retrieve her.

Abigail's stomach knotted as thoughts flew for what the urgency to see the man in charge of the continental army could possibly be until it stopped with a full force on one: Abraham. It was the only explanation she could come up with that made sense. The knots she already felt twisted tighter, realizing she hadn't seen her brother in weeks.

Lord, please let him be all right.

When they'd arrived to the house, Abigail followed Haywood's lead, stepping behind him through the threshold and into the formal entry hall of Washington's headquarters. The Black woman who'd allowed them entry disappeared down the hall and past the white, balustered staircase while they waited for the commander to see them. Distress about the news she felt sure to be concerning her brother caused Abigail's eyes to drift downward at the carpet which featured a repeated pattern colored in a series of muted greens. Normally, it would've been an inviting touch, but any sense of normal this evening was wiped away by a cold blast coursing throughout her body. When she managed to raise her head again, a grandfather clock stood tall and looked at her from a break in the stairs to remind her of the late hour. Only a few minutes passed when the Black woman returned and relayed General Washington's readiness for their arrival before she opened up a pair of doors to the study.

Haywood was the first to proceed, Abigail a short distance behind him. They both stood while the woman who'd let them in, came forth, picking up a plate Abigail could distinguish as the remains of a pawpaw fruit from the corner of the desk. The general himself seemed engaged, his quill pressed to a sheet of paper as his hand moved back and forth across it. Abigail swallowed, wondering if his letter had anything to do with why she was here.

"Please take a seat, Miss Thatcher." The calm, deep voice came from the man at the desk while he folded his paper carefully before sealing it with a red wax. The warm and almost regal-like smile that welcomed her made the knots in her stomach ease until she remembered the bleak expression of Haywood when he came to get her. The general's gaze shifted to the officer barely in front of her who looked unaffected by his own lack of invitation to take a seat. "Thank you, Haywood. I'll send for you when we've finished."

Haywood gave the general a nod before Abigail watched him proceed out of the room.

"Please, Miss Thatcher." Washington's hand gestured towards a chair across from his desk, again imploring her to accept his proposal. She complied this time. The setup seemed familiar, reminding her of her meetings with Haywood back at the camp; a desk always conveying a metaphorical boundary between them. It'd made her feel inferior and she'd grown to dislike it each time. But here, even with the barrier that still divided them, Abigail felt strangely comfortable, even a little more

350

calm since when she first arrived.

Washington's countenance was different than Haywood's; less critical and more genteel. Her shoulders relaxed into the cushion of the seat as the man's soft, methodical tone began to speak to her. All the while he spoke, she couldn't help but feel amazement by a man she knew so little about, yet was in charge of an army she'd been part of for nearly three months.

Washington hadn't removed himself from his own chair to stand over her like Haywood had done in previous days and she appreciated that, but even sitting she could tell her brother's description of the general had not been exaggerated. His upright frame towered over the mahogany desk he occupied, surpassing even Haywood's six feet by a couple inches, she guessed. He had a strong physique accompanied by a long face with a prominent nose and high cheekbones. She could see the remnants from the smallpox he was rumored to have experienced in his youth, but even with the scars, his countenance was both appealing and revered.

"Miss Thatcher. Thank you for coming on such short notice. Officer Haywood has spoken of your services at camp." The general smiled at her; a gentle warmth hidden in the gesture. "As you might have noticed the man is strict, but effective in his line of duty. He gives you a great compliment by telling me how hard you work to keep our soldiers clothed and fed and also about your work at the hospital. On behalf of the continental army, I thank you for it."

Abigail startled. She had no idea Haywood spoke highly of any of the camp followers, least of all, herself, but could this really be what this meeting was about? "Thank you, sir," she stammered while she suppressed her confusion for the time being. "Officer Haywood has been overly kind to say so. To be fair, more of my time has been occupied at the hospital and elsewhere than within the camp as of late."

"You're at the Lady Schreier's estate." It wasn't a question. He smiled again, reassurance in his demeanor. "Yes, I know. I'm aware of her condition and your service to her as well. I try to keep myself informed on all accounts concerning what's happening here in Cambridge. I also know Mrs. Schreier pledges her allegiance to King George." His smile faded, yet she still heard a sense of dignity and respect within his words. "However, even if a war divides us, we will not be so low as to forget our scruples towards one another, no matter how different our opinions may be. We are after all, equals in the eyes of the Almighty. That, Miss Thatcher, is why your work at the Schreier estate, too, is important and equally appreciated."

Though grateful for the commendation, something told Abigail a man of such importance would not likely send for her, much less this time at night, just to pay his compliments.

"Thank you, General Washington, but is that really why I've been sent for? To be thanked?" Abigail swallowed, hoping she hadn't caused any offense. She didn't want to sound disrespectful or make the man feel as if she didn't appreciate his praise. She just wanted to know why she had been summoned, even if she was scared to hear it. "What I mean, sir, is I quite accept your kind words, treasure them even, as I've hoped to be of help towards the men, but you shouldn't have troubled to send for me if this is the case. I would have been equally as happy to have received the recognition from Officer Haywood as long as I knew it came from you."

The tightness in her chest gave way to see a flicker of a smile again on Washington's face, letting her know the man hadn't taken any offense. But just as quickly as it appeared, it vanished, leaving behind a straight and contemplative expression that told her there was more and she wasn't going to like it.

"No, Miss Thatcher, I'm afraid you're right. It is not."

Abigail braced herself, hands pressed together in her lap as Washington continued.

"The reason I sent for you has to do with your brother Abraham."

Her heart dropped to her stomach. She hadn't seen Abraham in weeks, still clinging to Cleophes' reassurances that her brother was all right, but that, too, she realized was too long ago. "Do you know him, sir, apart from just enrolling in the army?" Abraham had admitted to his attendance at some of the meetings with the officers. She still didn't know why he'd been included, but something told her she was about to find out.

"Yes. Over the course of these few months, I have come to understand your brother fairly well, or as well as any man could in such a short time. I won't give in to such detail in the presence of a lady like yourself, Miss Thatcher, but do take my word on it when I say from experience that when faced with a common cause, the spirit of comradery can be established quite earlier in the world of war than otherwise in the civilian world."

Abigail pressed her lips, trying to make sense of what Washington was trying to tell her. "Do you mean to say you and my brother are friends?"

"I wouldn't exactly say friends, but we do trust each other."

She shook her head. "I'm sorry, sir. It's just that I don't understand how. Abraham came into your army with neither experience nor affluence behind him, and you, sir..." She didn't mean to but looked at the man and evaluated him from head to foot. She noted his well-tailored uniform, his tall and straight physique, nearly absent of signs of hard labor and even his mannerisms, polished. "You are a man of gentility. How can it be that my brother, born and raised on a farm among thousands of soldiers here in Cambridge came to be one to work so close to you?"

The general gave a short, bemused laugh. "I can ask the same question of how such a woman came to be so learned in the art of healing."

Abigail felt her mouth fall open, but he didn't give an indication of noticing it of which she was thankful for.

Washington's smiled faded again. "However, I see your point, Miss Thatcher. Your brother and I are different in many ways, as you've pointed out, but we have a common goal. It also occurs to me Abraham possesses a set of skills you may not be aware of?" A single white eyebrow raised above his blue eyes.

"Sir?"

"Have you ever heard of privateering?"

"Privateering?" Abigail whispered the word and tasted the bitterness of it in her mouth. Yes, she did know what it was, a more elegant way to refer to piracy. The only difference was the fact a privateer had been commissioned to rob a vessel rather than just take it for sole gain. And though, she admitted, she knew that much about the term because of Abraham, she still failed to see the connection to her brother. "Yes, sir, I'm familiar with the term, but Abraham has never been on a boat much less at sea, not our whole time in Falmouth."

Washington nodded. "That may be true, Miss Thatcher, but much has happened and has needed to for this war to continue. Your brother has been a part of that and has done the very thing you claim he knows nothing of for our side, learning of it from a Mr. Cleophes Lockhart."

"Cleo?" Abigail edged back in her seat.

"A former privateer and pirate for some time, so I'm told, and also a friend of yours." An easy grin appeared on the man. Washington really did keep himself informed on everything in the camp.

Cleo's past life had been a pirate and he taught Abraham to do the same? Abigail's mind went back to all the mornings her brother ventured to the harbor. Is that what he'd been speaking to Cleophes about? How to rob ships? Is that why she hadn't heard from him for so long; because he'd been away at sea, taking crews captive and stealing their cargo? "But sir," she stammered, hardly believing such news could be true, "to what end?"

"To a very good one, I can assure you, Miss Thatcher. One that will supply our troops with more fuel for their fires and food for their stomachs. One that will keep this army going and keep the war effort alive along with it, giving us a much-needed advantage over the British." He looked out through a window as if he could somehow see the ocean beyond the darkness. "We have only a few vessels out there, but we've been able to acquire these very things, including the firewood the British troops in Boston are no doubt in desperate need of and our own men will be grateful for upon receiving tomorrow morning."

His face grew stricken and Abigail tensed again, realizing more was about to be revealed. "However, it was during some of our earlier acquisitions from sea when I became informed of your brother's zeal, even if misguided at times, for patriotism. We needed information concerning our opponents and I needed someone I could trust. Your brother was eager to consent and has been a spy in New York for me."

An unwelcomed shiver ran up Abigail's back, the chair under her losing all sense of comfort. Yet, she remained in it, quite certain the man before her would not appreciate the outburst that wanted to come forth.

"A—spy?" The words sputtered across her lips, tripping over them. Suddenly things began to make sense, including Haywood's remark pertaining to her. "Someone like you." Now she understood. She was the sister of one of Washington's spies.

Washington nodded to confirm the information that still felt a little hazy to hear. "He has done well. Because of him our vessels have been able to intercept those departing from New York, but now…" He paused, letting a pensive breath draw out. Abigail clenched the edge of her seat as if Washington's next words might throw her from it. "Now, your brother has been captured by the British and is being kept in New York."

A low moan escaped Abigail's lips at the news she had half expected. It had not been exactly what she had prepared herself for. Abraham was not dead. She silently thanked God for her brother's life. Yet, that wasn't the end of it. Abraham was not dead, but he had been captured. What was the punishment for spying? The air left her lungs as the answer came all too swiftly. Death. Anyone found committing treason was put to death, and she didn't have to guess if spying for the enemy was at the top of that list.

"How long does he have before——?" Abigail's hands gripped the seat tighter, but she couldn't bring herself to finish the dreadful thought.

"The British general has informed me within the week, and I'm afraid he's being generous. Most sentences for spying are carried out with more immediacy." A genuine discouragement read from Washington's now hard, blue eyes. "I'm doing all I can to get your brother back, but if General Graves does not cooperate then I'm sorry to say Abraham will most likely be hanged." For the first time since she'd been in the presence of the man, she saw the general's countenance fall. "I am truly sorry, Miss Thatcher."

***

Tears came rolling down Abigail's cheeks as she sat in the parlor, relaying what had happened the night before.

"Is there anything we can do?" Charlotte's own cheeks were now dampened; an earnest concern written in her eyes.

Abigail bent her head, feeling like a brick had been placed on the back of her neck, making it difficult to turn her own eyes upward to the hope she knew they needed to cling to more than ever now. *Jesus, please hear our prayers for our brother.* Her eyes strained to reach Charlotte's. "I asked General Washington the same question before our meeting ended. He tells me he's doing all he can, and I believe him, but I'm afraid time is not on Abraham's side. The only thing I can think to do is pray."

Charlotte grasped a hold of Abigail's hand, the desperation in her grip apparent. "Then that's what we'll do."

Chapter 32

Garrett could feel the wet snow pile up on his boots as he walked along Brattle Street. His feet had already grown numb, a product of his shoe exchange, but still not a decision he regretted knowing what it had done to help Abigail. A sharp wind stung his face as it whipped passed, reminding him all too well of the news she told him last night that bit at him more than the news of Knox's guns. He didn't know Abraham, but he knew the man was Abigail's brother and that was enough.

At half a mile down the road, Garrett let his frustration cool along with his already frozen body. That's when he saw it. The church. Even as the doors of it remained closed, he believed the invitation from Isaac was real, always welcoming him to enter. Garrett wondered if Isaac was inside now with any more blunt wisdom to give like he'd done the day of their checker game. The immediate answer that came, as if the priest was in his head, was prayer, but there had to be more he could do to somehow make the events of this grave situation alter.

Today, Garrett felt neither a nudge nor pull to enter, but something else near the holy building tugged at his response entirely. Two men stood just outside of it close to the far corner. Garrett would've nearly missed the exchange if it hadn't been for what the man was selling, a pair of worn-out boots but in much fairer condition compared to the ones he had on now. He felt an unintentional movement of his toes inside his shoes, grateful they weren't chilled completely.

It didn't take him long to figure out who was in need of them. He watched the man whose feet lay barely protected by a pair of battered moccasins flinch at the unfair price. It didn't matter that Garrett agreed. The same man's shoes had lost nearly all the stitching, and the buckskin layer that was supposed to be a barrier to the outside elements was worn thin. The salesman knew that and so did his customer, eventually succumbing to payment to improve his chances to keep his feet dry for the rest of winter.

When the scene ended and the two men parted, Garrett headed back to the house, though he wished he'd have something to offer Abigail when he got there for her brother's sake. He rubbed his hands over his face, the friction of the ice against his skin making him feel raw. Just when he was starting to give his heart to God, this happened to leave his head spinning downward again. He tried to understand, but he couldn't. Too many bad things had happened to those he cared about. His father had been a good man, but he was murdered. Abigail was the most amazing woman he knew and now her brother may meet a similar fate if something didn't happen soon. Why was it that God let bad things happen to good people?

"For my thoughts are not your thoughts, neither are my ways your ways." A small voice whispered in his ear and echoed a verse Nikolai told him to look up in his free time. The voice grew more powerful in his head and demanded a trust he wanted to hold on to.

Garrett stopped, unable to do anything but respond. "All right, Lord, I'm listening and I'm ready to accept your ways are not my ways, your thoughts are not my thoughts, and your plans are not my plans. I don't know what your plan is for Abraham but help me to trust in you with it as I'm learning to trust you with my own life."

When he'd finished, Garrett continued his route to the Schreier estate. He still had no answers, but the discomfort in his chest from earlier had dimished. Maybe he'd yet to have an idea of what to do about Abraham, but he wanted to be there for Abigail and to do that he had to get back. The mission seemed clear until suddenly it wasn't.

Chapter 33

Garrett didn't see his face, but he didn't need to. He knew that limp from anywhere. The sheer sight of it again was like a second chance given to confront the man and he was ready to take full advantage of it. Garrett's heart hammered, wanting to head straight for Cleophes. He wished he wasn't a prisoner so he could arrest the old man on the spot. Instead, he decided it might be better to give Cleophes some space and see what he was up to, just not too much this time. He wasn't about to lose him like he had in the church.

The casual pace the man walked and the lack of stiffness in his posture, told Garrett Cleophes hadn't noticed him. Garrett hoped to keep it that way. Occasionally he'd have to duck into a small alley when the older man turned round, but he hoped the increase in distance he'd allowed between them this time might help ease any suspicions of being followed. The two of them went on this way for almost a quarter of a mile until Garrett watched with roused curiosity as the older man veered from the road and into a row of dense trees.

If Cleophes had been able bodied, Garrett would've surely lost him amidst the maze of ash, pine, and chestnut. Not to mention the other plants and the occasional stump that forced him to act more cautiously than he might otherwise to keep himself quiet and undiscovered. He watched again as Cleophes slowed his pace to arrive at a small clearing already occupied by a familiar pair Garrett recognized from the Blue Anchor Tavern: Jasper and Linus.

Both men wore irritation across their faces that told Garrett they'd been waiting for a while. Garrett stayed back, hoping the foliage of the Eastern White Pine he chose would be enough to hide him. He didn't aim to get in a struggle, but something about the whole ordeal told him that's exactly what would happen if he were discovered, and he wasn't so sure he'd be able to handle himself if things went awry. If he had to, he could probably handle the men one on one. He wasn't worried about Linus, who looked like he'd never been in a fight before or Cleophes who could hardly manage on his own. Even with Jasper, Garrett was fairly confident he could take him, if need be, but he wasn't so sure how things would go if he had both men working against him. That was counting only on brute strength and tactic and unfortunately that's not all he was facing.

He almost let out a curse that would've blown his position when he saw it. Jasper was armed with a pistol at his side. He was also the first to speak.

"Cleo." A sinister grin formed on the large man's face when he spotted the old man, "I was beginning to think you'd gone and double crossed us again." Jasper's brow furrowed as the next words came out bitterly. "You're late."

"Oh no, Jasper." Cleophes gave a nervous laugh. "I simply got held up. I wouldn't do that to you."

"Oh yeah?" Linus crossed his arms. "What happened the last time then? You didn't even show! You're lucky, I could talk Jasper down that night. Otherwise, you might not be standing, even as you are with that cockeyed limp of yours." The man's words were made to sting, but

Garrett saw no ill expression produced on Cleophes from the jab. He merely stood as if ready and taking it willingly.

"Aye, you're right, gentlemen, "I am in the wrong, but I've come to try to make it right."

"Then make it right." Jasper's voice raised with a touch of annoyance. "Where are my barrels? And don't say you already traded them. We had a deal."

"I didn't trade them…"

Garrett could read the hesitation in Cleo's response, even yards away. His own hair stood on end. That wasn't good. He just hoped Jasper and Linus weren't as observant as they were short-tempered.

"Good." Jasper's reply was sharp. "Hand them over then. I don't have all the time in the world here."

"I'm sorry gentlemen, but I can't…" The nervous stammer seemed to have replaced the once calm resolve Cleophes had earlier. Garrett didn't have a good feeling about this, though why he cared what happened to Cleophes Lockhart, a traitor to the Crown, he didn't know why.

"You can't?" Jasper pulled back before his eyes shot a deathly glare. His hand grazed over his gun holster. "What do you mean, you can't?"

"The truth is, I never had them." Cleophes looked up at Jasper who only stood with a blank expression that was hard to decipher. It made Garrett's nerves shake for the old man, not sure what kind of reaction to expect, especially knowing Jasper had a gun at his side. "As far as I know the barrels made it to Boston and are being unloaded by British officials there."

"What? My tea is in Boston? Being drunk by those Redcoats?" The anger in the larger man was unmistakable, his nostrils flaring. "You mean to tell me you did double cross us and are brave enough to show your face in this town? You've got some nerve, Cleo, I'll give that to you. It's a shame no one will know." Jasper tightened his grip on his pistol, aiming it right between Cleophes eyes.

"Now, fellows, let's naht be hasty." Cleo raised his hands as if in surrender, his voice shaky. "I wouldn't double cross you. You have my word."

"Oh, like you gave King George your word you would steal for him and then turn around and keep it all for yourself?" Linus was the one to interrogate, giving himself another chance to speak up, but unfortunately not on Cleophes behalf. "Face it, Cleo, your word doesn't amount to much."

The two enraged men took a few steps towards their target, the gap between them closing quickly. Cleophes shook, but it surprised Garrett to see he hadn't taken any steps back. The man stood his ground. Still, as impressed as Garrett was by such courage, if Cleophes didn't appease these men fast, he was going to get a bullet right in the middle of his forehead.

"Honestly fellows," the older man pleaded, this time with desperation. "I've become a changed man. I don't do those things anymore. Let God be my witness to that."

"Ha!" Jasper huffed a mocking laugh. "A changed man? You won't ever change, Cleo. A man like you doesn't change, not when he's been working for himself for so long."

"Aye! I mean it." Insistence bellowed in the older man's response. "I've changed. I'm naht stealing for myself and I'm naht stealing for anybody else anymore."

"Well, that's just too bad for you then, isn't it?" Jasper cocked his pistol.

With hands trembling, Cleo made a grab for the inside of his coat.

"He's got a gun, Jasper!" Linus shouted the warning.

Garrett jolted as he heard the gunshot and turned his head away to keep the shards of wood of the blast from cutting his eyes. When he turned back, he expected to find Cleo lying on the ground and the two others making their getaway as fast as they could out of the clearing. To his amazement and sheer bewilderment, he was wrong. Cleo still stood and from what Garrett could tell, unwounded. Both Jasper and Linus looked at each other dumbfounded.

"This darn thing. Misfired! No matter, it won't happen again." Jasper readied his pistol for another shot.

Garrett couldn't stand it any longer, certain if Jasper had another chance, he'd make his mark this time. The pull at his heart surpassed all the feelings he had for this Cleophes that drove him to respond. He just hoped it wouldn't get him killed too. "Lord, if this is your plan, help me." With a step of blind faith and resolve in the decision, Garrett went for it.

"Now gentlemen." Garrett stepped out from his hiding place from behind the white pine and secured himself between Cleophes and his accusers. "Let's not do anything we'll regret." The two men evidently too perplexed by his sudden appearance failed to see the same surprise in Cleophes' face.

"Cleo, who is this?" Jasper sneered. "You were supposed to come alone."

Cleophes' mouth gaped open. "I-I did come alone. Honest Jasper."

"Don't blame him on my account." Garrett chimed in. "He didn't know he was being followed. I made sure of it."

"And who are you?"

"Who cares, Jasper." Linus' nose scrunched as he made the interjection a little too eagerly. "He's heard too much. Finish him off too!"

"Am I glad it's you who has the gun." Garrett gave a short, nervous laugh that came out forced. The remark wasn't the best thing he could come up with, but it would have to do in their current situation. He needed to buy some time and figure a way out of this. "Your friend here seems a little too anxious to get blood on your hands."

Jasper looked to Linus like the comment struck a nerve. Good. If their friendship carried some doubt along with it, then that could come to his advantage. Jasper turned his attention back to Garrett and gave him a suspicious glance. "You look familiar. Do I know you from somewhere?"

With the gun still out, Garrett acutely perceived Jasper had moved his target from Cleophes to him. He made the quick assumption that revealing his identity wouldn't be the worst decision he could make today. That had been done when he'd decided to put himself between Cleophes and this man's pistol.

"No, we haven't officially met, but I've seen you two at the tavern before. My name is Garrett Ward."

"Garrett Ward." The man thumbed his brow, like it meant something he couldn't recall in that moment. "I've heard that name before."

The man's eyes lit, telling Garrett he'd figured it out.

"You're the lieutenant, the Navy prisoner!" Jasper's gaze shifted, slits of accusation taking their place. "What are you up to? Are you spying on us—getting information of your own?" Jasper didn't wait for an answer. "I'm sure there's a many few in this town who wouldn't mind if you just 'went missing'." The words came freely, a little too freely for Garrett.

"Now, gentlemen." Garrett hesitated, a part of him beginning to regret his decision to step in. A big part. "Remember, your quarrel is not with me." He didn't dare look back, keeping his attention on the barrel of the gun squarely on him. Part of him did wonder, however, if Cleo had tried to flee while the rest of them had been busy in conversation. That would've been just his luck after risking his own neck for a criminal.

"I don't know, Jasper. The way I see it, we can take care of two problems in one day." The suggestion that came from Linus seemed to make his comrade smile with satisfaction.

Garrett took a quick breath, doing his best to subdue the sweat that began to form near the base of his hairline. Not that it was an easy task with a gun still at his head and now cocked. This wasn't going how he planned, though planning hadn't exactly been part of it. If he didn't act quickly, it wouldn't just be Cleo left here on the forest floor. And that was counting the older man was still behind him instead of bolting when he got the chance. "Jesus, help me. I'm trying my best to trust you."

"I don't think you'll want to do that." The words spattered across Garrett's tongue like someone else had put them there.

"Oh yeah?" Jasper's brow raised, though the man took on a crooked smile. "And why is that?"

"Because your general—" Without quite knowing the rest of what he was going to say, Garrett let the reference sink in, hoping the mention of the person in charge of these men might give him some more time. It did.

He could see by both Jasper and Linus' confused and thoughtful expressions they were considering possibilities concerning their respected leader. Garrett went on and used the leverage he had just gained while trying to sound confident in his delivery. "Your general hasn't put me to death himself yet, which means I'm still useful to him." He swallowed hard, wanting to believe his own words, but doubt crept in with the reminder of how long he'd been at the camp. He hadn't heard so much as a word pertaining to his own side's concern for his freedom, but no point dwelling on that now. With the pistol still pointed to his face, he squared his shoulders, resolved to finish this no matter the outcome. "I don't imagine he would be happy to hear of my death, especially if that meant one of his plans to gain an advantage in this war was foiled by his own men. I'm sure the two of you could imagine what punishment for something like that would be." He let the weight of his words sink in. After a minute or two the men started to back off.

Linus looked to his friend for guidance and Jasper docked his pistol back into its holster.

Garrett wanted to exhale deeply but didn't dare. It was not the time to show his relief, not when they might make it out of these woods alive. More comfortable with the decision to take a glance behind him, Garrett did, amazed to see Cleo was still there. He gave the man a look that warned him to play along while signaling him to come forward alongside.

"I give you my word, gentlemen," Garrett straightened, his voice bolder now that the gun was back in its holster. "As long as Cleo and I here don't feel any further threat by you, we won't speak of this incident to your commander in chief."

"Oh, I'm not worried about that. I doubt he'd believe a word either of you would have the nerve to say to His Excellency. You," Jasper's attention was fixed on Garrett, "I hope you get back to where you belong so I can have a chance to see you in battle and finish things off properly. I bet the general would thank me then." The man shifted his attention to Cleophes and scowled. "And you, this prisoner may have saved you from getting a bullet, but we still have business."

"Aye, Jasper, I know. That's what I was aiming to show you before I thought I was a goner." Cleo again put his hand inside his coat.

"No funny business, Cleo, you sly fox!" Jasper grabbed his gun again from its holster. Cleo immediately put one hand up, but this time held something in the other.

Jasper's brow went crooked at the small bag. "What's that?"

"It's your money. I promise it's all here and with interest, too. I was just wanting to make it right. That's why I came, Jasper. I knew I had to make things right."

Jasper gave a huff, the tip of his mouth raised. He motioned for his comrade to retrieve the satchel and verify its contents. Linus only nodded and following the confirmation, the burly man repositioned his pistol to finally lay it to rest.

"Get out of here," Jasper snapped. "I better not see your face again, Cleo. And you." He turned to Garrett again, a sardonic smile creeping in, "I look forward to the next time we meet."

***

Garrett and Cleo didn't waste any time getting out of the woods and back onto a public road where their chances of being among other people and kept alive were much higher.

"Lieutenant, thank you." The Scottish accent of the older man was more pronounced in expressing his gratitude.

Garrett didn't say anything at first. He still wasn't certain why he'd done it, but part of him was glad that he did. It had been the right thing to do no matter who this man was, criminal or not. Now, however, after getting through the shock of the death they'd just escaped, Garrett considered the man's words while they'd been in the clearing. He looked at Cleophes, his mouth pressed. "Did you mean it?"

"Sir?"

"Did you mean what you said? You've changed, that you don't steal anymore?" Garrett eyed the man, letting him know he wasn't in the mood for games. Time was running out and he needed answers he could count on.

"Aye, sir." Cleophes' his lips turned into a smile. "I've been searching for a change in my life and I've finally found it through Jesus. Isaac has been helping me with it all, too. I'm trying to stay on the right path." His eyes dimmed as they trailed down to the road and back towards the trees where they'd crossed into the clearing, "but I'm naht always doing a great job of it, as you can see. I shouldn't have made the deal in the first place."

Garrett thought about that. He wanted to believe Cleophes, even as hard as it was with his shaded history. Something stabbed at his heart, realizing he too had his own dark past he'd been forgiven of and knew by the genuine brokenness in the man's expression, Cleo had too. Maybe this was the opportunity he'd been looking for, another part of God's plan he hadn't seen coming. Garrett just hoped Abigail was right and Washington's concern for her brother held the same authenticity.

"I take it you've heard about your friend, Abraham?" Now with the immediate threat behind them, Garrett was ready to see if this man was one of action and not merely words.

Cleophes' face went downcast. "Aye, sir. I'm sorry to say I have, and I understand it doesn't sound good."

"No, it's not, and to my understanding you're the one who helped him become a spy in the first place, after your lessons in privateering." Garrett saw his accusation had cut deeply and immediate regret coursed through. His intention wasn't to make the man feel responsible. "But we might be able to make this right too."

Cleophes looked up; his eyes hopeful. "Aye! What is it that I can do?"

Impressed by the man's willingness, Garrett was becoming more convinced he'd done the right thing in saving him. "Can you get me a meeting with Washington? As you might imagine, I'm not very welcomed in the camp. I doubt the general would take my request to see him unless someone he knew vouched for me." He gave Cleophes a knowing look. "Particularly someone involved in such a close-knit scheme as preparing one of his spies for his secret navy." Garrett watched with impatience as Cleophes rubbed his bristled chin, reminded again that Abraham's time was short.

"I might be able to, but he's going to ask for a reason. You can't just have a meeting with the commander in chief without a good one."

"Trust me." Garrett straightened. "If Washington wants to get Abraham back alive I think he will be very interested in what I have to say."

Chapter 34

Dearest Mother and Father,

Abigail tried to think of the next words she could say to her parents to soften the ill news she had to tell them. Nothing good seemed to appear in her mind. Every way she went about it, the right words just wouldn't come. But then again, were there ever truly right words to tell your parents it was likely they wouldn't see their eldest son again?

The quill between her fingers started to give weigh, the burden of what it had to convey becoming too heavy. Her hand let go and the quill released along with it, falling to the desk. Abigail stared into the mostly blank sheet of parchment she'd worked all morning on. Her progress had come up short. She closed her eyes, though soon regretted the decision. Images of what she imagined her brother going through flew through her head. Abraham wasn't an officer whose rank she found out did in fact matter about how one was treated as a prisoner. He wouldn't receive the same kindnesses Garrett had while he remained here in Cambridge. Her brother's chances to occupy a comfortable home or inn like the lieutenant were nil and his ability to roam about the town even less so.

She took a shaky breath and worked to subdue her thoughts from going in directions she'd rather they not, but in the end, trepidation won out. Were they keeping him aboard some disease-infested ship, crammed among other prisoners of war, or was he somewhere in the army camp, locked away in seclusion? Did he know what awaited him? The exasperation overwhelmed her. Was he being mocked and tormented somehow, perhaps for further information of Washington's plans? And what of Washington? Would he be good on his word in trying to get her brother home alive or was he writing a similar letter to her parents right now, telling of her brother's unfortunate but patriotic death? She had more questions than answers, answers that were what her parents hoped to receive, yet something she couldn't give.

The more Abigail thought, the wearier she felt, and frustration began to build. She couldn't do this now. She wouldn't do this now. Abigail believed Washington, and she hoped desperately the man was going to the furthest lengths he could to get Abraham back, but he also gave her no guarantees. And although she herself believed, prayed her brother was still alive, somehow writing this letter meant she'd given up hope. And she wouldn't do that. Not now.

She took in another breath, though deeper this time and made a point to observe the room she now occupied as a break from the task that seemed so daunting to complete. She was thankful for its use. Despite the little progress she'd made on her current effort, the library had served her in other ways, as it was of the more secluded rooms in the house. It gave her privacy, something she was not usually accustomed to back home with her four siblings, but something she hadn't conceived she needed here in Cambridge. The room in its humble appearance served her a great purpose: escape. With the thoughts that still whirled inside in her mind like a twister, she needed that more than ever now.

Across from her, a simple bookcase seemed nearly full. Abigail recognized some of the works but was at a loss for some of the others

Mr. Schreier contained in his collection. Most of them looked well-read, some of their covers frayed or bent while only a few looked untouched. It didn't take her long to notice the Bible encased within the collection, its own wide binding as worn. Abigail smiled, thinking of Margaret and her husband reading the work, confident their daughter would be familiar with it, too, in time.

Admittedly, she'd not read from the text since her journey to Cambridge and hadn't thought much of it until now. But looking at it prompted her to pull it from the shelf and open its dark leather binding to a very familiar passage. It was one she knew by heart but needed to see its promise again with her own eyes. The sweet words filled her with hope and served as a reminder her brother wasn't forgotten.

"For I know the plans I have for you, declares the Lord, plans to prosper you and not to harm you, plans to give you hope and a future."

Perhaps she didn't know what that future was for Abraham, but God did. What she did know and what she found rest in, was that no matter what happened to her brother, as much as she hoped such a dire future wouldn't befall him, he would be at peace. As fervent as her brother had been for the patriotic cause, she knew, too, his passion for the Lord was just as devout, and that was something she took courage in.

Abigail traced her finger over each word, whispering them softly aloud and taking in the promise one last time before she put the book back in its place on the shelf. Her eyes went to the letter to her parents that sat on the desk expectantly, waiting to be written. A small clock at the top of her workspace read half-past three. She was running out of time. If she didn't act soon, she'd miss the courier. Her parents had a right to know what was going on no matter how much she hated the idea of being the one to tell them. She closed her eyes and straightened, letting God's promise wash over her another time before she opened them again and picked up the quill.

***

"Your brother is still alive, and you will see him again."

Abigail gave Garrett a blank stare all the while Sophie laid nestled in her arms. She worked to soften her expression, though Garrett could see a clear inquisition in her eyes. "What do you mean, Garrett? We pray that Abraham is still alive, but we haven't heard anything from Washington in two days. How do you know we will see him again?"

Garrett straightened and took a deep breath, feeling both a satisfaction of the news he was about to disclose and remorse with what he was about to lose. He just hoped it wouldn't be for the rest of his life. "Because I've spoken with Washington." He smiled, focusing more on the good tidings he had to bring. "Just this afternoon as a matter of fact."

"And the king's general has agreed to release my brother?" The hopeful expectation in Abigail's voice was enough to confirm he'd made the right decision.

"He has."

"But I don't understand." She leaned back in the chaise. "How? Washington said he was doing everything. What's changed?"

Garrett took a seat across from her in one of the wingbacks, not exactly sure how she would respond. He wasn't looking forward to telling her the less than exciting part of his news. "It's not that simple, I'm afraid. General Howe hasn't just decided to release your brother, at least not without something in return." He paused as the more complicated details that loomed over him. He didn't want it to be this way, to leave Abigail like this without a plan afterwards. His deal with Hart to go to Boston would've allowed him opportunity to return to Cambridge after he'd revealed the news about Knox's arrival. With luck, Garrett's reputation might be restored and maybe his chances at captain back on the table, but even all that paled in comparison as pure conviction for what he was doing now told him it was the right move. He was thankful Hart understood that too, even if it took a full explanation of their plans to save Abraham in order to leave the tailor a little less than cross. Garrett locked eyes with Abigail again. "In this case it's someone."

The realization on her face came quickly. "You." He could hear the struggle in her throat. Garrett had to admit, it felt good to hear she cared, especially when this might be the last day he would see her again.

"Yes, but no. Not just me. It seems I was not enough to be traded for." Garrett felt his countenance shift. The pain of what Washington told him earlier that day came back and stung hard. He let out an unsteady breath trying to be strong, but the wound cut from earlier had cut too deep, affirming what he'd feared as the battle of his self-worth came on with a full vengeance. "That's why I've been here so long. Washington has been trying to trade me for some of his own men from the battle at Bunker Hill since I arrived, but for some reason I wasn't enough. Not alone anyway."

Even as he spoke the words, the bite of their reality made him wince. He hadn't been enough for Admiral Graves in Boston either. Washington couldn't tell him why Howe had refused his trade offer when he'd asked. As far as Garrett knew, he had no quarrel with the British general. The only reason Garrett could come up with was Howe was simply looking for the advantage. Nothing personal, or at least it was never meant to be personal. Even if Garrett couldn't agree with the concept, he couldn't blame a general for that, not when there was so much at stake in this war. And apparently getting one of his officers back was not advantageous enough, not when the man needed something more.

That's where Cleophes came in, but Garrett saved that detail to tell Abigail for the end on purpose. He almost bit his tongue, as if the gesture might prevent him from continuing, but in the end, he confessed. "Your friend Cleo is also a part of the deal. He'll be traded too." Instinctively, Garrett put his hands up, bracing himself for what he imagined would be one angry woman. "Trust me, that part wasn't in my plan. It was just supposed to be me for your brother, but Cleophes was there with me when I spoke the idea to Washington."

Abigail searched him, her eyes imploring. "Cleo was there with you?"

Garrett gently nodded. He would need to tread lightly. "He wasn't in the room when I met with the general, but he was the one that got me an audience with him. In truth, I thought he would've moved on once I was face-to-face with Washington. My only guess is he must've overheard the fact General Howe refused to trade for me alone." Garrett's lips pressed as he recalled the sheer determination in the man's stride up towards Washington's desk, his disability seeming only as an afterthought in the current moment. "Cleophes told us both he was ready to pay for his crimes, especially if he knew it would bring Abraham back safely. He said he was certain he'd be a valuable capture for King George, and I hate to say," Garrett shook his head, still disbelieving it had come to this, "but the man was right. Howe accepted."

Garrett studied Abigail's expression, remembering the first time he saw her, those emerald-green eyes glaring at him with sheer defiance. He'd expected to see a trace of that anger now that she knew all the details. Instead, her eyes merely pulled away from his own before they returned, inquisition clearly in them.

"So, you'll be going back to Boston?" The longing disappointment in her tone touched his heart, knowing he shared in it equally.

Garrett took a deep breath and let it go forcefully, the unknown surrounding him on every side. "I'm not sure what awaits me. Howe might send me back to England in case he believes I've somehow changed sides or gone soft while I've been here, or he may let me stay and fight. I doubt he will let me resume my command on a ship right off. I just hope in light of everything that doesn't mean permanently, but we'll see." He let a soft smile touch the hard moment between them. "But my leaving along with Cleophes' means you'll get Abraham back. Howe is good on his word."

Abigail gave a light shake of her head. "I hate to even ask this, but why both of you, why not just one?"

The smile faded from Garrett's face, knowing full well she was talking about Cleophes. Garrett's lips pressed tightly, the older man's courage still speaking volumes to him. "Cleo actually proposed that, but we knew your brother was running out of time. We needed to offer Howe a trade he couldn't refuse. A two for one deal allows him a sense of victory. It might seem small, but it's something he probably wants right now after dealing with the riots from the *Common Sense* pamphlet and supply shortages your brother has also been helping out with."

Abigail leaned towards him; her eyebrows drawn together. "And what about Cleo? You said he was a criminal to the Crown. What will happen to him after the trade?"

Garrett's jaw went stiff. He didn't want to think about what might happen to his new and strange friend. Cleo had boldly committed treason, making the king look like a fool. That alone was a death sentence, a detail he was pretty certain Cleo understood too. Wasn't that the reason the man had been on the run for so long? So, what was different now?

The answer came clearer than sailing on a day with a bright, blue sky. Jesus and the love Garrett still worked to wrap his mind around. Cleo was given a changed life, changing motives along with it, something Garrett was beginning to relate to. It was the reason he felt so strongly to do anything he could for Abigail and that included to bring her brother back. He'd been too selfish with trying to raise himself up that he nearly missed the sacrificial love of the true God, the true King. Any doubt he held with his decision was erased. It was the right thing, even if that meant he'd have to say goodbye.

"Garrett?" Slight impatience casted itself across Abigail's face.

"He'll be sent to England for trial. That's all I know for sure." His head went bent, feeling the gravity of the man's sacrifice. "He's doing a brave thing, Abigail, one of the bravest I've ever seen actually. My respect for him goes far beyond his past as a criminal. I know the situation isn't ideal on many accounts…" His chest constricted, thinking about having to leave her too, "but it will get your brother back."

"Are you sure there's no other way?"

"I'm not, but with your brother's timeline cutting short, it was the fastest solution we could come up with."

"Thank you, Garrett." Abigail's words came out with gratitude, but her eyes told him there was more on her mind with his news. He could read the stiffness in her posture while her hand continued to gently graze the back of Sophie's head, the white strands of the infant's hair barely distinguishable. "I wish I knew more to say. It's just so much to take in."

"I know and I'm sorry for that."

"When is all this supposed to happen?"

"Tomorrow, actually."

"Tomorrow?" The flicker of surprise grew bright in her eyes and burned into his.

Garrett rose from the wingback he'd occupied and took a seat next to Abigail. It had come too soon for him too, but they needed to act fast. "We all agreed the sooner we get this done, the better. We don't want to give Howe too much time in case he changes his mind."

She issued a series of small nods. "And does Washington not have concerns about you going back? You know about the smallpox patients and General Knox's arrival. You even suggested Washington's element of surprise was his advantage. Wouldn't he have reservations about that knowledge leaking out?"

Garrett smiled. This woman didn't miss a thing.

She eyed him suspiciously, apparently not liking his choice of expression. "What?"

"It just sounds like you've thought of everything."

"Well, evidently I haven't because Washington is still agreeing to your going to Boston where you'll be among your comrades."

Garrett shrugged. "All right, almost everything, then. There's a reason your commander is the one leading this army." A certain kind of respect came with revering one's opponent bellowed. He'd learned in his meeting with Washington the man not only knew of his attempts for finding an escape route where he'd posted his men, but also the plan Garrett had made with Hart. The man really did know everything that was going on in this town. The whole time Garrett thought he'd been let free to wander, Washington had someone watching his every move. He'd promised Garrett he'd do the same with one of his informants in Boston, a promise if Garrett blew the news about Knox, he'd be facing the same fate as Abraham before Howe agreed to the trade.

A tightness wrung at Garrett's neck, not entirely sure if he was willing to take that chance. His experience thus far didn't exactly give him assurances his own side would help him if it came to that. "He has the situation covered. I'll just leave it at that."

"Do you think we'll see each other again?" A shadow passed over Abigail's face and Garrett's insides grew warm, wanting to believe this woman was meant for him to cherish all of his days.

"I certainly hope so. Things happened so fast for the trade that right now I don't know the details of what to expect, but I'm choosing to trust God with it. I'm learning that's the best way to go." He offered a smile and was glad to see one resurfacing on her face too. That was, until a troubling thought stole the moment. "I just hope I don't see you on the battlefield. Have you figured out what you are going to do?"

"Not yet, but I get the feeling I'll know soon. We're seeing fewer cases of smallpox now, so I imagine Dr. Adams won't be with us for much longer. Other than that, I'm anxious to see Abraham, even if I don't know what to expect. I just hope he'll actually talk to me now that his cover is blown."

Garrett frowned. He had a good knowledge of what happened to army prisoners who weren't officers and was less than optimistic Abraham had been an exception. "It's likely your brother hasn't been getting the same treatment I have while he's been captive. I don't want to alarm you, but there's even a chance you may not recognize him. One thing I can be sure of though, you'll be the first person he'll want to see."

Chapter 35

Abigail awoke, her stomach fluttering with anticipation. Today was the day. Today, she would see her brother alive thanks to Garrett and Cleo. Her heart nearly collapsed inside her chest for both men and their different sacrifices. Cleo's sacrifice was evident, even if she had trouble believing it, still surprised by the man's past as a privateer for the King of England. But then again, her own brother had been a spy for Washington, and she hadn't known about that either. Now, Cleo was giving himself up, like a lamb to the slaughter, willing to give what may very possibly be his life for her Abraham's. How could she possibly thank him?

Abigail's heart stirred too for Garrett and his own loss. Maybe he hadn't walked into an almost guaranteed death sentence, but he was walking into an uncertain future. She saw his pain clearly yesterday when he told her he wasn't enough to be traded alone. Her heart ached for him then and for his goal to make captain that seemed so far out of reach now. He was going back to his own side of the war, to his comrades, but other than seeing Nicholas again, she wasn't so sure he was looking forward to it. And there was a part she wasn't looking forward to either; saying

380

goodbye to the man she fell in love with.

With Charlotte still asleep beside her, Abigail gently rolled out from the covers to wash her face and get dressed. She grabbed a stack of papers from the nightstand and headed downstairs, the sweet aroma of maple syrup tingling her senses in every good way. Despite her stomach protesting otherwise, she didn't stop at the kitchen, but continued her way out. She needed to get into town before the trade began at noon. Haphazardly, she reached for her coat from the hall tree and strode for the door. Her hand grabbed the knob, swinging it open more quickly than she had time to react to as the momentum behind it lurched her forward. Her feet stumbled beneath her body to regain their balance, but in the end, she tripped right into Garrett's arms.

"Wow, you're off to somewhere in a hurry this morning." The smell of sea salt and sage mixed with morning sunshine captivated her senses. His arms around her were firm, catching her from her fall before gently releasing her from his strong embrace as her feet touched the carpet of the entryway again.

"I have a letter to take into town for the courier and I wasn't sure how much time I have before the trade. Do you need me to take one for you?"

That rogue smile she'd grown so dear of flashed across his face all the while knowing the time was coming up short when she'd miss it dearly.

"No, I'm hoping the next time I see Nicholas it will be face-to-face." Garrett eyed the papers in her hand. "For your parents?"

She nodded. "I thought I would give them some notice before we came home."

"Home? I take it that means you've decided not to stay with the army after Dr. Adams leaves?"

"I think it's time for me to go back home at least for a little while. The last thing I wrote to my parents was the news of Abraham's uncertain fate. I'm sure they're more than a little worried and I'd like to see my mother again. I don't know what Abraham will want to do when he returns but

I'm hoping he'll come with us." She took in a shaky breath, thinking about what this day meant for Garrett too. "Are you nervous about today?"

"I am, but I also know it's the right thing. I'm ready. How about you?"

"I'm nervous too." Abigail recalled Garrett's warning about Abraham, trying not to let her imagination get the better of her for what to expect, but it proved difficult. Visions of the inside of a prison ship haunted her mind, hearing from Garrett conditions aboard such a vessel were not only unacceptable, but downright unsanitary in the most horrible ways. He told her some of the details, including the lack of food and spread of disease, but he spared her the others. She packed a small bag of ointments to have just in case, before she'd have a chance to really look Abraham over and, if need be, take him to the hospital.

Garrett's warm eyes met hers as he grazed a finger down past her temple. The brush of his skin was light to the touch yet filled her with desire. "It'll be all right."

"I know, I'm just starting to fully take in it's going to be some time before I see you again."

He grinned, but kept silent.

"What?"

"It just feels good to hear you say that. You know there was a time when we had our differences."

Abigail knew he meant Falmouth and though the day of the destruction still echoed in her mind, even its reverberation had become quieted by everything that happened. She knew it would always be a day she'd remember, but no longer was it a day she felt any bitterness like she had when she first arrived in Cambridge.

"A lot has changed."

"It has and I'm glad for that too." Garrett took his hand from her cheek to reach inside his coat pocket. "Here, I have something for you." He pulled out a piece of jewelry she'd immediately recognized.

"Your mother's brooch?" Her hand went instantly to her hip, prepared to scold him. "Is that what you've been up to so early this morning?"

A guilty smile crossed his face. "I just wanted to have it polished one last time before I gave it to you."

The sarcasm in her expression faltered. "Garrett, I can't take that. It's all you have left of your mother. You said so yourself."

"Which is why I'm giving it to you. Just think of it as my way of reminding you I'll be back when I can. Trust me. I'll be wanting that brooch." He gave her a teasing grin before putting the heirloom in her apron pocket and bringing his hand to the side of her face again. He pulled her closer towards him, his strong arms wrapped around her, the mere impact of his touch making her tremble in a way she hadn't realized she'd longed for. She wanted to kiss him, and his eyes looked intently into hers with that same desire, eventually granting the wish into a reality. His lips met with hers, their touch both tender and passionate. Without persuasion, she felt her arms wrapping around his neck and as if reading her mind once again, he deepened the kiss, the taste of its sweet nectar causing a warm rush to run throughout her body and to the tips of her toes.

A moment too soon, he pulled away, his dark, brown eyes full of longing. He smiled then looked down at the stack of papers she'd been holding on her way out, now scattered on the floor. "We better get these sealed for you." Together, they gathered them up and put them in order before Garrett took hold of the pile. "Wait here, I'll be right back."

Garrett returned soon with the papers in hand, now neatly bound and waxed with his original seal.

"There." A warm smile lit his eyes. "Now, you can be assured your parents will get your letter in its entirety. I'll let you get into town so it can be delivered on time. Do you want me to walk with you?"

"That's all right. I think I'd like some time alone before everything begins."

He nodded, seeming to understand. "All right. Then I'll go pack my things." His lips were tender as they touched her forehead before he handed her the sealed letter to her parents and disappeared up the staircase.

"I see Garrett gave you a souvenir to remember him by." Abigail nearly tripped again at the unexpected voice from behind the wall, but this time Garrett wasn't there to catch her. She stumbled backward, regaining her footing and marched straight into the parlor.

"Charlotte, were you eavesdropping?"

Her sister gave an innocent smile with sly intent. "Only enough to see the gift Garrett gave you."

Abigail's hand went to the inside of her apron pocket, pulling out the brooch. "It's really special. It was his mother's."

Charlotte's mouth slowly tipped. "It's lovely, but I wasn't talking about the jewelry, Abby."

Abigail's cheeks burned to what she imagined resembled a bright crimson.

"So, are we really going back home after all this?" Charlotte crossed her arms while seated in the chaise, though her expression lacked any defiance.

Abigail didn't have to guess "all this" meant the trade with Garrett and Cleo for their brother. Everyone in the Schreier household seemed to be gearing up for it in their own way. Rebekah had made Garrett's favorite breakfast this morning: oatmeal with maple syrup and cornbread. Even Margaret joined in, having a new pair of Hessian boots fashioned to replace his old ones. "I'm hoping we all are. I don't know what Abraham will want to do, but Washington's approved his leaving under the circumstances if he decides to. I guess we'll see soon enough. Are you ready to go back to Aunt Sylvia's?"

Charlotte gave a single nod. "I like Margaret and Rebekah and little Sophie is a doll, but I'm ready to see Mother and Father, not to mention our own siblings. I bet Henry has been spending more of his time in the barn with the animals and Olivia's changed so much since I've left."

Abigail's chest twisted. She'd already missed the first quarter of her youngest sister's life. It was time to go home.

Charlotte's nearly perfect brow bent a degree. "But in truth, Abby, I'm a little surprised you're not staying. Abraham is one thing. He needs some time off, but what you're doing here is important. Even with Mrs. Schreier on the mend, you're still needed at the hospital, especially with Dr. Adams leaving soon too. Do you know what the army's going to do when that happens?"

She did. "A different physician will be taking over in his place, a Dr. Eric Young. I'm told he's already signed on for a full year if the war continues."

"Couldn't you study under him?"

Abigail shook her head, a prickling poked at the back of her neck as she recalled the first and hopefully last time she'd have an audience with the man. "I don't think so. I've met Dr. Young already, and he isn't a man who approves of women in his work setting or appears to view them as his equal. I feel certain he would refuse to teach me. When Dr. Adams introduced us to each other, I think he hoped the man might continue with me as his apprentice, but Dr. Young only mentioned he believed my talents might be more suited to stitching and mending clothes, not patients." She shrugged, not entirely surprised. "I've been fortunate to have the experience I've had under Dr. Adams' instruction, but I also know not everyone is as accepting of women as he is. It's going to be some time before the rest of the world is ready for such a partnership outside of just administering home remedies and births." A dapple of hope welled inside her. "But who knows, maybe this war can be a part of that."

Charlotte frowned, her concern running deep. "I'm sorry, Abby."

"That's okay. Don't worry. I'm not giving up on it, just taking some time to figure out some things and trusting God with all the rest."

"This house is certainly going to be empty in the next few days." Margaret and Rebekah entered the parlor. Sophie snuggled in her mother's arms with her bright blue eyes wide open as if taking in the sights and senses of the world around her. "If it weren't for Alex's arrival within the week I'd be more than a little disappointed, especially with having to look after Sophie by myself."

"Now, Margaret, stop that. You'll be fine. Besides, I already told you, Nicholas and I aren't steppin' one foot out that front door 'til we see Alex pass through it."

Abigail's brow faltered. What were these women getting at? "Rebekah, you're leaving?"

The dark brown crows' feet at the corner of Rebekah's even darker brown eyes grew pronounced as she gave a solid grin. "Yes, Miss Abby. It turns out the news Margaret meant to tell me at dinner the other night was interestin' to me, enough to do somethin' about it. I told you Margaret's been writin' my past owner in Georgia to see about my kin and she's finally heard an answer back." Rebekah straightened like a long-carried burden had flown from her shoulders. "Turns out the man and his wife I worked for have both passed on, but their daughter and her husband have taken over the place. The daughter admitted to only discovered Margaret's letters just recently while goin' through her parent's belongings, some of the papers still sealed. She wrote Margaret straight away to say all of the slaves were sold when her parents died except for one: a Mr. Elias Andrews." The woman's eyes illuminated brighter than the morning sun. "Abby, that's my brother's name and a place to start. I'm gonna buy Elias' freedom with the wages I've earned here under the Schreier roof and do the same when I find the others as long as God gives me the courage to do it." A twinkle in her eye sparkled with some mischief. "That is, just as soon as me and Nikolai are married."

With the current news overshadowing the events that would be taking place that afternoon, even if just for a moment, Abigail couldn't help but embrace Rebekah with a hug, overjoyed. "Rebekah, that's wonderful. I'm so happy for you."

"Thank you. I'm still a little nervous, not about marryin' Nikolai, mind you, but about goin' to find who's left of my family. I'm thankful God has provided a man in my life who helps me find my courage by reminding me where it comes from. Take it from a woman who knows what love looks like." She gave Abigail a knowing glance, the message reading loud and clear as the image of Garrett took shape in Abigail's mind.

"What about you and Sophie? We can't just leave you two by yourself, can we?" Charlotte's eyes drew from Margaret's to Abigail's for answers.

"Don't you worry, Miss Charlotte." It was Rebekah who answered. "As I mentioned before, I'm not about to leave 'til that babe's father is home and promised to be here for some time before his next campaign." Rebekah looked to Margaret, her eyes heartfelt and warm while a firm hand touched the lady's shoulder. "And don't you worry either. You're gonna do just fine as a mother. You already are. I knew it the day Dr. Adams and Abby here took her from your belly and you held her for the first time." Her smile grew. "But even so, I'll be back to see you and that sweet angel often. You can count on that."

***

Abigail walked out of the Blue Anchor Tavern, her letter ready for the courier when he came through to pick up the town's mail. Her pace quickened as she made her way to the hospital. There were others she wanted to say goodbye to, including the Bates and Thomas and she wasn't sure if she'd get the opportunity after the trade. Still, a few things remained at the hospital for her to do including saying goodbye to the remaining patients she'd cared for.

With the sight of the army hospital in view, Abigail sucked the air in deep, letting everything that transpired over the course of the past few months wash over her. She'd have to thank Dr. Adams, too, along with the list of others who'd helped her here in Cambridge.

A mixture of disappointment, uncertainty, and gratitude entangled inside her chest for the calling she both found and lost in such a short time. Even with her heart telling her it was time to go, she couldn't help wondering what was next–what she would do when she reached Falmouth again. Would she be able to find contentment back on the farm, or did God have another plan? She silently prayed for a renewed trust before she opened her eyes again, now a little more ready to do what felt like ending a chapter in her life, a chapter she wanted to hold onto.

"Morning ma'am." Mr. Douglas stood faithful at the Vassall door and greeted her with his customary flat expression. Abigail sensing then she'd miss it too. "I hear your brother is going to be joining us again."

"Yes, he will be." Her response came somewhat hesitantly, though why, it was unclear. Something told her news about Abraham being a spy was certain to travel quickly among the camp. Had the news about the trade spread just as fast?

"'Heard, too, that prisoner that was with you the evening you came to get the doctor will also be off our hands. Sounds like a good trade to me." That answered that.

Abigail forced a smile before she proceeded to the door, thinking how differently she felt regarding that detail.

Mr. Douglas gave a brutal clearing of his throat. "You also have a visitor, ma'am."

She turned with peaked interest, looking about, though it was only Mr. Douglas in view.

The hospital guard gestured his head towards the house. "He's already inside. Dr. Adams said it was okay when he arrived this morning."

Abigail turned back to the door and entered through, holding an expectation for who she might find on the other side of it. Her mind went straight to Thomas or a now recovered Mr. Bates, but her eyes lit to see she'd been mistaken on both accounts. "Cleo! I wasn't sure if I'd see you before—" Her words dropped, puddling at her feet.

"I know, Miss Abby, I wanted to say my goodbyes too. Thought I'd start off here with you." Cleo gave a weak smile, barely revealing his missing tooth. "My guess is if you know about the trade, then you know what I've done to be a part of it."

Her heart welled up with emotion. "I do and as thankful as I am that you're willing to risk so much for Abraham, I can't ask you to do it."

The man's smile grew two-fold, the absence of a tooth now evident. "You didn't, Miss Abby. No one did. I'm doing this out of my own volition. It's my chance to make things right, to atone for my sins in my past."

"Cleo, you know you don't need to do that."

"I know. I know Jesus has washed them all away, but I still want to. I'm just glad it helps get Abe back. I'll face what's coming to me willingly knowing that." The side of his mouth raised a little higher. "It seems God is going to finally let me be with my wife and daughter again. I suppose that's all I really wanted. Now, I can face death with some honor, knowing I helped someone in the process."

Abigail did her best to choke down a sob bundling in her throat. "You certainly seem at peace with it. I admire your courage."

Cleo shook his head. "It's naht courage, miss. Take it from a man who's been a coward most of his life, running from his due punishment. I just know it's the right thing to do, and I suppose since I found the Lord, death doesn't seem so intimidating anymore."

She watched wordlessly as Cleo removed his Monmouth cap and bowed before her with that same light humor she'd remembered on the docks in Falmouth the first time they'd met. Again, her heart swelled with an indebtedness to this man as he placed his hat back over the tufts of hair on his scalp. He took in a long breath, letting it out again easy, the gesture also telling Abigail their conversation was coming to a close. "I'm certainly glad I was able to see you before this evening, Miss Abby. It'll be a better memory for me than the one I'll have later on at the trade tonight. Until then, Washington has advised I take some time for enjoyment and goodbyes, and I imagine I should take the man's advice." A flash of a smile caught his expression again as he drew past her and out the door.

Abigail allowed her gaze to linger as Cleo made his way down Brattle Street, thankful and heartbroken at the same time. A tear made its way downward against her cheek. She knew the peace that Cleo felt was real, but even so, that didn't mean it would be an easy road.

Chapter 36

"Excuse me, sir." Abigail bumped against a middle-aged man as she worked to make her way up to the front of the crowd where she could see the trade happen. She hadn't expected a turnout like this or she would've tried to get here sooner. Garrett had gone over the logistics of an official exchange, including what likely to expect with this one, but he never mentioned having to work to find a clear view of it just to see the men in her life she cared so deeply about go through with it.

"It's like the whole town is here." Charlotte came alongside her, but not before she had to veer around a married couple who'd unknowingly stepped into her path. That had been after she'd just side-stepped out of the way of an army officer.

"I think it is." Abigail tried to look for an open path that led up towards the field where the trade was supposed to take place. "Garrett didn't say anything about a crowd like this and I think he would've mentioned it to let us know what to expect."

Charlotte shrugged, the signal conveying she had little more to offer as far as an explanation went. "Maybe he forgot?"

"Maybe." Abigail wasn't so sure, although he did have a lot on his mind. They all did. "I don't know, but I think I see the field. Let's try this way. There's fewer people over here and I bet we could get closer to the front." She cautiously, though with purpose, went forward, Charlotte following her lead close behind her. They'd almost broke through to the front without any accidental touch or need for an outspoken pardon when her arm brushed against the back of another woman's dress.

"I'm sorry, ma'am." The apology came quickly and without much thought, Abigail's mind more fixed on what was about to happen and whether she was going to miss seeing it. She was about to walk on when the shaggy red top of a young boy's head made her look twice, instantly recognizing him at the woman's side. "David?" Her eyes rose questionably to the woman he clung to. "Mary?" Abigail blinked and recalled the day all too well when mother and child were sent out of the camp on the wagon with a fate uncertain. "How? I thought—?"

Mary Russel rested a hand gently on the top of her son's ruffled head and smiled. "We've been staying at Mr. and Mrs. Fuller's since we were driven out of camp. Mr. Haywood got us a room there for the time being after it all happened."

Abigail flinched, hardly believing. "Officer Haywood set up a room for you after sending you out in the first place?"

Mary's jaw went tense. "He had to send us out. It was Washington's orders to since I wasn't workin' like I should've been doing. I don't know what happened. I guess I just got overwhelmed with what I couldn't do versus what I could do, and the next thing I knew David and I were on a wagon on our way out." She looked down at her son, an expression of a mother's concern wrapped in her features. "I wasn't sure what I was going to do or where I was going to go until Mr. Haywood met us at the edge of camp where they dropped us off and took us to the Fuller home." The strain in her expression softened into a smile. "They're really nice, and

Mrs. Fuller has shown me how to properly manage a household and do more things that are useful. Mr. Haywood has also taken up a room there too and spends time with David when Mrs. Fuller teaches me something I need to know."

"That's wonderful, Mary. I'm glad you're all right. Are you planning to join the camp again when they march on?"

Mary shook her head though Abigail didn't miss the rosy color glowing from her cheeks. "We have plans to go to Virginia when that happens. Mr. Haywood wants to show me his home and other things the future Mrs. Haywood will oversee while he returns to the war effort." A wry smile tipped upward before fully blooming. Abigail's jaw would've dropped if it wasn't for the woman's joyful expression she didn't want to ruin.

As if on cue, Haywood came up beside Mary, giving Abigail a slight nod before he took David by the hand like he'd known the boy all his life. "I need to get on my horse soon, but I have a spot for you at the front." He offered his arm and Mary took it before he glanced back at Abigail, signaling he'd extended the invitation to join them. Without a need for coercion, she and Charlotte followed behind until they reached the edge of the field. The hairs on the nape of her neck stood on end to see the back of not only a man she recognized, but dearly loved.

***

Garrett found himself in what he could only gather to be a mutual clearing located between Boston and Cambridge and where neither side seemed to hold the advantage. That would change, however, when Knox arrived, carrying cannon and other artillery. But as to when that might be, Garrett wasn't one of the privileged to know.

He wasn't alone in the field and that was by far. He'd imagined a few spectators outside the officials orchestrating the trade, but not a crowd this size, certain the rest of Cambridge was standing just a few yards behind him. "I've never seen a crowd like this at an exchange. Is there something I don't know about?"

Cleo stood beside him, looking straight ahead as if daring his future to take the first move. Garrett had to admit, he'd been impressed by not only the man's offer to do so in the first place, but also his determination to continue with it, knowing his own time for being a free man was coming to an end.

"They've never seen a trade before. Looks like the whole town showed up including our friends from the other night." Cleo tilted his head to the side and Garrett caught the man's hint in an instant.

Jasper and Linus had front row seats, though stood with arms crossed like they weren't happy about it. Jasper caught Garrett's eye, his lips curling into a malicious smile like the one Garrett had seen that night in the clearing. It did well to remind him of the burly man's promise for what would happen the next time they met in battle. Garrett had already made eye contact, but he wasn't about to encourage the man any further by showing he'd understood the message even as clear as it was. Instead, he switched his gaze over to what lay ahead.

Washington sat almost regally upon Blueskin, his half-Arabian gray horse. Three other officers on their own mares joined him, Haywood being one of them and looking as stiff as usual.

With their sights towards Boston, in the direction of which the King's general should be, an empty field stood. Garrett's own countrymen hadn't shown yet, and it past the agreed hour, but Garrett was fairly confident they would. A general's word held a certain accountability to it, and though he'd not seen the man's response in writing, Washington clearly held the impression Howe had agreed, his own resolve unflinching as he sat atop Blueskin. Still, a shred of doubt lingered for Garrett, a predicament he knew well of before he'd been stationed in Boston, a predictament that kept a constant strain on Parliament. It was the simple fact that agreeing for an exchange of prisoners meant recognizing the colonies as an independent nation, a country of their own. That was the whole precedent for this war, and something Parliament was just not willing to do.

There was also the possibility that General Howe had simply changed his mind. That wasn't a far-fetched idea either, considering the conflict between the mother country and, in her mind, the disobedient child. Howe no doubt had endured his share of that during the release of *Common Sense* and his willingness to deal with the leader of those that stood behind its principles may have very well crumbled.

"Mr. Ward, sir."

The youthful male voice among the crowd of men he stood with made Garrett turn round with a startle.

"Thomas? What are you doing out here?" Garrett tried to hide his alarm, but could see by the boy's frown, the damage was done. "I'm sorry. It's not that I'm not happy to see you, but you better get back to the crowd. I don't want anyone giving you trouble thinking you made a friend of the enemy. I imagine Jake and his gang wouldn't let you forget it either."

Thomas shrugged with an indifference. "I don't care about them anymore, sir. Not that I wish them any bad will, I just figured I could do better with friends. Besides, I wanted to say goodbye. I got caught up with things this morning, and I'm afraid this might be my last chance."

Garrett smiled, moved by the boy's persistence, even if the timing was off. "Thank you, Thomas. I'm glad you came over. It means a lot that you did." His smile faded, the reality of where the next time he'd see Thomas might be hitting hard. "Although, I'm not looking forward to see you on a field like this in a different setting."

"Actually, sir, you won't have to worry about that."

Garrett pulled his head back, his brow lifted. "Oh? Does that mean your determination for joining the other men on the battlefield has waned?"

Thomas' shoulders slumped slightly. "No, Mr. Ward, my determination is intact, but my responsibility over my family is calling and this time I'm willing to listen. Turns out my earnings here in the army aren't enough to justify me staying here any longer. Mother says I'll be more useful to her and my siblings at home as we prepare for the spring, and I suppose she's right. I'll be leaving for Salem in a few days, I gather."

Garrett did his best to hide the breath of sheer relief, knowing it hadn't been an easy decision for his young friend, but in the end, the release of satisfaction gave way. He was glad his chances for seeing Thomas among the lines of combat were gone, even if for the present, but he also knew what that meant. Thomas wouldn't be avenging his father, at least, not in the way he had set out to do.

"I can't say I'm sorry to hear that, Thomas," Garrett said, admitting the truth freely. "But I also know that's not what you wanted."

"It's not, sir. But seeing as I'm the man of the house now, I have to do what I can to provide for my family, even if that means postponing my own plans." The side of his mouth raised. "At least for a little while. It's what my father would've done, I'm sure of it."

Garrett smiled, feeling a certain pride for the boy. "Your father would be proud of you."

The other side of Thomas' lips drew upward and revealed a full smile. "I hope so, sir. I also hope you don't mind me saying he'd be proud of you too. If circumstances were different, I think you would've liked him, sir."

"I'm sure I would have." The sharp clearing of a disgruntled throat cut at the moment between them. Garrett caught the disapproving eyes of Haywood down on him and Thomas. Reading the message loud and clear, Garrett worked to resolve the problem. "You better get back to the crowd. Things here should be starting soon."

Thomas nodded to both him and Cleo before his eyes veered upward to Washington on Blueskin with a childlike marvel.

Garrett watched Thomas walk back towards the crowd, his own amazement less directed at the general on the gray horse and more by the young boy who'd somehow in the course of a few months, became a man. When he turned back to face Boston again, Garrett noticed Washington's gaze pressed on him, his mouth slightly pinned with curiosity as he looked between him and Thomas. For the briefest of moments, the two opponents seemed to share a mutual understanding before the continental general's chin ascended again to stare at the empty field with calm expectation.

When another quarter hour passed, tensions rose. Garrett scanned the crowd in search of the only face he truly cared to see. He smiled when he found her, having taken a place at the front of the mass behind them with Charlotte by her side. Abigail caught his glance and smiled back, the gesture becoming more like home to him each time he got a chance to view it. She was wearing his brooch, something he hadn't requested of her. Yet, seeing it displayed proudly against her chest now made him feel more than a little heartened by the day's event, giving him a renewed hope.

"General, sir, it looks like Howe is approaching."

Washington's countenance never wavered, only acknowledging Haywood's observation by following the officer's motion to the far side of the field. Garrett too could see movement just before the clearing on the other side. He guessed tensions behind him that concerned the other party's reluctance to follow through with the deal shifted to see their adversary in full view.

The British general, like Washington, was on horseback with Admiral Graves at his side. In between the two, a single man and the only party on foot of the three, Garrett guessed to be Abraham. The insides of Garrett's stomach knotted, observing his treatment had been a far outcry from his own. It was clear by his newly shaven face and coarse, cut hair, the officers had given him a chance to clean up, but those things alone couldn't hide the remnants of what he must've experienced during his imprisonment in New York. As the men drew nearer, Garrett could only surmise the man who walked towards them now was a little more than a shadow in comparison as far as physical appearance to the one he'd met in Falmouth. His face was gaunt and pale, the product of malnutrition and lack of sunlight. It had to have been for many days and despite having washed his person, his clothes were worn and filthy.

Garrett couldn't help but glance back at Abigail as she took in the ghastly site of her brother. Her eyes were locked in the direction of Abraham, but otherwise she looked composed. He knew her well enough to know she was either trying to be strong for the benefit of her brother and those around her or she was utterly shocked. Maybe a little of both. Garrett wished he could be beside her, to be there for her. But he couldn't. Washington had begun his descent towards Parliament's general and unfortunately, that was his cue.

Garrett shifted his eyes over to Cleo, a stiffness in his neck and shoulders taking hold. The Scotsman gave him a nod as if to convey he was ready for whatever happened next. The two of them followed in suit behind the other rebel officer who trailed their leader. When each side had approached their desired distance, closing the space between them, they stopped. Garrett guessed they were about fifty yards away, close enough to easily catch the benign, yet authoritative expression of Howe as he looked only towards Washington. Garrett, too, caught sight of Graves. The admiral gave him a fleeting glance before his attention was drawn to Cleo and stayed there. Garrett's stomach knotted, knowing that was the part of the deal his commanders were more interested in.

The prisoners faced each other too, Garrett reading both recognition and surprise in Abraham's haggard expression. Unlike Cleo and himself, Abraham hadn't been privy to the details of the arrangement, but he didn't say a word. None of them did, afraid that doing so might somehow forfeit the deal. As directed, each man went to their designated sides as they were signaled by the motion of a single nod from their captors, a gesture they recognized and immediately obeyed. Then it was over. Once both sides were present, the whole thing took no more than five minutes.

Now, as Garrett stood among his own comrades, facing the rebel mass towards Cambridge, his breath still held and would until both sides parted and his feet were in Boston. Once that happened, he would be able to relax, even if a large portion of his heart yearned for a part of Cambridge he had to leave behind. Garrett took one last long look at the woman he had come to care for, to love, making sure he grabbed every single detail he could until the next time they were to meet again, if ever.

Chapter 37

"You look like you've seen better days."

The jibe had come from Charlotte, taunting her older brother with a sarcastic tone and probably hoping to make light of a very serious outcome. Though, Abigail thought, it was not hard to suspect she was right. Abraham truly did look like he'd seen better days. But as obvious as the statement had been, what wasn't clear was what exactly had he been through? Even knowing it was Abraham standing across from Garrett and Cleo in that clearing, she barely recognized the sickly, thin figure that somewhat resembled her brother. What had he experienced on the other side of the war?

"Abraham." Abigail broke in, now close enough to touch his hand as the siblings made their way back towards Portsmouth in a carriage Washington had loaned them. Even from the front of the field where she'd had a better view of the trade and first captured his appearance, she really had no idea the extent of his injuries until she'd finally seen him up close. She looked at his colorless face like he hadn't been outside for weeks and wondered. "Where did they keep you while you were imprisoned? Do you know?"

"Inside an old sugar house."

"A sugar house?" She recognized a nod, the struggle of the small gesture evident in the weakness he was still feeling. He nearly collapsed in her arms and would've if it weren't for Haywood and another officer saving him from it and bringing him to the Schreier house after he'd refused the hospital.

"Yeah, but there wasn't anything sweet about my time there." Though raw from the conditions he suffered, his voice grew with agitation. "They put us all in a basement where it was dark and wet. I don't remember it ever being dry down there or having something to eat that wasn't wet, either, but the dampness of the food when we got it wasn't something our hungry stomachs were going to complain about." He grimaced. "Although the pork and moldy bread they gave us on occasion was hardly ever enough for everyone, sometimes even infested with worms. That didn't stop our sergeant from stealing it though—the vicious and cruel scoundrel." Abraham drew in a forced breath and shook his head. "I'm just thankful I'm out of there. Otherwise, I'm sure it was just a matter of time before I'd be like some of the others, sewn up in my blanket and tossed to the corner of the yard to be picked up by the dead cart."

Abigail's stomach dropped. She stole a glance with Charlotte, neither one of them revealing the fact that was obvious: their brother had no idea of his impending execution scheduled for later that week.

"I'm thankful too." The words were genuine. And for the present, Abigail thought it unnecessary to give her brother all the details of his imprisonment. "You already look better after yesterday." She managed a weak smile as she recalled the wounds she'd dressed and the symptoms that were on the verge of appearing more like typhus. After giving him a mercurial ointment for the lice and other pests he'd probably run into, she was glad not to see a rash on his chest or stomach. Still, his weakened pulse and dry cough combined with the conditions he'd described, were enough to let her stay cautious.

Abigail's vision blurred, water beginning to take form in her eyes. She felt indebted too, for Rebekah, for the warm bath and the beef broth with bits of roasted meat and bread Abraham managed to get down the night before. Margaret was also a saint, not only to offer him housing for the night where he stayed in Garrett's old room but allowed him to partake in her husband's wardrobe when his own clothes were deemed more fit for the fire than to wear again. And she was thankful Abraham, knowing how bent he was for the patriotic cause, did not refuse the generosity and hospitality, no matter where it came from.

"Well, I feel better. Much better, actually, whether I look it or not." Abraham managed a smile.

"The bath was certainly an improvement." The side of Charlotte's mouth raised into a droll grin.

Abraham gave a mild huff, but the jab seemed to strengthen his countenance. "Yes, well, I'm sure I looked a bit rough. I'm just glad to be out of there. Anywhere but there is better."

"I'm glad you feel that way." Abigail was also pleased her brother hadn't given her too much protest when she'd told him her plan was to return to Portsmouth following the night of the exchange. She could see he'd been through enough of the war effort at present and she purposely took advantage of it. "Mother and Father will be so relieved to have you home." She paused, thinking how long their time away had been. Aside from their brief stay when their mother had taken a turn for the worse, they'd spent three months in Cambridge. An eternity when prior to the war they'd never been away from their parents for more than a night. "I imagine to have all of us home."

"You say that like you're happy about it, but I'm not so sure I believe you." Abraham's eyes narrowed on her.

"What do you mean?"

"Abby, I was a spy in New York where another part of the king's army is stationed. I know when something's off and your face couldn't be more telling. Besides, when I left, Charlotte was still in Portsmouth at Aunt Sylvia's and now she's here. Was there something I missed while I was gone?"

"There was something that happened while you were off playing spy." Charlotte jeered, a twinkle in her eye telling Abigail exactly what her sister was about to reveal. "Or should I say, someone happened. I'm guessing that's probably why our sister is a little torn when we're on our way to see our family again."

"You met someone?" Abraham frowned, a brow arched, before his mouth drew into a slow smile. "Really? Is he from the camp or in town? What's the name? I'm sure I'd know it if I heard it. I met quite a few men before I left on my assignment."

"Oh, I don't think you'd know of him. He's from out of town. He's a lieutenant and goes by the name of Garrett Ward…" Charlotte paused, giving their brother time to consider the name, "…of the Royal Navy."

"A king's soldier, Abigail?" Abraham shook his head with vehemence. He looked at her as if pleading that their younger sister was but jesting again. "And of the Royal Navy? The same Royal Navy who blew up our town?"

The speculation and disapproval in his tone made her stomach turn on itself. How was she supposed to defend Garrett for the time she'd been able to know him and see more of who he truly was? Where was she supposed to start? Abigail knew what her brother was feeling because she'd been there before, but her time with Garrett and the Lord's forgiveness had helped her move past the hurt.

"Actually—"

Before she could get in a word and try to cool things down, Charlotte stepped in, a little too eager to disclose the next detail.

"He was on the same ship." Her younger sister's chin lifted.

Abigail cringed, realizing how bad it sounded, especially to her brother who'd just been released from the opposing side's prison.

Again, Abraham looked at her, though this time his face blank as if she'd done the unthinkable. "I don't know what to say, Abby. I don't understand."

"You should say thank you, if you ever meet him."

Abraham's agitated expression turned to Charlotte, the words coming out forced. "Thank you?"

She nodded, unflinching. "He's the one responsible for your freedom in the first place."

"How do you mean, exactly?" Their brother's eyes scrutinized her. "Washington made the correspondence and orchestrated the trade. General Howe told me as much, even if little else." A bitter resentment was in his tone.

"Huh." Charlotte huffed, an ere of condescension in her own. "Then I guess one of the things he left out was the fact you were going to be hanged within the week. Thanks to Garrett, that didn't happen. Washington may have set up the exchange, but it was that Royal Navy officer who came up with the idea." She shrugged. "He and Cleo at least."

Cleo. The mention of her brother's sacrificial lamb made Abigail's heart sink, wondering what the man was going through.

"I imagine they have him in one of those sugar houses like the one I stayed in by now." Abraham's answer was composed as he read her mind. She pulled back, studying his expression. It was more relaxed now. She imagined he'd be more perplexed on the issue of seeing his friend face-to-face at the trade and wanting answers. Perhaps he knew more than she thought, even if he had been blindsided by his scheduled death sentence.

"So, you know why he was traded, why they took him?" Abigail met her brother's gaze with expectation.

Abraham inhaled sharply and gave a single nod. "I've known about

404

Cleo's past for quite some time. He's the one who trained me for my first mission after all, before I became a spy for Washington. I also know he's been on the run from it for twice as long, which is why I can't understand why he'd agree to such a trade. He knew what he faced if caught." Abraham eyed her as if with accusation, his glare making her insides turn. "So how did your lieutenant persuade him otherwise?"

"As far as I know, he didn't. Cleo volunteered."

"Volunteered? Did your lieutenant tell you that?" Abraham tipped the side of his chin, looking at her doubtfully. She challenged his scrutiny with the truth she knew, the truth of both men and their courage.

"Yes, but only before Cleo himself confirmed it." Abigail remembered the conversation they'd had on the day of the exchange, the peace he seemed to have within him. It was a peace that truly did surpass understanding and she could see the disbelief on her brother's face now as evidence of it. "I believe Cleo has changed, Abraham. He's not entirely the same man you knew before you left. He's found peace even from when I last spoke to him." She squared her shoulders, not wanting to diminish what the man had sacrificed. "And he did it for you." Hearing the irritation in her tone, she softened her words. She didn't mean to be difficult, but she needed him to understand. "Both of these men agreed to the exchange to get you back."

She had to force down the knot that had formed in her throat. Seeing Garrett go was just as hard as she'd imagined it would be, but she couldn't dwell on that now. Her brother went silent. Again, Abigail didn't know what he was thinking, but this time it didn't matter. He didn't know the details of the trade or what happened during these months he'd been gone, nor did he seem to care. At least not right now, and she supposed she couldn't blame him for that. Like his ignorance with what had transpired in Cambridge during his absence, she too was naive to think she knew what he'd been through both in and out of prison. And she did well to remember that.

An awkward silence fell during the rest of the carriage ride that was all but claustrophobic in such a small space. Even Charlotte said little after she'd brought up the topic of Garrett. For once, Abigail wished that wasn't the case. Especially now with Abraham's dissatisfaction so apparent.

Wanting to evade her brother's stare as if she'd committed some wrong, Abigail averted her view out the window. She thought, too, of how different she expected this moment to be; reunited with her siblings, her brother who was just days away from death, and going home at last. She'd been certain the carriage ride back to Portsmouth was to be a chance to come closer together, to relay how much they missed one another and what they had experienced along the way. She couldn't be more wrong.

Division reared between her and Abraham over Garrett and irritation with Charlotte for bringing up Garrett's involvement in the attack of their town. She hated the feeling. The only solace she took was knowing her own agitation with Charlotte was short-lived, reminded her sister had only spoken the truth. She just hoped Abraham's own anger towards her would ease, but the timing on that remained uncertain. Abigail made it a point not to mention Garrett again to her brother. After all, she thought, realizing she still wore his brooch at her chest and even though she believed he'd be back for it, there was still the question of when. It was a question for which neither she nor Garrett knew the answer. So, she determined, until Garrett really did decide to fulfill his promise, she'd focus elsewhere, on things and people she'd actually have contact with. Maybe in doing that, her relationship with her older brother might be restored sooner rather than later.

Abigail concentrated on the horses' trot-like rhythm outside. Her eyes struggled to stay open. The carriage wheels beneath them rolled over the path towards Portsmouth, the snow acting like a blanket as it covered the otherwise troublesome rocks and roots, making the ride smoother than it would have been otherwise. The combination of the uninterrupted motion and the sound of the horses' hooves was like a lullaby rocking her to sleep. With eyes heavy and emotions spent, she let the slow canter of the song do just that, letting her mind be renewed in a deep, unburdened rest.

***

When the horses' continuous trotting became less rhythmic and the carriage began to slow, Abigail awoke. Downtown Portsmouth. Just a few miles away from her aunt's home. She breathed in as if gulping fresh air again. Soon she'd be with the rest of her family. She couldn't wait to see her mother, having heard little of her condition since Charlotte arrived in Cambridge. Abigail let out a quiet, eager gasp. And Olivia, with the months she'd missed to see her grow. Her heart did a double twirl at the thought of seeing every member of her family as they finally found themselves pulling into their aunt's estate.

Her father and their aunt rushed out the door as if they'd been waiting for the arrival of someone extraordinary. Olivia sat high upon her father's shoulders while Henry stood by Aunt Sylvia's side. Her father squeezed her tight, his warm embrace filling her with comfort before he did the same for Abraham and Charlotte. The whole scene felt right and joyful except for one thing.

Abigail suspected her mother might be absent upon their arrival and was anxious to see the final face in the Thatcher family she had yet to see. She pulled herself free from the fold her of aunt's loving arms and turned to her father again. "How is Mother doing? I haven't heard of any news since Charlotte came to Cambridge."

Her father's eager smile to see them diminished along with their aunt's and just like that, all the rightness of the world in that moment faded, too.

Abigail's stomach coiled. "What's wrong, Father?"

"We thought it best if you all were here to see for yourself instead of writing. You were already concerned with what was going to happen to

407

Abraham. We were, too, until we received your most recent letter about the trade. Dr. Jenkins is inside now with your mother, but he says she doesn't have much time, maybe just weeks, even days."

"I thought she was getting better?" Abigail deviated to Charlotte, searching for answers, having been the bearer of the positive news, but she looked as confused as Abigail felt.

Their father spoke for her. "We hoped she might be, but she's not."

Abigail stepped towards him, her heart pounding. "May I see her?"

"Of course, you can see her, Abby." His mouth went somber. "But I should warn you, there's not much more we can do for her, and I think once you go in there, you'll see Dr. Jenkins is right." He gave a sigh, his eyes full of tenderness. "I know you want to help her, but she's accepted what's about to happen, and I have, too. You'll see what I mean." He handed Olivia to Charlotte.

Abigail followed him into the house and up to the room where she'd been at her mother's side at her last visit. There, they waited outside the door until Dr. Jenkins was finished.

Her father motioned for her to go inside, but not before he put a gentle hand on her shoulder. "She's very tired, Abby, more so than the last time you were here. It takes a lot out of her just to keep breathing. Say what you want to say, but don't expect too much from her."

Abigail nodded, looking into her father's eyes again, now full of acceptance for what was happening. Her father loved her mother, yet how could he be so calm knowing the woman he cherished was slipping away? Cleo came to mind and the peace she saw on his face the day prior came back, Abigail recognizing the same expression on her father's face now.

"How are you doing this—being so calm? I feel like half my world is crashing down, knowing Mother is dying." Abigail saw her father struggle to create a heavy-hearted smile, the openings under his brow now glistening. It was then she understood he was right there with her.

"I know exactly how you feel, Abby. Believe me, I do. But I also know more about your mother's condition than you do. She's had it a long time and the both of us knew this would come. As hard as it still is, we've had some time to prepare for it as best we can."

She wrinkled her brow. "She's had it a long time? How long?"

"Before we were married. At that time the doctor told us of her weak heart and warned she should stay away from anything too strenuous, including bringing a child into this world."

Abigail met her father's gaze again, seeing nothing but love in his pale, blue eyes.

His smile returned, one mixed with compassion and loss. "But your mother wanted a family, and I just couldn't find the strength to say no. Each time was risky, she knew that, growing weaker after, but she always said it was worth the risk. When Henry was born, we knew it was best to stop and counted ourselves blessed. Then the Almighty surprised us with Olivia. I'm afraid time as far as getting older has not been to our advantage, but we have no regrets and I know if your mother could, she'd say the same." He nodded in the direction of the room, taking in a forced breath. "Take your time with her. I'm going to go back and see about Charlotte and Abe. I suppose it's time I told them the same information I just shared with you. When you're done, come our way. I'm sure your brother and sister would like to see her too."

Abigail watched him go, the sound of his footsteps trailing the hall and down the stairs. Like her last visit, she took to her mother's bedside, though feeling a little more crushed in spirit this time, after her conversation with her father. With every in and outward motion of her lungs, her mother struggled for breath. The wheezing Abigail first noticed a few weeks ago was now more pronounced. Her mother coughed a few times but remained asleep as if the rough disruption that came from her own body could not even pull her awake. Abigail's body shook, fearing that very thought might be true.

Love Beyond the Ashes

She stroked the top of her mother's forehead like her mother had done so many times for her as a child, feeling then, nothing but love in her touch. The thought made her smile, then cry, grateful for the mother the Lord provided while Abigail also clung from letting her go to be with Him in the heavenly realms.

When another hour passed and her mother hadn't awoken, Abigail knew it was time to go and let her other siblings have their turn. She planted a firm kiss filled with emotion on top of her mother's pale head, not fully knowing, but somehow sensing this would be the last time she'd be with her mother in this life.

Chapter 38

Garrett stood across from the admiral's desk. He wasn't invited to sit down in the empty chair across from it. That alone was a clear indication this meeting wouldn't take long. Not that it amounted to much. He cared little for how much time he'd spent in the man's office. What he cared about more was what Graves had planned for him now that he'd returned.

"I'm sure you're glad to be back, Lieutenant."

"Yes, sir. It's good to be here." Garrett's words came out automatically. They were of course expected of him, yet he couldn't help but feel they weren't exactly true. He may have not been a prisoner anymore and back on his own side of the war but having lost that title also meant he lost a few other things, namely, Abigail. He fully meant to see her again, but he wasn't sure how long that would be. Days, months, years? Only God knew for certain.

"Now that you're with us again, I imagine you'll want to know what's in store for you." Graves' jaw lifted as if somehow the gesture pulled Garrett's spirits upward with it and he considered the possibility of his promotion to captain back on the table.

Was he foolish to think so—after so easily losing his ship and crew of the well-trained and skilled Royal Navy to what he surmised to be the newest navy out there? A familiar desire stirred inside; one he hadn't thought about for months. Garrett took a moment to consider what the promotion had meant to him, how much it had meant. Too much. He knew that now. He'd let the advancement of his rank come to define him, to make him feel like he mattered in British elite society, yet in the end that path had only led him down a dead end.

There was certainly nothing wrong with wanting to do better, be better. But he had done it for the wrong reasons. Now, he didn't feel those reasons held the same weight they used to. It wasn't his rank or commanding his own ship that defined him anymore. Garrett understood that now. It was a relationship with God, with Jesus, that somehow filled the hole in his heart he hadn't grasped he had, making him feel whole again. Anything compared to that just didn't seem to matter as much as it used to. So, whatever the admiral was about to say next, it would be okay.

"I won't spare you with pleasantries, Mr. Ward." Graves continued, his hands together at their fingertips on top of his desk. "That's not my way. Instead, I'll go ahead and say things as they are." Garrett saw the admiral's jaw grow tight with determination, he recognizing the look as one holding unfortunate news. "At this time, as I'm sure you will understand, Lieutenant, your request for promotion has been denied until further review and of course, your debriefing." Graves released his fingers as he relaxed the rest of his body back into his chair. "You spent a good while behind rebel lines and as a customary precaution, you are to be sent to the Motherland of where you will be received back into society life."

Garrett bit the inside of his cheek, not so much for his declined promotion, but more for the fact his superior hadn't mentioned an end date to his time in 'society life' and when he'd be able to get back on a ship. "Admiral Graves, sir, may I ask how long my time stationed as a civilian might be?"

"There's nothing official at present, but your captain has suggested six months."

Garrett swallowed down his disappointment. Half a year. "Six months, sir? Why so long?"

"It's double the amount of time you spent on the side of the resistance." Graves made the remark like it was purely customary. "Do you have a problem with that, Lieutenant Ward?"

Garrett did have a problem with it, but he chose to stand down. "No, sir."

"Good. Captain Edwards will also be accompanying you on the voyage and will be providing me with the necessary report upon your person. I'm certain you understand that too."

Garrett gave a resolute nod, fully accepting his deserved consequence. "When am I to expect to leave, sir, if you don't mind me asking?"

"You'll set sail for England in a month when the winter recedes and conditions prove more bearable for the journey. Feel free to enjoy your last few weeks in Boston with your comrades. I imagine they'll be a welcome sight after so much time among that rebel camp." A slight smile curved upwards on the general then down again. "But do take caution, Mr. Ward." Graves gave him a warning glare, his tone matched with disdain. "The civilians here have become less civil towards us since the publication of this awful *Common Sense* piece. We've had to threaten imprisonment among these challenging people and in many cases have found ourselves carrying such threats out to keep the riots to a minimum. Such actions seem to be working for now, but even still you can see it in their eyes we're not welcome here. I suspect it's but a matter of time before they break loose again. All they need is a little spark and these people will rally like a consuming flame." The man let out a disgruntled sigh. "Let's just hope we find a way to squash this rebellion soon. I'll be happy to get out of here. Perhaps that's why Captain Edwards wants to leave as soon as his men can handle the trip. Though if that's the case, I can't say I'm not desirous to do the same and move on from such a defiant people as these."

Garrett thought about that. Nicholas' father had never been someone he considered easily intimated. The captain's position and reputation as a hard man earned him a most respectable influence over any navy member, new or experienced to life at sea. Any order the man commanded was quickly carried out and without question. So much so that the man's prominence followed him in society, at least the society of his mother country. But here things were different. The people here could care less about his prestige and seemed unwelcome to the very notion of a king's soldier. It was a land determined to be separated from its origin and to make that happen, chaos in the form of riots took place.

Garrett could easily see how a man who was used to having order and power might otherwise feel overwhelmed by the very idea that not everyone was under his control. Still, he had to remember that was only an assumption, one of which he had no proof. But whether it was true or not didn't matter. Either way, Garrett would be returning to England and would have to be accompanied by someone. It was just as well it was the captain, reminded again of what more the man was to him: the man who'd taken him into his home, into his family.

There wasn't much more Garrett wanted to say to Admiral Graves or ask of him. He'd found out what he needed to know and seeing as his time was short in the Boston area, there was one person he wanted to see before he would have to ready his things by morning. He waited silently, expecting a formal dismissal. Yet, it didn't come. Instead, his superior only changed course.

"Lieutenant, before I let you take your leave, there is another matter I wish to address." Graves' tone raised with inquisition; his eyes fully centered on Garrett's who felt the scrutiny even from across his desk. It was then the issue of Henry Knox came beckoning and Washington's warning right on its heels. If Garrett told about the rumored battery of arms, he was almost certain Washington would find out and fulfill his promise to take him prisoner again, but this time without the consideration of his rank.

An image of Abigail's brother, Abraham, shot forward with him in the field at the trade, Garrett doing well to hold back the grimace he felt wanting to push itself outward. The thought lacked more than appeal. Never mind there was the possibility that the rumor of Knox really was in fact just that, a rumor—a plan to lead his opponents in Boston astray. Garrett heard the information from Thomas back at the Schreier estate, but he'd never heard anything more about it or seen Knox around either and he wasn't about to treat Washington with less caution than he deserved. The man wasn't to be taken lightly. Garrett could easily see the continental general planning a different strategy to overtake the city if he had to.

Unfortunately, the decision wasn't that simple. The call of Garrett's allegiance to his country and King and, more importantly, his duty to the Navy also made their demands. In the past it had only been a means to an end, his rise to captain, but now, while the glory of the position and its status diminished, Garrett's loyalty had not.

Graves' leaned forward into his desk. "You spent a great deal of time over in enemy territory and within the grounds of Washington's main camp. Did you happen upon anything concerning the rebel commander's next move while you were there?"

Garrett sat silent for a moment, still weighing his options. They were both heavy with consequences. Divided, like the two sides of the war he was currently a part of, he could only think to give what he knew to be concrete. "Nothing of certainty, sir. I was in the continental camp for some time, but Washington and his men didn't forget my position in the war or how I came to be in Cambridge in the first place. With that in mind, I couldn't be sure if anything they mentioned was accurate or mere ploy in deception." He watched as the admiral reclined back into his chair, satisfaction written across his face once more.

"Yes, Lieutenant, I suppose you're right. This whole war affair has been most surprising. I made the mistake of judging these people too quickly. I was certain order would soon be restored upon our arrival here––even expected the people to be thankful for our military presence and what we stood for, yet that couldn't be farther from it." Annoyance captured both his countenance. "I will not make the same mistake with Washington by labeling him incapable of such schemes. Thank you, Mr. Ward. That will be all. You may go."

***

A month later, Garrett found himself just where he wanted to be, at least while he remained in the Boston area. Nicholas sat across from him in the safe confines of the wardroom to the captain's ship, the one they'd sailed on to get to the colonies. It had been his friend's suggestion after rumors to the hostility of the Boston people proved true, to settle in a place they were welcomed and catch up before Garrett's ship had to set sail for England.

Just glad for the opportunity to see Nicholas after hearing he'd been out on duty patrolling since the week of the trade, Garrett consented to the idea easily. He took a sip from his glass, holding a rich combination of melted chocolate and a splash of port. Nothing like getting a warm dose of sugar in the morning before a long voyage home. As the dark blend of flavors stimulated his senses, he listened, finally able to hear of Nicholas' account of his assignment from the King himself.

"But as amiable as King George may be and my visit having gone just as well, I'm afraid the situation for why he sent for me is troubling. It's no wonder His Majesty wants the knowledge of it kept secret." Nicholas' voice shrunk to a whisper. He looked around the wardroom and to the

416

door as if watching out for anyone else that might be present and partial to their conversation. They were alone. Even still his friend's body bent in closer over the table, the whole of it looking tense. "If word gets out, this war might be over more quickly than we thought and not because we'd hold the advantage in military and numbers."

Garrett had been in Cambridge long enough to see the so-called misfit army he'd labeled was more capable than his own comrades previously thought. Lexington and Concord along with Breed's Hill all proved that as well as his own time spent during his imprisonment. He thought, too, of Henry Knox and whether the threat was true, still having a hard time himself believing the man had hiked 300 miles over snow and ice with a battery of cannon in tow. But he wasn't about to deny the rumor completely. Was there something more Nicholas knew to their efforts? Garrett's ears perked as his friend's tone grew more critical, revealing the secret he'd been wondering over since Nicholas got his new assignment.

"There's a large sum of debt that has already piled up from this war."

Garrett frowned, expecting more, but Nicholas' pause only proved disappointing. "That doesn't sound so bad, Nick—at least, not as bad as I imagined for whatever was going to come out of your mouth. Debt certainly isn't desired, but it's almost always a part of war." Garrett eased back into his chair, the urgency waning for the need to be covert. "And something I can't see a reason for being so secretive about. Isn't it common knowledge countries often have a financial deficit while in conflict?"

Nicholas shook his head, the firmness of the gesture telling Garrett he not only disagreed, but Garrett hadn't fully understood. "That may be, but I'm not talking about just one war, Garrett. The Seven Years War alone nearly doubled Parliament's debt. Now we're in the middle of another. Think of what implications that will have to our economy, to our own countrymen." Nicholas slammed his glass of the sweet concoction on the table, nearly spilling half of it over. "The fact is, we can't afford to stay in this war."

"Yes, but surely a power such as Parliament has it handled, or a plan, at least, for when the war is over."

Again, Nicholas disagreed. "I'm afraid not. The solution for the prior war costs, the Seven Years War, was to tax the colonies. As you already know, that didn't fare well. Not to mention trade with them has all but fallen apart. Even our merchant sailors who do continue to attempt to trade are now being seized by enemy vessels."

Garrett flinched, aware the last item Nicholas mentioned was a part of the work Abraham and Cleophes had been involved with. He was also beginning to understand Nicholas' point and comprehending what that kind of debt meant. If Parliament's financial burden couldn't be alleviated by other means, it would fall to the hands, or rather the pockets of the English people. And those pockets were already strained enough.

"Okay." Garrett relented; hands raised as if the dramatic effect might help his friend see his argument had been made. "So, what do you have to do in all this? What does His Majesty require of a lieutenant instead of captain to help remedy the situation?"

"Actually, he does require a captain." Nicholas' mouth slowly curved upwards as the truth dawned on Garrett.

The downward direction of his lips turned into a heartfelt grin. "You made post?"

Nicholas' smile strengthened as he straightened in his chair. "I did, and I've been busy with my new position ever since. The King has given me orders to command a fleet to take enemy ships."

"Take enemy ships? As in privateering you mean?"

"Yes, at least to help make up the losses we've acquired from the seizure of our own merchant ships."

"Is it working? Have you held any captures?"

Nicholas shrugged. "A few. It won't be enough to make up for the debt, but it's something."

Garrett took on a wry smile. "So, that's what you've been doing the past three months? Privateering in secret?"

His friend shook his head. "The privateering hasn't been a secret at all. Both the admiral and my father know about my orders to do so and that I've been given them directly from His Majesty. They just don't know why I've been ordered to do it. I've been instructed by his Royal Highness to keep the details of the debt secret, even to my superiors."

"Have they questioned you about it further?"

"No. I know well enough my father would never question the King's order. And from what I can tell, the admiral appears to hold the same view."

Garrett considered his friend for a moment. Nicholas had been entrusted with vital information that remained highly confidential. He knew more about what was going on than his own father and the admiral, both highly respected and well-positioned men. What did he think about all this?

"So, what's your take on things, then? Is this war about to be over before it barely began? Will the King and Parliament take our troops out of the colonies because the cost has become too high?"

A solemn expression crossed Nicholas' face. "I don't know. From a man who doesn't carry both the weight of his people and his country's pride on his shoulders, I couldn't answer that truthfully. I know King George speaks well of the people, and I'm certain he has thought about their burden with the debt, but I also know there lies another conundrum for him. One quite difficult to ignore, if I may add." Nicholas' shoulders slumped like he was carrying the hardship himself rather than the King. "To pull out of this war recognizes the colonies as they desire to be: independent from Britain. It's a declaration our King did not count on facing, I'm sure. But it has nevertheless happened. From the King's perspective, these people have forgotten from which country they came.

I suspect no man could just let an insult like that go without consequence."

Garrett thumbed his glass, considering what he might do if in the same position. As he went through possibilities, he couldn't be sure of the best outcome for pleasing both parties. The only thing he was certain of was the mere fact he was glad not to hold such responsibility. "No, I can't say I wouldn't feel the same, nor what I would do in such a position of power." He just gave in to the slightest hope the war might be over sooner than he thought.

Nicholas took the last sip of his breakfast before roughly returning the glass to the table. Garrett got the impression his friend was finished with this particular subject and he wasn't going to push. He'd heard enough.

"Now that you know about my secrets, it's high time I know more of yours." Nicholas folded his arms across his chest, revealing a knowing grin. Garrett was glad his friend was more relaxed. It made it that much easier for him not to worry about having to hide the smile now across his own face. "Here I am doing everything I can for His Majesty to continue the war effort while you're off falling in love with the enemy. It doesn't sound like imprisonment was too bad for you."

Garrett could feel the heat rise up to his ears, even if the remark had come out in jest. He'd already mentioned Abigail more than once in their letters though he had been careful not to mention her name, making sure she wouldn't be tied into things if their letters were intercepted somehow. As far as he knew, they hadn't been.

"You mean Abigail."

"Out of all the women in England who were smitten by you, you decide to fall for one here in the colonies rebelling against us. I always knew you were up for a challenge, Garrett, but this seems like a little much."

Garrett half-rolled his eyes, throwing Nicholas' continuous bantering aside. "You'd have to meet her sometime. She's worth it, I assure you."

"Must be. Although, I suppose she can't be that bad if she passed on your letters." Nicholas shrugged. "Anyway, I'm not about to try and make you see reason. I know a lost cause when I see one. You're already thinking about how you're going to get back."

Garrett gave a huff. He forgot his friend knew him so well. "I don't know. I'm ordered back home at present, but I don't know how long that will be. And I suspect your father is going to be on my back to make certain I don't do anything rash."

Nicholas' brow lifted. "Oh, I don't know about that. It'll be hard for him to keep such a close eye while he's still here in Boston."

"But Admiral Graves said The Captain was assigned over me, which reminds me…" Garrett paused, mindful time for their departure was upon them and he'd yet to hear the low baritone of Nicholas' father carrying out orders to make sail or drop in for a visit with them in the wardroom. "Isn't it about time for me to depart? I haven't seen your father at all this morning."

Nicholas gave a languid smile. "And you won't. Sorry, there's something else I forgot to mention. Graves may have said 'Captain Edwards' would be monitoring you but not necessarily The Captain Edwards."

Again, the light dawned as Garrett's understanding came into full view. Garrett smirked. "You're my escort back."

"I am."

"What about your assignment for the King?"

"I'm still on it, which is why we're leaving as soon as we are. I have to get to London and give an official report."

Garrett nodded, then recalled another detail discussed in the admiral's office. "Six months of civilian life?"

Nicholas raised his hands from the table unapologetically. "Hey, everyone who knows who we are also knows we're basically brothers. I had to be harsh or someone else would be taking you back."

A small laugh broke forth. "Thanks."

"So, you think you'll be heading back here to the colonies when your six months are up?"

Garrett let out a deep, determined breath at Nicholas' question. "I want to. There's a promise I intend to keep, but I also know I have responsibilities with the Navy. Those need to be handled first."

"That's certainly honorable. I know it's not easy for you."

Garrett shrugged. He didn't know if it was honorable or not, but a voice inside him said disobeying his orders to run off to Abigail wasn't the right thing to do. He would just have to wait and see. He'd have to wait on the Lord to make the first move. He just hoped it wouldn't be years before he did. "I'm just going to wait and see what God has in store. I don't feel pressed to move to the right or left just yet."

Nicholas drew back, the surprise he felt evident. "The last time I tried talking about God, you weren't so inclined. Now, you're the one bringing him up. That's new."

"I'm not exactly the same person these days." Garrett gave an easy smile. "Don't worry, it's a good change."

"Something's certainly different. You don't seem as intense. You haven't once mentioned what happened to your promotion to captain."

Garrett hadn't realized his failure to speak of it, but it wasn't as important these days. "I guess it doesn't mean as much to me as it used to."

"Well, God or not, whatever it is, it's a good thing." Nicholas gave a heartfelt smile again before he took a stand and grabbed his naval coat from the back of his chair to put it on. It was the first time Garrett noticed the gold laced buttons that lined his friend's new uniform. "We better get out there. It's time."

Garrett put on his lieutenant coat, grateful to still have it despite everything before he followed Nicholas out of the wardroom. When he arrived at the main deck, Garrett gulped down a surge of fresh sea air, the sweetness of what he knew and missed from his time as a captive, filling him with gratitude for it again. He watched with pride as Nicholas took his position atop the forecastle, giving orders Garrett would not be carrying out, at least until after his debriefing back in England.

Today, he was just a common passenger, looking to stay out of the way, though strangely unbothered by it. He stared off the stern of the ship as it began making its descent from the Boston harbor back to the mother country and felt an almost longing. Not for the city just before him but rather the smaller town that lay just west of it, even knowing she wasn't there anymore. Garrett could only gather it was his memory of her there, where he'd truly met her, understood her, and ultimately fell in love with her that drove the feeling. He closed his eyes as if doing so might somehow take him back to it. When he opened them again, however, the distance between him and the memory lengthened as the expanse of water did the same, separating his ship from the nearby town.

That was when he heard it, the boom. It was the all too familiar sound of a cannon blast, but the charge hadn't been from their ship or any ship in the harbor. It pierced his ears from a distance and his pulse shot high. Garrett took hold of his spyglass and aimed it in the direction of the land they'd just left minutes ago. He almost stumbled backwards as the picture began to focus and reveal the truth he hadn't been certain of in the admiral's office. Henry Knox.

Chapter 39

Abigail wiped the sweat from her brow, jotting a few notes from the night into the journal Garrett had given her before she put the book back into her satchel. She was satisfied with the work she'd done. It'd been a long night, but Mrs. Bennett's newborn was welcomed into the world without any complications. For that she was truly thankful. What was more, she had helped to make that happen.

After having gone through Margaret's delivery with Sophie and aiding Dr. Adams in the process, Abigail couldn't help but feel a further desire to continue in some fashion of the medical field. It wasn't the same full-fledged work Dr. Adams had been teaching her in his profession as a doctor, but it was something she could do, especially after the miracle she'd been fortunate to be a part of back at the Schreier estate. Bringing a child to its mother's arms for the first time did have its rewards and was satisfaction enough when she considered the dead ends she'd faced since her return back to Falmouth.

She'd learned her suspicions about following her dream were true, only confirming the uniqueness of the man she'd been allowed to study under while in Cambridge. Dr. Cabot, who made calls between Falmouth and Cape Elizabeth, was nice enough in conversation, but against the idea of having a woman under his supervision, especially after taking a young man who was already set to attend Harvard in the fall. That is, if the war didn't continue to be an obstacle for the college.

Abigail wrote to other schools, following the encouragement of Dr. Adams who'd done the same on her behalf, but each letter came back with no offer. Even as women began expanding their roles within the home while husbands and brothers were fighting in the war, it seemed the world— even the new one here in the colonies was not yet ready for a woman in such a field. Perhaps, one day that would change, but right now as she lived and breathed, it hadn't.

With her heart still set on what she'd learned in Cambridge and a desire to continue to help others, She found something her current society could agree with and that also appeased the longing she had. She was a midwife, or at least, well on her way to becoming one thanks to Mrs. Smith, the town's midwife, who'd agreed to take her on as an apprentice.

Abigail hiked up her dress above her ankles, deciding to take the path through the woods and back home. She was in a hurry this morning and the main road would take longer, especially without a horse. She breathed in the crisp air. The walk back was refreshing. Satisfaction from her recent delivery filled her and the warming temperatures of late told her spring was budding. If she'd taken the same route back home a few weeks later she'd see the beginnings of anemone, mayflowers, and azaleas along with tulip trees starting to make their blooms. She let the lids of her eyes fall shut. The warmth of the sun's rays penetrating through the leafless branches of the trees and onto her face felt peaceful. She savored it, knowing the moment wouldn't last long.

When Abigail opened her eyes again, an acute awareness took hold of the late morning. Soon the sun would be at its peak, and she'd promised she would help with the spring planting. But if she didn't hurry, she was afraid the burden of clearing the beds from weeds and debris while working the organic material into the soil would be left entirely alone to her sister.

She quickened her step, making the quarter of a mile back home in almost half the time. To her pleasure Charlotte had not been alone in the garden. Sitting up straight, quite on her own now and close enough to the dirt to get her tiny hands dirty was Olivia. Her youngest sister was the first to spot her, clapping her hands as she did so. Abigail beamed with affectionate pride as Charlotte brought over a pile of compost from behind the barn. The new earth smelled fresh and full of life.

It was a new season to look forward to while they still embraced the old. The past few months had given them things they'd least expected— things they'd learned about themselves and each other. But it had also taken from them too. Their town boomed with its rebuilding, but their mother could not be replaced, Abigail knowing a part of her own heart would always miss her no matter how peaceful she felt about it.

Her mother passed away just days after Abigail and her siblings arrived back to their aunt's estate in Portsmouth. Each day her mother continued to draw in less and less forced breath, Abigail sitting by her side until the end. They'd held the funeral back here in Falmouth and buried her next to her grandparents.

Abigail went over to the garden to swoop Olivia up in her arms before she gave her a raspberry on her cheek. The babe giggled. Looking at her served as a remembrance of Margaret's daughter, Sophie, and Abigail wondered what new feat the young infant was accomplishing these days. She'd written enough to know Mr. Schreier made it home and Rebekah and Nikolai had gone to Georgia. Abigail even had a trip planned to visit the Schreier estate later in the year after the summer harvest. It was a trip, she admitted, she looked forward to, eager to see those who had become dear to her and to meet Rebekah's brother who'd just been purchased his freedom. The only downside, she thought, was that being in Cambridge was also a reminder of who wouldn't be there.

The thought of one man made her all too mindful of another. She hadn't mentioned Garrett again to Abraham and had only discussed the topic when asked by Charlotte or her father, though he hadn't asked much. She wasn't certain if her actions were the reason or if that time had lapsed for her brother's anger towards her to wane, but it eventually did. No longer did Abraham avoid her every chance he got or eye her like she'd caused him a great wrong—not like he had done on their way back from Cambridge. She'd seen a change, one that told her Abraham's irritation was dissipating. In fact, after days without so much as a word, he finally spoke to her to relay he'd be down at the harbor, no doubt expecting her to pass on the information if anyone asked. It wasn't much, but it was a start.

She hadn't seen him today, having been occupied herself at Mrs. Bennett's for the last part of the night and morning, but she guessed that's where Abraham was now. He'd been going down to the harbor every day since they arrived back in Falmouth. Her brother didn't say it, but she knew he went down there for Cleo, as if returning to the place they met could somehow bring him back—that it could somehow fix things. She knew Abraham wondered about his friend's fate because she too wondered. Perhaps she hadn't shared the same kind of bond Cleo and her brother had, but she had shared a kinship nonetheless with him. And the man's fate was something she thought about time and again ever since the trade back in Cambridge.

"Well, look who finally decided to show." Charlotte took a short reprieve from adding some compost to the garden. She placed her soiled hands upon her hips, using a tone that sounded more like teasing banter than annoyance. "How is Mrs. Bennett doing?"

Abigail put Olivia down, placing her back in her original spot close to the dirt for her to play again. She gave a tired sigh, feeling the night's work catch up with her before she smiled. "Exhausted after such a long delivery, but quite happy I suspect. A brand-new baby boy was in her arms when I left."

"That's four boys, not including her husband. Poor woman, we better send her something over for all her trouble. She's supplying a good part of the army."

Abigail laughed. "I think she'll be all right, but that's a good idea to send something. Mother would've agreed. I'll work on a chicken soup later and I think Mr. Bennett is a fan of Indian pudding." She did a quick survey of the garden. Nearly two-thirds of it was already completed, the weeding done and soil amended. All that was left was the planting. She gave Charlotte an apologetic look. "Sorry I'm later than expected."

"It's all right. I figure the work you're doing can't exactly be rushed." Charlotte's head tipped towards the far side of the garden. "Why don't you start there at the end and plant the cauliflower."

Abigail set herself to work. The dirt felt good between her fingers as she dug the holes and scattered the seeds. It was easy to get into a rhythm and let her gaze drift at the view before her. It was one that was all too familiar.

The last time she'd been in the garden was the day her town was stampeded by cannon fire. Not even a year ago. Yet, the destruction hadn't been enough to keep Falmouth and its people from thriving again. Thanks to the help of the community, her parent's home had been rebuilt in record time. The barn too nearly restored. Soon, it would inhabit more than just the horses they'd taken to Aunt Sylvia's on the day of the blasts.

Abigail's eyes drifted to the house, the side of her mouth tilting upward. It was not as it once was. The new floors did not creak as the old ones used to and the smell of the restored timber had an odor of fresh pine, masking the years of life once in it. It was different but not necessarily bad. Like her town, she too had been changed by the war, a war she had to remind herself, that still went on even if she was no longer a part of it.

She breathed in deep, her sight back on the wide expanse of water while she continued to sow the seeds. Like the day of the attack, the sun shone across its surface. It sparkled as if the wavelike dance was taunting her. She couldn't help but think of Garrett and whether she'd see him again. She wondered where he might be now. In Boston? Somewhere out there at sea? Had he made captain like he hoped, like she hoped for him? Her countenance faltered somewhat thinking of the other possibility he mentioned. The one where he hadn't reached his goal but was even now on his way back to England. She imagined him on a ship, sailing farther away from her, and her heart sank like an iron anchor hitting the water's depths. The longing only grew with each thought of him. Her eyes closed, as if doing so might bring him to her and it did for a moment until she had to open them again.

"There wouldn't be a certain someone on your mind now by chance?"

Abigail startled. She hadn't noticed Charlotte come up beside her.

"Relax. I'm just taking some seeds from your pile to the other side of the garden. We can finish by meeting in the middle." Charlotte gave her a look as if to say, 'but while I'm here, you might as well talk.'

"What makes you think I was even thinking about him?"

"Oh, just the way you were staring at the ocean like it had something you wanted. My guess is a certain lieutenant." Charlotte's eyelashes batted with girlish flirtation.

Abigail couldn't help but reveal a smile. "My mind wandered there for a moment. I'll admit that much." She straightened, then made the holes in the dirt before she put more seeds in. "But right now, there's no point in dwelling on such matters." Not when the thought of Garrett made her heart ache.

"You don't think he'll come back?"

Abigail stiffened, Charlotte asking the very question she'd been wondering herself even after Garrett had given her his mother's brooch. She reached for the jewelry on the left side of her chest and felt an instant reassurance by the solid reminder of his promise.

"No. It's not that. I just don't know when he'll come back. For all I know it could be a decade the way this war is going or rather, not going at the present."

"Maybe that will change since the winter is almost over."

Abigail shrugged. She agreed with her sister. The weather conditions were already improving and with it, people were coming out more often. It was likely the fighting would ensue once again, but for how long? "Perhaps, but still, I don't know how long it will last."

"Well, maybe that doesn't have to matter."

Abigail angled her head, not fully understanding where her sister's optimism stemmed from. "I should think that it would. Garrett's not likely to return until it does. I don't see how he could."

"I'm not certain how he could, either, but I'm going to disagree with you just the same."

A half-hearted laugh drew from Abigail's breath while she covered the rich soil over the seeds she'd planted. "And why is that?"

Charlotte gave a rueful smile as if Abigail's question had been one her sister hoped she'd asked.

"Because he's coming up the hill just now with our brother, that's why."

***

Abigail blinked one, two, three times before what she saw with her own eyes combined with Charlotte's declaration finally made sense. She looked in the direction her sister referred to, towards the harbor. Her view did not disappoint. Abraham was indeed approaching them and there, by his side was Garrett. Abigail's heart quickened, until she comprehended the significance of it. She looked to Charlotte, making sure the sight had not been her imagination. Charlotte grinned and her question was answered. No, it was real and for the moment she couldn't explain it. Her brother was walking alongside a man he claimed to despise while a war still pressed on, but she took it willingly.

Suddenly alert her mouth hung open, Abigail promptly closed it and managed to rise from her kneeled position in the garden. Charlotte had done the same and grabbed up Olivia in the process. She also perceived Charlotte's attention, though clearly aimed towards the men approaching them was more focused on a third party that accompanied them. Abigail admitted to a familiarity in his own right but standing next to Garrett's side now she knew it had to be Nicholas.

"Abraham? Garrett?" Abigail's eyes shifted from one man to the next, still unconvinced she wasn't dreaming.

Her brother's mouth tipped. "I know. It's not what you expected. Believe me, I get it. I'm still having a hard time myself grasping the thought of walking next to a Royal Naval officer, much less two of them on friendly terms. Never mind the fact I'm escorting one of them straight to my sister." His gaze drifted to Charlotte. "Why don't you show Captain Edwards here around the farm before dinner while we wait for Father and Henry to return."

"Dinner?" Abigail stepped back, her eyes widening.

Abraham's smile deepened. "They're going to be dining with us tonight, unless that's not all right with you? If that's the case, just say the word and I'll be happy to take them back to where they came from."

The twinkle in his eye gave way to his humor despite the sarcasm she heard. Still, she wanted to make sure. "No, that's fine."

"Good. In the meantime, I'm going to go and let Father know we have company. He and Henry should still be visiting Mother. Besides," Abraham eyed her and Garrett in a way that made her cheeks go hot. "I think you two have a few things to catch up on."

When all parties had left them, Abigail refocused her attention to

Garrett, quite certain her bewilderment to his welcomed, but unexpected arrival was all too evident.

"I told you I'd be back. You still have my mother's brooch, I hope." His wry grin made her smile.

"Of course, I do." She pressed her lips firmly. "But Garrett, I have so many questions. How are you here? I thought…"

"You thought I wouldn't come until after the war ended. I know. I thought that too. I was on a ship on my way back to London and almost out of the Boston harbor when we heard the cannon blasts. We immediately reentered and docked to aid in the defenses, but in the end it all proved at a loss."

"Knox made it after all?"

"He did—showed up with his heavy artillery in Boston as promised. Washington took the city.

Abigail frowned, still feeling like her questions needed more answering. "What does that mean for you, then? Surely, you've been ordered somewhere else. Won't they need you, especially after a defeat like that?"

'I'm not so sure. I was headed for civilian life in London for a while, but even so, things got a little crazy after the attack. Most of the troops went to Halifax where the British headquarters are for safety and to regroup." The side of Garrett's mouth raised, and she saw a gleam in his eye. "But you wouldn't believe who I ran into during all that chaos." He paused, allowing a moment for her to think and her mouth dropped open.

"Cleo."

"Yep. It turns out a couple of those cannonballs Knox sent our way tore into one of the buildings some of the prisoners were held in. No one was hurt, but it seems some of them are unaccounted for. Have I covered everything?"

"For the most part, yes, but I do have one more question to ask."

432

"Go on."

She eyed his selection of wardrobe. It didn't have an ounce of similarity to the royal blue she'd grown accustomed to. She softened her tone, afraid more had been taken away from him in Boston other than his chance to command a crew again. "Where's your uniform?"

To her relief, his mouth cracked into a smile. "Nicholas and I thought it might be a good idea if we didn't draw too much attention, especially knowing what happened the last time we were here. We didn't think the locals would care much for us otherwise"

Abigail took a moment to consider before she nodded in full agreement. Maybe her family was willing to forgive for the burning, but that didn't mean others in town would. "Good idea. And you and Abraham?" She gave him a pointed look. "How did you end up so close?"

Garrett laughed. "I wouldn't count us as close friends just yet. Your brother and I have an understanding that goes beyond our differences and responsibilities of the war. We might be adversaries as long as the conflict continues, but when it comes to you, Abigail, we couldn't agree more." He gave her a grin that warmed her heart.

"And what of your plans now for the rest of the war? Won't you have to return to your post?"

"I'm not certain." Garrett took in a sharp breath, before he let it out again. "Eventually, I imagine I will, but right now I'm headed to London to follow through with my orders there. I'll be a civilian for a while until I'm deemed fit enough to resume my position as lieutenant. But thankfully, Nicholas has taken charge of me. That'll help."

"I imagine so. When will you be leaving for London?"

"Tomorrow."

Disappointment rose within her, realizing his stay was brief. "I see." She took the brooch from her dress and held it out to him. "Well, let me go ahead and return this to you. I wouldn't want you to be halfway to London and forget it."

"Thank you. I would like to take it with me." Garrett took a step forward and drew closer to her. He grasped her by the hand that still held the keepsake, though he failed to take the jewelry from it. "But I was hoping it might stay put and you might agree to come with me. That is, if you answer a question for me, first." She stilled, Garrett taking the opportunity to continue. "Abigail, will you be my wife?"

Her answer came easily. Garrett took a final step in, closing what little space remained between them and kissed her with both an affection and desire that sent her heart reeling. When he gently released her again, she couldn't help but take a step back once more, not because she hadn't enjoyed herself in that moment but because she couldn't believe everything had happened in the way it had. It was something she owed God for. Her town had been burned, inflicting her with pain and grief, but little did she know God had a plan and not just for her. He had given her an opportunity in Cambridge to prove to herself she was more capable than she thought she was, meanwhile providing friends along the way. But then there were others-others like Garrett, someone the Almighty had put into her life, someone she hadn't expected to fall in love with, and someone, too, she could see God at work in.

She also thought of Cleo and of his sacrifice she would never forget. It was a gesture that wouldn't have happened otherwise from a man who'd been living for himself for so long unless something about him had changed. The only change she knew of in the man's life and one he declared was Jesus.

Garrett gently kissed her on her forehead, before he took hold of her hand again. She couldn't be happier and thankful for the adventure the Lord provided and this man who would soon be hers. As they walked back towards the house, it occurred to her that she'd never been on a ship or even out past the harbor. She turned towards Garrett, about to tell him about her inexperience at sea, but the smile upon his face wiped away any doubt from her mind. She smiled too; pretty certain another adventure was awaiting.

Epilogue

"Now, Mr. Moore, I would suggest you work to get some good food into your meals—some fruits and vegetables if they can be had. In the meantime, I'll see if I can find some oranges or lemons for you to eat. If you do that, you should start feeling better in a few days' time."

"She's right. I've never had scurvy, but I've seen enough of it to know I don't want it. If you don't do as she says, you'll have fewer teeth in your near future and we still have a good number of days until we reach London." Garrett came down from the main deck into the cockpit and gave Abigail a hearty wink. She shook her head and offered him a droll look in return. "How are things going?"

"We're doing fine. Mr. Moore and I are almost finished, and I just have Mr. Cutter to see about a minor cut he suffered while rigging one of the sails.

He smiled. "Good. When you're done, I have something I think you'll be interested to see."

Her candor grew to intrigue. "Really? What is it?"

He shook his head. "You'll know soon enough. Just come up and find me when you're done."

Abigail watched him disappear back up to the main level before seeing to her next patient. When she'd completed the dressings for Mr. Cutter, she quickly went to the hold of the ship and returned with a few lemons to make Mr. Moore a lemon juice for combatting his first signs of scurvy.

Abigail voiced a low chuckle. Part of her still couldn't believe this was happening. Little did she know that when Garrett had asked her to marry him and come with him back to London, he'd also been planning not just a future for himself but for her too. He'd brought a doctor on board as part of Nicholas' crew who was even willing to take her on as a student. She smiled to herself. Even if it took a little nudge from his captain to do it.

She was already learning more too, not having seen the same things here at sea that she had back on land in Cambridge. Besides the minor cuts and bruises that came with manning a ship, she'd helped treat a small number of fevers and a broken arm from one of the crew members who'd been hauling in the sail canvas during a rain they'd encountered, each case now inscribed within her notebook. Abigail made a point to add her first case of scurvy to its pages later after Garrett showed her what he thought would be to her interest. Curious on what it could be, she dismissed the men and returned to the main deck to go find him.

"There you are! How is Mr. Moore doing?" Charlotte rushed up in front of her, unexpected enthusiasm of her sister nearly knocking her backwards.

Abigail managed to recover swiftly enough to see a suspenseful delight in her sister's eyes that was already making her forget her near-fall towards the lower level. "He'll be doing better soon enough as long as he does well to follow instruction."

Charlotte squealed, though Abigail felt certain the response had more to do with their future plans than of poor Mr. Moore.

"Can you believe we're going to Paris, just like Aunt Sylvia?" Her sister squealed again, the high-pitched sound, Abigail observed, noticed by a few of the crew members who'd stopped what they were doing to gawk in their direction. "I can hardly wait to compare notes when we visit this next winter, although I'm thankful she's offered to care for Olivia until my return. I'm sure Father is too. He'd certainly be fine on his own with Henry, but he seemed welcomed to the idea of having a womanly touch close by for our younger sister." Charlotte's face grew ever brighter. "Aunt Sylvia has already advised we must make a visit to see Notre Dame and at least get a good look of Versailles if we can."

Abigail smiled over Charlotte's excitement but also felt an elation of her own for the additional details to their trip. Once Nicholas finished his report to Parliament, he was going to take them to Paris while he worked to find out where France's support was regarding the colonies. It, like London, had been a place they'd wanted to see but never in her life had Abigail thought she'd be on a ship headed towards the very city.

"I'm excited too and for when we dock in London. After nearly a month at sea, it'll be nice to see some dry land again." Abigail glanced around the deck, her eyes eventually coming to a standstill as they found the man she searched for.

Charlotte followed her gaze and as if knowing her very desires, hooked Abigail's arm within her own and strode her towards Garrett. "Here, I'll have you up there in no time."

They went by a group of able seamen who'd by now grown accustomed to them being onboard and offered an occasional nod or smile as they passed until they reached the forecastle of the ship.

"Miss Thatcher, Mrs. Ward." Garrett gave Abigail that warm smile that always made her feel wanted. He stood by Nicholas who'd just finished giving a command that made some of the men climb the masts and adjust the sails to a changing wind. With the order accomplished, he followed Garrett's lead, offering his own smile and pleasantries to the two women, though his object of affection was clear. Abigail recognized the tenderness in Nicholas' as he looked at Charlotte, who returned the stare, beginning to see more blossoming out of what was currently friendship.

She felt the touch of Charlotte's arm loosen within hers as she left her side and drew over towards Nicholas before they began a conversation between each other.

Abigail raised her chin to Garrett, expectantly. "So what is it that you think I'd be so interested in, Mr. Ward? And why did I have to come up here to hear about it? Why couldn't you just tell me before, down in the cabin?" She could see he caught the playfulness in her tone and gave her that roguish grin she'd come to love.

"Well, it's more of something you have to see with your own eyes to really have an appreciation for." She hadn't noticed the spyglass at his side until he held it out to her. "Here, take a look."

She took it, bringing it to her eye and gasped. "Land!"

After nearly a month and who knew how many miles away from her family's farm, they'd reached it: the land her grandparents sailed away from to discover a new one, just as she would soon be discovering the one they'd left behind. Abigail took the spyglass away from her face and looked at him, her eyes narrowing. "But Garrett, I thought you told Mr. Moore we still have a good number of days before we reach London?"

His grin never faltered. "I know, and I think one is a very good number, don't you?"

Comprehending his jest, Abigail met it with a smile before putting the spyglass up to her eye again. She felt her breath catch with anticipation to the discovery of uncharted territory, at least to her and Charlotte. The rush of adventure ran through her body with joy despite the war that still pressed on, dividing this land and the land she'd come from like the long breadth of water that separated them.

She knew it wouldn't last long, but in the meantime, she could rest, knowing Abraham would be back on the farm and not in it. Not only would her brother be there to help her father until Charlotte returned, but to heal from wounds, she sensed, that went deeper than the cuts and bruises he'd brought home with him from his imprisonment. She wasn't certain if he'd find his way back into the war or not, but at least for now he was safe, and he and Garrett were the farthest they could be from facing each other on the battlefield. Finished with the glass, Abigail handed it back to Garrett.

"Nervous?"

"A little, but mostly excited."

"Good." Garrett closed the small gap that remained between them and put a strong arm around her. She instantly caught the scent of sea salt and sage as a cool wind passed over them and through the sails of the ship. "I wouldn't want you to be having second thoughts, now."

Abigail shook her head with undeniable certainty. "I don't and I certainly don't plan to." She smiled before allowing him the same question. "And what about you? Are you nervous?"

"You mean about getting reinstated to a lieutenant or the part where I'm going to be standing in front of the King of England to do it?"

She laughed. "Either? Both?"

The side of his mouth raised. "I'm a little nervous about being in court with not knowing what to expect, but Nicholas has reassured me I'll be all right as long as I follow his lead. As for getting my old job back, I'm more astounded it came about so fast. Nicholas told me six months, but he didn't tell me he'd be able to go over Admiral Graves to shorten that duration quite considerably. Not to mention, having King George issue it."

"I suppose he's been of good service to the King."

Garrett nodded. "I have no doubt about that. He's good at what he does, and he's a good man for it."

Abigail looked into his dark eyes again, her heart full of happiness for the friendship Garrett and Nicholas had but also the man she'd married. "So are you and what you're planning to do once you get reinstated."

"I'm not so sure anybody's going to really know once I go through and make the changes I'm planning to for the prisoners and their so-called accommodations, but it's the right thing to do. If it were me, I'd like a little more decency in how I was treated, war or not. I know many have already died simply out of starvation and disease. I hope it makes a difference for the prisoners we have now and in the future."

"It will and even for those in the past. I know it does for Abraham." She squeezed his hand tight and smiled both as a reassurance to him but also as a response of her gratitude for what he was doing. Garrett wrapped his arms around her as they both stared in the direction of the water where land would soon be within their sight and without need of an instrument to view it. No doubt challenges laid before them there, too, just like there'd been in the colonies and just like there would always be in this life. God had been with them and had taught them along the way in Cambridge, and Abigail was just as sure as He'd been with them then He'd be with them there, too.

Acknowledgments

There are a few people I'd like to thank for helping me reach the completion of this book. Their contributions have been invaluable to me, and I will never forget them. My gratitude goes to…

My family—Donny, for his support and patience these past three years, for his edits and for his work in detailing the cover design. My children, Ayla and Evie, though still quite young and unaware of their impact, for encouraging me to try and be a better mother each day.

Brandon Wagoner, for not only being someone I've been able to go to for guidance and answers, but who's also been instrumental in bringing the book into publication.

Anne Donnell, for her remarkable generosity and skillset in editing the manuscript. She has done me a great kindness.

And for Jesus Christ, who knows my innermost being and loves me all the same. May this book glorify that magnificent name.

Made in the USA
Columbia, SC
20 April 2022